THE IMMORTAL TRANSCRIPTS II

FEVER

LISA BORNE GRAVES

AUTHORS 4 AUTHORS PUBLISHING
Marysville, WA, USA

©2022 Lisa Borne Graves

Published by Authors 4 Authors Publishing
1214 6th St
Marysville, WA 98270
www.authors4authorspublishing.com

Library of Congress Control Number: 2022930411

E-book ISBN: 978-1-64477-136-5
Paperback ISBN: 978-1-64477-137-2
Audiobook ISBN: 978-1-64477-138-9

Edited by Rebecca Mikkelson and Brandi Spencer

Cover design ©2022 Practically Perfect Covers. All rights reserved.
Statue from cover image:
Statue of Mars by Johann Gottfried Shadow
Charlottenburg Palace (Schloss Charlottenburg)
Berlin, Germany

Interior design and layout by Brandi Spencer.

Authors 4 Authors Publishing branding is set in Bavire. Titles and headings are set in Goudy Trajan and Mr Darcy. Text messages are set in Source Sans Pro Semibold. Handwriting is set in Reey for Lucien, Architect's Daughter for Callie, Allura for Archer, and Moinho for Chase. All other text is set in Garamond.

THE IMMORTAL TRANSCRIPTS II

FEVER

LISA BORNE GRAVES

Authors 4 Authors Content Rating

17+

OLDER TEENS AND ADULTS

This title has been rated 17+, appropriate for older teens and adults, and contains:

- Intense implied sex
- Graphic violence
- Strong language
- Moderate alcohol use
- Moderate fantasy drug use
- Depression and suicide
- Domestic violence

Please, keep the following in mind when using our rating system:

1. A content rating is not a measure of quality.

Great stories can be found for every audience. One book with many content warnings and another with none at all may be of equal depth and sophistication. Our ratings can work both ways: to avoid content or to find it.

2. Ratings are merely a tool.

For our young adult (YA) and children's titles, age ratings are generalized suggestions. For parents, our descriptive ratings can help you make informed decisions, but at the end of the day, only you know what kinds of content are appropriate for your individual child. This is why we provide details in addition to the general age rating.

For more information on our rating system, please, visit our Content Guide at: www.authors4authorspublishing.com/books/ratings

DEDICATION

For my best friends, I could ask for no better crew.

WORKS BY LISA BORNE GRAVES

Celestial Spheres

Fyr
Draca
Bladesung

Wundor (June 2023)

The Immortal Transcripts

Quiver
Fever
Shudder
Glimmer (February 2024)

Stand-alone Titles

Apidae
"Dare"

TABLE OF CONTENTS

NOTE TO READER

The following is a faithful transcript for the use of the newly formed International Republic of Immortality (IRI) in its inquiry behind the altercations involved in the Olympian sector. As far as the signed witnesses state, everything was recorded with complete honesty, arranged chronologically, and written separately so as to not influence one another's accounts. ~~The IRI reserves the rights to this manuscript, and it is by no means to be reproduced nor shown to any creature mortal. Mortals who read may be subject to permanent silence.~~

In case we are executed for our "crimes," I pass this on to you, mortal, in hopes to continue our memories into the future. Welcome to our world.

CHAPTER 1

I was in that dreadful, dense fog again, the kind that wraps around and chokes you like a tangible, oppressive presence. It meant I was asleep. These dreams were troublesome because the fog meant prophecies, but if a prophecy was coming, it was much needed with the debacle we were all in. If I, Apollo, god of prophecies and much more, could save my friends, I'd risk anything. Wasting no time, I slipped into a serene scene that poets depicted as Elysium, but the thought of it was far from peaceful. I was alive, so it frightened me. Who wanted to visit the land of the dead and talk to ghosts while he slept?

Oh, it was beautiful: the rippling barley in a slight breeze, the sun radiating through the fog, lighting up the world yet easy on the eyes. Even the gilded gates and endlessly tall stone perimeter didn't feel as if they trapped me in, but more sinister forces out. Safe, heavenly. A babbling brook could be heard on the wind. Knowing what it looked like gave me an advantage in life. I could not fear death if I ended up here in this wondrous place. Not that I could die—easily, that is.

This is where the oracles brought me, or I wandered into their realm unconsciously—I was never sure how it worked. In the field of barley, one of the seers stood in front of me, as beautiful as ever—with her bronze skin and hour-glass figure—her palms being tickled by the plants as they swirled in multiple directions in the four winds. She turned when she heard my legs brushing through the barley, and she smiled, yet the smile didn't reach her ebony eyes. I swallowed the lump forming in my throat. It wasn't going to be a good prophecy. Last time, just months ago, she was a playful flirt, and the news hadn't been great. To see her somber, a deep foreboding crept over me, making my flesh prickle with goose pimples, an odd sensation since it had never happened to me before. The ichor in our blood regulated our temperatures, so a chill, a sweat, none of that occurred to my kind. But I was in a dream, so all laws of nature were moot here.

"Themis—" I guessed, since she had been an oracle before I was born.

"Hush! Never say my name." She looked around, frightened.

"Why? Who sent those dogs? What are you afraid of?" I referenced the last time I'd seen her. What would've happened if I'd died in my dream? While people slept, Morpheus, god of dreams, gave souls to his uncle Thanatos, god of death, but those were mortal lives, not gods. But Morpheus couldn't give them to his uncle anymore; Thanatos was dead. Last time, Themis had foreseen love changing the immortal world forever. And he had. Love, under his mortal alias Archer Ambrose, fell for a mortal Zeus refused to let him be with, and then everything spiraled out of control, resulting in the death of Thanatos. To see Themis again so soon was not good. Apparently, there would be more to deal with. Simple prophecies were sent through my living oracle, who contacted me via phone call or email. A direct line to Elysium? That was straight up apocalyptic.

"We don't have time for long-winded explanations that you'll never understand anyway. Surely, after all these years, you've realized that dead oracles aren't supposed to talk to you. It takes me tremendous effort and help to get you here."

"I'm sorry, but why do you do it? Why not use my mortals, my living oracles?" I asked.

"No one can be trusted. No one."

"No one but me, the god of truth," I amended. After all, she'd brought me here for a reason and must have had faith in me.

"Not even you anymore."

I stopped, going rigid. "What?" She might as well have punched me. Not only was it insulting, but if you couldn't have faith in Truth, who could you trust?

"Things will never be the same again, Apollo. You need to choose your alliance, for you alone will tip the scales in this battle." Was she referencing how Zeus had punished Archer, whose family was on his side?

"I have chosen a side." The fact she used the word "battle" was not lost on me. Would it become more than a couple gods disgruntled with Zeus? Would it come to war? I had so many questions but so little time with which to ask them. I already felt a pervasive darkness creeping in that told me this interview would be cut short.

She looked at me skeptically, lifting one of her brows. "Have you?"

"Archer is my best friend, my family. I'd never go against him or Dite or Ares."

"No?" she challenged, making my stomach drop.

I could imagine a number of ways in which our friendship would end, rocky as it was at the moment, but never could I imagine going *against* him in what sounded as if it could be a full-fledged Olympian war. Never. "Why don't you just tell me so I don't do whatever you're hinting at? Will there be a war? And why in Hades would I ever go against the combined forces of Love and War?"

"You know far better than anyone else that I can't give you details. Everything has to happen just so. They won't allow us to alter the course," she whispered the last bit. She was referring to the Fates, the powerful beings who ensured all that would occur, creatures beyond anyone's control, even Zeus's, the god of us Olympian gods.

"Do they know you are slipping me secret prophecies?"

"Of course not!" She looked around as if the Fates were here now, watching us, and maybe they were for all we knew. "No matter, they can't harm me. My string has already been cut, but yours..."

I swallowed with some difficulty. They could cut my life string at any moment just for being here—if goddess mothers' tales are to be believed. They usually only dealt with mortal fates, but after certain events, I questioned the extent of their power.

"Look, they'll notice I'm gone soon," she began hurriedly.

I pulled her into my arms, hoping to gain the prophecy via that luscious kiss again, but she pushed me away, giving me a Cheshire grin. She was all that was feline and seductive. Themis placed her hands on my temples, and images shot forth into my mind. I closed my eyes so I wouldn't be distracted by her beauty.

Archer was standing on what looked like a mountain, smoke around him, his face full of despair. Archer punching me in the face. Callie, dressed in white, giving me a look of hatred. Then the images began speeding up: Zeus angry, lightning, Hymenaios frightened, fire, Chase and Athena shaking hands, water, drowning.

"My son—" I was cut off by her lips on mine. I wanted answers but couldn't pull myself away from her. I closed my eyes. Kissing her was better than Elysium, or so I deduced from my small glimpses of the entrance. I heard the nefarious baying in the distance that told me I was staying too long. I yanked myself away from her, took a moment to watch those luscious lips turn into a greedy little smile, and gave her one of my own. Then I ran for the gates. I heard the dogs coming closer, but unlike last time, I would make it out easily. I opened the gates, escaped into pure fog,

5

and the ground beneath me vanished. My stomach dropped. I was falling for ages, so much so, I lost track of up from down, my left from right. There was nothing but a wispy pale gray fog.

Then I opened my eyes to find I was in my bed, in my room, in Manhattan, with more questions rolling around in my head than answers. Fear for my eldest son kept me from sleep, not to mention seeing Callie, the woman I loved, apparently marrying another.

CHAPTER 2

Callie

It had been the worst Christmas ever. Every holiday sucked because each was likely to be the last one with my father, and my god-boyfriend was dead (so they said). Not only had I lost the person I'd thought was *the one*, but it was also compounded with the fact I'd soon lose the most important man in my life: my dad. Before Death tried to take me, I had Archer, a future, a life, a boyfriend to help me through the upcoming hardships. At first, the pain of the news that Archer was executed had been so acute, I could hardly function. Then I slipped into the denial stage where I could not let go, let alone believe Archer was truly gone. There was something utterly wrong with the statement "Archer Ambrose is dead."

Impossible.

There was another reason it was a crappy Christmas. While girls my age, including my friends (those mortal, that is), were worried about not getting the latest phone or gift cards for shopping sprees, I was fighting off spiking fevers from an unknown illness.

Right now, across from me, Emily was whining about not getting everything she wanted for Christmas. Didn't she realize that you can't always get what you want? People were dying, and lots of kids at other schools probably got less or nothing at all. I was sick, and all I wanted was my father to live, not some stupid phone.

I gazed around my peers in the cafeteria, who were chatting and eating, all their faces cheerful. Everyone was buzzing with what colleges they did or didn't get into. They were all excited for the next chapter of their lives, impatient to get out into the world. I was accepted to all the colleges I applied to (by some miracle because I hardly remembered taking my finals last semester) and chose to attend NYU. My heart wasn't into college. It would just fill up my time like everything did now: school, hanging out with friends, dinners with my dad—they were simply distractions. I was numbly going through the motions of life. I wasn't truly alive without Archer; I merely existed. And I was angry about that. I should've never given my heart away, let myself fall in love so deep that without him, I was a mess (a pathetic one).

"Did you do anything interesting over Christmas?" Linda asked me.

She was trying to include me, which was nice. I had been off in my own world as I tended to be these days. Lucien had told everyone Archer was dead, trying to make things easier for me, no doubt, but the fact they all ignored he had existed was worse than them talking about him.

"Not really. My dad can't do much, and I was sick." I didn't think Linda would understand the truth: *Death had come for me. Archer killed him to save me—by the way, Archer's a Greek god, didn't you know?—and now his family is lying to me.*

"Well, we'll have to do something to make up for that." She gave me one of those sympathetic smiles that showed me how pathetic I was.

Lucien (aka Apollo) looked away, ignoring me. There was guilt in his eyes every time they met mine.

I pushed the food around my plate, not hungry. Doctors had at first thought I had food poisoning—that was until the fevers kept returning. Then they spent a couple weeks ruling everything out. Now I was waiting to see a psychiatrist, neurologist, and a half dozen other specialists to rule even more out. My dad believed they were stress induced, but that didn't explain the original cause. Lucien kept his views to himself, but it was obvious he was at a loss as to what it was, which had to drive him mad, being the god of medicine and healing. He helped as best as he could by lowering my fevers with the touch of his hand and making strange herbal concoctions for me to drink that kept me at a steady 100 degrees. He sent a couple blood samples to Athena and basically said she'd figure it out. If she didn't, it would mean I was the ultimate freak of nature (his choice of words, not mine). Like I could feel any worse.

No one listened to what I thought was going on. I thought Zeus was torturing me, much like he was slowly killing my father for unearthing their identities and finding the original Mount Olympus. Regardless of where these fevers came from, I almost welcomed them. They kept me numb, out of it, and when I was that way, I couldn't feel the pain of Archer's absence as much. This being the first day back to school was a harsh reminder of the void he left behind.

I would keep going because I had to. I'd made a promise to the god of love to never hurt myself. He'd broken his promise to come back to me one day. Or had he? Perhaps what really kept me going was my foolish hope that Archer was still alive and that I would see him again. I envisioned him somewhere far away, trying desperately to get back to me as he'd faithfully promised. I closed my eyes, hoping I could recall the details of his face.

"Callie?" Lucien's voice called me back to reality. Where was I, and what I was supposed to be doing?

"You all right?"

I looked around. Our entire lunch table was staring at me. Third period—I had been in study hall and now in lunch. Emily rolled her eyes and whispered something to Mary Beth. They laughed, but Mary Beth recovered herself and gave Emily a look of censure. Emily was making fun of me again, something she had always been prone to do.

"I'm fine," I muttered, embarrassed. I had yet again let myself get carried away in my thoughts, my memories. It was so hard to focus on the real world and all the pain that came with it.

"Linda was talking to you," Lucien supplied, trying to help me out. His guilty eyes darted away from mine.

"I'm sorry," I said sheepishly. "What were you saying?"

"We were talking about going shopping after school on Friday, Fifth Avenue," Linda said.

"Oh sure. I could really use new clothes." I looked down at my loose jeans. I hadn't had an appetite, so I'd lost some weight, and now my clothes were all ill-fitting. My jeans sagged and wrinkled. I didn't feel stylish at all.

As we left the cafeteria, Lucien moved closer to me and leaned in to whisper, "I got a text during lunch."

I turned so fast to look at him, my neck muscle strained with a sharp pull. He straightened, realizing that our faces were awfully close together. I hadn't meant to invade his space, but Linda's territorial grasping of his hand told me it didn't go unnoticed (great). He kissed Linda's forehead and gave me a significant look that told me it would have to wait. Things were weird between us. I pretended I hadn't overheard him arguing with Archer over their feelings for me.

Fourth period was the longest class of my life. I had no clue what the health teacher was talking about. I had to keep myself from running to fifth period, AP Physics, where I could finally get an answer from Lucien.

I sat, tapping my feet in anticipation. Then he entered, met my gaze, and looked to the floor as he approached. It wasn't good news.

Still, I was desperate. "Archer?"

He looked away from me as if I stung him. Then he peered up, his eyes intense and perturbed by my mention of Archer. "Callie, stop this nonsense. He's gone." The god of truth was a terrible liar.

"No, he's not. Lucien, I know he's alive. I can *feel* it."

He sighed and looked out the window at the rainy day, frowning. Sun god—I wanted to laugh out loud. He really was affected by a lack of sunlight, which would explain his grumpy mood. "That kind of thinking is only going to hurt you more."

I swallowed hard, a lump forming in my throat. I pushed the tears, the feelings, back into myself as if I were a bottle and then put the cap on. "The text?"

"From Athena." His voice was hushed as other students chatted idly. "She found nothing abnormal in your blood, just that the sample showed leukocytosis."

"What does that mean?" I challenged.

"Thought you'd know, smarty pants," he mocked me. "Only tells us that you're fighting off something, which we knew already, but she can't localize what's attacking your system."

"Great, so I'm a medical phenomenon?"

"She wants to perform a DNA test, but fresh samples are needed."

"No. She had her chance. No more needles. If she couldn't figure it out from the first samples, then I see no point for more."

"Callie," he pleaded. "She just needs a saliva swab of the inside of your cheek."

"I'm not a lab rat, Lucien!"

Mrs. Hapner began talking, so Lucien couldn't respond. I proceeded to ignore him for the rest of the class. He even tried to pass me a note, but I refused to look. I was definitely acting childish, but there was this intense rage fueling me, an anger that wanted to lash out at everyone, even those closest to me. I wondered if it was part of my illness or if I was just that resentful because Archer was gone.

When the bell rang, I took a deep breath and then turned to face him.

He pressed his lips together tightly, probably put out that I denied him, a god, attention. I had put him on hold, and he was not happy about it. He was so full of himself.

"Callie, she also said Aroha was on her way back to New York." (Crap.)

I felt dizzy, my stomach churning with a multitude of conflicting emotions—fear, guilt, dread, desperation, and hope. The last emotion confused me. I guess since she was his mother, who had to pose as his sister (still so weird to think about), I could garner the truth from her. If she seemed absolutely devastated, maybe I could digest the fact Archer was dead, try to come to terms with it. If she seemed no different though, it might mean they were hiding something and that he was somewhere in the world alive and well, missing me. The hope grew and squelched the anxiety in my stomach.

"I would, uh, suggest keeping your distance until I see what she has to say." His tone was soft and gentle. More drippy-sweet sympathy on his honeyed breath, something I realized they all smelled like—honeysuckles. It could work as my god-dar (like a radar) to differentiate them from humans.

"What she has to say?" I could not hide my astonishment. "She must want me dead. I deserve it."

"Callie, don't be so absurd. Archer made bad decisions. He ignored warnings to stay away from you. He killed a god. You're not to blame at all, and if Aroha can't see that, then she's an idiot."

I sighed and gathered my books up. The room had emptied, and the teacher looked expectantly for us to leave. I hurried into the hallway but hadn't gotten far when a powerful hand grabbed my wrist. Still, even now, my heart skipped a beat thinking of Archer's touch.

Lucien let go as if he sensed my unease. "You can't keep blaming yourself. Archer wouldn't have wanted that."

I nodded and then went on my way. He didn't follow. I made it all the way home and through the door before I fell apart, crying my eyes out. I couldn't handle the stress of trying to act normal, to pretend the gods didn't exist, to pretend my heart wasn't shattered into a million pieces.

I vaguely remember our servant, Raphael, carrying me to bed; my father coaxing me to eat soup; Raphael taking my temperature, feeding me pills. Then I drifted off to sleep.

I awoke in the middle of the night to see my phone in my hand. I couldn't recall how it got there. Had I grabbed it off my desk in my sleep? Had I been holding it the entire time?

I scrolled down to his name on my phone for the millionth time since Archer had left; as the second name on the list after my old friend Amy from Minnesota, he was inescapable. This time, instead of dismissing it, I did something different. I texted him.

Please. Know you're alive. I feel it.

As I expected, there was no answer. I then opened my photos and stared at the one of Archer and me together, the only one I had of us that his annoyingly gorgeous cousin Belle had taken. I studied every feature of his face, trying to memorize it. Then I prayed to him, hoping he would hear me.

After a torturous hour of staring at a photo, imagining future possibilities that could no longer occur, I put my phone down. Why was I so delusional that I couldn't grasp the fact he was gone? Psychoanalyzing myself kept me up half the night. (I was absolutely headed to a padded cell.)

Because I hadn't slept well, I missed my alarm in the morning. I was running late for school, rushing down the hall, trying to put my keys into my bookbag while I walked. I dropped them in the process and stooped down to pick them up. A faster hand snatched my keys up.

I stood back up, raking my gaze over the effeminate clone of Archer: Aroha. She gazed at me smugly and bitterly, but something was missing. There were no hints of grief or depression in her eyes. I knew they wouldn't physically manifest on her as they would on me, like the dark circles under the eyes and such, but she wasn't as upset or angry as she should be.

"You may want to hold onto things a bit better, Callie, or they might just slip through your fingers." She smirked, knowing I caught onto her double meaning.

"Aroha—"

"Don't!" She glared. "Don't talk to me." She raced down the hall at immortal speed, a blur, and then was gone around the corner.

There was no point in trying to talk to her. Aroha had always disliked me, and without Archer around, she would have no problem lying to me (or doing worse). Even Lucien, the god of truth, was lying to me. Something in me was absolutely certain of it, like my sixth sense called out with the truth.

I voiced this the next day, much to Lucien's dismay.

"For the last time, Callie, I'm not lying!" Lucien protested. "You need help, you know that?"

I probably did, but that wasn't the point.

"Even Dionysus couldn't cure your stubborn insane inability to—"

"Then why didn't Aroha want to kill me? Why isn't she taking more time off from school to grieve? Why does she look so happy and content that Julian Creswell is obsessed with her? She's not acting like Archer just died!"

"Keep your voice down. First, it's been a month, Callie. She wouldn't graduate if she didn't return. You may not think that is important, but we came back here to New York for her. She wanted a college degree from here last time, but women weren't allowed then. I'm sure she is throwing herself into that goal to forget her son. She needs to make up finals. Second, everyone grieves differently. She puts on a façade that everything is fine. You have willful denial."

"Lucien, look me in the eye and tell me that Archer is dead, that he is no longer on this Earth."

He groaned and covered his face. Then he threw his arms down, exasperated. "I have already! A dozen times now. You need to stop."

"You never looked me in the eyes and said 'dead.' You're not supposed to lie, Lucien."

He squared my shoulders and gazed into my eyes, "He's dead. Please, grasp that." His eyes flickered up to the left.

I didn't want to call him out yet. We'd move in circles then. Instead, I wanted to see if I could enter Lucien's thoughts. I'd somehow connected with Archer's mind and had seen he'd wanted a baby. What a crazy sentiment, but in hindsight, part of him would still be with me. I'd have a purpose.

I shook the thought and willed myself into Lucien's mind. I met resistance, but a few thoughts got through. *Wish he were dead...worse...never love me...why...angry*—the thoughts stopped.

He stared at me funny. "Why are you looking at me like that?"

"You're lying."

He rolled his eyes and gripped my shoulders, frustrated. I couldn't call him out on the lie without admitting I was reading minds, so I had to let it go. I had always been uncannily perceptive of people, but after the fevers began, it went to a whole new level.

"He's gone." Lucien said.

"Gone where?"

"What do we have here?" Aroha's vindictive voice sent chills down my spine. "Forgot about my brother already?"

I batted Lucien's hands away to see Aroha cocking her brow at me, with a glowering Emily by her side. Emily and Aroha were apparently buddies now, most likely drawn together by their mutual hatred for me (just lovely).

Lucien looked at me, hurt. Why did he have to look at me that way, touch me? It made people jump to the wrong conclusions.

"My bad. I thought I was the only one here actually remembering him. Where are your tears, Aroha?" The rage flared from me out of nowhere. I felt power, strength, and a huge amount of anger. I was suddenly in her face. Then I whispered so Emily couldn't hear, "I know he's alive."

Then I lurched at her as if I were about to attack her, making her flinch, before I quickly walked away. I turned around to see her reaction. She glared at Lucien, who shook his head. Emily missed the exchange, still examining me like I was dirt on her shoe.

"He didn't say anything, Aroha. I read his mind. Didn't you know? I'm psychic." I called to her.

"What. A. Freak," Emily announced.

I'm sure everyone was looking at us, but I couldn't care less. I took pleasure in seeing Aroha's mouth drop open in shock before I fled the scene.

When I got into the bathroom and splashed some cool water onto my feverish face, the anger abated. I was shocked and appalled at how rude I had been, how much I was giving away in front of others. Where had I gotten the audacity to challenge gods? I might regret my hasty actions later, but deep down, I knew now they were lying. *Wish he were dead*, Lucien had thought, so Archer must be alive.

When I got home from school, two immortals were standing in front of my apartment door. Lucien sheepishly had his hands in his pockets, avoiding my gaze, while Aroha (the full-of-herself Aphrodite) had her arms crossed, her maternal gaze narrowing on me.

"What do you two want?"

Aroha answered my question with another: "What did you mean by 'psychic'?"

"I didn't think your vocabulary was that poor, Aroha."

"Callie," Lucien scolded.

"What? Why should I answer you when all you do is feed me lies?"

Aroha sauntered forward, her expression unreadably blank. "Let's have a civil conversation." She grabbed my arm in a crushing grip but managed to make it look like we were happily arm-in-arm. She led me down the hall to her apartment, and I wondered if I'd leave alive. This goddess was scary sometimes.

The sight of the door dashed my confidence and spite. In there, the memories of kisses and words of love and promises would come back.

She unlocked the door and entered, Lucien pushing me gently forward. Inside, everything was the same. Archer's chemistry book was still on the coffee table, haphazardly tossed aside when we had given up on doing our homework and gotten lost in each other's lips. Lips I wouldn't kiss again, according to these gods. I inadvertently looked toward his room to see the door closed.

"Go in if you like," Aroha said quietly. "Take what you want before I dispose of it."

My heart skipped a beat, and my legs went weak. Doubt was setting in. She was getting rid of his things. She finally sounded sad, grieving, full of pity for me and herself.

"Sit." Lucien steered me into the direction of the sofa, the same one Archer and I had spent our days upon, watching TV, holding each other, kissing. Part of me wanted to bolt from the apartment to avoid the agony the memories would bring, but the other part of me wanted to curl up on the sofa and lose myself in the past and stay there forever.

"Callie, you owe me. Everything in my life is ruined because of you—"

"Aroha," Lucien scolded.

"No, Lucien. Stop protecting her! All you boys have done was protect her, and for what?"

"Go ahead." I said. "I know I deserve it. And it's not like you can hurt me any more than being without him does."

Lucien walked back toward the all-glass wall and stared out into the city. He was endlessly frustrated with me when I said such morbid things. I was stubborn, pathetic, and I knew I was pushing away my only real friend left because of it.

"Chase and I were getting back together, and now it's all ruined. No one can make it through what we just had to deal with—"

"Stop it, Aroha!" Lucien interceded again.

How could love create such havoc? Be so destructive? I foolishly had believed that our love only affected us, but when it was taken away, it affected many lives. I had done this to all of them. I should've stayed in the dark. Now, even a life of lies with Archer seemed like a better option than knowing the immortal world. I just wanted Archer back.

I lost track of their argument, tuning out the words and letting myself sink onto the sofa, into the memories. I swear, I could still smell Archer's scent on the pillow and inhaled it. My heart pounded in my ears, and I shivered. A fever. I'd welcome it to leave here and stay in the warmer cocoon of memories. I lay down fully, closing my eyes, picturing him.

Archer's gorgeous face was in front of me. He looked thinner, paler, his eyes dull and vacant. They didn't glow like they used to. Was I envisioning him dead? No, he blinked. A tear leaked out, and he wiped it away with the back of his hand. Something was off, not right, since this wasn't my imagination if I couldn't control what I was seeing. Was I asleep and dreaming?

The scene around him came into focus as if someone brightened a picture. He sat on a stone wall, his legs dangling over the sea, palm trees behind him, as if in some tropical locale. A city was in the background but unfocused. He held his cell phone in his hand and peered down at it.

"Oh Callie, you really are too cruel," his melodic voice said quietly. It had been so long since I'd heard him speak. *The wind blew his hair, making ripples across his scalp. It was growing longer, curling more.*

I was frozen, afraid to speak. If I were dreaming, I didn't want to wake. I longed to hear him say my name again.

Archer slipped the phone into his pocket and leaned back on his elbows. "You see way too much." He looked up, directly at me, as if he could see me.

Then the scene began darkening. I tried to hold on, but it slipped away, and Archer was gone.

"Callie." A voice brought me back. Two hands were on my temples, feeding healing heat into my head. I opened my eyes to see two concerned, intensely green ones staring into mine. Honey-scented breath wafted over me, making me think of Archer. My stomach flopped sourly in realization it was Lucien instead.

"What is wrong with her?" Aroha watched above me.

"She's sick. She's been having fevers."

"Well, fix her, then. That is your specialty."

"I'm trying to, as you can very well see, Aroha." He growled. "I don't know what causes them. Diagnosis comes before a cure."

"I'm fine." I pushed him away. I was tired of them talking about me as if I weren't there.

"Lie back a moment," Lucien commanded. "You were completely unconscious. You'll need a minute."

Although I hated to admit it, he was right. My head swirled, and my stomach churned. I lay back down.

"I saw him. He's alive. By the sea. Why did you wake me up?"

"She's hallucinating now? Take her to the mortal doctors. Let them deal with her."

"I'm not hallucinating. I saw him as he is now, thinner, paler, his hair longer. I've always sensed things about people, and the fevers make it stronger. My dad is the same. It's genetic or something." I gave Lucien a significant look in reference to Psyche.

Lucien gave me a slight shake of the head to remain quiet, which meant Aroha still didn't know who my ancestor was.

"What's going on, you two? Tell me everything, Callie, and I might just tell you something in return." Aroha smirked at me. Her eyes, so much like Archer's, unnerved me. But she had answers. I would tell her anything just to hear her say he was alive.

CHAPTER 3

CHASE

A month in Belize City wasn't enough to improve Archer. I had never seen him so depressed. Well, maybe once or twice before with better reason. He was only ever melancholy when a loved one died. When Psyche and he dissolved their marriage, he had been equally disappointed and relieved. This breakup with Callie was much worse, just like when his daughter died, just like when his siblings died. Even after Aroha and I had lost three of our four children, I was able to push on, persevere. Grief can easily transform to fighting, but Archer was no fighter, a lover through and through. He gave Callie his entire heart, mind, and soul, and it was as if she had died and taken all three with her to the Elysian fields.

I wanted to throttle him, beat some sense into him, berate him for being so weak. A son of mine pining after a girl—embarrassing, laughable, but the feeling and negative thoughts about Archer were easily suppressed. Oh, I had a temper that no other god's could match. I've done things—such horrid things—things I never would dare to tell others about. Waterboarding? Created by me. Hangings, beheadings, war, The Code of Hammurabi—me.

And then something profound happened. It had happened before in small spells of time. I would feel free. It was as if war was chaining me to being this horrific person. I hated everyone, including myself, and then— No, not chains. More like that book with the doctor guy. I'm no reader, so I forget his name. Hyde is his alter-ego, the villain. That's what it felt like. I was Hyde most of the time, the poor innocent doctor dormant inside, but every now and then, I was somehow free. The doctor took over the angry beast. It happened when I met Aroha and fell in love with her, but then Hyde won, and I was terrible to my family, longing for war, lusting after it. I never wanted anything more than Aroha or war—depending on who was winning in my head. For years now, decades actually, the doctor-me had won. Chase was a nice person inside and out; Ares, a war-driven monster. And now Chase wanted nothing more than to help his son—even if thoughts of beating some sense into him rose every now and then.

I was in new territory: away from war, with my son, trying to use my tactical brain to play detective. Something was going on with Callie. I wondered if she was this thing that freed me from myself, but it had happened before her lifetime too. I had simply gone through the motions of what I had started in Afghanistan, so it had been very easy for my estranged wife to convince me to leave the front. Still, something kept coming back to Callie. I couldn't speak to Archer about it yet. I didn't want to give him false hope or make him needlessly worry. It was clear that she was a demigod whom Zeus feared. And that fear, I believed, directly linked to our ability to defy our gifts: aside from me leaving the war, Lucien was able to lie, and Archer actually fell in love, while also going completely against his nature to kill our kind. If Aroha had changed, it wasn't obvious except for how easily she'd fallen for me this time.

Archer entered the kitchen, where I was yet again trying to research info on Callie and not getting far. If only I could research like Athena. If only the scoundrel Lucien would reply to my emails and texts. He knew. He'd almost told us. If I were in New York, I could get him to tell me in minutes—pound his spineless, selfish, lying face until he choked on his own blood and fessed up what he knew. A glorious image, but Archer needed me. I had never been there for him, pushed him aside as equally as he ignored me. This time, I would stay. I would push Ares down into a cage just as my father had done with the defiant Titans during our first great war. Had I known my father planned to lord over us and control our every move, I don't think I would've helped him win that war. Regrets are for the weak-minded though. The future is the path.

"What are you doing?" Archer asked.

"Researching."

"You? Researching?" He scoffed and sat down in front of the breakfast I'd made him, the toast he would pick apart and pretend to eat. He had a thick book in his hand, but I couldn't see the title. Most likely it was something tragically depressing. I wasn't past book-burning at the moment. It was very useful to have the masses attack the intellectual stronghold of their own countries to make them fall from within; it was easier to control the ignorant. Somehow, I didn't think it would work on Archer, him being neither ignorant nor whole enough to break down. Archer was already broken. He had taken to reading morbid books and not sleeping or eating. We could go without those latter two, but I'd have to get him some nectar at some point. He was already thinner, his cheekbones more defined, and there were black rings under his eyes.

He was torturing himself. Each day, it got worse. No war tactic yet had come to me that could solve this. After thousands of years, it finally dawned on me how much there was to learn out there, and I had only fixated on war, politics, and geography.

"Well, if you've got that attitude about my researching skills, I won't tell you what I'm researching." Picking on him seemed to be the only thing that elicited a half-smile from him these days, but it felt cruel, kicking a man while he was down.

"Do you even know how to use one of those?" He motioned toward the laptop.

"You do realize warfare is rampant with technology these days, right?"

He nibbled on the toast. Good. If I could keep him distracted, maybe he'd absentmindedly eat a whole slice.

"Okay, let me rephrase. Do you know how to use that thing without killing people with it?"

Ouch. I didn't react. He had a tendency to try to bring me down—misery loves company, so they say. And he needed it. I pushed down the Ares temper that would've punched someone at such an insult. It was so easy to do now that I doubted anyone knew he was still in me; I was positive I showed no outward reaction whatsoever.

"War can save people, you know. Some are killed through collateral damage, but some are saved from oppressors. You remember why I walked out last time, no? Hitler was out of control, and I had to help the allies."

"With atom bombs that destroyed entire cities."

"That was Nemesis," I retorted. She was the goddess of vengeance and often worked with me.

Well, Dite would tell it differently. I imagined her saying, "That horse-faced mongrel would do anything to get you in bed, Ares." And she'd be partially right, but never did I give in to Nemesis's advances. I was also careful not to scorn her either. I had seen what retaliation she would unleash if I was cruel to her.

"Well," Archer fumbled for a moment. "You had a hand in the Hitler situation in the first place." He really thought that of me? The kid had a viper-tongue.

"I was only on the ally side, remember."

He scoffed. "Doubtful."

"Why would you assume if you don't even know? There are others you know. It was called a *World* War for a reason. That was Thor and

Odin's mischief. They even admitted they lost control of Hitler thanks to Loki."

"Ugh. I don't want to hear about war." Archer groaned.

No, he only wanted to read morbid poetry about lovers who can't be together or kill themselves or die in the name of love.

"I'm sure you enjoyed yourself anyway," Archer added.

"I did, naturally."

Archer looked up from his book and gave me a wry smile. Then it fell. He scrutinized me. "What research are you doing?" His voice took on an accusatory tone.

"Looking for answers, Son. That's all for now."

"About Callie?" He swallowed hard after saying her name. It was the first time he'd said it to me. We hadn't talked about her. I'm not your heart-to-heart talk kind of god. I'm a doer, a solver, a fighter. I don't do emotions—other than the ones that incite bedroom activities or bloodshed. According to Athena, I was Freud's Id personified. I kind of got what she meant—like primal urges—but I think she was insulting me when she said that.

I nodded, gauging his reaction.

"It doesn't matter that she's a demigod anymore. Zeus would never..." He took a bite of toast, staring off in deep thought.

I had to say something before he slipped back into a depressive state again, but I didn't want to give him false hope. "The answers always help in planning."

"What are you planning?" He was wary, untrusting. "You're planning a war?" His mouth dropped. "With Zeus? Your own father? The god of gods? Are you insane?"

Well, that could've gone better, but at least he was shocked and not melancholy.

"War doesn't have to be on the offense, you know. I always plan a defensive move and retaliation move. It would force Nemesis—as you inadvertently brought her up earlier—onto our side that way too. I know my father. He wants Callie dead. He won't stop. Eventually, ten years, twenty, he will strike again. I need to find out why. I need to find a way to protect her."

"Because you like war or for me?"

What a complex question. "For you, of course, but truly for everything. You heard the prophecy Lucien withheld. Our world is changing, and it has something to do with Callie. It never was about you. It was about *any* god being with her. She is why you fell in love, why Lucien lies, why I left war—"

"You're planning one now!"

"I'm planning how to protect her and you. The old me would've stormed Olympus by now."

"You would have." Archer smiled weakly. He picked at his toast, and when he found the courage, he asked, "Have you found anything?"

"Nothing concrete yet. Just theories. I'll tell you when I know something for certain." Only, that was a lie. I would only tell him things that wouldn't hurt him. One of my theories felt so way off that I could hardly think it, let alone voice it. Callie—if she was the one freeing us from our roles—was like free will. But she was a demigod, and there had never been a god or goddess of freedom. Zeus had always reigned over us. But the idea of losing that hold over us would terrify my father into a war. Food for thought.

"Is that why we're near the Blue Hole? Are you going to recruit Poseidon or something?"

I stared him down. We were by the Great Blue Hole, the underwater sinkhole to the humans, but to us, the entry to Poseidon's home, Atlantis—the real one. "We're here so Zeus can't watch us, as I know he is longing to do." There were places my father couldn't see us—sites with high volcanic and magnetic activity, domains ruled by other god families, and his brothers' kingdoms. "But what would be the point in recruiting gods who cannot leave the water?"

Archer looked down at his toast and sighed. He seemed disappointed, almost as if he wanted me to somehow break Poseidon from his prison and raise an army to beat Zeus. If only I could. By my spear, Poseidon and Hades would jump at the chance to destroy my father if someone untethered them from their worlds. It would be utter chaos or could be a beautifully orchestrated war if properly mapped out. Too bad it was impossible.

Archer stood up and said he was off to the rooftop patio to read. I nodded, needing the privacy to call New York anyway. Once he left the room, I looked at his plate. He had eaten two pieces of toast. Progress!

I immediately called Lucien, who answered with, "What is it? Is everything okay?"

"Yeah, why? Another prophecy you're going to hide from us?" I countered.

He paused. "I'm hanging out with Linda." Then he said in a hushed tone. "Should we even be talking?"

"For the love of Hera, Lucien, relax. I'm alone right now. So, is that a yes?"

"I'll call you later."

"You won't. You're ignoring my emails."

"Because he most likely will hack in to see them. I taught him everything he knows about computers, and you know who I learned from."

Lucien was being careful not to say Archer's or Hermes's names, so I realized how careful I needed to be when he was in front of mortals.

I heard Linda ask something about computer hacking, but it wasn't clear.

"Likely excuse. You better call me back tonight," I said.

"I will."

"You better. Don't make me sic Dite on you."

"Ugh, I will, okay?"

Lucien hung up first, my annoying little half-brother. I deleted the call log just in case Archer would pry. Then I emailed Athena because she was just not a phone person—awkward to say the least. She and I worked together now and then because she was the goddess of justice, which went hand-in-hand with war. She wouldn't blow me off like Lucien.

After that, I texted Aroha, asking about Callie's parentage.

She texted back with, **Are you Prometheus or something? I'm here with Callie right now. She just showed me something interesting.**

What?

A carefully preserved letter from Psyche herself, asking the mortals to take care of her child: Marshal Psyches or later known as Syches.

Damn if that didn't hit me hard. Callie was descended from a demigod as she said, but she was Psyche's. This would not bode well in Archer's condition. It might drive him insane.

I'm not telling Archer that, I typed.

Of course not! And I won't tell this girl that he's alive. She is prying, though. She's insisting he's alive somewhere in the tropics and says she's psychic. I think we broke her mind.

But she's right. We are, I typed. What did this mean? How was she seeing where we were? Psyche's descendant or not, this was too powerful for your average demigod.

There was a long pause before she sent back, **Where are you?**

If she is seeing things somehow and professes to be psychic, I shouldn't tell you, Love. What if she can read your mind?

I hate this. I miss you. Her words made me smile, and my mood lifted. Gods, I missed her already. Unlike our poor child, at least I knew I would see Aroha again. I hadn't seen her since the late 1930's until this recent, welcomed, intrusion into my life. That's roughly eighty years, so I could manage until the Callie situation resolved or she passed from old age. I wish I hadn't taken it slow, had Dite physically again, because it was all that was on my mind at the moment. But regret was for the weak. I don't do weak.

The other day, I did promise her I'd tell her something if she told me all of this. What should I say?

Stall her, lie. You're good at that.

Ha ha. Takes a liar to know one.

Touché. I smiled.

"Who's that?" Archer's voice made me jump. He was grabbing a water bottle from the fridge.

"Your mother." I was about to pretend I wasn't talking to her or anyone, but I'm sure I had a cheesy smile that told him the truth.

Archer froze for a second but then opened the water bottle and took a swig. "About what?" He was trying so hard to be nonchalant that he failed terribly.

"You wouldn't want to know," I insinuated, knowing full well that Archer wouldn't want to hear any more. It had always been the best method to deter his inquiries.

"Gross." Then he gave me a disgruntled roll of his eyes and went back outside. I heard his footsteps plod up on the roof again.

I looked down at my phone to see Aroha had answered: **I'll think of something. She's quite tedious, though.**

Our son needs you to care for her, protect her, so be nice.

For how long? I want to be with you two. She ignored my request for her to be kind to the girl, which was worrisome.

I know. Just for a while. I want us to be together too. I'm trying to figure out a way around the punishment.

Don't you go starting a war.

Not going to start one, darling. Preparing for an attack. He won't let her live, no matter what, Aroha. I just know it.

I hope not. Gotta run. This mortal is nosey. I love you.

I love you too.

I deleted our texts, as Lucien suggested, in case Archer would snoop, and leaned back, closing my eyes, thinking. My mind strategized ways to prevent my father from killing Callie. Any move he would make would be deadly. I hoped my possible retaliation would prevent it. I needed allies first. Although my father was hardly on good term with the others, I had some alliances left over from certain wars. Trusting other war gods, though, was a bit problematic. Our alliances shifted often. If Zeus demanded the girl's life or attacked, I might not have any other options but to trust in other immortal tribes.

My phone rang. It was Athena. I knew she wouldn't beat around the bush like Lucien—god of lies. But a phone call? I was flattered.

"Athena?"

"Where are you, Ares?"

"Safe. Where are you?"

"Safe."

We chuckled over neither of us trusting each other enough to give over a location.

"The girl is still in New York? Is she safe?" Her second question was a strange one. Maybe she knew enough to help me after all.

"Yes, in New York, but you were there for the ruling, so you know she's not."

"How is Archer taking it?"

"Just about as well as he took to Hedone's death."

She sighed out a heavy breath. "I don't understand our father."

"I emailed you because I think you do, Athena. I need to know."

"Know what?"

"Your theories, because I want to see if they match mine."

"I honestly don't know. My theories vary greatly, but I'll tell you some probable ones. You go first, though."

That was something I could agree with. I finally had a plan: alliances, find them. The more on our side, the better, so if Zeus made a move, we wouldn't be alone. Another strategy to start on: break up Olympus. That would take some scheming help from Athena, and my wife—who was the queen of breaking people apart, even though she was supposed to join them together. Athena was halfway on our side, so I just needed to convince her to go against Zeus. We could do this. I would be ready for Zeus's strike.

CHAPTER 4

Archer

Without Callie, I was nothing. It sounded pathetic, but the embodiment of Love could not exist without love. I was barely alive, losing the joy I had in anything, as if Callie were truly dead. Only she wasn't. Knowing she was alive out there was killing me. How I longed to be with her but knew that I couldn't. Zeus would kill her, damn it.

I stopped thinking of him as my grandfather or my relation. He was the foulest villain in all this mess, and my hatred for him—something I'm normally not adept to feeling—grew in me each day. My anger gave me something to focus on, aside from thinking of the girl I would never see again. It grew and festered inside, building in pressure until I felt like I would explode. Rage. That was the emotion. I was becoming my father, and I didn't want him to know that.

I was munching on toast, reading *Romeo and Juliet*, much to my father's dismay, when he brought up the subject I wished to avoid for the umpteenth time. "Don't you think it's time—"

"Nope. He didn't give a timeframe."

"Let me finish." He growled at me and took a deep breath.

I was pissing him off. Good, maybe he'd leave me alone so I could wallow and fade into nonexistence. Even better, maybe he'd start a fight to help me lash out—not that I would win. He was the strongest of us.

"Archer, we don't have to find a Death. But we are near the Great Blue Hole. The water gods get leave to go to the surface to mate." He gave me an annoyed don't-be-stupid scowl before continuing, "Zeus can't even control Proteus on that score. He puts Lucien's roster of women to shame. I'm willing to bet there's at least one demigod in this city."

"And if they are marked to be Death?" I pointed out, just wanting him to drop it. I didn't want to hear his condescending lecture about water gods I already knew everything about.

"Hades is on the other side of the world, Archer."

"But Thanatos got around everywhere to take souls."

"I don't think Thanatos would spend more time than he would have to in Belize. It's doubtful we'd find his progeny here. It doesn't matter. We figure out the parentage before we choose."

"It still will get me closer to choosing a Death. I can't do that to Callie. Not until she's over me."

"It won't get you closer. It will buy you time with Zeus." Chase was quiet for a moment. "We're going out tonight."

"Oh, so is that a command?" How dare he tell me we were going out when all I wanted to do was stay in my room and be alone and suffer in solitude.

"Do I need to make it that way, or will you come peacefully?"

I said nothing but inwardly seethed at him.

"Do you have anything better to do?" he pressed, raising his thick brows in that arrogant way.

Of course, I didn't have any excuses, and it didn't seem like not going was an option. I wanted to fight it, to argue with him, but he was so different and caring; part of me was unnerved by it, and part of me was basking in the parental attention I had been denied for thousands of years.

So, that night, I found myself at a seedy bar with music blasting and bodies gyrating to an eclectic playlist of music—Latin, pop, and reggae, *Garifuna* rock—and I was drinking enough rum to fell a mortal man. Ichor burns off mortal alcohol, so it was a pointless exercise, but trying to sling back enough to get drunk seemed like a challenge I needed at the moment.

Chase came back from the dancefloor, a girl on each arm and two trailing. Great, what was he up to? Picking up girls was not on my agenda for the night, and it was even weirder that my dad was doing so in front of me. They were all fairly pretty, of course, because Chase would seek no less than the best looking. They all varied in skin-tone and looks, aside from similar hues of dark hair and eyes, as if Chase were trying to bring me a sample tray of sweets to see which I wanted from this culturally blended country. It was all pointless. Even though he took the pains to profile for possible local water-god descendants, none of their eyes held the mystique a demigod would possess. They all paled in comparison to Callie.

My father introduced me in both English and Kriol, and they joined me at the bar. I ignored their stares and winks, how the one brushed her chest up against my elbow. The girl to my left all but said she wanted to leave with me for a tumble. One thing was clear: I wasn't going anywhere with this woman.

After a while, I think she realized I neither wanted her nor really wanted to talk to her. All the girls faded away, except the one who felt she'd won Chase over the other ladies. Not much later, he kindly dismissed his worshiper and paid up. We wandered home in the dark night, the noises of the city still alive despite the hour.

"You could've gone off with her. I was fine," I told him.

"I didn't want to. I'm going to wait for your mom. She has four more years in New York if plans stay the same. I pulled them to distract you, much good it did. But I was entertained in seeing you try to get out of the one's clutches, though."

"Wow, thanks. What's the point?" I tried not to think about how Ma was with Callie, how she would simply abandon her in four years, as would Lucien most likely, and by then, her father would be dead. Callie would be alone.

"We're looking for a demigod. Every day, we'll go out into the city for something, and every night, we'll hit the busy bars or clubs—somewhere different each time until we find one."

I inwardly groaned. And each day and night, he made sure we did so, only letting me shirk this duty on Sundays since businesses had shortened hours and fewer mortals were about. January gave way to February when we finally came across a demigod.

We were in yet another dance club when I saw a girl on the dance floor moving with unearthly elegance and rhythm. Her dancing was eerily impeccable and graceful as she relentlessly rolled her hips back and forth, doing the regional *punta* dance. I didn't know how she didn't exhaust herself dancing the night away nor how she could stand men throwing their sweaty bodies up against hers so suggestively, but this was a different culture, a modern time period, and as all other male gods liked to mockingly point out, I was "an uptight prude" when it came to sex. Whatever. I wanted one woman and one woman only, and I definitely had those kinds of feelings for Callie.

Objectively, the girl was pretty, with dark skin and thick, straight jet-black hair. She was short and curvy in the right areas. She finally stopped dancing and made her way off the dancefloor, fanning herself, her nails painted a bright red. She passed us to go to the bar, and I noted large almond-shaped eyes and full pouty lips.

Chase nudged me.

"Her. She has to be one," I said.

"So, seduce her." He nodded over at her.

"No way. You do it."

"She's beautiful, Archer."

"So, you go for it."

He shook his head at me and sighed. "I guess we'll do it the long way. You'll have to befriend her."

The girl turned from the bar, holding a drink, and spotted us. We stuck out as the rare Caucasian tourists for this part of town. She appraised Chase briefly, and her eyes raked over me before she made her way to her giggling girlfriends, who were all now staring at us. I looked away. There was no way I was approaching her here, now, like this. She would expect something from me here at a dance club, even if she were innocent. She'd try to get a kiss at the very least.

I'd find her the next day and purposely run into her.

CHAPTER 5

Thankfully, by the grace of my nemesis Dolos—god of deception—Aroha was crafty enough to avoid telling Callie that Archer was alive. However, I knew enough about Callie's relentless tenacity to know that if she found out, she would become unbearable to deal with. Aroha seemed to stave her off by telling Callie she wasn't allowed to say anything without Callie being killed, but one day, she hoped she could tell her the truth about what had happened.

As expected, the lies backfired on Aroha. No one needed an oracle to know how Callie would react. She hounded Aroha relentlessly, and Aroha's patience was quickly wearing thin. My own patience with Callie was at a breaking point—and I secretly loved her. I'd do anything to destroy the bond between her and Archer and help her move on at this point.

Callie's birthday was fast approaching, which was pretty crappy for her because she'd be too depressed to enjoy it. Linda insisted we go out shopping together to buy Callie gifts. Per usual, I never knew what to get a woman. They were impossible to shop for, and Linda made it even more difficult. She scoffed at the lovely present I had picked out. "What's wrong with a bracelet? Look, it has an arrow on it, to remind her of Archer."

"First off, that's a bit romantic, don't you think? It'll give her the wrong message," Linda chastised.

"Callie doesn't think of me like that." Even if I wish she did.

"That's not what people are saying."

"People, meaning the jealous, psycho friend of yours."

"It's not just her."

The fact she answered me proved she knew Emily was just that.

"You and Callie spend a lot of time together," she said.

Great. I knew enough about women at least to know where this was headed. Instead of calling her out, I played the typical expected role of male ignorance. "With Aroha and you, yeah."

"I know, but don't do a bracelet, please. She's a mess about Archer still, so reminding her of him is a bad idea."

"That's true," I mused.

Linda was growing jealous, which was tiresome. If I broke up with her, though, what human friend would Callie have left? She'd let Archer hijack her life and then abandon her.

"Here," I said as I saw an antique bookshop.

"A book?" Linda asked as if I were crazy.

"Not romantic, is it?" I shot back.

She frowned at my reproachful tone.

I weaved through the aisles in the tiny shop, looking for the reference section. Mostly, there were old dictionaries and encyclopedia sets, but then I read the covers at immortal speed and found the one I was looking for. I gingerly took it off the shelf and opened it to see the print date: 1942. One of the original editions in amazing shape.

"Greek mythology?" Linda asked, raising a skeptical brow at me. "Won't her dad have one of these?"

"I'm sure. But this is a first edition of Edith Hamilton's version. It's the best." To Callie, I'd say it was the most accurate. Hiding myself from Linda was tedious too.

"Didn't know you were a mythological expert too. Do you have club meetings with Callie I miss out on?" Her tone was mocking and kind of catty.

"More like I talk about it with her dad. He's so intelligent, knows so much."

"Her dad?"

"What's wrong with that?" I challenged as I took the book up to the counter to pay.

The old woman running the store looked at each of us as if she anticipated something kicking off between us. If not today, it probably would soon. Not only was this jealousy unbearable, we were at a crossroads. Linda and I were hedging our intimacy toward sex, and although I really, really, really wanted that...she'd get frighteningly attached.

"Well, either it's dorky, or you're trying to get on his good side to date her."

"Well then, if you insist those are my only options, I'm a dork then, aren't I?"

"I didn't mean it like that."

"You did, or if you didn't, you're annoyingly jealous of a girl whose boyfriend just died." There, see how she liked the either/or logical fallacy thrown back at her.

"I..." She was lost for words.

"Ultimatums aren't nice are they? Please stop trying to force me to admit rumors that aren't true." I forked over the cash, which was pretty hefty, and hustled out of there.

"I'm sorry. You're right. I've been so fixated on what Emily said that I forgot Callie is the victim here," Linda admitted, which surprised me greatly. She weaved her arm in mine and put her head on my shoulder.

I kissed the top of her glossy black hair. I wished her jealousy was unfounded and that I could love her more than Callie.

"I've been thinking about Callie's birthday and how she hardly has any friends—"

"Thanks to Emily."

Linda sighed, annoyed I disliked her "bestie." I avoided this ridiculous slang as much as possible. It was so hard to keep up with in multiple languages, and it was outdated so frequently. "And the fact she's still fairly new. Anyway, I thought since Valentine's Day is her birthday—"

"Wait, I thought you were joking, like the day before or after?"

"No," she looked at me oddly. "*On* Valentine's Day, February 14th. Why does it matter?"

Oh, the irony! It had been turned into a greeting card holiday by modern mortals, and they'd adopted Archer's Roman alias, Cupid, as a symbol for that very day. If only they knew the real origin of Valentine's day; it didn't involve saints, candy, and roses until much later—more like animal sacrifices for Pan and a dating game gone overboard for Hera. Everything was so uncanny and strange. I needed to research more. I should cooperate with Ares. I had called him back, two days after I'd promised, and told him all I knew about Callie, but Aroha had already done so. I told him of my prophecy, except the bit where Themis said I wasn't to be trusted and that there would be a war. The last thing I needed was them harassing me or the war god knowing his favorite pastime was on the horizon. I told him to keep me out of his findings and his alliances until it was time. I blamed it on my unstable ability to lie. It was the best I could do to protect them and myself, possibly from each other.

Linda was staring at me, awaiting an explanation.

"It doesn't matter. It just sucks, considering the situation."

"Exactly, which is why I thought about having a Valentine's party at my house. Don't tell her, though. I want to combine it as a surprise party for Callie. She insists she doesn't want to do anything for her birthday but dinner with her dad, but it would make her so happy. She needs to know people care about her."

"If she doesn't want to do anything, maybe we should respect that."

"I thought you two were like best buds?" Linda scoffed. "Callie's too kindhearted to impose upon her friends, who are mostly dating people. She thinks she'll be a third-wheel and spoil our night. But if it's a group of people, she won't feel that way."

Was she right? Did I not understand Callie? Surely, a sad mortal would need company on the day of love, so Linda had a point. Callie should not be alone and would make the Cupid association.

"I just thought you were bent on going out." I expected I'd have to go over-the-top for this ridiculous day. Archer and Aroha had trained me well in the art of romance. It all felt cheesy, fake. I was a realist. Formerly, I had always told the truth. Fantastical romance was a subterfuge and a lie, but apparently, some girls liked it.

"Well, yeah, but we can do an early dinner when she's with her dad, and then I go home while you pick her up with some excuse that I want her to come over for some girl time."

"Okay," I agreed, although it made me uncomfortable. I didn't know how Callie would react. She could emotionally breakdown and cause a scene, or she could be ecstatic. She was pretty unpredictable at the moment.

Monday morning, Callie showed us her true emotional range after she entered the cafeteria. She came in weepy after holding herself together well over the last couple weeks. The fevers were relentless for her still, which didn't help her mental state. She held a manila envelope.

After neither Linda nor I could get her talking, I pried the envelope out of her rigid hands. I think she only gave in when it was clear it could tear. I opened it and pulled out three large black-and-white photos. The first was taken of Callie pondering over a book, unawares. She was stunning. I had forgotten how gorgeous she had been before fevers and grief ravaged her body. She still inspired desire in me, but before, she'd had more to her figure and had been full of so much liveliness.

The second photo was Archer and Callie together, his arm draped around her shoulder, them smiling at the camera, both full of the exuberance of new love. He shouldn't have allowed the photo. This was probably not his fault. Avoiding a photo was harder these days, with cell phones and social media, and much easier to remove the evidence later down the line thanks to Zeus's task force. Then again, they really only bothered with things that alarmed them, things mortals noticed.

The third photo was of Archer alone, looking away as if he hadn't known the camera was there. In the photo, Archer had a jacket draped over his shoulder, and his face was at ease, staring at something with his intense, brightly lit eyes. I didn't need to see what he was looking at; his expression was beholding Callie.

I slipped the photos back into the envelope and handed them back to her. She'd torture herself with them, but I couldn't keep them from her.

"Jannie from yearbook gave them to me," she mumbled.

I gave Linda a look, so she took over soothing Callie, walking her to the bathroom, where she could cry in peace. Emily rolled her eyes and made a joke to Mary Beth, but at least Mary Beth had the decency not to laugh or give in to Emily's vindictiveness.

I sat down with my tray. "He's dead, Emily," I lashed out. "So you can stop your petty jealousy and grow up. And stop those asinine rumors too. I'm with Linda."

The girl's mouth dropped, but then she closed it and straightened herself up and shot me a haughty look as if she were Aphrodite herself. "Thanks for the advice, Lucien, but anyone who has eyes in their head knows you're dying to pick up Archer's leftovers. And as for Callie? She's simply playing you and all these guys, pretending to be a victim."

"Is she now?" Aroha's authoritative voice sliced through the cafeteria.

Emily turned to see Aroha standing behind her with her tray.

"So, my brother, God rest his soul, meant nothing to Callie? Is that what you're trying to say?" After being buddy-buddy with Emily and talking trash about Callie, Aroha defending her was the last thing I expected.

"I—" Emily gaped.

"You what? We can't hear you, Emily." Aroha's volume was loud enough for surrounding tables to hear.

The silence rippled down the line. The entire cafeteria was listening now. Faraway students were standing to see, straining to hear.

"I—"

"She's speechless for once! What a miracle!" Aroha said, despite not allowing the girl to speak. This comment elicited a few giggles. "Anyone who saw my brother and Callie together knew they were in love, true love. How dare you sully the memory of my brother with lies!"

"Aroha," I warned her that she had gone far enough. She was legitimately furious, not an act, and I didn't want her to lapse into godly feats.

"And this guy? No offense, Lucien, but he looks at every girl that way. He's a guy! It doesn't mean he would act on it. You're just bitter because he doesn't look at you the way he looks at us. All jealous because you're basic, nothing, just a sad girl trying to push others down to make herself feel better."

I dared to look at Emily, who was staring down at the table, dejected, angry, and most likely trying not to cry. She deserved it, but I knew Aroha would take it further. I think Callie had grown into an extension of Archer, and no one messed with her son.

Linda and Callie had returned, and everyone was staring.

"What's going on?" Linda asked.

"Emily was just leaving our table," Aroha said.

Emily stood up quickly, her face crimson with embarrassment and shame—one would hope—and she trudged back to her old table. Aroha glared at the table; the girls saw Aroha's glower and shook their heads, denying Emily. The mortal moved to another table, and Aroha's eyes followed. I caught Linda and Callie up to speed. Callie tried not to smile, too kind to gloat, but she sighed with relief. Linda watched her friend, torn. When I turned my attention back to Aroha, she was still playing the game of intimidation.

"Aroha, let the girl sit down. Stop glaring at everyone."

"I will after she sits alone for the day. She needs to learn to stop hurting people." Aroha put her arm around Callie and rubbed it in support.

Callie sighed again. I hadn't realized until now how much stress Aroha and Emily had put on Callie. I was doing a poor job looking after her, and I was beginning to realize that I didn't know Callie as well as I had wanted to believe, which meant she and Archer had had something I could never have with her. But I really wished it were otherwise.

CHAPTER 6

Callie

Aroha came over while my dad was at the doctor's, and she was acting nice again (very suspicious). She had been kind to me lately, but I didn't trust her, and she kept prying into things and wasn't telling me anything about Archer. At least she'd stopped insisting he was dead, but she refused to talk about him at all, diverting the subject each time.

Now, she wanted to know about my mother.

"I'm not telling you anything else until you tell me he's alive," I insisted. (Take that!)

She gave me a haughty look as if to say I was so lowly, she was offended I would dare to refuse her. She was such a snob, but she had the answers I needed. Aroha crossed the room and took out our photo albums without asking. Then she flipped through it in superspeed, my eyes trying and failing to keep up. Archer hadn't let me see those abilities, except when he was trying to save my life, so it was still surreal.

"You could just ask, you know," I scoffed at her.

"Is this your mom?" She held up the album.

"No, that's my aunt."

Aroha tried another book.

"There aren't any pictures of her there."

She put the book back and stared me down. Neither of us said a word.

I crossed my arms in challenge. I wasn't going to tell her anything if she didn't spill the beans first.

Then she was out the door at immortal speed and back in the room, holding a box.

I jumped.

She smirked, and her eyes squinted upon me, returning my challenge. She was up to something.

"You tell me about your mother, and I'll let you see Archer's keepsake box."

The offer was too tempting. She'd never tell me he was alive, so getting a part of his past would be the next best thing, to know part of him I hadn't been allowed to know. I wanted to see anything that had been Archer's.

"There's a wooden chest in my father's closet, top shelf. It's locked, though, and I have no clue where he hides the key. Everything about my mother is in there. He'd probably show it to us if you just wait."

"Have you seen everything in it, or did he just show you pictures of her?"

The idea of my father hiding anything from me was shocking, and yet her accusation wasn't farfetched. He would go get the photos and show me whenever I'd asked. I never was allowed to open the box or see what was inside. I had always assumed it was something private, like love letters, but now my mind was spinning webs of possibilities. "You think he's hiding something?"

"I have no idea. Athena wants to know about your mom. Probably to complete the biological picture and cure these fevers. Plus, Chase is asking too. He thinks he needs intel so he can protect you. Stop looking so shocked. What kind of parents would we be not to protect whom our son had sacrificed himself for? It would make it all pointless."

I flinched. She hadn't spoken of Archer's death in weeks and now did with such ease. To distract myself, I opened the box and looked inside to see Archer's things. I picked up a round frame.

Aroha dropped down next to me, making my heart leap up into my throat. I hadn't even seen her leave the room. This was messing with my head.

"Stop moving like that around me!"

"Thought you said your father would be home soon. Trying to speed things up." She held up the wooden chest.

"How do you plan on opening—" Before I could finish, she was trying to pick the lock with some paperclips she must've grabbed off the desk in Dad's office.

I focused back on the picture in my hand. It was an old oval wooden frame, and inside was a painting. It looked in the style of the Renaissance when people were painted pale, round, in extravagant dresses. The woman was beautiful, ethereal, and my stomach lurched. Was this Psyche? I took in the voluminous strawberry blond curls, bowed little pouty lips, flawless skin, and a pug nose—and then I saw them. Looking right at me were vibrantly blue eyes. Archer's eyes. This must be Hedone, his daughter. If he left something so dear behind, he must be dead. My denial was starting to slip into dread.

Aroha paused her lockpicking to look over. "Hedone," she said with a mixture of pride and sorrow. "She looked just like Archer, like me."

"What did her mother look like?"

"Pretty. Short. Curvy. So pale. Red hair and green eyes. It was an exotic look back then for us in Greece, but the curvy figure was attractive at the time. Don't worry, Callie, she didn't hold a flame to you."

The compliment was kind, but I was the one who was green-eyed—with envy. Ridiculous to be jealous of a ghost (but there it was all the same). I looked through the rest of the box. There were photos of places, not people, but it was extraordinary how many locales Archer had photographed all over the world. There were pictures of sights I only dreamed of seeing—some of buildings and wonders of the world, some of picturesque settings, beautiful sunsets, bright blue oceans and skies, and snowcapped mountains. The pictures started out black and white, then to grainy color, ending in vibrant crisp modern hues. The things he had seen left me in awe. He had lived such a long life, and I had lived a mere blip in his lifetime. And it was my fault he was gone.

"What was your mother like?" Aroha cut through my morose thoughts.

"I don't remember her. She died when I was five."

"That's awful. How?"

"A car accident."

I moved on from the photos to find little carved figurines of bowmen and Spartan soldiers. They looked exactly like the ones in my dad's case. He had been right all along. It was crazy how Dad's ideas were true.

"Your grandparents?"

"All dead. My mother's parents were dead before I was born. My dad's passed by the time I was ten. Why?"

"Your mother's past seems so unclear. If we could've talked to her parents, it could shed some light on these fevers."

"I don't think that would help. My mother and aunt were adopted, and my aunt isn't related to her by blood."

Aroha paused briefly, thinking, before she continued picking the lock, a futile endeavor because now she was trying various speeds when all the combinations of clip positions hadn't worked. I knew it was futile. In my rebellious pre-teen years, I'd tried my hand at it too and had never unlocked it.

Among Archer's keepsakes, I found a small cigar box that was locked with a tiny padlock. Aroha looked over and shrugged as if she hadn't seen it before. Then she snapped the lock clean off with little effort and handed it to me. I cringed at the thought of her strength. She could snap me in two with her bare hands.

"Why not smash that open with your goddess strength?" I asked her in reference to my father's chest.

"Because your father would know I snooped...and I just had my nails done."

I hid my eyeroll from her so she wouldn't murder me. Inside the cigar box were more photos. Eagerly, I sifted through them. They were of people. The first was of just Aroha and Lucien. The second was of Archer. Seeing his face again, his eyes staring at the camera, sent a jolt through me, and my stomach turned. I closed my eyes, unable to face the pain of seeing him and knowing I'd never see him again. *Callie,* I heard his voice whisper in my head, a faint memory of what it had sounded like, already fading away. I couldn't remember the timbre of his voice, the luminescence of his eyes, the feel of his lips on mine. It was all slipping away from me. I swear I could hear waves crashing and Archer murmuring, yet I couldn't hear the words.

"This is too much for you?" Aroha's concerned voice cut through whatever strange hallucination I was having, and it yanked me back to reality.

I opened my eyes and gazed at her. There was genuine concern on her face, her superficial mask gone.

"No." I flipped through the photos. They went back in time. Mostly, it was the two of them, sometimes Lucien. Their clothes became more dated, the pictures fuzzier, and then they became black and white. In these photos, there were other people—all young, beautiful, except that older bartender I met once (wait a minute). When had I met a bartender? "Who's this? I think I met him. A bartender?"

Aroha glanced over briefly, then went back to picking the lock. "Dionysus. You did meet him. Mnemosyne wiped your mind clear—or so we thought. You figured Archer out after an attack."

"The man with the scar," I confirmed, memories fluttering back. I had believed they had been dreams. Archer had let them mess with my brain (betrayal of the century).

I flipped to another picture, trying not to think about the past. A couple stood next to each other: a woman with light hair and eyes, and a man with darker skin. His eyes were dark, as was his hair, both perhaps brown, but it was too hard to tell in the black-and-white photo. A flicker of an image danced across my mind. I'd seen him before. *There was noise, water, his face, hair wet, eyes horrified.* That was it. I tried to recall what seemed like a millisecond of a memory, but nothing more came to me. "Who's this couple?"

Aroha leaned over. "Athena and Prometheus. And they weren't a couple. Athena doesn't do love. All brains, no emotions." Then she sighed. "Ares would scold me for being judgmental, but Athena and I had many fights about the lack of rationality of love, so I am biased. Athena is...different."

"How so?"

"She's just, I dunno." Aroha paused her lockpicking and pondered for a moment. "Anti-social, socially awkward. She prefers books and learning to people, and when she's in this hyperfocus mode, there's no getting through to her. You might as well be talking to a brick wall. There's nothing *wrong* with her. I just cannot fathom never being in love for over three-thousand years and stubbornly believing that I wasn't missing anything. Love and rationalism are like oil and water, Callie. Athena and I don't mix."

Although I wanted to hear more about Athena, whom I had always thought by far the most talented goddess (not that I would admit that in front of Aphrodite herself), I didn't want to hear about feuds. I shifted to the other god in the photo. "Does Prometheus really see the future?"

"Yep. But he's impossible to find."

"I thought Zeus could find everyone?"

"No, just mortals and Olympians. Prometheus is a Titan. Different family, people. Greece was tribal back in our beginnings. I wasn't around yet for the massive war they had, but Ares said they had 'Near East' values. They're the first to discover immortality, or so I've heard. Lots of gods think they were the first." Aroha set the chest down. "This is impossible."

My mind thought about what she was saying. I wasn't as familiar with Mesopotamian mythology like Dad, but I knew that "Near East" described that region. No wonder Zeus killed Cronus—who, I guess, wasn't his father as the myths said—and put him in Tartarus. No wonder he chained Prometheus to a rock to have his liver pecked out repeatedly. He couldn't control them. Zeus was a control freak.

Aroha looked to the door, then was off in a flash and back sitting next to me as the door opened. Dad hobbled in, followed by Raphael. Aroha pointed at the next picture in my hand, the chest gone. She had heard him coming and put it back. "Artemis, Lucien's twin sister."

"Pictures of gods?" Dad asked eagerly.

"Come sit. I'll show you," Aroha offered, charm dripping off her voice.

Raphael and Dad gazed at her fixedly, and my father hustled as fast as he could to sit next to her. Goodness, she was using some godly charisma to try to cajole answers out of Dad. She was a sneaky one. Little did she know, my dad would never fall victim to her charms.

CHAPTER 7

CHASE

Archer was dragging his feet about adopting Lena—that was the name of the girl we'd met in the club. I had to find it out for him. I had pulled a bunch of girls, hoping he'd go for a distraction, but he was the faithful kind. He would never be with another woman while Callie lived. I found myself envious, so when one of the girls invited me back to her place—and my gods, her dark skin and vibrant eyes were delectable—I refrained. The Ares in me wanted fulfillment, yet the clear-headed Chase was in control, who loved his wife and would be faithful to her, even if they were apart. He and Aroha were together in spirit and emotion, so he must be patient about the physical. The day he saw her again, though...

I stopped thinking about myself in the third person and turned my thoughts back to the Archer-Lena situation. Forcing him back onto our mission of intel on Lena, who we suspected was a demigod, was hard. We followed her back from the club she frequented—at a distance—to see where she lived. Once she was inside the house, we cut down a side alley to head back to our apartment. She lived with an older woman we presumed was her mother, but no dad or siblings seemed to be in the picture. One way or another, we had to find out if she was demigod stock. There was a good possibility, since those few of Poseidon's clan who could slip through Zeus's barrier took advantage of it. The Caribbean and Central America were littered with water-stock demigods. We were drawn in by demigods, sensed they were like us in a way, and both Archer and I got that vibe from the girl.

We hadn't made it far when I sensed a presence and stopped Archer with my arm. He looked at me, perplexed. I nodded in the direction of where I'd felt it. Gods like me—involved in war—have heightened senses; we have to, or we'd never survive. Sure enough, a man stepped out in front of us, blocking the alleyway. He was short, tubby, dark-skinned with receding black hair. Like a lot of people in Belize, he seemed to have a mixed ethnicity of Kriol and Mayan. I wondered if I had erred in choosing this location. I was hoping for Poseidon spawn, but was Lena part of the Mayan sector? That could be a bit problematic. Zeus viewed their desire for blood sacrifice, which a few of them still practiced, as outdated. I thought they were fascinating and badass. I'd love to trade war stories with a Mayan. "Excuse me, friend. We're just passing through," I tried, hoping by Posiedon's trident that this was his stock. Otherwise, a fight would be on. On the other hand, that would be fun. Ares was jumping for joy at the chance, anger and protectiveness bubbling up inside, adrenaline rushing, nerves firing off like mad. My body was ready for a brawl.

His black eyes narrowed on me. "What do you want with my daughter?"

"Daughter?" Archer challenged.

My mind was busy fantasizing how I'd incapacitate him by grabbing the metal from the lighting fixture on the building next to me, slamming it into his head, and when he was stunned, tackling him to the ground while I called for Archer to grab the rope being used to dry clothes up above us to bind him.

"Lena," the man answered.

I shook my head to get rid of my aggressive thoughts. "Ah." I gave Archer a significant look.

Lena was a demigod, but whose? Interbreeding between races of gods had always been frowned upon, so she wouldn't be Mayan and Olympian. Zeus put a stop to it not long after Archer was born. Even my mother, Zeus's wife, was originally a Titan—yeah, Dionysus fudged that one on purpose when telling the myth to mortals to make us look bad. He was the unwanted son of a mortal and looked two decades older than most of us, so he got his revenge. Now the mortal world thought I was a product of incest. Dionysus is lucky I didn't murder him for that. We hated each other for thousands of years, but I couldn't care less about my false lineage these days when humans thought we didn't exist.

"Who are you?" I asked. I was becoming confident he wasn't an other, but who was he? A demigod himself?

"Never mind that. What do you want with Lena?"

"To make her immortal," Archer said.

I whipped around to look at him, shocked he was giving so much away. What if we were somehow wrong and this man was mortal?

"What? You don't recognize him?" Archer asked me.

I looked back to the man, trying to figure out who he was. Right before me, the man's hair changed colors from the roots to the tip, like black ink was running out of it. His hair turned blond as his skin lightened. The eyes became pools of blue-green. Then his body elongated and thinned until he was almost eye-to-eye with me. Proteus stood before me, the shapeshifting spawn of Poseidon who could break through Zeus's barrier and come to the surface whenever he wanted. He also could see all time—past, present everywhere, and future. But he was a slippery little eel—literally. You had to get a hold on him to get the answers, and he could get back into the sea, change to a fish, and swim away before you could blink.

"Lena means a lot to me. Her mother means a lot to me."

"Proteus," I greeted. I was on edge, ready to pounce to make sure he didn't turn into some gull and fly away.

"We need to talk. I want her immortal, but I won't condemn her to the Underworld." He didn't greet me back but got right to it. I liked that. Get the business over with first, catch up later.

"If you know about that, you must see she will go there," Archer challenged, quick to connect Proteus's words with what the shapeshifter had foreseen.

Zeus ran a tight ship, and few immortals would know Archer was selecting three demigods as part of his punishment. As far as the rumors went, the charities reported to Aroha that the only leaks were Archer murdering Thanatos and being punished accordingly. Then again, who knew how much Proteus could see?

Proteus frowned. Archer was right.

"I make the choice," Archer continued. "I have to make three precise immortals, according to Zeus. She won't make a good Death, and I do not want her as my companion, so that leaves her to be a gift to Hypnos. No Hypnos, no immortality."

"She's a human being, not a gift," Proteus snarled.

"Watch your tone," I told him, stepping between him and my son to remind him whom he was dealing with.

"I know what she is," Archer responded. "In this day and age, she doesn't have to be with him or marry him. It's just a stupid gesture Zeus is making me do. She won't be stuck down there since she's a water demigod. She'll have no real domain suppressing her."

"No deal." Proteus slashed his hand through the air with finality.

"Okay," Archer said nonchalantly.

"Okay— *What?*" I turned around to face him.

"We find someone else. Simple as that. Let Lena age and die." Then Archer walked around Proteus, who seemed shocked.

How Archer shocked an all-seeing being confounded me, but I simply followed him. He had a plan, so I would trust him.

The next day, Lena and Proteus—in his true form—came knocking at our door. Man, Archer was good. The manipulation skills he'd learned from his mother—and yeah, myself, I suppose—were astounding. He'd make a great army interrogator, not that he would ever follow after me. No, those children were gone who'd worshipped me and never left my side—Deimos and Phobos. Death is a part of life and of war. They died nobly trying to save Sparta. No Greek could ask for a better death.

Archer let them in. Lena was shaky, terrified, and eyed us as if we were about to devour her. Proteus urged her to sit down. She looked ill. Archer and I exchanged a look of confusion, for Proteus said nothing about why they were there or what was going on.

Proteus smoothed her hair down lovingly and then looked to me. "She's had a bit of a shock and needs a minute. I explained things to them—her and her mother—and then I transformed. Her mother is a god-fearing woman and begged me to make Lena immortal, so here we are. Lena is not so spiritual, so her mind is processing our existence a bit slower."

"You?" She looked at Archer with an accusatory glare. "You're one too?"

"And him." Archer pointed to me. Then he sighed as if this was a chore he was forced to do—which I suppose it was—and went into the little kitchenette area. He grabbed a bottle of beer from the fridge, popped off the cap with his thumb, and held it out to her. "For the nerves."

She looked up at him, her eyes scanning him, and she took it. I could see a glimmer of appreciation in her eyes for Archer. She found him attractive, very much so. When I looked at Archer, though, I saw disinterest. The tiny spark of hope that he could move on and keep Lena as a companion left me.

"Do you want to live forever?" Archer asked her.

"What's the catch?" She took a huge gulp of beer.

"You won't be able to stay here. You'll go to the Underworld." Proteus had to pause during her sharp inhalation and more beer chugging. "I don't want you to go, but you won't be stuck there. I can bargain with Hades, get you time up here. Most likely, you'll be Persephone's attendant, friend, bring her gossip from up here."

Archer shifted uncomfortably. It didn't sit right with me either that her own father was leaving out details. "Proteus," Archer cut in. "Tell her all of it. She needs to know before she agrees."

"And if I don't agree?" she asked.

Archer shrugged. "If you keep your mouth shut about all of us, Zeus might let you live, but he's not too keen on water-demigods."

Proteus gave Archer a look of rebuke.

"I'm so lost." Lena whimpered.

"You two." Archer pointed at us, taking control. "Outside. Call Hebe to be on standby, and let me tell her everything. Alone."

Proteus looked at me for answers. I shrugged, not sure what Archer was up to. He probably didn't want the three of us competing to tell a story; he seemed rushed, although we had all the time in the world. Archer wanted this over with.

We retreated outside. It felt weird to bow down to the commands of my son, but I had to let him lead. Anything was better than him whining and moping about Callie like the pathetic lump he had been. I called Hebe. She was intent on keeping me on the phone for a minute, seeking permission from our father on the spot. I hung up. My phone was untraceable, but Hermes might be able to trace Archer's.

"Hebe tried keeping me on the line."

"Trying to pinpoint your location? Poseidon's trident, this is worse than I thought." Proteus whistled. "Glad I can hide underwater when this goes down. We must meet them somewhere else."

"Will something major go down?" I hedged. He would know.

"We're gods. A lot of major things will go down throughout all of time. You'd need to be more specific." He was avoiding the question. Before I could press for those specifics, my phone rang.

Hebe. I answered to my spitfire little sister cussing me out for hanging up. She had gotten Dad's permission, and Hermes and Demeter would be coming with her once I texted her it was finalized. She asked for my location. I said I'd text her the details, thanked her, and hung up. My little sister—a whopping five-foot, one-hundred-pound, baby-faced goddess of youth—was being sent with bodyguards. I was her brother, and I loved her. I'd never hurt her. I learned two things from my naive sister: Dad was very suspicious of an ambush, and they needed our location. The Great Blue Hole was masking our presence as I had hoped.

"Bodyguards coming with her. You going to stay?" I asked Proteus.

"They don't frighten me. They're coming because of Eros."

I was lost.

"You don't think he'd try to incapacitate your sister, call on his old buddy Zephyrus, and race to New York to make his girl immortal?"

I was about to protest, but he was right. I had no idea what Archer would do.

The door opened, and Archer stood there. "She's in."

"What did you say to her?" I asked.

"I told her the truth." He shrugged.

About what, I wasn't sure. We filed in regardless.

Proteus called out for each of the four wind gods, but none came. Then he started shouting. They were busy and frequently despised being used for transportation.

Archer sighed. "Let me. Zephyrus?" he said quietly.

A second later, there was breeze whistling, and Zephyrus walked in the door, his soft feminine face taking in Archer's with adoration. I subdued Ares, who had not been fond of the wind god trying to seduce his son when Archer had been an impressionable teen, but it never panned out, and they ended up merely as best friends. After his love was not reciprocated by my son, he moved onto others, including Lucien, but that might be Dionysus fibbing, or it could be true. Who knew with Lucien, the god who loved all but never could keep love in his grasp. I was different now; Chase didn't hold grudges against delicate men nor chastise them for not being able to win a fight as Ares had. Back then, I had wanted Archer to be a fighter, not a lover, but I think, in the end, my kid turned out very well at being both—a lover who could defend himself well. And it was clear that, no matter what, Zephyrus would still do anything for Archer, including protect him. There was beauty in loyalty that I admired.

He greeted us all—me warily. No one trusted me not to throttle them. I can't blame them. I have done my fair share of throttling. He asked us where we wanted to go. We couldn't go to New York. The only other place I had was an apartment in Afghanistan. As soon as Hebe's entourage saw Proteus, plus Lena's ethnicity, they would know what part of the world we had been in anyway.

"Rio de Janeiro," Proteus said.

We looked at him.

"What? I've got a place there we can use to make it seem like you are there. You're hiding from Zeus, right?"

"Not hiding," I corrected, my ego a little dented from the accusation. "Forcing my dad to mind his own business."

"My bad." Proteus put up his hands, laughing. He looked as if he wanted to say more but refrained.

Archer, being cleverer than me when it came to everything except war and governments, probably was in tune with what I was thinking at the moment: Proteus might've slipped up, revealing we would hide in Belize for real at some point. It made me glad I was cautious, but Archer was fidgeting nervously.

Zephyrus's wind instantly transported us to the exact place Proteus asked for. I opened my eyes to see a beautiful glimmering blue-green ocean, beige sands under my feet, and spun to see a cluster of tightly packed buildings and high-rises with greenery-covered mountains behind them. Zephyrus walked towards the city to go exploring and stay away from our visitors, and we followed Proteus—Archer nervous, Lena terrified, and me ready for battle. Proteus let us into a modest apartment, while I texted Hebe, and then we acted as if we were simply at home.

A minute later, the knock at the door announced their arrival. Hebe walked in first, her dark hair braided in little pigtails, and her large black eyes landed on me. "Ares!" She smiled her toothy grin, skipped into my arms, hugging me tightly before I could register how I should greet her with all the family tension.

"Li'l sis, I think you have even more freckles since the last time I saw you." I tapped her nose, teasing her.

She slapped my hand away, giving me a fake look of censure. Hebe had never grown up, not really. Adult issues such as sex, parenthood, or money never interested her, which was fitting since she was the goddess of youth. Her other job, and why she was here, was "cupbearer," a ceremonial role where she gave ambrosia to immortals but, more importantly, to demigods to make them immortal.

"Liar." Hebe laughed. She took in the rest of the room, and I noticed her companions.

"Hermes." I nodded at him. "Aunt Demeter. It has been a while."

"Yes," she said, her disdain for me apparent. She and Zeus were siblings and had a very close relationship—weirdly close—but Dionysus lied, of course, when he exposed our myths to mortals about

Persephone being Zeus's daughter. Carmanor was the real father, a god of unknown parentage, and they had a brood of kids but never had been a happy, whole family. I hadn't seen the guy since Roman days. I bet Demeter killed him long ago.

Demeter never liked me, because she hated Hera and Dite and a lot of other gods. There are many inappropriate names other gods called her, but Dite and I had settled on "shrew" long before it had become a common expression for a cranky nag of a woman. Perhaps we had invented the slang usage of it. It was hard to know what we had influenced over the ages.

"What brings you here?" I asked her, trying to get her to admit they were bodyguards. I was picking a fight. I wanted her to say it so I could flip out and insult them for thinking I'd hurt my sister. I thought Ares was easily at bay, but he was rearing his evil, impulsive head. My pulse quickened, the adrenaline and cortisol releasing into my bloodstream. Chill, Ares. Of all things, why was Demeter the one setting him off?

"This beautiful girl is going to the Underworld to be with my daughter. I had to meet her." Demeter ignored Archer completely and doted on Lena, playing with her hair.

Lena's expression was priceless: fear and annoyance at some strange woman touching her.

I almost laughed, which halted the adrenaline rush.

Archer was hugging Hebe, and when he pulled away, I scrutinized his hands. He didn't try to steal the ambrosia vial that was somewhere on her person—thank the gods. He smiled at his aunt—because who could resist the pull of her innocent happiness—but it didn't reach his eyes. He was distressed. I could feel his emotions through some inexplicable tie I had with him, some genetic trait that coincided with our glowing eyes. I knew then that his mind was most likely plotting how to get that vial to Callie, but he wouldn't act on it...I hoped. Regardless, I was ready for anything, even if it was stopping him.

"Let's get this going?" I suggested. It would be better to end my son's temptation as soon as possible.

Proteus hesitated, but the rest of the gods wanted to get it over with too. Overruled, he sat on the side of the armchair Lena was nervously perched in.

Archer went over and squatted down to her level. "It's just a drink, like a shot, but tastes much nicer. You'll feel giddy, light-headed, and you might faint, but when you wake up, you'll feel like a million dollars."

"How would you know? You said you were born a god."

Archer stood back up and looked down at Lena, who seemed to only have eyes for him. If he could just let Callie go, he could be happy with Lena. She would worship him, but I knew—like me—he only would truly love one woman. Lena wasn't Callie.

"My wife had been mortal first," he said quietly. I knew he was uncomfortable talking about the past. "I saw the transition, and she told me what it was like."

"You're married?"

"No, you'll most likely meet her in the Underworld if she hasn't moved on," Archer said firmly. He was losing grip on this now-apparent feigned civility with Lena.

The girl looked down at her hands sadly. She did have hopes Archer would want her to stay.

Hebe came forward and gave the girl a reassuring smile. She pulled out a small vial and uncorked it, making a little popping sound that drew Archer's attention. I saw him go rigid as if he was ready to spring into action, or perhaps he was trying desperately to stay still. Hermes watched him like a hawk, his expression for once worried, not smug. I wondered what his orders were if Archer went for the vial. I grew anxious too. The tension built in the room. I had to calm down as all their moods would reflect mine. Archer's eyes were lighting up brightly with emotion, but which emotion was winning? I wasn't sure. All I could feel was his distress; it overrode his other emotions. His hands balled into fists. I took a step closer so I could jump in between Hebe and him if I needed to.

Hebe didn't let go of the vial but held it to Lena's lips and tipped it back.

Lena swallowed the contents and then smiled. "It is sweet." She beamed at Archer.

He did not smile back, but his eyes dimmed, and he relaxed.

It was over. We only had to go through this two more times. By the beard of Zeus, how in Hades could we do this? I was exhausted simply from the anxiety.

"I'll be in my room," Archer muttered. As he walked by, his eyes looked dead, and his expression went back to that morose scowl he wore lately. He went into one of Proteus's bedrooms and shut the door.

We had to wait until the Olympus entourage left to drop the ruse that this was our place. Then Zephyrus came back and knocked on the bedroom door Archer was hiding behind. Archer asked to be left alone, not even letting his friend in. Great. He was back to square one.

CHAPTER 8

Archer

I was in utter despair. I had ached to steal that ambrosia from Aunt Hebe and to somehow give it to Callie, but it would never happen. Even if I were miraculously successful, immortality couldn't protect her from Zeus.

A few minutes later, Zephyrus knocked at the door, which meant my aunt and her entourage had left. I told him I wanted to be alone. I felt bad, but I'd talk to him when I was more up for it. Right now, my thoughts were dismal.

Not long after, my father came in to tell me Lena had passed out. He wanted me to go wait by Lena's bedside, to calm Proteus, who was a nervous wreck.

"Tell him that's normal for demigods. They get a fast, intense fever, and then once it subsides, she'll be immortal." My impatience was obvious, from the look on my father's face. But I wasn't going to sit by some girl's bedside for hours on end, wishing it were Callie.

"He knows that. We all know how it works." Chase sighed, disappointment in his gaze. As if I could feel worse.

Gods get a little ill on and off when the full powers kick in during puberty, but demigods do it all at once when the ambrosia brings their immortal recessive gene forward. This was what Proteus should obviously realize.

"You were different though," he mused, leaning on the door frame. A small smile played on his lips, thinking of the past. "You were a sickly little baby."

This was news to me.

He noted I was interested. "Your mother never told you?" He rubbed the back of his neck and stared me down. My father didn't do well talking about feelings, and from his hesitancy—and the fact Ma never told me in my long lifetime I had been an ill infant—it had to have been emotionally taxing for them.

I shook my head.

"No, I wouldn't suspect she would." He crossed his arms. "It was a very hard time for all of us. Zeus wanted to leave you out in the wild—"

"Like the Spartans." I cringed.

"Yes, stoicism was an admirable trait back then." His mind was wandering back to the old war days, so I had to say something to bring him back to the topic I wanted to hear about.

"You didn't let him?"

"I tried to convince him subtly it was a terrible idea. I couldn't fight for you properly. They all thought you were Heph's, see?"

"Why would Zeus want to leave me for dead?"

"Gods normally aren't ever ill, not even as children. I think he knew Dite was cheating but thought you must be half mortal, so not Hera's grandson."

"Hera and Heph pleaded your case; Zeus summoned Apollo, who was sowing his wild oats somewhere at the time, and when he arrived, he was perplexed but figured it all out. Apollo knew you were mine, and he knew you were a powerful god who was inheriting your powers much too early."

"But how in Hades did he withhold that truth?" I was sitting upright now, my mind reeling.

"That's the question, isn't it? He was able to lie then. He's able to lie now, but not often in between. My dad was unstable then, as he is now. Something is going on, and maybe it's cyclical, and maybe history is repeating itself—I have no clue. All I know is, Lucien proclaimed we needed to carefully spike your fever. Heph warmed you carefully, and you had a horrible night. We didn't think you were going to make it. Anyway, the next day, you were well and floating around the room, buck naked."

I laughed aloud at that. "Why wouldn't Ma ever tell me that story?"

"Because you pissed on her after that perhaps? She has her pride. Plus, I was there with you guys when I shouldn't have been."

I didn't know what to do with the story or how to feel, but I laughed at the thought of infant me floating like those crappy cherubs in those paintings and peeing down on her. I must've put her through more Tartarus than she deserved. She had paid me back ten-fold by now, I was sure.

"My point is, I know exactly what it is like to worry your child won't make it through a fever. Show some compassion, Archer, for Proteus if not Lena."

I nodded and got up reluctantly. Dad and his ridiculous narrative lessons. I had been wrapped up into the story before I realized it would turn didactic. To deny what I should do would be childishly stubborn.

I sat and talked to Proteus for a while, reassured him with the description of Psyche's transformation, even though it prickled my grief deep down to do so. All thoughts of my ex led to our daughter, but I squelched the thoughts. There was nothing to be done but to wait for Lena's fever to break, marking her change to immortality, and hope for the best. Proteus stayed by her side, which left me redundant, so I eventually slipped away into the room I had claimed and lay down, staring at the ceiling.

My phone went off. It had been quiet for a while, the occasional text from my dad when he went to the market and wanted to know if I needed anything. And Callie had texted once. I refrained from answering, so I thought she had given up. When I looked at the screen, her name was at the top. Relentless girl.

Aroha's not depressed. Chase didn't come back. Lucien's lying. Why won't you tell me the truth? I know you're alive. I *feel* **it.**

A desperate urge to text her back took hold of me. My fingers itched to respond. I hated hurting her, but wouldn't the truth hurt so much more? I wanted to text her that I was alive, loving her and wanting her, but there was no hope of us ever being together. She was being punished with me for my crimes, and it was unfair, damn it.

I know you're reading this. Phones tell you when someone has received it.

I hadn't thought of that. Should I respond? No, I should let her move on. Why hadn't she yet? At the very least, she should've acknowledged my death. Surely, two months was enough time to digest the fact I'd never come back, promises be damned. But the answer was simple: Callie felt the same as I did. We would never get over each other. It was love, true love, the kind that destroys beings when not fulfilled. I was seeing firsthand what damage my family—particularly the love entourage—could do to humans.

My phone rang, making me jump. It hadn't rung in months, those closest to me keeping up the façade of my death. It was Callie. Was something wrong, an emergency? Was she in danger? I worried and longed to hear her voice, so much so that my thumb pressed talk, and I held it to my ear, my self-discipline leaving me completely.

"Archer?" Callie's voice pleaded, sending a knife through my heart, as cold as Zelus-the-ice-demon's daggers. Her pain was my pain, but equally agonizing was my longing to hear her say more. "Archer, I can hear you breathing. Please." Her voice cracked, and a sob escaped her.

My throat constricted. I couldn't say a word, even if I tried. I held my breath and closed my eyes, envisioning her, bringing her to me from my memories—her smooth skin, warm and trusting eyes, slender wrists, and that place where her jaw sloped up toward her ear. The place I would die just to kiss one more time.

"I love you," she whispered. "Please, just say something so I know you're alive and I'm not crazy. Talk!" Her pain was peaking, making her wail.

I couldn't bear another moment, but I was powerless to hang up. When she started crying uncontrollably, I ended the call. What could I have said? Us together was impossible. I realized in that moment, all hope had left me.

The phone rang again. I rejected it. She tried again, and I rejected it again. But she wouldn't stop. I had to say something, but I couldn't bear hearing her voice again.

Instead, I typed her a message: **I'm as good as dead. I can never see you again, or he will kill you.**

Talk to me, please, was instantly fired back.

Too hard. You need to move on.

Never.

Despite the emotional turmoil I was feeling, her conviction made me smile slightly. My tenacious, hard-headed girl. I was glad to see she was still strong after all I had done to her life. But it was wrong to smile. She had to understand there was no chance of us getting back together.

You must understand that we will never be able to see each other again. I'm sorry, Callie.

Then I want to die.

Don't you dare say that. You promised me. I need to know you are alive out there. It's the only way I can cope. Please, try to forget me.

After my last text, I shut my phone off. I couldn't take any more, and there was nothing else to say but to repeat ourselves. Frankly, I was worried I'd let her convince me into anything, damn the consequences. Except a voice niggled at the back of my mind. My punishment didn't mean I couldn't talk to her. Would that be enough? Could we bear a long-distance relationship that would never result in us being together? I needed another loophole. I needed her. One night, one day. It was so tempting. If I could get her somewhere safe off Zeus's radar...

I tried to banish the thought from my mind. We gods were selfish, and often mortals suffered from our interference. I would not do that to Callie. I lay there and tortured myself with many possible happy futures with

Callie that would never occur, trying to stop myself from turning on my phone and talking to her. I had to see her anyway I could, and after a half hour had passed, temptation overtook me.

I closed my eyes and mentally projected myself up into the sky and traveled far. I found myself in New York. I zoomed down into Callie's bedroom. She was in her bed, fast asleep, her phone still clutched in her hand. She was beautiful, but like me, there were circles under her eyes, and she looked thinner. She wasn't eating or sleeping much, but it was much worse for her. I couldn't die from that, while she could.

Chase had been threatening to send me to Fiji, where Zeus wouldn't hesitate to force-feed me nectar or ambrosia. I didn't want to be under his watchful eyes, harassed by his gloating attitude at seeing how his punishment was taking its toll, nor tempted to destroy all of Olympus to steal ambrosia to make Callie immortal. It was a scheme that often crossed my mind, but it wasn't plausible; I'd never get away with it. Not even my dad could swing that.

Beholding Callie, I couldn't resist, so I tried to touch her. Impossible without my body being there, but I could feel the faint sensation of her cheek against the back of my invisible fingers. She murmured my name in her sleep as if she knew I was there, as if she could feel me. That was impossible, though. I needed more of her, a better connection, so I thrust myself into her mind to see images spiraling out of control.

A volcano smoking. There was a bookbag and a notepad in a plastic bag. I was climbing up the steep incline toward the dangerous area. Then the image blurred to Callie in a white dress, her wedding. She was kissing Dan, then Dan morphed into Lucien, and Lucien morphed into me. Suddenly, we were somewhere else. Lucien was there. I punched him. This faded away into another scene, where I was standing on a boat, Zeus in front of me looking mighty pissed off. Lightning struck me. There was water, and Callie was drowning.

I was thrown from Callie's mind and yanked back to my body like a rubber band snapping. Or had I woken up? Had it all been a dream of mine?

I grabbed my phone and turned it back on. Sure enough, texts came in from Callie, proof we did have a conversation.

I'll never forget you. You're too much a part of me. Followed by, **I love you.**

The phone came to life in my hand. I answered it without thinking of the consequences.

"Were you here?" Callie blurted out.

"Not physically."

"What was that?"

"It was your thoughts."

"It was my dream," she corrected me. "And somehow you were with me in it?"

"Yes. I entered your mind. It's a god-thing."

"No. It must be a demigod thing because I can read minds too. The fevers, they make me better at seeing people's thoughts. And my dreams...I think I can see things that could happen."

My heart beat wildly in my chest. Us kissing, a wedding—could it happen? But she thought of others before me. No, no, these were simply dreams that she wanted to be true. But she saw Zeus was there, trying to kill us. Maybe her fear of Zeus projected into her sleep since we had just texted prior about how he would kill her. If she somehow saw these things for real? That would mean she was extremely powerful for a demigod, like Nostradamus had been.

There was silence in the conversation long enough for both of us to realize what had just occurred. She now had irrefutable evidence that I was alive. There was no taking it back. There was no going back, no moving on for me. I'd have to be with her, or I'd have to die trying. I knew her well enough to accept that she felt the same. I'd known answering the phone would start a chain of events that would not end well. Why had I let myself give in? Why was I so weak when it came to Callie?

"I'll only ever want to be with you." She broke the silence with affirmation our thoughts were aligned.

"And I you," I allowed. I would not say those three binding words again and ruin her chance of moving on. "But it can't—"

"Don't you dare tell me it can't happen. We just saw our wedding." Her tone brooked no argument.

I should tell her it was just a dream, and it looked like her marrying other people too. I could tell she was clinging onto this so tightly in the hope we had a future together. "Callie..." I breathed into the phone.

"You can't give up on us, Archer. You need to find a way for us to be together."

"It's impossible."

"It can't be."

"Zeus will kill you."

"I don't care."

"Don't you dare say that! I care. You need to live, damn it!"

I heard my father call my name. I had gotten so loud, he had probably overheard me. Great. Now he'd give me the third degree about who I was talking to.

"Callie. I've got to go. Don't tell anyone we've talked. Don't tell anyone you know I'm alive. Take care of yourself."

"Wait. Don't hang up."

"Callie." I tried to be stern.

"Please. Promise you'll call again. Every day."

"I can't. Look, my dad's coming. I have to go."

"Then text me."

"I'll try. Email. That's more off the grid. I'll text you a new email address, and you should create a new one no one knows about." I ended the call, created a new account, and texted her my new email address. I stowed the phone under my mattress at immortal speed, right before my dad entered the room.

"Who were you talking to?" Chase asked, looking around.

"Myself."

He looked at me oddly. "Sounded like you were arguing."

I laughed. "Yeah, okay."

"You look...happy?" The poor man was probably wondering if I were insane, or he was onto me and Callie.

"Do I? You just said I was arguing with some phantom." I shot back at him, being sure to hide my happiness about talking to her. I couldn't tell him the truth. He'd either dash my hopes or stop me. I had to communicate with Callie now that she knew I was still alive. She was like a drug, an aphrodisiac. I was hooked.

He hesitated as if he were about to say something but thought better of it. "Lena's fever broke. She seems fine. Come see."

"I'm good. Let's take her to the Underworld tomorrow."

"No. Proteus wants time with her. You could be a little bit nicer to her, you know. She's one of us. If things go badly in the future, the more people on our side, the better."

My mind was elsewhere. I was thinking of more loopholes. Zeus had said I couldn't "see" Callie. I could talk to her it seemed, email her. I wondered if...they always said love was blind. What if I were truly blind? Could I be with Callie? Athena was a stickler for exact wording. She would back me.

"Dad?"

"Yeah," he said, leaning against the doorframe. His face was screwed up in a mixture of confusion and concern.

"When you took the arrow to your eye in the Battle of Thermopylae, how long were you blind?"

He was stunned by the question and answered hesitantly. "My eye healed in hours, my sight in a couple days. Why?" But before I could make an excuse for asking such a question, understanding spread across his features. He ran his hand through his long hair and came into my room. He sat on the edge of my bed. "Don't even think about it. You'll put yourself through so much pain, you won't be able to go anywhere. Then you'll heal before you can even make it back to New York. If you somehow make it there, you'll get Callie killed. Zeus is waiting for your failure."

I didn't say anything.

"Give me time, Archer. Please. There is always a way around things. There is always a battle that can be won. I need time."

"How long?"

"A year. If I can't figure it out by then, it's impossible."

"You've got six months," I said.

But I wasn't referencing the idea of gouging my own eyes out after that time passed by. I was thinking of more sinister plans. Two months without Callie was unbearable. Six months? I might be creating a Death to take me away from this world by then.

CHAPTER 9

Valentine's day. I dreaded it. I was no romantic. I was honest. Still, I put on the show many men do just for tradition's sake or, more likely, to not get berated, nagged, or dumped for failing to do something a girl could brag to her friends about. I took Linda to dinner and presented her with flowers, chocolates, and a bracelet that cost a pretty penny. Linda did not disappoint, so easily pleased by superficiality. Callie wouldn't fall for that. The girl would prefer a poem or song written for her, a picnic in Central Park, and honest words of love. Words I withheld daily.

I was worried to distraction about her. Linda was going forward with this ridiculous party for Callie and other sad singles who might be alone on Valentine's Day. Sure, it was sweet of Linda, but would Callie spike a high fever from the surprise of it all or freak out and cry? She was unstable, and time hadn't helped her. As of late, she'd improved a little, which gave me hope the party would run smoothly and that maybe she was finally admitting Archer was dead and would eventually move on.

After dinner with Linda, I dropped her off so she could prepare for the party. Somehow, everyone kept it secret from Callie—not that she picked up on much these days in her feverish out-of-it state. I was to pick up Callie on my "way home" and drop her off at Linda's under the pretense that the two of them could watch chick flicks and eat ice cream.

Callie was ready when I pulled up to her building. After a few pleasantries, she went silent and stared out the window. My few questions felt as if I were bothering her, so I went quiet too. I pulled into Linda's parking garage, contemplating how Callie would react to the surprise party. I parked in a visitors spot and turned the car off.

"You're coming in?" she asked.

"Yeah. Left my jacket," I lied. It was a good excuse since it was cold out, and I hadn't bothered to wear one.

"I feel like I'm imposing. I mean, it's Valentine's Day and all. Linda probably wants to spend it with you."

"Not at all. You coming around was all her idea."

"Because she feels sorry for me."

"No, because you guys are friends, and she wants to spend time with you. She and I went out to dinner already, and she was spoiled rotten and probably wants to tell you all about it."

I wasn't sure if she heard me or was even listening. I expected a halfhearted laugh, not sudden silence. She closed her eyes, leaned back onto the seat, and sighed. Her hair was pinned up, and she wore a blood-red dress, making her skin appear paler than usual. She had wanted to change clothes after having dinner with her father, but I got her dad in on the plan, and he convinced her not to slum over to Linda's in sweats. Even in sweats, she'd be stunning. I longed to reach over and touch her smooth skin, hold her in my arms and protect her, kiss her soft lips, which were painted a matching luscious red...

I looked away from her, suppressing the urges. If I knew Archer well—and over two thousand years as his best friend proved I did—he'd be checking in on Callie constantly, torturing himself as he watched her move on.

"Callie?"

"Shhh," she said quietly. A small smile played upon her lips, her eyes still fast shut. When she opened her eyes, she was smiling, beaming, and I was at a loss about what just happened.

She climbed out of the car, and I followed. "What's with you?"

"Nothing." She was lying. I didn't need my truth radar to know. Her smile said it all.

"You saw him again." The accusation in my voice was blatant.

Callie looked as if she had been caught in the act of some heinous crime.

"How is that possible?" I demanded.

She pressed the elevator button and crossed her arms. "It's possible because he's alive, no matter what crap you try to say otherwise."

"Even if he were, Callie, demigods can't transverse space telepathically like we can."

She shrugged.

"Don't shut me out. Explain it to me."

"I don't know, Lucien. I think of him, and it's as if I'm there, wherever he is. I can't always do it, but when I sleep or have a fever, I see him more."

"That explains why the dark circles under your eyes are disappearing. Sleeping a lot lately, I take it?" I was bitter and unable to hide it. It was an unhealthy way of sleeping, prolonging the grief she felt for Archer's absence and most likely longing for something that could never be. I had foolishly assumed she was getting over him.

"Lucien, I know what you're going to say—"

"Then I don't have to say it, do I?"

The elevator ride was silent, each of us fuming for our own reasons. I sensed her eyes on me twice, but I couldn't look at her. She'd read me all too well. Part of it was explainable. Simply put, Callie had capabilities genetically passed down from Psyche. But something about them was off. Either Callie had hid them from us, or they were getting stronger. The latter was unheard of. No demigod ever naturally developed more powers. They had limited talents, like Einstein's intellect and Nostradamus's foresight. The only time they gained godly abilities was *after* they ingested ambrosia, like Heracles. And the other reason I held my tongue and ignored her was because I was furious with her tenacity. I was jealous, I acknowledged, so Callie—the perceptive mortal—knew it too.

The elevator opened, and we walked down the hall to Linda's place. I rapped on the door three times as instructed by Linda.

"It's open!" she called.

I opened the door and motioned for Callie to go first. When she entered, everyone shouted, "Surprise!"

I squeezed through the doorway behind her, eager to judge how she was handling the situation. She had covered her mouth, and her eyes were wide as they took in the small crowd and then came back to me. She shook a bit from head to toe, and tears welled up. Just great. She might just lose it and spike a fever or, worse, lose consciousness. She must already have a mild temperature from what she said about seeing Archer minutes ago. I awaited the fallout.

But she rallied and threw her arms around Linda, then Mary Beth, and joined the party. Emily was there, which kind of ticked me off, but Linda wouldn't ditch her catty, superficial "friend" because they had known each other since kindergarten. I resented Emily and her treatment of Callie. She relished in Callie's grief and was the worst excuse for a young mortal that I had come across in years. Despite Emily, Callie was okay. I relaxed since my fears about the party were unfounded.

"Lucien," Linda called me into the kitchen not long after everyone calmed down and mingled.

I went into the kitchen to see Linda standing with a middle-aged woman.

"My mother wanted to meet you," Linda said, blushing. There was something endearing about her at times, which kept me from dumping her while I was infatuated with someone else.

I did a double take. The woman looked nothing like her, so I assumed Linda was adopted. Her mother was blonde-haired, blue-eyed, and a bit thick in her figure. Definitely not the lithe thin figure of Linda, and not at all Asian.

I did my boyfriendly duty and played the role of a perfect prince for her mother. I lied, saying I was headed to Princeton for a pre-med program. The truth was, I hadn't bothered about good grades enough to get in this round, but I had a few different medical degrees already. It became boring after a while. I didn't even apply to a college. I had no clue what the future held. Part of me wanted to watch after Callie; the other half wanted to be far away from her. None of me wanted to see Archer again, which tore me up. I had no clue how we'd *let* Callie destroy our friendship and lives, but we had.

Her mom gave us a cheesy grin and excused herself to hide away in her bedroom to let us teens have fun, but that was because Linda was straight-laced. There was no alcohol or drugs at this party. In my lifetime, I had seen it all. This would be a boring, innocuous, human party. Safe for Callie.

"Your mom is nice," I said to fill up the silence.

"Nice?" She laughed. "Lucien, ask what you really want to know."

"What?"

"You're wondering." She clasped my hands in hers playfully.

"And what am I supposed to wonder?" I leaned into her, kissing her lips gently.

"What everyone wonders."

"And what is that?" I asked distractedly, kissing her neck.

"If I'm adopted."

"Oh." I pulled away from her since her tone was serious. "Yeah, you don't look a lot like her, no, but why would that matter?"

She smiled at that. "My father was from China. He ditched my mom when she was pregnant with me."

"I'm sorry." I frowned, not knowing what to say.

"You're so cute when you're sad, but equally tragic. It's no big deal. Probably better off without him, to be honest." Then she kissed me to take my frown away.

Someone cleared her throat, which broke us apart. "Sorry," Aroha said sheepishly in the doorway. "Callie's got a fever."

I pulled away from Linda. Her hand grabbed my wrist tightly. Without reading her mind, I knew it was territorial, a command, and maybe an ultimatum: Callie or her. The choice was clear in my head, but I couldn't let Linda know that. She'd be awful to Callie, and she was Callie's only friend except for Aroha and me.

"I can take her home. I'll stay with her until she feels better," Aroha supplied.

My touch would make her feel better. I could swear it was the Fates hinting to me that she and I were meant to be. She was suddenly ill, and I was the healer god.

"I should come with you. I have that EMT training," I said.

Aroha scoffed. "It's a fever, Lucien. Stop by on the way home if you're that worried. But stay here. It's Valentine's Day." She nodded towards Linda.

I turned to see Linda's glare slip back into a pleasing countenance. This was irritating. She was jealous, and yet I knew that very same feeling personally, daily. "Yeah, text me later if she's not better."

Aroha smiled and left. I was worried about Callie but could see no safe way out of this Dionysus-forsaken party.

"I'll take away your worry," Linda whispered. She took the lobe of my ear in her mouth and sucked on it, distracting me immediately from whatever I had been worried about. My mind was rendered useless and fixated on steamier subjects. "I got you a Valentine's gift. Only, I can't give it to you tonight," she continued. "I want to do *it*, Lucien." She giggled next, most likely in reaction to my eager whiplashed expression.

The idea of having her was enticing, and yet it was wrong. My fantasies about bedding Linda shifted to Callie, and the guilt was overwhelming. I couldn't go further with Linda. It wasn't right. I normally didn't care about using mortals. We did it often, but this felt different.

I pulled away. "I should go." The rational, chivalrous part of me came to the surface.

"What?" It was merely a whisper, a breath of wind. "I practically throw myself at you, and you say you have to go?"

Great. This would cause a scene if I couldn't calm her down. "I'm sorry to be so blunt, but we probably shouldn't...you know."

"Why not?" Her tone shifted to anger as her eyes narrowed at me. "I see." Then she pushed me away and paced the kitchen.

I let her. It was better to let the mortals do the talking, see what she thought caused the problem and then simply agree with her.

"You've always kept things from me, been closed off, never fully honest. You don't want me to meet your parents. You never want to talk about the future. You did all this because you don't honestly want me in your life. I'm just some substitute, and I deserve better than that. I'll always be second best—to Callie, I assume. Archer's dead, and you're so eager to fill his place."

"Archer was my best friend, Linda. I'd never..." The guilt and the lies made me pause. I was a terrible boyfriend, but I was an even worse friend. I veered back to truths; they were easier to say. "I promised Archer I'd look after Callie while he was gone, and then he died. It was a stupid promise. He was paranoid, but now I have to see it through."

"How very noble of you, and I wouldn't mention it had you not enjoyed your job so thoroughly." She punctuated the statement with a bitter laugh.

Anger flickered up in me. What if Archer were truly dead? Her words were catty, selfish, and insensitive. It showed her true colors, and I didn't like this version of Linda. "How can you even say that?"

She shrank back, wide-eyed. I never showed my anger to her, raised my voice at her, to any mortal really.

"Sorry," she mumbled. "It's just with what people are saying about the two of you. I can't help it, Lucien."

"Yes, you can. And if you're referring to the gossip-monger Emily, why would you even listen to her? You're smarter than that."

"It's other people too, Lucien, not just her. And it's not that I believe them. It hurts me to hear these things, even if they are only rumors." Great, now there were tears in her eyes. I still had no idea what to do when women cried.

"What do you want from me, Linda? What do you want me to do? Ignore *our* grieving friend who needs us?" I tried to make her see how unreasonable she was being through my thick sarcasm laced with guilt-tripping.

"Yes." She studied my face, trying to gauge my response, but I'm sure all that appeared on my face was the shock that she would be so bold and callous.

I looked at her as if she were insane because, to me, her behavior was teetering into the unhinged territory. Maybe Dionysus was doing this. I dismissed the thought. He had no qualms with me and didn't stoop as low as making mortals insane for sport. "Are you serious?"

"It's a simple choice, Lucien. Callie or me." She crossed her arms and glared at me. But I could see through the lies, her front. She was terrified.

"Well, when you put it that way and give me an unfair ultimatum, I'm left with only one choice: Callie."

Her face sank. She hadn't been expecting that. She thought I loved her, that she could control me, but she had no idea she was dealing with a higher being. Linda was a blip in a long roster of women, while I was much more in her young, inexperienced life. This breakup would hurt her more than me.

I turned to leave before she could say anything more. I didn't look back but said bye to a few people who insisted on trying to talk to me on the way out. I felt bad doing it on Valentine's Day, but she shouldn't have pushed me to it. How could she let jealousy guide her to make such selfish demands? Callie needed us, being physically and mentally unwell. What kind of friend was she to desert Callie?

I decided not to go to Callie's to check on her, but to head home. In the elevator, I texted Aroha just to check in and make sure I wasn't needed. Linda made me realize in her jealous fit that I needed to watch my behavior around Callie. If people were talking, Aroha would catch wind, and the last person who needed to hear Callie and I were speculated as being together was Archer. He was stupid enough to act rashly and endanger Callie again.

When I started the car, my phone pinged, and I glanced a millisecond at it, hoping it wasn't Linda begging me to come back. It was Aroha.

Fever under control. Father's servant caring for her. We need to talk. She's seeing things she shouldn't.

Tomorrow, I texted back. I'd had enough tonight. The last thing I wanted to deal with was the high-maintenance Aroha, another sometimes-unhinged female. I was done with women.

CHAPTER 10

Archer

Archer,
I miss you so much that I can hardly breathe when I think about you. Thank you for letting me email you. I'm so happy you answered the phone. The confirmation that you were alive has brought me out of my funk. Before, I had nothing to live for, to look forward to. There's my dad, of course, but when he's gone, there's nothing. I can't bear to think of a future without him and you, so I will let myself dream that we will be together one day. I know you'll tell me not to hope for this, but it is the only thing that will keep me going. I have hope, something left for mortals, according to your myths. I will hope one day that I will get to see your face again, feel your arms around me, your lips on mine. I miss you so much, Archer. How do I go back to an empty, boring life after the world you have opened up to me? I love you.

I'm yours for life,
Callie

What torturous words to read. I wasn't sure what broke my heart more: the fact she was depressed without me or the fact she sadly hoped a miracle would bring us together. I dropped my phone and rubbed my eyes in frustration. I had the impulse to go to her right now to end this suffering. Thankfully, my conscience remembered Callie would die if I did that, and it was fortunate I couldn't travel on a dime like the Four Winds. I had to say something to deter her unhealthy, hopeful dreams; she needed a dose of realism, but I didn't want to break her heart.

Dear Callie,
I have no idea what to say in response to your email. It breaks my heart to hear this. I miss you too, and I feel the same, but please take care of yourself. I've been visiting you

in my mind, and you have lost weight. Please eat, please sleep. Go out and have fun with your friends. Knowing you are having some semblance of a life without me will help me get through this. As for a mundane existence, you have no idea. I was bored out of my wits until I ran into you by that elevator. I'll never regret that, nor saving you. I'm sorry everything turned out the way it did, that it makes you feel so wretched. I have no words, no empty promises to give you. I'd rather never see you again than cause your death. Move on. There is no end to this that will satisfy us.

Yours forever,
Archer

As I read it over, a realization dawned on me: I didn't trust Dad could do it. I had given up on him in one hasty email. The truth of it stung, and I was overwhelmed. What was I to do now?

I heard footsteps moving from pavement to sandy gravel, showing someone was approaching the stone wall I was sitting on. I quickly clicked the send icon. I closed my email and opened the internet to the page of Jordan I had been viewing earlier that day for our trip. I had never been there, and the idea of the others who lived in that area unnerved me. When you're a god, the unknown is a frightening prospect. I didn't like going into areas that weren't ours or that weren't free like the Americas, where no godly race drew territorial lines around them—for the most part.

Lena plopped onto the wall beside me. We had come back to Belize for her to spend time with her mother, and here she was annoying me instead.

"You moved too fast," I said to her, not taking my attention away from the phone. The puppy-dog eyes she had been giving me were annoying, so I didn't want to see them again. She thought I was attractive, if the amount of time she spent staring at me was an indicator, or she was hoping I'd fall for her and keep her here with her father and not send her to Hades.

"These people would never notice."

"Some mortals are perceptive."

"Like your precious Callie," she said with disdain, punctuating with a scoff.

"Yes, like my precious Callie," I said without the censure she gave.

"Then why didn't you steal that stuff that girl came to give me to drink? You could've given it to your girlfriend." Lena's tone was curious, the venom having left her voice.

I decided to play nice. None of this was her fault, and I had been less than kind. "I couldn't. There are laws we follow, rules in place."

"I saw the look in your eyes. You wanted to steal it. For a moment, I saw ambition and rage. I think the smallest nudge would have had you murder those people and take that immortal elixir to Callie."

I didn't want to admit there was truth in her statement. I had sickeningly thought of incapacitating my aunt and murdering Hermes in a quest to make Callie immortal. It had been a fleeting thought, but this was what love had done to me. The fact the scheme quickly left my mind did not assuage the guilt I felt for even having the thought. "It would be pointless. He'd kill her. We can still die, you know, by fire."

"Great, and I'm going to Hell, where there is loads of it." She sighed and traced her finger in the sand.

"It isn't Hell, no fire and brimstone. Sorry to disappoint. Its main drawback is it's dark and there are lots of dead there, ghosts if you will."

"So, you've been? For your wife?"

I didn't say anything but stared out at the ocean. Let her think what she wanted. I hadn't been back there since I said goodbye to my siblings. I couldn't go when I should've, and I still wouldn't go now to deal with it. Part of me couldn't face the idea of my daughter Hedone leaving for another realm to become whatever we gods become when we reach Elysium. Even if she were a spirit living with Hades and Persephone, she would still be there in a sense. And, selfishly, knowing she existed somewhere felt better than allowing her to disappear forever. I took in a ragged breath, trying to dispel my guilt.

"But you'll condemn me there?"

"You had a choice," I snapped. I spun my legs around and hopped down off the wall.

Grudgingly walking mortal speed, I left Lena and the crashing waves behind. I made my way back to our apartment, climbed the stairs, but I stopped at the top when I heard raised voices muffled through the door. My immortal ears could still make out the words. I held my breath and did not move so they could not hear me.

"No, Proteus. You can't change things now. You of all people should know she will remain in the Underworld. You see the future."

"I've seen many futures, my friend, some good for you and some bad, but your son—"

"If you know something, tell me now!" My father growled.

"Okay, okay, lemme go." Proteus muttered something, and I quietly crept closer to hear better. He was still muttering obscenities toward my father. When he calmed down, after my father's threat to his bodily person, Proteus said, "He will try it Ares, more than once."

"Try what? To go to New York?"

I sank against the wall and slid down, my stomach a jumble of bubbling nerves. Dread swept over me. I knew what Proteus meant. The thoughts never left my mind. Every day, I thought about a way to end my existence, but the drive was squelched by the thought of what Callie might do if I died.

"End himself. I don't know if he's successful. I can't always pinpoint time in my visions, and they are incomplete at times."

My father said nothing.

"Watch him closely. Watch his girl closely."

"Is it because of her? Does something happen to her?" My father asked quickly.

I held my breath, dreading the answer. That would be a reason I'd go through with it. If Callie died...

"I've seen confusing things, Ares. I doubt Prometheus could even decipher the mess the future holds. She dies; she lives. I've seen it all. Everything is changing. We sense that, even deep down under the sea."

"Proteus, he's my first child, my only one with Dite left, I can't..." my dad's voice broke. The god of war was trying not to cry.

I was about to throw up from what I was putting him through. I stood up, floated down a flight of stairs, and walked up with a heavy step so they'd hear me. When I opened the door and walked in, my dad turned away from me, and Proteus looked sheepish.

"What's going on?"

"We were wondering what abilities Lena will have. Someone who could read the future would be best right now," Chase said quietly. He turned to look at me, and I tried to ignore the thinly-veiled sadness in his eyes. He was looking at me differently now, great.

"My bet is on shapeshifting." I tried to sound upbeat, but I couldn't even fake it.

Proteus studied me as if he knew something more. Maybe he had known I was right outside the door. Maybe he wanted me to know what I was capable of doing. If so, why hadn't he said something to stop me? Was I supposed to die?

I fell asleep that night, troubled but somewhat content. Callie and I had emailed back and forth for an hour. It ended too soon, but her time zone was ahead of mine, and she had school.

Proteus's words bothered me. I wasn't thinking at all about taking my life at the moment. I was finding happiness and a need for existence through simply communicating to Callie in what ways we could. But would it be enough? Would our love fade and we get over each other given time, or would we always feel so bittersweet when we spoke? I longed to hear her voice, to visit her in my mind, and when I did, I was so happy. When reality crashed upon me, though, that this was it, that I could never have more of her or see her again in the flesh, Proteus's words didn't seem so farfetched.

When I awoke the next morning, something was tickling my arm. I blinked my eyes open to see dark brown curly hair splayed on my shoulder. I froze, my pulse racing. I knew that hair, that skin tone, slightly darker than mine and Mediterranean. Callie. I jerked up, disturbing her. She peered up at me with those dark almond-shaped eyes. My fingers dug into her shoulders. Callie was here in front of me, flesh and blood. I couldn't move. Or speak. My heart thumped wildly in my chest. She simply stared at me and I at her. How was she here?

"Callie?" I asked, touching her cheek. Her cheek was so smooth and warm. I wanted her instantly, Zeus be damned. Her breath hitched as I pulled her closer. By the gods, this must've been some fantastical dream I was having, but I would take what I could get. It felt so real, though, her here—the bed pressing down under our combined weight, her warmth against me, and the sight of her perfect face. Callie. I felt alive for the first time in what felt like ages. "How?"

She pressed her lips against mine, and I reacted, kissing her back. If she'd rather take advantage of the situation than talk, I was all for it.

Instantly, something was off. The feel of those lips, how they moved against mine, how she eagerly pressed her body against me, her hands roaming downward to my pant line. It felt weird, and Callie had never been that forward. I pushed her away a bit too roughly, and she fell onto her butt on the ground. She gaped at me. Even the expression of her shock was wrong. This was not Callie. Was I forgetting her already to the point my dreams couldn't realistically conjure her anymore?

Then she pouted. I realized two things: Callie was not a pouter, and this mirage hadn't said a word.

"How are you here?" I pressed.

She shrugged. It clicked in my head, and I wanted to kill her. I wanted to hurt her in any way possible for breaking my heart like this, pretending to be her when I so desperately needed to see Callie, to be with her. The craving and need for Callie rekindled but not tied to this fake vessel. And yet, I could not wound her, for she looked exactly like Callie. Even counterfeit, I could not lay a finger on her or shout at her.

"Lena, you're a horrible person. Get. *Out.*" I buried my face in my hands, trying to not explode with the multitude of emotions bashing around in me.

"What gave me away?" she asked.

I came out of hiding to glare at her. Callie's skin and hair slightly darkened, her hair straightened, and her body shortened and became curvier.

"Everything. Get. Out," I spat, trying to hold in my anger.

Lena gave me a look of sympathy and guilt. She got up, but instead of leaving, she came over to the bed, touching my shoulder. "I'm sorry, I just saw your photo of her, and I thought you might like me and let me stay if I could look like—"

"Now!" I shouted. I didn't realize I'd pushed away from her until I was up on the ceiling, glaring down on her.

Lena was frozen, shocked, her chin trembling.

"This is nothing compared to what some gods will do if you upset them."

She bolted from the room.

I let the gravity I hadn't realized I'd defied take hold of me again. I fell onto the bed and buried my face in my pillow. The gods, I missed Callie. It was too painful after the fake kiss to even think about, yet my mind replayed every moment I had with Callie, again and again, until I thought I might lose my mind. I didn't think I was far from it, to be honest. Maybe insanity would be a reprieve from this feeling of hopeless despondence.

CHAPTER 11

Callie

It was Friday night. I was sitting at home with Dad, watching TV, while Raphael puttered about in the kitchen, cleaning up after dinner. He didn't let me help when I offered (chased me out of the kitchen with a spatula actually). I'd wanted to help so I could stay busy. Staying busy kept sad thoughts at bay...momentarily. If I never stopped, I couldn't think or brood.

"No plans tonight?" Dad asked as he pored over his book edits on his laptop for the millionth time. He didn't look up at me or at the TV. Some history program was on. We didn't really watch TV, Dad and I. It was just soothing white noise.

"No." I picked up some of his scattered papers to have something to do—maps, graphs, family trees that he was revising after he cajoled Lucien into talking about the past. I don't know why he was asking about my Friday night plans. I hardly went out anymore, so me sitting here every night was a common occurrence.

"Whatever happened to that girl, Emily?"

I pretended to be engrossed in the family tree to avoid Dad's probing gaze. "She hates me because she had some four-year crush on Archer."

"And Linda? You were still hanging out with her after Archer...er...left." He could not say "died" or didn't believe it either. I wasn't about to point out his hesitation. "Why don't you see what she's up to?"

"I would, but she hates me now too."

I finally dared to look at my father, but instead of the pity I expected, I saw confusion. He really didn't understand my life. It was my fault for shutting him out. We used to talk about everything together, but then puberty and boys and things we couldn't discuss on equal ground parted us. Now, I felt as if the situation with Archer made us drift even farther apart. It was both our faults. He was obsessed with his books and studies, and I was obsessed with...Archer. And Dad didn't even know he was alive, that I knew it, or that I was contacting him.

"Why would she hate you? I'm sure it's a misunderstanding."

"She and Lucien broke up because of her jealousy of me. She thought something was going on between us since he was taking care of me so much."

Dad got a pensive look on his face. "Explains why he's kept his distance lately too."

I nodded. Then something on the family tree drew my attention, something I had never bothered to connect before. "Dad, Archer is Lucien's nephew." I laughed that I had never realized it.

"And? They always were in the myths and antiquated texts. Wait—'is,' Callie?" (Crap.)

"Don't point out the fact he's gone, Dad. It hurts," I tried.

His eyes narrowed on me. (Double, triple crap.) "Callista Thea Syches, don't you lie to me." Dad raised his voice. He was angry, rigid.

"Open that trap, girl; your dad doesn't need to be stressed out in his condition," Raphael chided.

Guilt washed over me. I glared at Raphael, but he raised his brows in challenge as he adjusted pillows behind my dad.

"You think I'm blind?" Raphael continued. "Always texting, on your computer, talking late at night in your room, smiling when you read responses. If you have no friends, as your dad just found out, who is it then?" (Absolutely busted.)

I was shocked Raphael was so observant, and I had been so stupid as to not hide things better. I floundered and then met my father's disappointed gaze.

"I figured they wouldn't actually kill him," he said. (What!)

"How could you not tell me that then? I was depressed, half alive when I thought he was dead," I attacked.

"How could you not tell me he was alive either?"

We sat in silence for a moment. Something had shifted entirely between us. I had this silly profound feeling that I had grown up. I hadn't told him anything, hadn't depended on him, while I dealt with my grief by myself and fought for the truth. I didn't *need* Dad anymore, but I wanted to. It was an overwhelming concept. If I could have Archer in my life, maybe I wouldn't fall to pieces when Dad passed. Or maybe I could just hold it together as I had when I thought I had lost Archer forever. I was surprising myself with strength in the hardest times.

"I think I'll head home for now?" Raphael asked awkwardly.

Dad nodded. "I'll call you when I'm ready for bed."

Raphael left to go downstairs. Once Dad's health had deteriorated too much, he set Raphael up in an apartment in our building. He wanted to give Raphael privacy—so he said—but I knew it was my Dad's last attempt to hold onto his dignity; he didn't want a live-in nurse or to admit that we were crossing into hospice territory.

"I'm talking to him. We can't be together, but it...hurts less to be able to talk to him."

"Is that a good idea?"

"Probably not, but I'm beyond caring about it. He will find a way back to me. I know he will. He will keep me safe."

"I don't doubt it," my father said quietly. "The god killed Death for you."

There was another awkward silence. Things weren't the same anymore.

"Happiness in life is everything, Callie. I might be dying because of my curiosity, but I had a happy life of discovery. Playing it safe is stifling."

Was he telling me to be with Archer?

"I should be telling you to stay away from him and that safety is paramount, that you should do nothing to anger Zeus, and I'm not telling you to go looking for trouble, but Callista..."

I met his watery gaze and wanted to stop him. He was talking as if these were his last words. I felt our distance growing and the feeling I could survive on my own becoming stronger, but I needed more time.

"...you are much stronger than you think." The comment felt loaded, but how? Maybe he just had faith in me, impressed by how Death hadn't killed me. "There's something I need you to see—not yet—but when I pass. It's about your mother." (Oh man, he was about to cry.)

"Dad, don't. This is not goodbye. And you don't have to talk about her. I know it makes you terribly sad. I'll tell Aroha to stop questioning you about her. I saw that it bothered you."

"Aroha," he said, blinking away the tears that had been forming.

"What about her?" I hedged.

"What is she up to tonight?"

I shrugged.

"Maybe you should call her, go have one of those girls' nights."

A Greek goddess having a chick-flick night? I wanted to laugh in his face. Instead, I smiled at his suggestion and texted her, really just wanting to make him happy. Aroha was back and forth with me these days. It was my fault that I'd ruined her current life, and at times, that sentiment slipped through the veneer of her kindness. Maybe, just maybe, we could truly be friends one day. All I knew was that, by her side, I might eventually see Archer again.

I was surprised when she texted me back that she wanted me to come around to hang out. Her text even gushed with excitement. I told Dad, which made him smile. That grin on his face meant everything to me.

"Before you go, I have something for you." He sifted through his paperwork that Raphael had spread around him until he located a small envelope. He held it up, which meant I had to get up off the sofa and grab it. Dad was having trouble getting around these days but refused to use a wheelchair.

I felt the envelope. Something small and hard was inside. I opened it and dumped it into my hand. A tiny silver star pendant landed in my palm, attached to a chain that snaked its way out.

"It was your mother's," Dad said quietly.

My heart soared with happiness I hadn't felt in a long time. My mother's necklace. I looked at him expectantly for more. He rarely ever talked about Mom.

"I'd tell you more about it and what it meant to her, but your friend is waiting for you."

I wanted to protest, to insist Aroha could wait. As if they were in on this conspiracy together, my phone beeped with a text. My father smiled as if to say "see?"

"Please, Dad, just quickly tell me about it."

"Oh no, it's a story that will take time, and you should never keep gods waiting."

My phone beeped again. I looked at my phone. Aroha was mighty impatient. She must've been as lonely as I was, which made me feel bad that I hadn't reached out before.

I gave my dad a look, and he chuckled. Then I grabbed my key and went to the Ambroses' apartment down the hall. With trepidation, I knocked on the door. Memories of Archer opening the door and kissing me senseless came back. I squashed them. Aroha opened the door, clad in a robe, her hair wet, and face clear of makeup. I hadn't seen her like that before, without the whole superficial façade on. She was radiant with a natural beauty that far surpassed the done-up version of her.

"Wow, you're pretty," I blurted out.

Aroha raised her brow and smirked. "Don't tell me you prefer the fairer sex now, Callie? Sometimes I do have that effect, you know."

I pulled myself together and pushed my way in with a scoff. "No. I just have never seen you without your face painted like a movie star. You look better *à la naturelle.*"

She beamed and laughed.

"So, what do you want to do tonight?" I asked, not knowing what goddesses did on the weekend.

"Ah, come, come." She frightened me with a girly squeal. Aroha grabbed my hand and pulled me into her room.

Unlike Archer's plain and smaller room, this one was the master suite and was opulent. My eyes were drawn to the massive vanity that had three mirrors—the kind where the side ones angled in—with a glowing white LED frame surrounding each. It was a Hollywood-actress vanity, with at least six drawers and a furry padded stool to top it off. She literally had a white faux fur comforter and pillows and a matching rug by the foot of the bed. Everything was white—except the carpet was gray—and the walls were a light blue. I felt as if I were on a cloud in the sky. I touched the furry pillow on her bed, and it was so soft. That's when I noticed two outfits lying on the bed. Pajamas and a vibrant red dress. On the other side of the bed was another set of pajamas and a black dress.

I gave her a quizzical look.

She gave me a sad maternal-type half smile and played with my hair. "You're naturally beautiful too." Her tone wasn't that tight-lipped condescending one she often used. It was genuine. I was seeing the true Aroha (but who really knew?). She then pointed at the bed. "With the state of things and how we both feel and your desire to hang out, I knew it must be a girls' night, but I wasn't sure which kind. Go out, flirt, and drink a little, and come home to pig out? Or stay in, pig out, watch cheesy movies, and talk about everything."

I eyed the black dress and thought of trying to talk to college guys in bars. Not me, not ever. The teal PJs looked silky and inviting. "Pajamas."

She laughed. "An Archer choice through and through. You were fit for each other, such a shame." She picked up the dresses.

"If you want to go out, I will."

"I know," she called from the massive walk-in closet as she put them away. She came back out. "I'm happy to stay in on one condition...let me be myself with my movements and such. That's what I miss the most." Aroha's eyes teared up. "Acting mortal is painstaking. And when I can be me now, it's alone."

I pulled her into my arms. We hugged, and she—the goddess of beauty (my mind was reeling)—cried on my shoulder. And it broke me. I could never fathom what it must be like to spend thousands of years with your child, have him be your best friend, and then to suddenly give that up due to a punishment.

She yanked away from me and was gone and then back in her PJs. I shook my head, trying to process the immortal movements.

She smiled, although her eyes were still teary. "What was I thinking? We're both grieving. Why would we want to go out? Let's put on *The Notebook*."

I ignored her grief comment. I refused to let her indulge in that lie. "Not that movie. I hate it."

Aroha scooped up the teal PJs and threw them at me. She shifted her mood to suddenly laughing. "Ugh." She rolled her eyes. "Typical. Don't tell me you love *Romeo and Juliet*? If so, you and Archer are meant for each other."

I hated love stories that ended in death. I wanted to reject her comment, but I got fixated on her word choices. "Are?"

Her face fell. "If you do this to me, make the pain of losing my son worse, I will make you leave."

"I *know*, Aroha." I pulled my phone out of my pocket. I put my thumbprint on it to unlock the screen and opened my messages. Not wanting to face her potential outburst, I left it on the bed. I went into her closet and changed into pajamas, knowing well we had a lot to talk about after this. With her immortal speed, she should've read through everything in Archer and my texts by the time I changed. The amount of transparency I was giving his mother might upset Archer, but I needed her to know. I needed her to see how much we loved each other, couldn't live without each other. I wanted her on our side, if there were sides. I had to confide in someone. I just hoped she didn't go into the super personal emails we had shifted to.

Tentatively, I entered her bedroom, wondering if the PJs were a bad idea since she might kick me out at any moment. She still held my phone and met my gaze. Her expression was blank, but then she was right in front of my face. I braced for a verbal, or perhaps physical, attack.

"Who else knows?" She wasn't angry, which took me by surprise.

"My father and his servant. Raphael suspected and called me out on it. Why? Will Archer be punished further? He told me it was fine we talked as long as he never came back."

"Calm down, Callie." She braced my shoulders and gave me a tight smile. "We will talk about this tonight, but there are two people who cannot know."

"Who?"

"Chase and Lucien. Chase and Archer have become closer than ever before. I can tell. Archer has been happier, and Chase thinks he's doing it. We can't take that away from him. And Lucien, are you kidding me? He might decide to set the sun forever if there's no chance with you."

"But there isn't."

"Callie, if it could cause another world war, you don't mention it. Lucien is...enamored with you."

I didn't want to think about Lucien's misled feelings. "Agreed, I won't tell him. I just had to tell you... I want us to be friends, and this was such a huge lie between us."

"It was. I'm getting so weary of lying day in and out."

What must that be like? I had seen Archer struggle by hiding a large part of himself from me. Aroha must hate living this façade of a mortal life.

I took my phone back from her, clicked it to photo mode and switched it for a selfie. She posed with me in our PJs. We looked good. I sent it to Archer with, **Girls night with Mom.**

Aroha hit me with a furry pillow and took my phone from me. She typed superfast and handed it back to me. "Come on. We have to agree on a suitable yet sappy romantic movie."

I peered at the phone. Aroha had written, **Your secret is safe with me. Don't tell your father about it, though. I would be honored to be her mom.**

My heart picked up in pace for another very different reason. Not only was Aroha accepting me, but she was hoping for a future with Archer and I together, rather than brushing off my comment.

Full of glee for friendship instead of a boy, I joined her in the living room.

"*Pretty Woman?*" Aroha asked.

"Never saw it."

"Deprived child. Sit." She pointed at the sofa as she raced at immortal speed around the room. The smell of popcorn assaulted my senses, and the TV was on before I registered her movements. "I've missed this."

"What? Girl time?"

"Yes," Aroha said. "No, to be honest, girl time with someone who isn't envious of me and whom I can act normal in front of." Then she turned away, getting bowls ready for popcorn and pouring sodas.

I wasn't sure what to say in response. I was beginning to realize the gods were just as human as we mortals were.

CHAPTER 12

Archer

After Lena's nasty trick, I demanded we get rid of her as soon as possible. Proteus didn't like my rude attitude toward her, but at least he didn't defend her actions. Lena had inherited his shape-shifting abilities, much to my embarrassment. Proteus wanted her to stay for a few more days to say goodbye to her mother and friends. I wanted to wash my hands of her, already regretting my choice of making her immortal.

As a compromise, Dad settled on leaving for Hades two days after the incident. We flew to Amman, Jordan, the country currently housing the entrance to the Underworld. After layovers and connecting flights, we landed in Al-Karak, a city near the south coast of the Dead Sea, and checked into a mid-grade hotel. I didn't like being under Proteus's and my father's watchful stares. Proteus's all-seeing eye knew something. He was watching me with a cautious yet pained expression. He probably knew what I was up to, but he didn't call me out about it or stop me. Perhaps things had to happen a certain way for the future to pan out the way he wanted. Maybe everything would work out for me for once. Callie and I deserved to be happy, damn it, even if it could only be for a year. A year of happiness had to be much better than this constant sorrow for both of us. It was completely selfish, but I was done living without her. A life without love is no life at all.

The first evening, Dad met with some others who were in the area, and he made me tag along, most likely to babysit me, because he wasn't involving me in their plans. They were speaking in Arabic, one of the few languages I didn't know. I had never spent much time in this part of the world since my father had often been here in the past for wars, and I had made it my life's work to avoid him. He greeted one as Hadad and the other as Ashur, so I had an inkling what he was up to. The latter was a war god, so my dad had to contact him. War gods sought each other out when entering each other's "territories" to make peace or lay terms. The other, Hadad, was a storm god, so this was most likely our cover to get into the entrance to Hades, which was currently in Lot's Cave. The entrance changed often due to the sea now being more of a touristy place than it had been a hundred or so years ago. Lot's Cave was a tourist destination for some biblically inclined people, but not nearly as busy as other areas.

The meeting ended peacefully, and Dad and I left.

"So, what's the plan?" I asked.

He eyed me. "What do you think it is?"

Great, he was getting all Socratic on me. He had done this when I was young to launch me into self-discovering lessons. As a teen, it made me want to rip his head off. I think I tried once even, but he was always ready. There was no such thing as a surprise attack on Ares.

I rolled my eyes at him. "God of storms, so…"

He smiled and patted me on the back. Then his hand squeezed my shoulder, stopping me. He looked wary about what he was going to say; it couldn't be good. "Are you sure you don't want to go with Lena and Proteus into—"

"No."

"Archer, just hear me out."

"You'll say the closure will be good for me, and you're probably right, but I'm not going."

He shook his head. "No, it won't be good for *you*. It will always hurt, a gaping hole in your heart for eternity. But it will help Hedone. You're keeping them trapped—"

"Enough!" I stormed off away from him, back to the hotel. I knew he was right. Ma had had the same conversation with me about a dozen times. I could never bring myself to see the ghost of my daughter and ex-wife, to conclude their unfinished business–whatever Psyche's could be because I knew it wasn't me. When whatever was holding them back was wrapped up, they would pass on to Elysium, where they would be at peace but not exist anymore in my world. We gods are selfish creatures, and in this respect, I would cling onto my nature to protect myself.

Thankfully, Chase didn't bring it up again. I was forced to play tourist with my three companions, and although I was hardly interested—my mind coming up with grand schemes of escape—I did enjoy myself in the Dead Sea. I had never been in the salty waters nor felt that peculiar buoyant feeling of weightlessness in water. It felt as if I was defying gravity—my "flying" ability but in the water. It made me think of my half brothers and the water sports we had played with our godly talents. My spirits were lifted momentarily from the cleansing dip and the positive thoughts I had while feeling weightless and reminiscing.

That evening, we took the tour-guide route to the cave but ditched the car after almost an hour of driving and went the last bit on foot. Our Mesopotamian friends led us quietly through the night, and we climbed up the steps to the top of a covered platform.

Two men stood on security watch underneath the partially covered metal structure that protected patrons from the sun. They spoke to us in Arabic and then English. "You cannot be up here at night. Come back in the morning when you can see it properly." They seemed uneasy about our appearance as if they never had anyone bother to stop by this late.

Ashur nodded at us and tapped the railing gently with his finger. Hadad turned and looked at me with a smile before his eyes rolled back into his head and lightning struck the metal scaffolding, making the mortal guards jump. I jumped as well, my instincts thinking of Zeus, who would be even angrier if he could read my mind. The wind picked up, funneling through the two unprotected sides, blinding all of us with sand, and then rain poured. Despite the paneled roof and single glass wall, the rain slashed in at us through the tunnel and gaps. I had to grip tightly to the railing to stay grounded, my hands slick with water.

I heard my father shout something about "holding tight."

That's when I knew it was time to do the opposite. I let go.

The hurricane force winds sucked me off the platform and up into the sky, and I let those winds carry me away. The force whipped me back and forth, my leg hitting something hard, stone most likely, and then the wind dying down. Soon, I was descending, dropping free of Hadad's storm. I gracefully landed in the desert sand. I wasted no time calling Zeph.

He appeared instantly in a whirlwind of sand. He looked around as he always did, a bit curious of the location he was suddenly summoned to. "Eros," he said, a bit nervous. "What in the Hades are you doing...near Hades?"

"Long story, but I need to get out of here, immediately."

"Is that a Hadad storm?"

"Yes."

Zeph shivered at the thought. "You don't have to tell me twice. Where to?"

"Manhattan."

"Got it."

My heart thumped wildly in my chest, and I grew excited and anxious at the same time. Zeph didn't know. My punishment and all I had done hadn't spread to all immortal ears. I feared he might refuse to take me, persuade me it was wrong, but his compliance came readily. My suffering would end tonight. I knew when I saw Callie, I would only feel bliss and love and relief. There wasn't time for regret; that would come later. If Zeus killed her, I would follow.

Zeph and I landed in an alleyway, a few blocks from my old apartment. I was so close to seeing Callie; I imagined I felt her presence. Like two magnets trying to find each other, the attraction was strong. I needed her. And then, as soon as the euphoria peaked, foreboding crept over me, making my skin crawl and my breathing heavy. I leaned on the brick wall, trying to press down the rising bile in my stomach.

"You okay, Eros?" Zeph's blue eyes squinted in concern, and his soft boyish face tilted, trying to read me. He was the gentlest of the Anemoi, the four wind gods.

"You're not up to speed with Olympian news, obviously?"

"You know I don't ask my passengers questions, like who that girl was and why she was made immortal. I'm staying clear of Fiji. Zeus wanted me to wear a tracking device to keep tabs on whom I was taking where. Boreas told him to shove off, and I joined in. Well, you know I'm not the defiant type. I simply handed the tracking device to Boreas, and he smashed both. Notus refused to even show up to the meeting—hot-headed, you know."

Notus, the south wind god, was responsible for that grueling summer heat and being hot-headed, but the north wind god Boreas was harsh, cold, and cruel, much like the winter winds he cast. The joke wasn't lost on me, but I was thirsty for info from Fiji and torn about seeing Callie.

"Eurus?" I asked about the east wind, trying to stall.

My thoughts were hardly with the wind god drama at the moment, but I was already regretting coming here. If I saw Callie, I'd never leave. One year. Then Callie would be dead. She deserved to live. She deserved to be happy. My father's belief that Zeus was hedging on me to fail so he could kill her resonated in me.

"Eurus, of course complied. Unlucky, melancholy sod," Zeph chided.

We were silent for a moment.

"Are you all right, Eros?"

"No. No, I'm not. Get me out of here, Zeph. I was about to make the mistake of an eternal lifetime."

"Heavy." Zephyrus whistled. "Let's get you out of here, then. Where to?"

"Montserrat, please. I'll fill you in on what has Zeus in a hissy fit when we get there. Let me just send off a text real quick."

"I could do with a day off. What do you say we make a day of it?"
I wanted to dismiss him. I knew what I had to do now. I had run out
of options, but if Zeph could distract me—maybe somehow help me—I
should hang out with him. If this was the end of the road, what would be
better than spending time with an old friend?

CHAPTER 13

Callie

I called him. My calls were ignored, but he'd have to answer eventually. How could he? Archer told me he needed me to move on, to stop the emails, the texts, that he couldn't bear to keep this going. In. A. Text. (Coward!) I felt like he'd stabbed me in the heart. I could not live without him. He had said he couldn't go on without me. It wasn't just teenage melodrama. It was this profound binding nonsense gods did to attach humans to them—or true love (maybe both); we were connected. We both knew this, but after all we had been through, he was giving up on us. I felt betrayed, but more than anything, I was angry.

Finally, he answered. "Callie, I said not to call—"

"And I say no! I'm not giving up on you."

"I'm going to break our bond, make you love someone else."

"Don't you dare!"

"Callie..." His voice was weak, defeated. He was giving up on more than me, which was terrifying.

"Archer, why? Why are you suddenly doing this? These last few weeks have made me happy."

"And me."

"Then, why?"

"That's the point. This is prolonging the inevitable. We can never be together, and we have been kidding ourselves. I'm going to let you love another, okay?"

"You mean you're going to force me against my will to love someone to get over you. Say what you truly mean to do, Archer." I was irate. How could he plan to take away my freedom just to end the love between us?

I knew the truth, although I hated to admit it: it was his nature. These gods had meddled with mortals for thousands of years on a daily basis and thought nothing of forcing us to do their bidding. I had never before thought about what they could do and the power they wielded.

"It's what's best."

"For you. If you do this, Archer, I'll never forgive you." I couldn't stop him, so I had to convince him through words.

"No, for you, Callie. You could live a normal life with a mortal man, have a family. With me, you can't have any of that. There is no way, no hope for us to ever be together; please, see that."

"I won't."

"He will kill you." Archer took a deep breath. "I was there, New York. I was blocks away from you, completely ready to come back, but I realized how selfish it was. We would have one happy year, and then your life cut much too short."

I wanted to tell him to come back, to hell with it. I didn't want to live without him or my father. I wanted to give in and just be happy, even if fleeting, but I didn't say the words. Deep down, I knew he was right. In my depressed state, I didn't want to think moving on was the right thing, but I had to live. I had to let him free me from this uncontrollable, intense love. It was too much for me to be a part of and then lose. If he could end this suffering, I should let him. Yet the words wouldn't come.

"You know it is the right thing to do. Your silence tells me you know it, Callie, even if you won't admit it."

"Don't make me love someone. Just make me stop feeling this way." When it came out, it felt like knives slashing through my barely beating heart.

He drew in a ragged breath. "It doesn't work that way. I have to make you love another to break the bond. You'll be happy."

"Forced to be."

"I'm not that talented. If I make you love some random person, it will fade if he's not right for you, and then you'll be free." He breathed heavily in the phone, as if he was barely holding himself together. "Look, I have to go."

Too soon. It might be the last time I spoke to him. "No, please, don't hang up."

"I can't say the words at risk of binding you more, but you know my heart, Callie."

"I love you," I rushed out, knowing he was hanging up.

"Goodbye."

My phone made the tell-tale three beeps, announcing the end of the call. Gods never said goodbye; Archer had told me this. He meant it. I would never talk to him again.

There was a tap at my bedroom door. I took a deep breath, pulling back tears that wanted to spill, and got up to open the door. Raphael told me dinner was ready.

I trudged out with a brave face for my father. I sat down, and we talked about trivial things. It was so hard to feign happiness, but I got myself through it. After dinner, I was helping Raphael with dishes—Dad retiring right after dinner—when a peculiar feeling came over me. My heart lurched, and I thought of Dan Egan of all people. My imagination envisioned me kissing him before I shut it down. My blood ran cold. I lost the grip on the glass I was drying, and it went crashing to the floor.

I instantly tried to pick it up, but Raphael took my hands up in his and looked at them. His expression was strained; then he smiled. "Lucky I stopped you from cutting your fingers, isn't it?"

It was a strange thing to say, but my hands weren't sliced up. I thought I had to have cut them on the sharp shards that gleamed menacingly in the light, but sure enough, I was fine. I didn't think much of it and was distracted by the pounding of my heart echoing in my head as if I were running.

"Are you okay, Callie girl?" Was *he*? He was looking at me oddly.

"I'm just...tired."

"Go have a lie down. Let me do my job."

"I think I might."

I had made it into my bedroom and shut the door when a piercing pain struck my heart. I thought I was having a heart attack for a moment and bit my lip to not scream out. I flopped onto my bed. I screamed into my pillow as a third wave of pain hit me. I lay there immobile. Then a moment later, the sharp pressurized feeling eased out of my chest, and I felt a weight lift off my shoulders.

Archer had made me love another. It was heartache (literally). I thought of Dan. Warm feelings flowed over me. I felt a fluttering, almost an instinctual, hormonal stirring, and it made me angry. What happened to my free will? I guess that's what happens when you try to be as powerful as gods. It comes back to bite you. I'd never forgive him for this.

Archer. The thought of him made me smile. Love washed over me. I felt whole, complete. Whatever he did hadn't worked, not fully. He made me feel something for someone else, but not love. Something told me that this love I had for Archer had nothing to do with the bind. He acted as if that's all there was between us. But I had loved him before he said the words, so when they were taken away, why would that change?

"Because it should have changed everything," Aroha said in disbelief by our lockers the next morning. "Callie, seriously. You shouldn't feel anything for him. What you're describing sounds like two or three of our arrows."

"Arrows," I scoffed (I was bitter). I'd told Aroha about my heart pain because she was the only one I could confide in who could give me answers.

"Metaphorical, but they do pack a punch. Or so I've heard. I've never been as silly as my son and tried one on myself. Lucien knows the sting of the arrows of love most."

I inventoried my mythological knowledge. "Daphne."

"He was in love with a tree...for ten years, thanks to Archer."

I couldn't help but smile and giggle when I saw Aroha trying not to laugh.

"But in all seriousness, for you, Callie, he would need two to sever your bind and a third for you to fall for another. I know you don't want to hear it, but this is good. You can live a normal life."

"Stop saying that! Everyone keeps saying that. What is 'normal?' You've all—including my father—thrown me into this world. How am I supposed to forget it? Fall in love and marry a mortal, have two kids, white picket fence around my four-bedroom house, a cushy job, and a dog named Spot?"

"Most mortals long for that, you know."

"I'm not most."

"You don't need to tell me that, my dear." Aroha and I began heading to homeroom. "But what do you want?"

I laughed. "I bet you a majority of eighteen-year-old girls would tell you they have no clue, so I'm one of them, but before, I had a future with Archer. We never planned it out, but my mind did. And without that, all I see is my father dying and me being lost and alone."

"I will look after you."

"For how long?"

She looked away from me, biting her lip, so I knew then that my friends would abandon me before long too. "I can only stay here safely for a few more years. I was planning on college. We could be roommates even."

"Roommates?" Lucien's voice cut in. He had come up behind us.

The three of us talked about NYU, and it felt kind of okay to admit plans, to foresee a future with my two friends. Linda and Emily walked by us, the former glaring and latter smirking at me (huh?).

"So why is Linda giving me death stares? I mean, why didn't you smooth it over and tell her she had no reason to be jealous?" I asked him awkwardly.

Aroha laughed and patted Lucien on the shoulder. "You have fun with that one." Then she just abandoned us, running to catch up with her next male victim (okay, a bit harsh of me), leaving me alone with Lucien in the almost-deserted hallway.

Lucien blushed a little because it was a difficult situation. He didn't want to confess his feelings, and I didn't want to hear them, but surely Linda should be over her jealousy, seeing that Lucien rarely spoke to me these days. "She made me choose between being with her or being your friend."

"Whoa." How could she make an ultimatum like that? She had no idea she was trying to bend a god to her will, so of course she expected him to choose her. She was silly for doing it, which made me feel sorry for her.

"I chose you."

"Because you think I need you or because Archer wants you to look after me, but you don't have to." I had to stop him from saying stupid things he might feel.

"I chose you for those reasons but also because I judged her for making such a cruel request. You needed her friendship, and she let rumors run her life and believed there was something going on between us." That wasn't fabulous but better than what I had worried he'd say.

"Great," I muttered.

A few stragglers in the hall were looking at us as if trying to see gossip they could spread. It was only natural, since Lucien hardly hid his feelings well, that others would pick up on his feelings for me. I had none for him, though. I hoped he realized I'd only ever love Archer.

"Is that such a bad idea?" Lucien hedged. His eyes were expectant, longing, and yet there was a hesitant dread in them. He knew I loved Archer and yet still had some misguided hope.

"You're my best friend, Lucien." I rushed off before I could see the disappointment spread across his face. It had to be done. And I would find a way to be with Archer one day.

CHAPTER 14

If only I were like Dionysus, made immortal in my thirties, the possibilities in this modern world would be limitless. It felt like eons since I had been actually legally allowed to practice medicine. Being eternally eighteen utterly sucked, the endless high school and college circuit, over and over and...

The drama these pubescent mortals conjured up was ludicrous. Linda, led by Emily, was creating so many fantastical rumors that I had to distance myself from Callie at school. Not majorly. I spoke to her in passing during physics and minimally at lunch. I didn't want her to feel completely forsaken.

I had hoped this clear sign of distance from her object of jealousy would make Linda come around, befriend Callie again, or at least be civil. It didn't. Linda ignored her or joined in when others ridiculed Callie, and it was getting bad. Callie was being mocked and bullied, yet she hardly cared or noticed. She was a shell of whom she once was, and I hated Archer the more for it.

I even tried to repair things with Linda, become friends again, but after three millennia, I still had no idea how to deal with an ex. I usually was the one to muck up the relationship and stayed far away from them. How could I be so old and not understand basic human social behavior when it came to the fairer sex? With all my godly talents, I've never had the knack for relationships.

Graduation couldn't come fast enough. I didn't want to stay, even though Callie might need me, as a *friend*, as she'd so candidly slipped into our conversation this morning. I wanted far away from here, from her, from all my fellow Greek immortals. I wanted to pull a Prometheus and go off the grid, a life neither Zeus nor anyone could track or control. And yet...if it were possible, I might just take Callie with me, masochist that I was.

Then, after first period, Linda fell in step with me in the hallway. She gave me furtive side-eyes.

I gave her a reassuring smile, trying to show her it was fine to talk to me.

"I need to talk to you in private. It's about Callie." She looked around as if she didn't want to be overheard. "Meet me under the stadium bleachers during lunch." Then she hurried off down the hall.

It was peculiar behavior for the strait-laced Linda to break the rules by leaving the school. Her choice of locations was a bit strange too. For all of time, under the bleachers has been a place where most couples would secretly meet to make out. I remember kissing Euterpe in the shadows of the Hippodrome back when I was young. It has always been the place parents forgot about, where kids could let loose. When people are so enthralled by the games, they forget to watch over their daughters. Had Linda not said it was about Callie, I would've completely gotten the wrong idea. I still would've gone, though. I'm a guy, one who missed the feel of a girl in my arms, her lips on mine.

At lunchtime, I slipped outside through the backdoors of the gymnasium. Linda was already there when I arrived, sitting on a concrete base that held up one of the highest posts. She looked at me, her deep brown eyes shining. She didn't smile in greeting, but stood up, dusting herself off.

I walked toward her and stopped when we were a couple feet apart. I jammed my hands in my pockets, awkwardly, not knowing what to do with them. They twitched, wanting to pull her close. "So?" I prompted.

"I want you to be honest with me for once." Her tone put me on the defensive, and fantasies of kissing her dissipated.

"What's that supposed to mean?"

Linda's eyes narrowed suspiciously. What was she up to? "Is Archer really dead?" Her eyes searched mine.

I froze, willing myself not to react in any way. Somehow, she knew; she wasn't actually asking me. I read the truth off her. "I thought this was about Callie?" I stalled. How in Hades, Olympus, and Atlantis did she know?

"It is." She glared at me. "I see you won't tell me anything." Then she blinked, and I saw tears forming.

Ugh, girls crying was my greatest weakness. I stepped closer to her, taking her chin between my thumb and fingers, remembering the feel of her delicate, soft skin.

She backed away out of my grasp, suspicious. "You'll feed me some lies or tell me the truth will hurt me. Did Archer move away? Is he in trouble or something? Did he fake his death? What's going on, Lucien?"

"Why would you think that? After Callie being depressed for months, and Aroha and I..." I wasn't even lying, but it was still hard to mask the truth. I didn't want to hurt her anymore.

"Aroha is hardly depressed," Linda scoffed. "And Callie is a different story altogether."

"What do you mean? Why don't you get to the point?"

"Callie's on her phone all the time—"

"So is everyone we know."

"She's texting and talking to Archer. If he is truly dead, then she is crazy, Lucien."

A coldness formed in the pit of my stomach. Surely, Archer wouldn't be stupid enough to go back on his conviction to let Callie go. He couldn't have. "She must just be going through his old messages. I admit it's not healthy—"

"No, I heard her in the bathroom talking to him. She thought she was alone, obviously. It seemed like they were arguing. Last week, she was getting texts that made her smile. Haven't you noticed she's not as depressed?"

"Maybe she's finally getting over him." As soon as I spoke, I knew it was a desire of mine and not what was truly happening. Callie was forever bound to Archer, unfairly in love with him.

Linda laughed, a nervous, tight laugh. "No one has a love like those two and ever gets over it."

"Huh?"

"You wouldn't understand." It was an insult. She thought me callous and unloving, and when it came to her, she was right. I had been incorrigible.

"He can't be texting her, talking to her," I said quietly, sticking to the truth I knew. I was afraid Linda might end up finding out too much and be on Zeus's hitlist next.

"Is he alive, Lucien?"

Unable to meet her gaze, unable to lie—not because I couldn't but because it rankled and hurt me to do so to her—I nodded. I looked up to see Linda's ashen face, her lip trembling. She knew there was something much more going on, and my mind scrambled with excuses of why we'd lie about his death. Not knowing what else to say or do, but feeling as if we were at some dangerous crossroad, I pulled her into my arms and tucked her head under my chin. She went rigid at first but then softened in my arms, feeling most likely as I was—comfortable, familiar. Then she shook in my arms.

"Why are you crying?" I didn't understand girls. If Archer was alive, why would she be crying? It was mind-boggling.

"I'm happy," she murmured. Then she seemed to realize she was in my arms and backed away, wiping her tears away. "I'm so happy for Callie."

"Don't be. He's not coming back."

"Why?"

"Can you just be there for her like you should've been? She needs you." Not wanting to give away more, I took off. I walked as fast as a mortal could. Such measured steps felt confining. I needed to feel immortal again. It was painfully tedious to go through life so slowly.

"Lucien!" She ran to catch up to me, and I had to let her. "I don't understand."

"Remember what you said earlier? The truth can hurt you, Linda. It's a family affair, so just leave it at that. His family will never let him come back to New York or be with Callie."

"Lucien—"

"No." I stormed off, letting her have the anger that I wanted to direct at Archer.

After school, I went straight to Callie's apartment. When I pounded on the door, I realized the anger at Archer hadn't quite left me; instead, it had seethed and grown all day, and knowing my temper, it was about to transfer onto someone else.

She opened the door. When she saw it was me, she smiled. "To what do I owe this pleasure?"

I pushed my way in. "You alone?"

"Yeah?" Her brow adorably furrowed in confusion at my tone.

She closed the door, and I snapped, "What in Tartarus are you two playing at?"

Callie's eyes went wide, and then she looked away. Guilt, lies, all across her face as plain as day. How had I not seen it?

She crossed her arms. "I have no idea what you're talking about."

"Callie." I ran my hands down my face, growling in frustration. "You're talking to Archer."

"Oh my God, he's alive?" she blurted out.

I glared at her. "I'm the god of truth, and you're crap at lying. Give it up."

She moved away from me with a sigh. "It's not his fault."

"Don't defend him. He's selfish. He's going to get you killed!"

"I was relentless. I called and texted him until he gave in. You don't understand. We have a connection. I see him in my dreams. I *knew* he was alive."

"How long have you been talking?"

"Oh, stop acting so self-righteous, Lucien. A while, okay? But you can stop this hissy fit, because it's over. He 'freed' me or, at least, thinks he did. He broke it off with me and stopped answering his phone, email, everything. Happy?"

"No." I was jealous as all Hades, but I disliked seeing her pain more. "What do you mean, he thinks he freed you?"

"He shot me with his lousy arrows to make me love someone else. I think it's Dan."

"Callie. I'm lost."

"Sit down."

Once we were seated on the sofa, she launched into the tale of how he was shooting her with arrows to break their bond. Between what Archer said and what Callie felt, he had used three arrows. I remembered the sting of those. He'd hit me with ten of those suckers and made me mad with love for Daphne before her father turned her into a tree. I had obsessed over her leaves and roots for years. Humiliating. But wait...

"You couldn't feel his arrows, not really. Maybe a feeling of liking Dan, but—"

"No, it felt excruciating, a stabbing pain to my chest."

"Maybe you did have a connection like you say, Callie. I have no other explanation for it, but he severed it. You can move on now."

"It didn't work. I love him still, just as much as before."

"Only because you want to. You could forget about him, easily. You just need to move on, and his arrows will do the rest."

"I can't move on."

"You can!" I grabbed her forearms in hopeless desperation for her to see reason.

She looked down at her arms in my hands. Then those gorgeous mahogany eyes locked onto mine.

"You're beautiful," came out of my mouth on its own violation, my brain mush. I was a ladies' man with a track record of women only second to Zeus's, and here I was as tongue-tied and awkward as a pubescent boy. My hands slipped up her arms, pulling her closer to me. So mortal, so fragile, yet she had such power over me. Her skin was soft and warm. An urge to kiss all of that soft warmth consumed me.

"Linda was justifiably jealous. I heard you and Archer arguing the night he left." She was looking away now, not at me, and I felt bereft.

"Lucien—"

I didn't let her finish. Hearing my name on her lips broke me, and I pulled her face to meet mine; only, she turned at the last second, and I caught her cheek in my lips, an inch from her mouth.

She batted me away and stood up, crossing her arms defensively. "Please leave." She put distance between us while walking toward the door.

I followed—immortal speed—and enveloped her into my arms, my lips brushing her neck all before she registered what had happened. She stiffened in fright and then relaxed in my arms. I pulled my head out of her neck and met her gaze. It was full of torn emotions, but I saw regard. I saw passion and longing.

"I love you," I whispered, leaning in to seal it with a kiss. It felt so liberating to say it aloud, to let her know.

But then she slipped out of my arms, slumped, her hands over her chest, her face in pain. I caught her before her head hit the floor. I scooped her up and placed her onto the sofa.

"Are you trying to kill me?" she demanded.

I realized she was covering her heart. She loved Archer. He had broken their bond and made her love Dan, and now I just bonded her to me with my impulsive but honest words. If it worked, Callie and I had a future now. Callie would be mine.

My cell phone rang in my pocket, but I ignored it.

"After all you gods told me about those words, you try to bind me to you, even though I love another? Why? How many arrows and binds can one mortal sustain? Archer said love can kill."

Guilt washed over me, but there was something important I had to know. "Did it work? Are you free of him?"

The phone had finally gone quiet. Callie's started to ring now from the table.

"No," she answered coldly, stood, and snatched her phone up, answering before I could stop her. I knew who it was before she even breathed out his name. "I'm fine. It hurt, I won't lie, but it's fading... No, I don't... Of course it didn't work. Archer, none of it did, not your arrows either. I love you, only you. Neither of you can make me love anyone else, so stop trying." She was pacing now.

Was this true? She wasn't bound to me? Didn't love Dan? Or was she placating him? In denial of her own feelings?

"I don't think that's a good— Okay, fine." Callie held the phone out to me with a smug smirk across her face, happy about the prospect of Archer chewing me out.

Maybe it hadn't worked. I avoided those bitter eyes, absent of love, and took up the phone. I didn't say anything, but he knew I was there.

"Are you insane or just plain stupid?" he demanded, full of the rage only a jealous lover could exude.

"Right back at you. You've been contacting her."

"Don't change the subject. I'm coming back."

"Don't you dare! He'll kill her."

"You're going to get her killed, you Koalemos." I ignored the fact he called me the daemon of stupidity's name. "Zeus isn't concerned about *me* being with her, but any of us."

I felt like someone threw a bucket of ice over me, and I was brought back to cold reason. The idea of my father killing Callie was overwhelming. Anything was better than seeing her dead, giving her up even if I must. But he had to as well. In all my jealousy, adoration, and agony over Callie, I had lost sight of what was best for her. Dan, any mortal, not us.

"And so will you. Stop talking to her, Archer. Stop spying on her." I knew that was the only reason he knew what I had done. He was metaphysically stalking her.

He took in a shaky breath. "Agreed. As long as you don't pull any more stunts like this. I'll free her from you, let her love Dan."

I wanted to back Callie and admit his arrows somehow didn't work on her, but he needed to believe that I'd bound Callie to me, or she could love Dan, that there was no hope for him. "I won't." I said, hoping I could keep up on that promise. I decided right then to leave New York. I couldn't be there for Callie without wanting more. I was weak.

The line went dead. I handed the phone back to Callie, who was disappointed he'd hung up. If he was smart, he'd destroy his phone and never contact her again.

"Callie, you can never see him again, know that."

She didn't say anything as I let myself out, but stood staring at the floor, her hand still over her heart. As soon as I left Callie's building, Hermes was waiting for me outside. Archer had been right. I couldn't have Callie either.

"I know why you're here. Consider me warned."

"What is it with this mortal toy that you boys can't stay away from? Does she have nectar flavored—"

"I'm warned." I didn't want to rise to his bait at whatever insults he'd throw at Callie, but I didn't want to hear it either.

"Glad to see you're more rational than Eros."

I booked a flight out of there the moment I got home.

CHAPTER 15

CHASE

I lost him! I should've known Archer was hatching some escape plan. How had I been so naïve, trusting? He had been too calm, happy even, which meant one thing: He'd left me in Jordan dealing with transferring Lena into the Underworld. The entrance to Hades being another "dead zone" for our godly radar, I had to search the area on foot for Archer. I could not tell Aroha I lost our kid; she'd kill me. But then, my mental worldwide search picked him up. He had fled to New York, to Callie. I was proud of his strategy yet furious at his defiance, lack of trust in me, abominable impatience, and foolishness. I'd find a happy Archer when I got there, for sure, but how long after Zeus killed Callie could he survive? I had been planning initial stages of finding allies—already securing the Mesopotamians, who despised Zeus—and Archer fast-forwarded us to the inciting incident of a war. All that is holy in Elysium, I needed the Fates to be on my side. This would be a war of all wars, the end of the symbolic unity of Mount Olympus, and the end of my life. I'd die trying to save my son from himself. But I would do my best to not let it get to that.

I headed to New York as soon as I could. The winds never worked for me, rarely the teleporting gods. I was always on my own. You take them into a warzone once, and they unfairly ban you for life. I had to travel as a mortal via airplane, which took ages. All the while, Ares battled toward the forefront of my mind, whispering little musings of war tactics. When the thought of storming Olympus and burning down the hotel in Fiji came to mind, I shoved the warmonger back and severed myself from his bloodthirsty daydreams.

As soon as I landed, I texted Aroha to pick me up. She was going to let me have it. Maybe I should've cushioned the berating my failure would lead to by calling her before I'd left. I had let myself believe it was best to let her sleep through the night—her time zone—and not let her worry. I never thought, till now, she probably knew Archer was there already. Aroha met me at the airport entrance, looking radiant and...happy?

Before I could speak, she distracted me with a mind-numbing kiss. She pulled away, and I touched her face, feeling as though it had been a millennium since I had seen it. Lust sparked in me, and I was determined not to waste our little time together, but her next words doused the fire in me like a bucket of ice-cold water.

"What are you doing here? Where's Archer?"

My stomach dropped. "He's not?"

The worry in her eyes alerted me. If Archer hadn't come to Callie, where was he? Why did I see him here, and where did he go? What was he scheming?

I quickly caught her up as we headed to her car.

"Since Callie has been *seeing* him, we need to ask her," she added.

This "seeing things" Dite had told me before, but Athena and I agreed demigods having such a profound ability was unheard of. Callie might be something else altogether. We were gods, after all. Who was to say other creatures did not exist? I'd run into all sorts of inexplicable beings in war, seen ghosts in the Underworld—anything could be possible. Athena disagreed with my theory and spouted her own about genetics and mutations and such. I pretended I fully understood, although I did get half of it. She was right that some of the behaviors were god-like. The others came to mind. If we could find where else she came from, we could form allies. There was the possibility that Callie wasn't really Psyche's. We were trusting a piece of old paper and Psyche's word. If she fully belonged to another tribe, Zeus could not harm Callie without retribution, so the idea could be merely wishful thinking.

On the traffic-delayed ride to her apartment, Aroha filled me in on everything, her nervous chatter nonstop. More unnerving things about Callie, how she and Archer had been communicating—behind my back—and what Lucen had foolishly just tried to do. A bind that did not work? My son's arrow failing? I was reeling from confusion and jet lag.

We were going to get to the bottom of this, though. Athena had sent Aroha a DNA kit to collect Callie's spit, so hopefully, we'd know soon. I tried to dispel the mystery and focus on the task at hand: finding my son before he did anything reckless. I dropped off my and Archer's luggage in Dite's apartment, then found myself pounding on the Sycheses' door. There wasn't a moment to waste, even to answer Aroha's questions about what I was doing or what I'd say. I didn't have a plan. No matter how many plans there are, in actual warfare, you have to run on instincts in the end.

The servant opened the door, and I could hear Dr. Syches asking who was there.

"The warrior," the servant said, staring me up and down as if rendered speechless. It was truly tedious dealing with mortals who knew of our existence. I wondered how long my father would let this one live. "And the love goddess."

Callie was right behind the man in a flash. "Is he..." Callie began but covered her mouth, her eyes brimming with tears, and she almost fell.

I pushed my way in past the starstruck servant and caught her as she sank to the ground. She looked awful. Her skin was pale, purple circles lined her eyes, and she was frail in my arms, bones on the surface. Just like Archer. The ire at my father for forcing this bubbled to the surface.

Dr. Syches hobbled up off the sofa as I carried Callie to one and placed her down. "What is it?" he asked, leaning most of his weight on a cane, and the servant, who finally snapped back to reality, helped the invalid man.

In comparison to him, Callie looked well. Dr. Syches hardly looked alive. The truth of it was, he probably shouldn't be. Just seeing the man made my stomach sick. No wonder Archer was trying to stall making a death. How could you resign someone to death, someone who didn't deserve to die, whom the Fates hadn't chosen, but only Zeus had? Then again, at some point, Archer would need to choose one, simply to put the man out of his misery. The line separating justice and mercy was a thin one.

"Archer is missing," Aroha filled in.

I took a deep breath and focused on the objective. "He took off in Jordan, most likely hitching a ride somewhere off Zephyrus. We just don't know where or why."

Aroha sighed. "At first, we thought this would've been the first place he'd come—"

"He's alive then?" Callie cut in, her tone full of what sounded like waning hope. Then she burst into tears, her father rubbing her shoulder, wanting to support her, but he could hardly hold up his own fragile frame. She wiped her tears onto the sleeve of her shirt and pulled her phone out of her pocket and handed it to me, her eyes full of guilt and desperation.

This was rough. Seeing her suffering, after Archer dealt with the same, riled me up with how unfair it was to keep them apart. To Hades with my father! The back of my mind fixated again on the storming Olympus idea. Every day, it felt more justified.

I looked at the screen and clicked on Archer's name. My anger at Zeus shifted to my son since it was clear from the time stamped on the texts that he and Callie had been communicating. I was about to scroll up to see how long this had been going on, how long my son had lied to my face, but the words there at the bottom knocked the breath out of me:

Callie. I'm finished living without you. Please move on and live your life. Goodbye.

"Chase," Aroha asked. "You're white as a sheet. What does it say?"

I couldn't form words or move. My eyes simply met Callie's tortured ones, and I saw the truth.

"He...he had told me gods never say goodbye unless they meant it. He said it once, as an official breakup, but...but like this...again...I think he's saying it forever." Callie took a moment to get the words out as she was trying to suppress sobs. She was explaining what we had already feared: Archer was going to end his existence rather than live without her.

Aroha yanked the phone from my hand and cried out when she read it.

"Twenty minutes ago," Callie said, her large brown eyes wide.

Aroha dialed him from Callie's phone. I snapped to it and grabbed Callie's shoulders, shaking her probably harder than I should. I could break her in the state she was in. "Where, Callie? How would he do it? What was he planning? Anything would help. We have to stop him."

"I don't know," she said, defeated. She began crying afresh, and I almost threw her across the room for her present uselessness but withheld my rage. The whole point was to protect her, and the Ares part of me was trying to go wild in desperation to save his son.

Aroha held up her phone and Callie's. "No answer. And I can't see him, Chase."

"Chaos hasn't...it's not too late," I managed to get out.

"Someone explain—" Dr. Syches began.

"No time," I barked.

"I'm trying to help," he defended.

"You can't," I scoffed. Mortals always seemed to overestimate themselves.

Aroha squeezed my arm as if to tell me to stand down. "He's exceptionally clever, dear. He might be able to help. We have no idea where to start." Then she looked at the man and rapidly explained to him how we could sense our kind, envision and find them no matter where they were, except places off the grid.

"So any disruption in magnetic activity and magmatic hotbeds are off the grid?" the man mused. "My atlases, Raphael, quickly." The doctor was in think-mode, and the servant hustled about with books.

Good, at least he could feel useful and not annoy me while I racked my brains for ways to stop my son from taking his own life.

"Callie?" Aroha asked, sitting down next to the girl.

Callie's face was pale, and she stared off, her gaze unfocused. For a moment, I thought she suddenly went catatonic for some inexplicable reason, but Aroha felt her forehead and withdrew her hand, a look of shock across her features. "She's burning up!"

"A fever," her father mused, poring over a book, half listening. "They're frequent. Raphael, please get her some fever reducer and a cold compress."

"No," Callie said, her eyes locking on mine in her feverish haze. "I see him when I'm sick. I could find him."

I thought she was delirious until her father said, "Too dangerous, Callista."

"I'm dead if he dies, Dad."

The old man's gaze left his books and met his daughter's. I saw defeat spread across his features. Could she really do this, find him?

"I'll get an ice bath going for her, if she reaches 105, we'll dunk her," the servant offered.

"No, you track her temperature, Raphael. I'm on it," Aroha ordered. Then my wife moved at immortal speed. I heard water running, ice being thrown in; then she was down the hall with a bucket, most likely to the ice machine downstairs or the kitchens—I didn't know the layout of her building.

Callie lay back on the sofa to get comfortable and closed her eyes. I wanted something to do. I couldn't stand here waiting for the slim chance of a sick mortal to tell me where Archer was. Her father pored over maps. Raphael ran a digital thermometer across her brow. It beeped and flashed, and he held it up to show me it said 102 degrees.

"She does see things, you know," Dr. Syches said casually, "when her fevers spike. Her descriptions sound like an out-of-body experience. Her dreams are about the future."

"She tells you this?" I was skeptical. This all sounded ridiculous as no humans could do these things. Few immortals could even boast it.

"No." He looked up, his eyes vibrant for the first time. "I can read minds—not yours, though. I can't read immortal minds, it seems. I knew your son and wife were different because of that very failing of my talent. Every human I have met, I can read. I get glimmers of Callie's thoughts, dreams. She's very good at blocking me, most likely due to lifelong conditioning."

"Same with us. Zeus can read ours until we learn to block him." I gave him that allowance, for what he could do was profound. A mortal who could read other mortals' minds? Definitely a descendant of Psyche, who saw into souls. But for Callie to dream of the future to mentally locate Archer was beyond the realm of a normal demigod. Something was freakishly off, which explained exactly why my father wanted her dead. She was something he couldn't control, a mortal full of too much power, one he didn't want mating with a god. This was why Archer couldn't be with her.

Callie thrashed around, her forehead becoming damp. Her father clenched his jaw, obviously uncomfortable with putting his daughter's life on the line but willing to risk it.

"104," Raphael announced.

Time seemed to tick by slowly. Aroha finally stopped coming and going and stood next to me. She watched the girl in anticipation. I wrapped my arms around her waist and tugged, but she wouldn't sit. The doctor opened book after book, jotting down notes—most likely areas we couldn't see our kind. With Zephyrus, Archer could be anywhere, though. I'd have to check them all if Callie couldn't come through.

"105," the servant said.

Aroha—her maternal instinct in hyperdrive—was scooping up and dunking the girl in the ice-water tub before the mortal men registered her actions. I was in the bathroom right after them. Once she hit the water, Callie's eyes shot open, and she gasped, sputtering water out.

"Callie?" Aroha asked, her arm still under Callie's shoulders, propping her up.

Callie's eyes were swimming, but they came into focus and then observed the tub of ice water she was in. "He's with that man, the one he had been scared of. He was creepy, a bad leg, fiery red hair. He left your mom—I mean, left you—a note, remember? Addressed to Aphrodite?"

Aroha's head turned toward me. "Heph," she whispered and looked away.

Her ex, the man I'd stolen her from more than once in our long lives. He had hated Archer more than anything else on this Earth, since he was the result of an affair, and it had broken the god's heart in more ways than one. He had lived for six years thinking Archer was his child and that his wife was faithful to him.

"Heph?" Callie asked, more lucid. She began to shiver.

"Hephaestus, god of fire," Dr. Syches supplied. I hadn't paid much attention to him and the servant as they hobbled up behind me.

"Who hates Archer," I groaned.

"Hephie would never—"

"Wouldn't he? He hates me. He'd strike me where it would hurt most."

I pushed Aroha out of the way and yanked Callie out of the cold tub. She was shivering. "Where, Callie? Where is he?"

Callie's brow wrinkled. "Blue waters, crystal clear. Poseidon, the Great Blue Hole, a volcano, an island covered in ash. I see it, but I just don't know where it is."

A chill ran down me that had nothing to do with the icy water drenching me. I placed the girl onto the sofa, where she shivered, while the servant was wrapping her up in towels.

"Plymouth," Callie said. She looked frightened as if she shouldn't know these things, and the truth of it was, she shouldn't. I was equally freaked out as she was.

"Montserrat," Dr. Syches said with conviction. "Active volcano that erupted and covered the city of Plymouth under feet of lava, ash, and mud. But the Great Blue Hole is a thousand or so miles away." The man typed in his phone for answers.

Geography was my strong suit, and when I recalled the place—a place I had only seen on maps—I remembered. "The Soufrière Hills."

Dite took in a sharp breath as I held my own. Volcanic activity was not something we gods sought out. Like fire, it could consume us. The "hills" were one of those massive active stratovolcanoes with many smoking holes that threatened to spew lava out at any time.

"You have to stop him," Callie said desperately. She was answering my greatest fears. My son had left me behind, sought out my enemy, and was hoping to die.

I went into plan-mode. "Callie, keep calling him. If you get ahold of him, do whatever you can to stop him. Aroha? Call Heph, and do whatever you can to stop whatever is going on down there. Buy me time."

Aroha was already dialing.

"What will you do?" Dr. Syches asked me.

I hardly knew. I needed to save Archer somehow. "Get there as soon as I can and stop any foolish actions he has in his stupid head."

"Ares," Aroha said.

I cringed. I would have to tell her I preferred Chase now; a new start for the new me, but time was too precious to waste on simple things.

She hung up the phone, apparently not getting an answer. Then she dialed again. "Save our son."

"I will." I left the apartment and stormed down the hall, taking the stairs down at lightning speed, needing the exercise to get my blood pumping, to get thinking. Once I hit the lobby and left through the front door, I slipped into the alley, calling to Iris. Per usual, she did not show, nor the other traveling gods. I kicked the dumpster in frustration. It would take me ages to get to Montserrat the mortal way.

"Frustrated?" A cold voice asked smugly. I turned to see Boreas, the north wind and winter god, an old friend of mine who also hailed from Thrace.

"Yes. Please. Can you take me to Montserrat, immediately?"

"What's in it for me?" He asked, twisting his pointy gray beard. "I don't mind the front as much as the others, but last time I took you, we were almost murdered in Hiroshima by one of those freaky bombs I'm sure you had a hand in inventing."

"For the last time, I had no clue about that bomb. And as soon as I saw it dropping, I told you, and you got us out of there. This is simple, not war related."

"Not war related? Strange words from your mouth," his said in his chilling drawl. "Still, why should I bother? What's in it for me?"

"Stick it to my father. Save my son. The whole lot. I'll owe you."

"Although those first two sound intriguing, to have the god of war in my pocket sounds infinitely better."

"Yeah, yeah, yeah. Please, quickly."

Boreas rolled his eyes at my anxiety and grabbed my wrist. I told him Montserrat, not wanting to end up in Soufrière hills. I felt as if someone squeezed me to death, cold crept over me, and everything faded to black. When I opened my eyes and found my footing, I was standing on a black sandy beach, the waves crashing behind me in what looked like paradise. In front of me stood a huge incline covered in greenery.

"Where am I?" I asked, wondering how far I was from the volcano or Heph.

"Brades. I don't pretend to know what is going on, but I took Hephaestus here about a decade ago. Over that hill is Brades Road. Head south. Can't miss him. Look for an amazing jewelry shop named after him and his best friend."

I thanked Boreas. He saluted me before he was wrapped up in his wind and vanished. As I climbed the incline, I realized it was more of a mountain. With the trees as coverage, I ran up to the top, pausing in the treeline to let the scratches from tree branches and brush heal. Ahead of me was open space, but buildings were clustered here and there. I walked toward the town, impatient to find Heph or just Brades Road.

I saw a post office and, not wanting to lose time, went in. Like a lost tourist, I asked a man sorting mail where the road was, and he pointed out the window to a cluster of trees. I could see the road was right there. I thanked him, hurried out, and cut across to the road. I headed south by charting the sun's position from this part of the world. I was walking down Brades Road when I saw it: a jewelry store named Fire and Ice. Heph and Boreas: a strange friendship of opposites. Heph was a smith of all sorts—gold, silver, black, etc., but he had always enjoyed crafting with metal and stones, particularly to lavish Dite with his jewelry—buying her love.

I walked in, hoping to see Archer and Heph talking civilly, but only a pretty, young mortal stood behind the counter. She flashed me a smile and greeted me. I wasn't sure what name Heph was going by, so I asked to speak with the owner. My father had a list of aliases and numbers he sent out periodically, but I'd never bothered to program Hephaestus's number into my contacts. It's not like we talked, ever.

"He's in a meeting right now. Would you like to leave your name and number?"

"Yeah, he's with a blond guy, right? They're expecting me." I gave her a dazzling smile to tip the balance, for she looked at me suspiciously.

She picked up the phone and shook her head as if to dispel my magical charisma. "Name?"

"Mr. Thrace," I said. I hoped the hint to my birthplace would clue him in to my identity, or he might assume Boreas. Then again, he might refuse to see me.

She spoke into the phone for a moment, hung up, and pointed to a door not far from the counter. "He said to go on through. He's in the workshop."

I thanked her and walked into the back of the store. Entering a room with metal, tools, and a god who could melt things with his bare hands—not to mention he had great motivation to melt me since I'd stolen the love of his life and he had never moved on—was foolhardy, but I had to find my son.

It was quiet. I saw a large heavy metal door different than the other two, which I assumed were an office and bathroom. I rapped on the door with my knuckles twice. The silence made me fear this was all in vain and Archer wasn't there. Wasting no time, I opened the door to hear speaking. He had soundproof walls.

Archer and Heph were seated as far away from each other as possible but at ease in chairs against opposite walls. They were sipping drinks, and the two empty bottles of nectar whiskey on the work table and Archer's flushed face told me he'd had too much to drink. Great. I guess this was Heph's way of stalling. The god could drink everyone but Dionysus under the table, so it was a safe bet he'd be the winner in this competition.

Heph's eyes narrowed when they locked on mine, as I'm sure mine inadvertently did as well. I tensed. Every drop of ichor wanted me to tear the man to shreds to protect my son, to prevent him from trying to abscond with my wife. He had stolen her heart twice, and I stole it from him twice as well. Before this mess, I would've had her in my life again. Taking a man's wife is one thing, but I had robbed him of fatherhood, hurting him the worst. Archer's existence was a torment to Heph: a reminder in looks of the woman who'd broken his heart, with the mannerisms and intensity of his rival.

I didn't know what to say and stopped just inside the workshop and closed the door behind me. I gave Archer a once-over to make sure he was okay.

He avoided my gaze, guilt in all his features. He nervously twirled his glass in his hands. "How'd you find me? This place is off the grid."

"Your girlfriend has an uncanny gift," I said vaguely to pique his interest. Then, against all nature and history, I met Heph's beady gaze and said, "Thank you." It came out like paste, but it had to be done.

"I didn't do it for you. I did it for Dite," he ground out. This was his nature always and not just with me. He was beastly, but Dite had the bewitching talent of turning him into an innocuous kitten.

"What?" Archer looked at each of us, crestfallen. "You said you'd do it," Archer directed to Heph. "I told you the whole sordid story so you'd do it."

"I was buying them time. Your mother was pleading, crying on the phone. However, now that I do have your dad here, it would give me great pleasure for him to watch you die."

My heart pounded, the pulse throbbing in my ears. He was the one god who could not burn. He could kill Archer and me with his bare hands, burn us until the ichor in our blood ignited. Ares came forward with plans: chains around his neck to restrain him and pull him down, flipping the pans of melted metal into his face to buy time, and the fire poker into the gut. Finishing him off would be difficult without a Death, and I would think it would take every gory, hate-filled, war-fueled feeling inside me to do what was necessary to dispose of an immortal who couldn't burn.

Heph stood up and paced his unbalanced gait. "You see, I wanted to hear why the kid wanted to die. Didn't have the gumption to do it himself, so he came here begging. It was *love*," he mocked, "always love backfiring. One less love god might be a good thing. The mortals might be better off without him."

"No," I warned.

He glared. I knew threats wouldn't faze him. No, I had to go against my nature, something I had been doing for months now, but by Poseidon's trident, I wanted war at this moment after that comment.

I took a deep breath. "We both know you'd never harm a hair on Dite's head. You do this, and she'll never forgive you. He's her favorite child."

"Don't listen to him, Heph. If you don't, I'll do it myself," Archer said.

"Heph, if you do this, she will ask me to end you, and I will comply." The threats came out after all. Here was Ares, god of war, returning after hibernation. It was good to know he was still in there when needed.

"You have always wanted to kill me but never figured out how. Dite used to joke about how brainless you could be. All brawn, all spite, no smarts—"

"Chains, liquid metal, fire poker. Then I'd have to cut you into itty-bitty pieces so you couldn't regenerate and throw you down into Tartarus among the pieces of Titans."

Heph's pacing stopped. He turned and looked at me, then the items around the room. Then he burst out laughing, a big hearty laugh that told me there would be no fight. "Ah, well, when it comes to murder and destruction, you have that talent, I suppose."

"A compliment from Heph. Things are changing," I muttered.

"No!" Archer stood up, his wiry frame on edge.

I subtly locked the door behind me to prevent his escape. "Stop this, Archer. If you're willing to die for her, then at least go back and make her happy first."

"He'll kill her!" Archer's eyes bulged with furious surprise at my words. He was losing it, maybe literally.

"So, say I kill you," Heph cut in. "Will this girl try to follow you?"

I could kiss the guy if I didn't hate him deep down. The man was cunning and stealing the words from my mouth. Since he was not directly involved, maybe Archer would listen to him.

"Why does Zeus want her dead?" Heph directed at me. "What do you mean things are changing?"

Oh, he was good. I'd never admired the man until this moment of precise psychological warfare against my son. And then he held up another nectar whiskey bottle and a glass. Not an olive branch, but it might have well been. It was weird, and Archer's expression reflected how odd this situation truly was.

"We should have a long talk," I said, placing the drink down on the table.

As god of war, I could feel upcoming attacks. I sensed Heph was about to make a move, but his energy wasn't hostile. He didn't want to hurt Archer, but was up to something.

"No, Dad, don't, please."

Heph's eyes darted to the chains I had mentioned prior. I moved as fast as possible, had them in hand. Archer darted toward the door, but Heph cut him off, threw him back into his chair. I wrapped the chains around Archer twice, and Heph took them from me. He welded them together with glowing heat from his hands.

"Dad, why are you doing this?" Archer screamed.

"Because I love you," I told him, quickly kissing the top of his head as he thrashed around.

"Heph, c'mon. You hate him. You hate me! And my mom. She's manipulative, evil. You know this!"

"Shall we?" Heph cordially handed me the drink I had placed down and grabbed his own. "Let him cool down." He pointed to the soundproof walls. "Outside."

Sure enough, Archer was cussing at us, and once the door closed behind us, I heard nothing. Outside, I took a deep breath of the salty air. "This is a nice place."

Heph laughed. We had gone out the back of his store, and there was a sandy lot, a couple plastic chairs, and a table that seemed to be an employee break area.

"Except, for me, volcanoes are unnerving."

"What are we doing, Ares? You say change, and I feel it. I feel...indifferent to Dite, and I want to murder you slightly less."

"I'm away from war."

"Making peace, it seems."

"I truly don't understand it," I admitted.

Heph and I then had the only civil conversation we'd ever had in our entire existence. He listened to everything I said, silently nodding here and there. I told him everything I knew and suspected, hoping against my better judgment he would choose our side. I felt like lines were being drawn. Perhaps I was drawing them, but my father kind of already had by denying my son what he needed to survive.

When I finished, Heph sighed, tracing his shoes in the sandy soil. Even in this hot climate, the god of fire wasn't overheated and most likely forever embarrassed about his clubbed foot. I had mocked him, made fun of him, and I never understood his self-loathing—I mean, there's Pan who can't even venture among humans with his hoofs—yet I could see Heph's feeling of discomfort at not being "normal." I was realizing my attributes were opposite his, another reason to hate the confident, athletic, and attractive man who'd stolen his wife.

"I'm not going to hurt your boy. I see too much of his mother in him and could never do that to her," Heph said once I was finished.

"Thank you."

"I'd prefer to stay out of it, but if I have to pick sides, it'll be whatever one Dite is on." Then Heph offered me his hand, clearly uncomfortable, and we looked at each other, shocked in that strange moment.

I took up his hand and shook it.

"Who would've thought that you, of all the gods, would be making peace with a man you detest," Heph said, staring up in the sky.

"I don't know, but things *are* changing. I intend to find out why."

"Are you and Dite back together?" he asked with feigned nonchalance.

I didn't want to lose him as an ally, yet both truth or lies might disrupt what peace was between us. "Father all but ordered it, and we were on the way for it to be so, but then Archer's life upended. I have no idea what will happen now."

"What will you do about him? Archer seems...serious." Heph didn't say it, but I knew what he meant. He believed Archer might take his own life, and I was starting to wonder if we should go back to New York, hide him and Callie as long as possible, try to keep them alive.

This depression had to stop. I wanted to see him happy, but that would sentence Callie to die. Could I do that? And if Callie died, how would Archer take it? It seemed every outcome in this scenario ended in my son's death. It all came down to my father's cruel ruling.

"I don't know."

"I don't understand your father. Once he found out Eros was actually his grandchild, he was the favorite," Heph mused.

This was all true. Heph was Hera's son with a mortal, and Zeus made Heph immortal in his late thirties. Zeus had done it to beg Hera for forgiveness for one of his thousands of indiscretions. When Zeus found out Archer was mine and not Heph's—not Hera's grandchild alone—he had been overjoyed. And now Zeus was putting him on the chopping block so to speak, the only grandchild left who was both his and Hera's who had been born a god. Why?

"You've got to do something. Force that kid to be rational."

"Since when is Love rational?" I laughed dryly. "Love has no order, control, or reasonable basis. It's completely against his nature to think beyond how he feels."

My phone pinged. I pulled it out and saw I had ten missed texts. The most recent were Lucien's, so I read them. I sighed.

Heph tried to slyly look over my shoulder at the message, most likely thinking it was Dite. I'm sure there were a few frantic texts from her, but I wasn't going to admit that to Heph. I'd text her once I had Archer safe and of sound mind.

"Lucien," I said. Then I amended, "Apollo. He's in Belize, waiting for us. Probably shouldn't have given him our address, but it'll give Archer a reason to live, momentarily."

"Huh?"

"Apollo kissed Archer's girlfriend and bound her to him."

Heph let out a whistle. "Let's go free the boy then." He got up, and I followed. "You might need to make sure he doesn't kill Apollo, though. We both know the power of jealous love."

He was right. Archer might just try to kill Lucien if I didn't intervene. Was it wrong of me to be just a little happy, anticipating Archer's self-hatred would turn on my little half brother instead?

CHAPTER 16

Belize was an eclectic, cozy place. When I arrived at Archer's apartment, the nosy landlady told me they had left last week and owed rent. I paid up for them so she'd let me in. It was empty, but their stuff was still strewn about, so they'd return. I hadn't announced my coming. I had to get away from Callie, and I had to apologize to Archer. Two brokenhearted friends could hang out in solitude together...if he'd forgive me.

I texted Archer, but he didn't respond. Perhaps he was childish enough to ignore me. Bored, I went sightseeing and exploring the city. That night—when it became clear they weren't coming home—I went to a club and let myself get lost in the arms of a beautiful woman. She wasn't Callie, though, so I went home alone. The next day was the same. This time, I tried texting Aroha and Chase. My texts were ignored. The third day, the same. I wouldn't put it past Archer to hold a grudge, but Aroha's and Chase's silences were unnerving. Something was wrong. When I mentally tried to trace them, Aroha was in New York still, and Archer and Chase were nowhere to be found. They were off the grid, but where?

There was nothing I could do but wait it out. Day four in Belize, I finally got a response from Chase.

OTW. Long story. Took forever to get to Belize from Montserrat.

They arrived that evening. Chase entered first, a look of exhaustion upon his face. I bet. Montserrat was almost two thousand miles away, and from how long it took them, I'm sure it took a series of boats and planes to get back, as Montserrat was a place hard to get to, even by modern standards.

Archer came in behind him. I hardly recognized him. He was emaciated, with dark rings under his eyes and a frantic, wild look in them. His skin was sallow as if he was sick, and his posture was hunched and weak. He had the beginning of a beard, and his hair was getting long, his usually impeccable appearance abandoned. His eyes narrowed as he took me in.

"Archer, I'm—"

My words were cut off by his fist. His appearance had been misleading. His punch sent me reeling onto the floor. I spit a tooth out, along with some blood, which sizzled a hole into the area rug.

"You're what? Sorry?" He crouched over me, grabbed my shirt collar, and yanked me up until I was sitting. The derision was all over his face and in his tone.

Chase stood to the side, just watching us. Archer's fist collided with my face again. I didn't block him or fight back. I deserved it. I had stabbed my friend in the back, an everyday Brutus, broken the god of love's heart, over a girl of all things.

"Enough, Archer," Chase said after the fifth punch.

Archer shoved me away but then started kicking me. I had never seen him like this, and the shock kept me from protecting myself. He was a lover, not a fighter. I finally blocked his leg after I felt a rib break.

"Eros!" Chase commanded. "Stop now."

Archer's face screwed up, fighting his elder's orders, desperately trying to defy his father.

He got another kick in before Chase physically pulled him away. "Go to your room, and cool down. Don't come back down until you are capable of using words to express your anger."

The scolding took me back to Olympian days when I'd watched my elder half brother scold the spoiled brat. It was the father-son dynamic all over again, ages later.

Archer glared at me, then his father. Just like back then, Archer reacted much the same: stomped down the hall and slammed the door. Then we heard a shout and a lot of things breaking.

"What the Hades happened to him?"

"Long story, but what you did sure didn't help," Chase explained. He offered me his hand and pulled me up to standing.

I growled in pain. "Could've warned me he was that mad in your text."

"You deserved it, but I had my reasons to fuel his anger toward you. I might've purposely taken the long way home to stoke his ire, but keep that to yourself."

"Wow, thanks." I muttered. My rib protested, so I gingerly sat down. I ran my tongue along my teeth until I found the hole—a bicuspid was missing. Not too bad. My injuries would heal in a minute, but growing something back took a few weeks, as Chase well knew. The man lived through what would kill mortals on a weekly basis, and I'd seen him lose limbs at least half a dozen times.

Chase plopped onto the sofa across from me with a defeated and worn-down expression. Taking care of Archer was apparently a full-time job. And from what he revealed, it was. He told me about the demigod they'd made immortal and taken to Hades, and Archer's premeditated escape and suicide plan to get Heph to incinerate him.

Then we pondered over the unexplainable ability for Callie to find him during a fever. I knew Archer was having as much trouble as Callie with the separation, but I didn't know it had gotten this bad. My heartbreak paled in comparison to his. Guilt flooded over me for that stupid kiss and those words. I should be the god of selfishness.

Chase handed me a bottle of nectar whiskey and nodded to the stairs. "Heph gave it to me. See if you can get him to drink some. He needs to take care of himself. He needs to see reason."

I trudged down the hall, dreading another confrontation, but all had gone quiet in Archer's room. Getting him to drink whiskey, a probability, but getting him to be rational seemed too tall an order. I knocked on the door.

"Go away."

"Archer, c'mon." I twisted the knob, only to find it locked. "Let me in."

No response.

"Look, I'm an awful friend. I shouldn't have done that to her, to you. I fell for her like an idiot, but she loves you."

I waited, but he said nothing.

"It didn't work, Archer, the bind. She still loves you—not Dan, not me—you."

I heard movement, and the door opened. He stood there, eyes still wild, but the extreme fury in them had died down. That emotional power he inherited from his father that lit up his eyes was dimming. Archer left the doorway, went and flopped onto the bed, and crossed his arms, shielding his face behind them.

"How is she really?" he asked, his voice hardly audible.

I ventured inside and opened the bottle of nectar whiskey. "Whiskey from Heph's private stock, 1600's." I took a swig. Instantly, I felt every last ache from my ribs and face fade away, and I felt whole again. Wow, this was good stuff.

"I don't want it."

"Best way to dull heartache."

"Liar."

115

"Fine, suit yourself. Thought it might soften the blow. You know, she's not doing any better than you are. She's barely eating or sleeping, and the inexplicable fevers are ravaging her body. She's a shell of whom she once was, just like you are."

Archer uncrossed his arms, and the amount of agony in his eyes forced me to divert my gaze. He took the bottle from my hands and drank down a few swigs before handing it back. Instantly, the purple shadows under his eyes lessened; the yellow from his skin faded to tan, and his eyes dulled to a calm stare. "What you did to her was terrible."

"And what you did wasn't?"

"Everything I have ever done to her is unforgivable, but you didn't have to compound my crimes. What did you do to her exactly?"

"Don't make me say it."

"I need to know."

"Know what? You know I kissed her and tried to bind her to me. It didn't work. We need to talk about that."

"No, I know that. Did she kiss you back? Did she enjoy it?"

I ran my hand down my face, not wanting to relive this in front of him.

"You know we're supposed to be irresistible to mortals, and she was so lonely and sad, vulnerable—"

"So she did?"

"Oddly, no. She pushed me away. Didn't even let me get her lips. Your focus is off. It wasn't her in any way. Stop thinking about all that, and start worrying about how Callie could locate you and why the bind didn't work, not how she could resist a god's advances."

His head snapped to look at me so quickly, he had whiplash. It was as if it were the first time he'd heard us admit she had extraordinary powers, even though Chase and I had already told him about it. "She's a mighty powerful demigod, that's for sure, but whose?"

I should've told him, right then and there that she belonged to Psyche; in fact, I shouldn't have been able to withhold the truth or lie, but everything about us was completely disrupted. "I wish I knew." Guilt ensued. I tried to stave it off by telling myself he had been ready to kill himself. What would the truth do to him?

"She almost seems like..."

I waited for him to say Psyche. How could he not see it?

"...Proteus, Prometheus, Epimetheus—a time-seeing god. But Lucien, we're not even thinking about other races of gods."

I shifted back onto the bind topic. "I still don't understand why my bind not only didn't work but how your bind is still intact and your arrows didn't work."

"True love?"

"Really, Archer? I'm too rational to buy into that. You and I have argued this for eons."

"No, I mean, maybe none of it worked in the first place: my bind, my arrows, and your bind. Maybe she simply loves me of her own free will. True love. No matter what abilities we use, she won't fall for anyone else."

It was logical, and it made the most sense, and yet nothing explained how that was even possible. "But how is she immune to the gods?"

"I have no idea." Then he looked at me. There was some life in his eyes at last. "What have you told her...about us?"

"A lot." I sheepishly bought time, swigging some more drink down. "She asks a lot of questions."

"You didn't have to answer them all."

I knew he was worried about what I'd said about his past—about Psyche and Hedone. I didn't want to bring them up. I didn't want to see how unhinged he'd become to know the woman he loved was a descendant of the first and only other woman he'd loved.

"She's annoyingly persistent."

This made him smile.

"I didn't give much detail, Archer."

He shrugged as if it didn't matter anymore what I told her, and maybe it didn't to him.

"What next?"

"I have to find and choose Death. Zeus was blowing up Dad's phone that the other death gods are getting hostile about being overworked and us not pulling our weight. No one is dying in Greece at all, and the mortals have picked up on it. Hospitals are filling up with people who should be gone, and no god can enter Greece who isn't Olympian without Zeus's permission, and he's too proud to allow help."

I noticed he was "Zeus" and not "Grandpa" now.

"So Thanatos had no immortal kids," I assumed.

If one of us died, the powers transferred to the eldest child of ours so that the mortal world would continue uninhibited. Not having any immortal offspring, Thanatos's powers simply vanished with him. It was true that the others had to pick up the slack of the Olympian sector, but they wouldn't dare touch Greece due to Zeus, who intimidated them all.

THE IMMORTAL TRANSCRIPTS: FEVER

The only god I had ever known to stand up to my father was the Nordic Odin. Plus territories were drawn along ancient lines that were still disputed. I rarely went to Italy these days, although it had been my favorite second home; it was as open as America now when it came to gods.

I doubt any death god would ever help Zeus kill off someone on his hit list, though; in fact, healer gods like me might even keep Callie's dad alive just to spite Zeus if they recognized his handiwork. However, they would not interfere with a Greek god taking away a soul that had been cursed by the chief Greek god, which made me think of Callie and how hard this would be on her. "Callie will—"

"Understand?" He laughed sardonically.

"There has to be a way."

"Around Zeus's punishment? If you know of any, I'm all ears." To proclaim Archer was bitter and resentful was an understatement.

"What about the others?"

Archer looked at me, astounded. "Befriending them and going against our own people will start a godly world war."

"I wasn't speaking of war, but of ambrosia or whatever they call their elixirs. Make her immortal behind Zeus's back."

"Still will be war. He'll wage it against them for helping us, or he'll still kill Callie. Gods can die." He ended by stating the obvious. "But thanks."

"For what?"

"Trying." He gave me a sad smirk.

Two weeks later, I left the melancholy Archer and the out-of-his-depth Chase because Aroha demanded my presence: the prom. Tedious, annoying mortal traditions. You don't jilt the goddess of love and live to tell the tale, though, so I scurried back to Manhattan because even though she knew my tux sizes, she needed me to go through the motions of all the planning. She was a love goddess after all. Sigh.

CHAPTER 17

Callie

Dan was staring at me as I walked through the lunch line. Aroha was next to me, taking over Lucien's position of babysitting me since he had left town. As much as I missed having him around, I was glad he was gone after that attempted kiss and confession. I could never feel anything for him like I did for Archer, whom I loved despite how he had completely forsaken me by not answering any of my texts, calls, or emails. But he was alive. I had to at least be satisfied I'd prevented him from being rash.

"He likes you, you know," Aroha whispered.

"Huh?" My mind still on Archer, it took a moment to understand she was talking about Dan. "Oh, only because Archer made him."

Aroha frowned at me. "He didn't need to if he had. He liked you more than me, if you remember well, until Archer intervened to try to make me happy."

"Oh." What else could I say when the most beautiful being on the planet (and vainest) admitted that a guy preferred me over the goddess of love and beauty? "Well, he's stupid, then, for not wanting to be with you."

Aroha laughed lightly. "Ah, if you were immortal, we could've gotten along for centuries, Callie. I do like you, despite not wanting to. The whole ruining-my-next-few-decades thing isn't fully forgiven."

I was spared responding to that comment (I had no idea how to) when we neared the lunch lady's register. We walked back toward the table. At least Dan stopped staring.

"Just think about it. A cover. If you have a boyfriend, Lucien will leave you alone, and maybe in time, you'll be able to move on."

"I'd rather you give me impossible tasks," I muttered.

"Oh, I do like you, Callie. I might just stay beyond NYU if you keep entertaining me." Aroha laughed wholeheartedly. Court jester to the love goddess for life (great).

We sat down, and I was stuck, thanks to Aroha's choice of seats (goddess of conniving more like), directly across from Dan. I tried to tuck into my food so I wouldn't have to talk to anyone.

"Hey, Callie." Dan smiled.

I felt warm all over. I didn't love him, so Archer's power didn't fully work, but I felt something (hormones, honestly). I knew they didn't work because I had seen the power Archer's arrows had when Dan had instantly stopped flirting with me and had become obsessed with Aroha, like a light switch. This didn't feel like that.

"Did you hear about Jenny?" Dan asked me.

"No."

"She majorly messed up her knee landing wrong in a gymnastics competition." Marybeth cut in to lead the story.

I tuned her out as she went into a long-winded story that I didn't want to know about while I was eating. I was blessed to never have been injured before, but the stories still unnerved me.

I looked up and met Dan's gaze inadvertently. He was smiling at me in a way that called me out for not listening. Neither was he, having already heard the story. Marybeth, however, was speaking to her captivated audience and didn't notice I was zoned out. I wanted to blame it on a fever, but I just really didn't care.

He rolled his eyes, and I couldn't help but laugh a little. Then he leaned over and said quietly, "I asked if you heard because this puts me in an awkward spot: Jenny was my date for the prom, and now she can't even walk."

"Oh, no. Is she okay?"

"She said she's done with gymnastics, poor thing. She has surgery next week, so no way she'll be allowed to go, but how fun would that be anyway?"

"That sucks. Who will you go with now?"

"You," he said.

Idiot that I am, I'd walked right into that.

"Oh, I...I wasn't planning..." I fumbled. (No, just say no.)

"As friends, Callie. Only as friends. Jenny and I were going as friends. I mean, who wants to start something with someone so close to graduation anyway." He shrugged, at complete ease when he was making me freak out inside. Now probably was not the time to remind him we both were attending NYU in the fall.

"You should go." Aroha nudged me.

"I don't even have a dress," I insisted.

"Oh, formal dresses? I have a ton, and we have roughly the same body type." What was Aroha doing? "We could easily hem one up since I have a couple inches on you, or you could pick a shorter length." She was being way too helpful (conniving indeed).

"Callie, c'mon. You only go to senior prom once," Dan said.

This was true, except for Aroha, who had probably gone to thousands of dances.

"I'll just check with my dad," I stalled.

"He has his servant and can text you if anything comes up. C'mon Callie. *Senior prom.*" She gave me such a forceful look, I wondered what might happen if I continued to make excuses.

"Okay," I told Dan.

He was beaming now.

"As friends." I added, hoping he truly meant that.

Not only did the all-too-helpful Aroha corner me into going to the prom, she kidnapped me after school. My dad was extremely happy to hear about the prom (Aroha blabs too) and told me to get lost and borrow a dress. I thought I'd be okay, and I was until I was inside the apartment and swore I smelled Archer's scent—earthy with a hint of honeysuckles. Likely, it was just Aroha's scent, but it was so intense in their apartment. She walked me away from Archer's closed door and to her room. Last time I was here, I never realized the size of her walk-in closet. Now I saw why—even though the setup was similar to our apartment—her master bedroom seemed smaller than my dad's. She gave up living space for her wardrobe: clothes and shoes everywhere. She walked to the back and sifted through the dresses so quickly, she was a blur, and I could hardly keep up. She muttered things at such a rapid rate, I only was able to catch snippets such as "wrong color" and "too old-fashioned."

Then she stopped. "Come," she commanded, pointing at a pile of dresses by my feet.

I scooped them up and followed her out. She was bossy all right.

She flopped onto the bed and picked up a magazine. "Try them on."

I froze. I never played sports, so the laissez-faire locker room behavior of just stripping down in front of someone else mortified me. This did not feel like gym class when a bunch of us tried covering what we could while we switched clothes. I had an avid audience. "In front of you?"

"Trust me, I've seen it all before. Nymphs aren't fond of clothes."

I tried not to think of nymphs, but my mind battled over asking what they looked like. I was overwhelmed enough. I couldn't handle more supernatural creatures at the moment. Absorbed, flipping through her magazine at a rapid pace, she seemed to care less about me getting undressed. As I bent down and picked up the first dress, I heard a *tsk* sound from her. I looked over and covered myself with the dress.

"Have you been eating? I can see your ribs." She stood up and came over to me, trying to get a glimpse of my body.

"Yes," I hissed, defensive and annoyed at her pushing me around all day and insulting me.

She pressed her lips together, not liking my tone. "Archer wouldn't want—"

"I couldn't care less what Archer wants!" My tone completely belied the statement, and Aroha knew it.

"I see."

Then she was out of the room and back in front of me in a flash. She had to stop doing that. It was jarring. Aroha held a small vial in her hand. "Drink."

"What is it?"

"Nectar. Archer said you had some before and handled it fine. Some mortals can; some throw it up. I don't know why Lucien hasn't tried it to stop these fevers."

"Will it stop them?"

"I have no idea, but this should be enough to make you healthy. Lucien should've tried it, but maybe we did forget to tell him about Zelus and Dionysus. So much happened afterward. You look ill, dear. Drink."

I grabbed the vial and tossed it back, feeling it burn all the way down into my stomach. Then a warm feeling spread throughout my entire body. I felt happy and whole. Aroha smiled and turned me to look in her full-length mirror. My cheeks were rounded out, my face tan again and not my feverish paleness that had left my bronze tone a garish green color. My eyes were more vibrant, shining with the energy I now possessed.

Aroha pulled the gown out of my hands, and I stood there examining my figure, noting my ribs weren't protruding as much. Of course, she poked me to make sure. My stomach growled. I had an appetite again.

"What does nectar do?"

"It's like vitamins for gods. The amount I gave you is what I have daily to look my best, but I could handle a whole lot more than you." Then she ran her hand down my hair, a more than kind gesture from her. "I'll cook us up some food. Please model the dresses for me, though, while I do."

This suddenly affectionate and maternal woman was scarier than the commandeering one as it was so unexpected. I slipped on a purple dress that was way too form-fitting for my liking and did as I was told.

Dress after dress, Aroha either gave me thumbs up or a frown. The last one was white, and when I came out of the room, Aroha's mouth stretched into a broad smile, and she put her hands to her heart. "You look like a bride."

I felt my face flare up. "Way ahead of yourself there, Aroha."

"That's the one."

"Whoa, I'm not getting married!"

"It was my wedding dress to Drew, my husband before we went to Germany and Lucien eventually met us. Drew was a very nice, handsome mortal," she mused.

It was kind of weird to listen to her talk about marrying and leaving someone in such a casual tone. Is that what I'd be for Archer one day? Would I be just some mortal he dated while in New York?

"It actually is a wedding dress? Then I'm not wearing it."

"Suit yourself. I'll save it for your wedding day."

I ignored that comment and the nagging image from my dreams. Was this the dress? "That was the last one."

"The pale green number, then. Makes you look tan and fits your simple taste."

It had been the second dress out of almost a dozen I had tried on. If I didn't know better, I might think Aroha was purposely torturing me.

Prom didn't feel like the rite of passage my father and Aroha had hyped it up to be. Dan was acting too friendly, making me regret going at all. To make matters worse, Lucien was back in town as Aroha's date and was doing a bad job of trying not to stare at me with a wounded, kicked-puppy look—two weeks of it. Aroha seemed to pick up on it all and stayed by my side most of the night as my guard dog, like Cerberus in the Underworld. Never before could I imagine her as Archer's mother, but her maternal instinct to protect was coming through. I dreaded talking to Lucien, but I needed to. We had ignored each other long enough.

We were awkwardly sitting at the table—Aroha, Dan, Lucien, and I; Todd and Marybeth were on the dance floor nonstop, sickeningly in love and oblivious to the rest of us (I might've been a tiny bit jealous), as well as Aroha's other four followers.

"Wanna dance?" I asked Lucien.

Aroha's head whipped over to look at me, while Lucien's eyes widened, and Dan frowned.

Lucien fiddled with his napkin, cleared his throat, and said, "Okay." It was a strange and powerful feeling to know you rendered a god almost speechless.

Lucien took me in his arms for the slow song but kept a proper distance away from me, staring over my shoulder at the other people around us. He was uncomfortable. I needed to get this over with.

I took a deep breath. "That night, the one before you left..."

His eyes darted to my lips as if he was recalling every detail of what he'd attempted that day.

I rushed to finish what had to be said: "I want to pretend that never happened."

His eyes met mine, and he gave me a smirk. "I have no idea what you're talking about."

"Thank you." I let out a sigh and moved onto the next subject I had to discuss that Aroha would chide me for. "How is he?"

Lucien's lips turned down into a displeased frown, his soft gaze hardening. "So that's why you wanted to dance, to pump me for information about him." (Oh crap.)

"I want to make sure he's okay, that he won't try anything stupid again. And I can't talk to him myself."

"Oh, *now* you have scruples about lying to your friends and torturing him and yourself?" To describe him as bitter was an understatement.

"I'm sorry if I hurt you."

"Me? Don't worry about me. Archer is the one you've destroyed. He's a shell of himself, broken beyond repair."

"Me too," I managed to get out, trying not to cry.

"You are human. You guys are weak—no offense—gods don't...I've only seen him like this once before, a long time ago."

"When his daughter..."

Lucien nodded.

"Tell him he can't do anything stupid, or I will follow him."

"Callie." He gasped and let go of me. "Don't say ridiculous things like that."

"Is there a problem, Veras?" Dan cut in, acting annoyingly territorial.

Lucien looked at Dan, then me, most likely jumping to incorrect conclusions (let him), but I didn't want Dan to be making more out of an "us" than there was or ever would be.

"No problem," Lucien said and fled the dance floor. The nasty look he shot me over his shoulder before he left the room made my stomach churn. He accused me of breaking his heart and betraying Archer's in one glance.

"Thank you, but I'm tired and I want to sit down." I told Dan and went and sat next to Aroha, trying to hold myself together.

"What did he say to you to make you so upset. I'll kill him." Dan's fists were clenched, and he was glaring at the doors Lucien had disappeared through.

"Nothing. Don't start anything. Please."

"I think this is a girl talk thing, Dan." Aroha emanated some of her charm by batting her eyes and twisting her hair.

Dan blinked a few times, stunned, but the anger left his features. He smiled and mumbled a half-coherent agreement. Then he walked off.

Aroha studied me. "What *did* he say?"

"Just that everything is apparently my fault."

What sounded like a string of expletives involving gods and items left her lips. She looked at me with those same sympathetic eyes everyone gave me lately. "He's an absolute victim-blaming ass. Don't listen to him. This is all on Zeus. He is the one who tried to tell Archer whom he could and couldn't love. He sent Death for you. Only, he underestimated—as he often does—the power of love. It surpasses everything and is the most vital power any god can wield, and beings like Archer and I have a hard time when we lose it. Archer was about to do something unforgivable, but that was his failing, his inability to stay positive, not yours. If anything, we're indebted to you for saving him."

"But Lucien—"

"No. He is not entitled to an opinion about anything dealing with you or Archer. He is bitter, jealous, and coming from a place of complete selfishness." Aroha touched my chin. "No tears tonight, Callie." Her eyes, full of varying emotions that were hard to discern, glistened as she gave me a sad smile.

Gods had a multitude of complex emotions like they felt everything simultaneously and so much more acutely. How had I not realized from the beginning they were different, and how did we mortals even stand a chance against them?

CHAPTER 18

Delusional. That's what Archer and Callie were. Impossible too. I was fed up. When I returned to New York for the blasted prom, Callie was still the same depressed and love-crazed girl I had left behind. Aroha was no help either. She defended her son, chastised me for not knowing what love was, and was unusually kind to Callie. They were on their way to being best friends. Just great. If I stayed here for four more years with Aroha, as the original plan had been, I would never escape Callie.

"You're staring at her again," Aroha teased.

I looked away from Callie and Dan dancing together, the welp only having eyes for her, while Callie was in her own world. "I'm trying to figure out what she is," I explained.

"You said the same about another girl once upon a time."

"That was different. That was more like where did she come from?, and who was her ancestor?, not *what* was Psyche? Her powers were clear. Zeus was the one who wanted her made immortal. Now it's quite the opposite." I kept my voice down, and the conversation flagged with the return of Marybeth and Todd to our table.

We made pleasantries, but soon the happy couple were lost in each other's company again.

Then Callie asked me to dance, after ignoring me for the most part. It seemed like all she wanted to do was put the past behind us, be friends again. My nervous energy of being around her after my disastrous move on her fizzled out. Then she had to fish for info about Archer. How many times would this girl break my heart?

I bolted. I had to get away from her, so I went outside the back of the school onto the loading dock. I leaned on the railing and sucked in the fresh air, finding relief. Too many mortal bodies cooped up in that hall and being too close to Callie was stifling and oppressive.

I stayed out there, trying to sort through my thoughts and calm down. A few minutes went by, and I started to feel at peace. Then Aroha came out. The look on her face was chiding. Great.

Instead of chastising me, she sighed and leaned on the railing next to me. "I don't miss Olympus or its long list of rules, but I miss being able to talk freely," Aroha said, staring off.

"I know. We should hang out more, just you and I. We haven't much with Archer being gone. We'll talk all about godly subjects until we long to hide among mortals again."

She laughed at that.

"Honestly, it is different this time, isn't it? With Archer, I mean?" I had this feeling, not like history was repeating itself exactly, but that when you live as long as I have, the past echoes and reverberates in the present in different ways. We had seen it all before and even from Archer.

"Yes." Her voice was thin. She was not the mighty Aphrodite at the moment, the woman who knew all mortals worshipped her beauty. She was almost that unaffected girl with no memory who'd sprung up out of the ocean at fifteen. She had been so sweet back then before Ares swept her away and filled her head with hubris and overabundant confidence. That ocean-sprung girl was in front of me, scared of the unknown, scared for her son, and all the materialism of the ages melted away.

"Archer is older," she continued. "He learned his lesson long ago. He is truly in love with Callie. And she...I'm beginning to like her due to her unreasonable dedication to my boy. There is something about Callie. I see it now—what you boys were trying to tell me—how she draws you in. It's not that she's prettier than me—she's not." The Aroha I knew was back now, building up her walls of superiority. "It's the fact she makes all of us like her without trying, like a charisma of sorts that seeks us to shelter her, protect her."

I simply nodded. It was all echoing, reverberating in time. Aroha was describing herself way back without even realizing it. We had felt that way about her back in Greece, wanting to protect the oceanic girl of beauty, even though we had no idea who she was. This was similar, but there was something more to Callie. We were willing to go against Zeus himself for her. A notion none of us could have possibly foreseen, even me.

"What do we do, Aroha? He's suicidal. She says she'll follow. Tell me they'll see reason in the end. We have to figure this out."

"My oldest friend, I'm sorry. The embodiment of Love knows how hard unrequited love can be, but you treated that girl abominably."

"Me? Save your maternal lectures for your son. He's the one who needs to hear them."

"This isn't really about Archer, and it's not even about Callie. It is about you. Blaming a girl for someone else's mental state when she is depressed herself and none of it is her fault whatsoever? Lucien, what were you thinking? Terribly done."

"I was mad. She'll get over it."

Aroha glared at me and crossed her arms. So she was out here to attack me, but instead took a more covert approach to get to the point. "You wrongly confirmed what she probably was thinking. You've been snubbed by a girl. Get over that. She is falling to pieces over a broken heart. Then you—one of her only real friends—pull this on her."

I was an ass, but she was completely downplaying how bad I felt. My heart was shattered too. I loved Callie, and to find out she didn't feel the same was gutting. "I'll apologize."

Aroha continued staring at me, her brows raised. She wanted more. "And?"

"And what?"

"Make it up to her. Swallow your pride, and be there for her, be her friend, and shut those feelings down." She touched my cheek, a maternal touch.

We had been friends for ages, through a lot together, but never romantically. Aroha and I were like brother and sister. There were spells of time we were apart—particularly her marriages to Ares—but after Psyche and Hedone were gone, it was the three of us: Archer, Aroha, and I always came back together. Nothing seemed right without that dynamic.

"I could ask...my other son...to back off."

I laughed. Her pauses, unable to admit Anteros—god of spurned love—was her child, improved my mood. "Oh, Dite."

She glared at me, but I couldn't help myself. Full belly laughter escaped me. Then her face upturned and she was joining in the merriment.

Once we settled down, I told her, "I don't think it's him doing it. I don't know why I love her. She doesn't encourage me. Her presence is addictive. I can understand Archer's sentiment, but to go as far as want to end himself after over three-thousand years because a two-month romance ended...unfathomable."

She let out a lighthearted huff. "How do you feel about truth, the sun, poetry? Put that intensity into your heart—imagine it for a second, Lucien—it is over thirty-two hundred years for him of love he's feeling. It's not that we love gods don't fall in love or feel it acutely. It bottles up and grows in intensity like a fine wine."

"He wasn't like this with Psyche."

"He was young then and foolish. It was lust, and love blossomed but faded. It wasn't true. He had values, unlike some gods we know. He had to marry her before taking her virtue. And you had a hand in that Psyche debacle. Don't pretend to be blameless."

"I was tired of hearing him go on about her. She was such a pale thing with that vibrant orange hair I wasn't used to, but he found it attractive." I referred to that strange period of time after the Daphne debacle where I was beginning to tolerate Eros for the first time, yet his immaturity still irked me since I was much older. I'd convinced Psyche's father to give his daughter up to a large serpent—mortals were so naive back then and terrified of us. Unlike today, back then, we showed ourselves, used our superhuman powers in front of them, and had them faithfully doing our bidding. It had been very controlled, and rarely had we exploited it. Zeus made sure of that.

Thinking back, my father didn't stop us enough, though. I convinced a man to sacrifice his daughter so my nephew could get laid. Archer had no intentions at the time to make Psyche immortal. She was his first—and only to this day—wife. Then Psyche broke Archer's rules and looked upon his sleeping form and recognized him for the god he truly was.

"Psyche had a rare type of beauty for us in Greece then. We didn't travel as freely to see other cultures," Aroha said.

"Are you saying you think Psyche was a descendant of the others?"

Aroha met my eyes and raised a brow that would stir most men's libidos. "Are you saying you think she was Greek?"

"I never thought about it. I thought... You were considered Greek. No one questioned it then. Where do you think she came from? Was she Scandinavian? Celtic?"

"I haven't a clue, but I'm beginning to think it might matter. Why don't you do what you do best, Apollo? We need it more now than ever."

Not that I was trying to be conceited, but I have always been hailed "the Greekest of all gods," multi-talented and possessing many gifts, so I still had to ask. "Do what?"

"Find the truth."

She was right. In this, my feelings had obscured my drive to know the truth. I needed to figure it all out—Psyche's lineage, the fevers, Callie's powers. I would stop getting distracted by beauty and find the truth. I would make amends with Callie, be her friend and nothing more.

CHAPTER 19

I was sick in the head. Seriously. I broke it off with Callie, ignored her calls, texts, and emails. Yet, every chance I could, I visited her in my mind, traversing miles telepathically to just get a vague glimpse of her. This did not bode well for my "getting over" Callie plan, which I was pretending to do because I had no resolve to forget her. Chase had to think I had given up, because I was done with lectures and pep talks and false words of promise that there could be a future for me with her. I was weeks from total madness, maybe less. Only Dionysus could gauge that. I would wait for her to move on, to love another, and then...I wasn't sure what I'd do. Painful as it was to watch her, at least I felt something.

Last night, I had tormented myself through the prom, watching Dan—no, he was no friend of mine anymore; now he was only "Eagen" to me. Then I saw him take her home and Callie slip away before he could say or do anything. The jealous monster in me was happy with her behavior, but deep down, I knew I should want her to move on and be with him. My arrows never erred, so she should love him, yet—if Lucien was to be believed—she still loved me. How? Not that I truly wanted her to stop loving me—well, the selfless part did—but the selfish being in me wanted her to never move on.

Here I was again, masochistically locating her in the coffee shop with Eagen. He and Callie sat across from each other, her warming her hands on her cardboard coffee cup. Callie was wearing an oversized T-shirt and jeans, so she wasn't trying to impress him. I bet she had a fever again. These troubled me. I hated to see her suffer and tried not to think about them, for if I did, I'd get anxious about possible causes.

"I'm so glad you came," Eagen said awkwardly.

Callie shrugged. "I didn't have plans, and I wasn't going to lie and say I did."

Well, that was a blatant letdown. I gloated, even though he couldn't see me.

"But you wanted to come, admit it," Eagen said cockily. His hands fidgeted under the tables, so it was an act.

Yeah, buddy, not the type of thing Callie would fall for.

She laughed awkwardly, and then they were silent. "Of course," she said lightly. "You're a good friend, Dan."

"Friend, huh?" He didn't look at her but stared at his iced coffee.

Oh, this was too much fun. I knew I was a terrible love god for watching this and enjoying the sight of him getting denied, but I couldn't help myself.

"Don't do this." Callie's tone was bold and slightly chiding. There was my girl.

Eagen's gaze darted up to hers, shocked. "What?"

"You said we were going to the prom as friends, Dan. And I know what you will say now. I could tell last night you wanted more, but I can't give it."

"Archer still, huh?"

"Yes."

He sighed. "I like you, Callie. I'm not going to lie. I know you're not ready, but time will help. We could hang out this summer, and we are both going to NYU... Maybe, things will change."

"I don't think they will."

"You can't know that."

"I do." There was such conviction in her voice that I started to wonder how far these feverish visions of hers went. She had prevented my death, after all. Did she see a brighter future for us?

"Give me a chance. Let's just hang out, you know? The summer, no pressure." He irritatingly kept saying that, although he meant the opposite.

I would bet a few mortal lifetimes that if I entered his mind, he was plotting ways to get into Callie's pants. The idea made me livid.

"Dan, I dunno. You want more than I do."

"There's this trip out to Cali I'm going on. I thought you'd like to come. It would be a good distraction."

"California," she mused. "I've never been." It was a blasé comment, and she was staring out the window, drinking her coffee, but Eagen grinned as if he'd scored the winning touchdown—not that he did often as he was a crap second-string quarterback.

"So, are you excited about NYU?" Eagen shifted gears, most likely trying to play it safe.

"I dunno."

"College! C'mon. Freedom from parents, independence, good riddance."

Callie froze.

What a prick! I wanted to punch him. I wish I could beat someone up in my invisible state.

"I don't want freedom from my father," Callie scolded.

Eagen looked at her blankly. He was an absolute tool. He was clueless. Everyone in school knew about Callie's father. Emily, the gossip queen, had made sure of that.

"I'm not feeling well. I met you because I didn't want to let you down, but I want to go home and rest."

"You're not even done with your coffee," he protested.

"They sell them in these convenient to-go cups for a reason, you know." She held up her cup as if to prove it to him. Then she stood up and rushed out, him trailing after her.

Satisfied she was okay and getting rid of the baggage, I came back to myself. The sun was baking my skin. I opened my eyes.

"Thought you were asleep," my dad said.

We were basking in the sun on the roof, which had been made into a makeshift outdoor lounge with a few plastic chairs. The sun was ridiculously hot, but we sweat very little, the ichor leveling our temperatures for us. The beach would've been better but wasn't close by. You had to jet across to a close island to find some sandy beaches that weren't consumed by mangroves.

"No, working." I felt guilty about lying. It was the only thing I could come up with that would explain my eyes being closed for twenty minutes.

"That's good." He was gazing out at the city.

Full of self-loathing, I closed my eyes to make myself a more honest being. For the first time in six months, I worked, matching two mortals together. It was awkward, the motion being forced, and wrong, even though their souls seemed to line up properly. Every couple I shot with arrows felt off, but I knew after a dozen that it was me. I selfishly didn't want to give them what I couldn't have. I gave up. At least I did something, and from what I saw in the world, my absence had little to no impact. I supposed Ma was finally working again. Oh, she'd be so mad at me for making her do it. I laughed at the thought.

"What?" Dad asked.

"I was wondering how Ma felt about working again."

Chase laughed wholeheartedly. "Oh, she's been whining about it all right, but it's her job too. I told her you'd help out when you were good and ready."

That night, I couldn't resist seeing Callie again. I closed my eyes and was instantly drawn to New York. Callie was thrashing around in the bed, saying "no" repeatedly, trapped in a nightmare. I placed myself next to her and tried to soothe her, but without a body or a voice, how could I? I pressed into her mind to see if I had any control there. Maybe I could somehow wake her.

Callie was slumped in bed, with something that looked like a jewelry box covered by her hand. The servant was there shaking her. For a horrific moment, it appeared she was dead. *Her father shuffled to the bed and pressed his fingers to her neck. He sighed in relief.* Thankfully, he found a pulse. *The servant was dialing on the phone frantically. Then she was in a hospital bed, unconscious, monitors tracking her health.*

I entered the room—not me, but a dream version of me—and looked at her, happiness flooding through me. I could feel it, despite this being a dream or vision or whatever it was. *I took up her hand, leaned down, and kissed her eyelids. They fluttered before they snapped open.*

I was thrust out of her mind, staring into the face of the now awake and scared Callie, who was panting and staring through me. She put her hand up and touched my face, which made me shiver with the odd sensation. I had never been touched or acknowledged by a mortal in my invisible state, which felt much more pleasant than the eerie feeling I had when I entered their minds in this state.

"Archer?" Callie's eyes searched but couldn't find me. I don't think she could feel me as I felt her, or she'd know I was right in front of her, wishing I could hold her in my arms.

I returned to my body, grabbed my phone, impulsively wanting to call her. I needed to hear her voice, to make sense of that dream, but I had been giving her space, letting her move on. I should continue to ignore her and let her go. A month ago, I had ghosted her. Surely, I could make it longer. I put my phone down, reason winning.

It was just a dream, nothing more. Because what she dreamed was the past coming back to haunt me. Minus the hospital, that was exactly how I had woken Psyche from her everlasting sleep. Contrary to the saying, history didn't repeat itself in that much detail. Human nature tended to make the same mistakes, but gods with boxes of eternal sleep being bestowed upon mortals would never repeat. I wouldn't see Callie again, and to think it was anything more than a dream might just be the thing that would break my heart and kill me.

CHAPTER 20

Callie

After the prom, the next few weeks went by in a foggy daze. The fevers were getting worse, or Lucien had falsely boasted about his abilities. Even his godly touch only brought the fevers down for minutes now instead of hours. On really bad days, Aroha gave me nectar, but by the following day, I'd be sick again. After Lucien gave me an apology and a promise of only friendship, he, Aroha, and I hung out together most days. Lucien didn't misbehave, and I was glad to have my friend back—although my trust in him was slower to return.

Throughout those weeks, Archer was still silent. Not only giving up on me, but now Aroha and Lucien seemed to have dropped contact with him or at least never dared to broach the subject when I was around. When pressed, they'd both tell me that Chase said Archer was fine. "Fine," a word defined as the opposite of how I felt. If Archer was fine, it meant he was through with us. It hurt, so I stopped asking. I refrained from harassing him with unwanted, depressing emails and texts to a number and email address that no longer existed (*he* was the cruel one).

This was what Archer had wanted. This was how I was supposed to live my life. I was told repeatedly by my mythological friends that I belonged with Dan. Part of me wanted to give in and date him, but using him would be cruel because I could never love anyone as I had Archer. He'd ruined love for me, and now I wouldn't feel that way ever again with anyone else.

"Cheer up." Aroha nudged me back to the present. "You're off in your own world again."

"Fever," I mumbled.

"Put a smile on your face. Fake it. Your Dad needs today."

Graduation day. She was right. The massive grin on my father's face in the crowd was worth faking happiness for. Maybe seeing how proud he was would make me feel...something. I plastered a fake smile on my face. My father snapped pictures on his phone. Lucien walked up to us, eyeing my father suspiciously, and angled his face away from the camera (rude much?).

He didn't trust my dad, which didn't sit well with me. What could my poor father do? Yes, my father wielded power over them: his book. But he'd never publish pictures and profess they were gods, because it would endanger me. Or would he?

"C'mon, you've got to be excited to get out of here," Lucien chided me. Mr. Sunshine was trying to make me see the brighter side of things, but it didn't work.

I shrugged.

"Graduating from high school is a once-in-a-lifetime milestone." He smirked.

His joke made me smile for real, and Aroha giggled.

"And how many times is this for you?" I challenged both of them, being sure to keep my voice down.

Emily and Linda were close by as we all mingled in the doorway, the principal struggling to get us to line up alphabetically.

"Lost count ages ago," he murmured, which elicited another smile from me.

Aroha moved to the front of the line, and Lucien and I headed toward the back. Since others were around, I tried to be vague and quiet as the conversation continued. "It must get tedious." I couldn't fathom doing high school over and over again. That would be Hell—or Hades. Tartarus? (I'd have to ask.)

"It does," he allowed. "And you know what else is tedious? Dan glaring daggers at me. Are you going to go out with the poor guy so he can stop being pointlessly jealous?"

Near the front of the line, Dan was glaring at Lucien, but when he noticed me, he smiled and waved. I waved back with a sigh. He just didn't do it for me (not at all).

"What will you do after graduation? Where will you and Aroha go?" I purposely changed the subject.

Lucien looked away, avoiding my gaze. (What?)

"You're leaving." I wanted to challenge him and argue, but it came out in a tiny whisper.

Eyes full of pain met mine. "We cannot stay forever."

"That's just it," I whispered. "You can."

He gave me a leveled look as if to tell me I was being silly, and I was. It would be cruel to ask him to stay if he truly cared about me when I didn't care about him (like doubly selfish). It would be stupid for him and Aroha to be near me, have news of me, when Archer was trying to forget me and vice versa. But I was so scared of being alone, and when my dad died, I would be. Maybe if Aroha stayed...

I was weak, so weak.

Lucien cursed under his breath. "Pull yourself together, Callie. Aroha might stay for a few years."

And then we were seated on stage, and the principal was addressing the crowd, so our conversation ceased. I could hardly focus on what the principal was saying. My head swam from the anxiety of learning I'd soon lose my only two friends and any connection to Archer, while another feverish fog overtook me. I felt myself drifting, like falling asleep with my eyes open, and my mind was disjointed from my body, floating up and away. I felt a pull then—like my head was a balloon, and my body was tugging the string back.

Only, when I was back "down"—for lack of a better word—I wasn't in myself. I was in Lucien's head, and I somehow was certain of that. (This was trippy.)

It is different this time, I feel it. I'm sure he does too. No wonder Archer is going crazy over this.

Archer suddenly appeared next to me. I was in Lucien's perspective, a memory. To see Archer again—even though he was thin and exhausted—made my heart pound with joy. Distracted by his figurative presence, I almost lost my grip over Lucien's mind. I clung on, hoping to see more of Archer.

He faded and then came into focus again. "But thanks." Archer said glumly.

"For what?" The voice came out of what felt like me, but I had to remember I was Lucien in this memory or vision or whatever it was.

"Trying."

There was a pause, silence.

"I want her to live too. I want to see you...not like this, happy if you can be."

"I won't ever be happy again, not without her."

"C'mon, time will—"

"No, it won't," Archer barked. "I'm going to die without her."

"Stop being so melodramatic. You can't die, so—"

"I will. I want to, and if I put my mind to it, I will find a way."

"Archer, you're talking mad again."

"I am mad!" Archer shouted at me (well, Lucien), his face screwed up in anger, but his eyes, which had been so gorgeous before, were devoid of emotion.

"You have to stop this. Just wait—"

"All I've been doing is waiting. And for what? All of you, time is your stupid solution. 'Never' Zeus said. If I'm with her, he will kill her after a year." *Then he stopped and took a deep breath. "Sorry, it's not your fault. You tried to help me from the beginning, warned me to stay away from her, told me I was getting in too deep. But as you well know now, none of us are immune to her, all victims of her beauty and charm. A sorceress of the heart."* *During this speech, the fight left him, and he was slumped and tired looking by the end.*

"You say sorceress, but what if—"

"She probably is of demigod stock, but what does it matter?"

Oh no, I wanted to control Lucien, to shut him up. I wanted to plead with him not to tell Archer whom my ancestor was. It would send him over the edge to know it was Psyche.

Lucien shrugged. "Yeah, doesn't matter now, does it?"

"Congratulations, Class of 2019!" yanked me out of Lucien's head and flung me back into my own. It took me a second to realize what was going on and where I was: graduation. The cheering was the crowd clapping and the students shouting with joy. I just graduated and missed it because I was living in the past, trying to use my weird perception to see more than I should. I seemed to have been in a memory of Lucien's, able to read his mind. Meanwhile, my present life was passing me by.

This self-scolding made me boldly ask Dan to join us for the graduation lunch Dad was taking us to. Aroha looked pleased, Lucien the opposite. Except for Aroha, the rest of us sat there uncomfortable, me most of all since my father inadvertently picked the same Greek restaurant Archer and I'd had our first date in. Dad did it to please the gods, I suppose. One thing he did not look pleased with was Dan tagging along, which made me wonder—but not attempt to read his mind. The way Dad's eyes narrowed on him, I assumed Dan was having some controversial thoughts.

"What is half this food?" Dan asked, leaning over my menu as if mine would have better explanations.

I cringed at his close proximity (and gave him a mental eyeroll).

Aroha, across from him, put her hand on his, drawing his attention away from me. "Let me help you. I love this place." She was changing her tune suddenly. Was she being a good friend, or was she competing again?

My father watched the exchange awkwardly from the head of the table and then looked at Lucien to his right. "So where to after this?" (Just stop Dad; this couldn't get worse right now.)

"I don't know actually. Might stick around." Lucien looked at me. "But then again, I might go abroad."

"Belize or somewhere like that?" Dad asked them.

Archer was in Belize! From the shock that rippled through Lucien and Aroha, I knew it was true. This had to be why I saw the Great Blue Hole in my vision. If I could just get there, see Archer, maybe I could convince him—what was I thinking? Lucien had told me through words and memories that I would die if Archer and I were together.

Wait. How did Dad know this?

Before I could be foolish enough to ask in front of Dan, he spoke. "I'm going out to LA this summer to see my dad, and I was hoping you'd let Callie go with me, Mr. Syches. She mentioned she had never been." (Whaaaaat?)

I was confused, speechless. Go to California with Dan? He assumed I would want to go off the mere admittance I never had been there, confident enough (or desperate?) to ask my dad and not me. It was all news to me, and when I gave Dan my bug-eyes, he winked as if this were some smooth move to get my dad's permission.

I looked at my dad, who seemed puzzled—and so worn out and old. He saw my expression right away and understood it. "Daniel, is it?"

"Dan."

"Daniel, I'm not sure if Callie told you. I'm an ill man, with limited time left with my daughter. She and I will talk about this later, privately."

I tried not to jump for joy and hug my dad for helping me out of this unanticipated situation.

Dan muttered something under his breath, his manners dissipating.

"No matter where we all venture off to this summer, I do have one hope that I ask of you, Callista. I want you to go to college."

"Dad," I groaned. I hated these difficult after-I-die talks. In front of others, they were nauseatingly painful.

"I hope you two"—he looked at Aroha and Lucien, snubbing Dan—"keep an eye on her after I'm gone, make sure she gets her education. She has an aunt and uncle here, but I'm not sure if they'll help much."

Considering we hadn't seen them once since we'd arrived, it was safe to say they wouldn't bother much with me. They had called once or twice, and Dad said it was about a loan. Who knows if he gave them the money.

"It would be my pleasure," Aroha said.

My eyes prickled with tears because she meant it. Somehow, she had become my best friend.

Lucien nodded. The look on his face was pure torture, though. After telling me he was leaving, my father was asking him to stay. I knew why. He wanted them to look after me, protect me. After all, there was the looming threat of Zeus, who wanted me dead, apparently (the god of gods wanting you dead, no big deal). They were promising much more than simply seeing me get a college degree.

"Callie, can I talk to you?" Dan asked.

I looked at him blankly, waiting for him to talk. I had no idea what he wanted and why he would interject into this amazing moment of realization that the gods were truly my best friends.

"Alone," he ground out. (Great, this sounded like loads of fun.)

The restaurant was small, and there were no private places to talk and, with the immortals around, not be heard. I led him outside. "What?"

"What is that all about?" he demanded.

"I don't know what you mean."

"Your dad being all controlling and then ignoring me. It's like you're in this little club with your buddies and dad, and you won't let me join."

"I'm sorry you feel that way." What else could I possibly say?

His wounded expression turned stormy due to the lack of empathy in my voice. I was barely holding anger back.

"You're not some little kid. You're going to LA, despite what he says and—"

"Hold up." (He just unleashed the demon.) "Number one, stop talking crap about my dad! He's *dying*, which once again you seem to have forgotten. He might not make it through the summer. I'm not going to LA, because I want to spend all the time I can with him. Plus, I don't want to go with you. You didn't ask me but commanded me like some caveman by putting me on the spot in front of my dad. Number two, or three—whatever—if we are some club, it's because we all went through something terrible together, okay? That makes us more than friends, almost family."

Dan gave a dry laugh and then looked away. "Archer, again, huh?"

I didn't respond.

"Callie, you need to move on. It's been long enough."

"Archer di..." It felt wrong to lie. "Archer's been gone for six months. Is that the timeline you stamp on when love should end?"

"I didn't mean—"

"It wasn't a breakup, Dan. He's gone."

"But you're still here. You and me—"

"There is no 'you and me,' Dan. I've tried to let you down easy. You even said you were okay with just being friends. I can't do this!"

"I know you loved him, but—"

"I still love him! I will always love him." I came out more harshly than I intended (but he deserved it).

Dan's face screwed up in anger. "Then, I hope you're prepared to live a long, sad, dried-up life." He stormed down the street, his hands in his pockets, his gaze down on his feet.

I took a deep breath, trying to rein in my warring emotions of rage and grief. I never could, never would, love anyone but Archer. I went back inside to the only people who understood me.

"Belize?" I asked Lucien.

"You can't go there, Callie," he retorted. Prophecy boy foresaw my plans.

"Where's Dan?" Aroha was craftily changing the subject.

"Gone. But I will go there. That's what shocked me. I've seen it."

Aroha gave me an eye roll. "Callie, you can't—"

"She's seen it." My father's face was flushed and weary. I did this to him, made his last months, weeks maybe, worse. "She had a dream during a terrible fever, and she was talking in her sleep, a one-sided conversation, but it was enough. I could tell she was speaking to Archer about Belize. I think they were here and then were going there. I don't know how far into the future she's seeing, but I heard it all the same."

I *had* had that dream, but my dad knowing about it was a surprise. It was a short one that lacked detail, so I had written it off as a fantasy, but if Archer was in Belize, it must be true.

"There's no way a dream is true. No mortal can see the future." Aroha was determined not to believe in my visions, even after witnessing them firsthand. Her face lost its usually fake joyful demeanor and became firm. She was agitated by our conversation. Why?

"She found him on Montserrat. You saw it," Dad pushed. I marveled at how he wasn't intimidated by her. He had known about them before I had and so was more acclimated to the idea of gods. How long had he known?

"Freak accident," Aroha tried, but her fight was gone. "You can't possibly see the future, Callie. And if you freakishly are somehow, you'll get my son killed." She was worried about Archer. My friend was drifting away, taken over by her maternal role.

"She won't go to Belize." Lucien met my gaze. "If her vision has them going together, he needs to come to New York; she'll stay put to make it happen." He was right, and why shouldn't he be since he was god of prophecies? Yet it felt like a threat, Lucien trying to control me and keep me here.

My dream was of Archer and me talking, but so happy that every look, word, and kiss, slowed us down. We were in a strange city, the skyline I had seen when I saw Archer through a fever: Belize. Now I had a name for the place.

"Dad? I didn't know it was Belize. How did you?"

"You said something about Caye Caulker. I know my geography." He shrugged as if it were that simple.

I was definitely researching Belizian city skylines to pinpoint his location tonight. Some strange hope was forming in me.

"I'm seeing more than just visions. I mean, I can do more." I gave Dad an apologetic look. "Sorry, Dad, I wanted to ask you how far your intuition goes, but I wasn't sure what I was doing."

"I can read people very well, but gods, or you for example, Callista, I can only sense things, like reading someone's mind through water or sand—emotions, intentions, not words. Are you seeing words, thoughts?" Dad seemed excited, animated.

I looked at my friends: Lucien looked uncomfortable, Aroha had a look that went beyond skepticism. My best friend, my mother figure, was abandoning me; I saw it in her eyes. She didn't believe me or was afraid to.

I took a deep breath. "The fevers bring the visions, but I'm reading minds without them, immortal ones."

Aroha and Lucien exchanged a look, and Lucien shook his head. Neither believed me. Aroha's look of disbelief turned into incredulity (I was seeing Aphrodite now). Dad's eyes gleamed with pride and something akin to confirmation. He had known I could do this. How?

"I read Archer's the night he left. He could tell you. And I read yours, Lucien, at graduation. You were thinking about the last conversation you had with Archer," I said.

Lucien shifted uncomfortably. Lucien's eyes bore into mine; the disbelief shifted, and his face clicked into place, as if everything he knew all made sense now, a knowing look. About what, though?

"Read minds, huh? Read mine, then." Aphrodite was definitely angry with me.

I wasn't sure I wanted to know what her mind was thinking at the moment. I also wasn't sure I could do it under pressure, on demand. At graduation, I'd had a fever, but with Archer, I hadn't had one; in fact, they hadn't started until after he was gone. I focused on her, staring her down, ignoring those challenging pretty eyes, so like Archer's. I pushed Archer from my mind (hard to do) and focused on Aroha, pressing my way—quite easily—into her mind. She must have been projecting her thoughts on purpose, it was that easy.

Unoriginal, Callie. You'll break my son's heart with these lies. I wish you'd never met him. I should've given you the impossible tasks. Here's my favorite: open Persephone's box.

I came back to myself. What horrible thoughts from such a pretty face. It stung of betrayal. She thought I was purposely trying to pretend to be like Psyche. I couldn't say anything or repeat her thoughts aloud. To say them would make them real. She had been my best friend for a short while. I deserved it in a way. Being in her mind, I could see it from a mother's perspective. She was cruelly overprotective. I had hurt her baby, and these abilities most likely were too similar to the last woman who had done that. Would I ever escape the ghost of Psyche?

"See? Nothing." Then she looked away as if everything were fine. "Ah, here's the food."

Then I endured the most awkward and silent meal of my life, Lucien and my father trying to keep superficial conversation going while I retreated into myself, trying to remember the details about Persephone's box and why I had lost my nerve to challenge Aphrodite (she was only a goddess, right?).

Lucien met my gaze at one point, eyes full of sympathy, but for what, I was unsure. Aroha—Aphrodite, whomever she was at the moment—was as silent and sad as me. Why had she done this? Breached our friendship and insisted I was lying? Losing her made me feel as if Archer was slipping away from me even further. What a dismal graduation day.

CHAPTER 21

I was growing bored and restless. My father pored over his computer daily, researching, he proclaimed, but he was elusive. I didn't ask. I didn't want to know. I was sure it had something to do with Callie, and I couldn't get my hopes up again. My father suggested every possible distraction, from us visiting other immortals to joining him on a warfront. He was itching to fight. I could see it. The tedious boredom was frustrating him as well. He hadn't worked in ages, and I barely had either. The world would fight and fall in love without our intervention. We had done our jobs so well for thousands of years that humanity was now capable of continuing without us for some time. The couples would pair up wrong as they do from time to time, and mankind would wage wars without my father intervening, and other gods would pick up our slack. In the scheme of things, I was one of about a dozen love gods and goddesses worldwide.

I really didn't have much to look forward to. Although Callie didn't know it, I was there in spirit; I watched her at the prom, wishing she were happy instead of living in this same melancholy daze as me. Things seemed to get worse for both of us, and I wondered if there was a point anymore. I worried about her dying if I went to be with her, but now I worried just as much about us dying because we couldn't be together. My thoughts had become so maudlin that I wouldn't dare speak them aloud.

So when there was a knock at the door one morning, I went to get it, hoping for any kind of distraction. I opened the door to see my face looking back at me. Well, not my own exactly, an identical structure, but the eyes hazel and the hair sandy-brown and straight, just past his ears.

"Bruv," he said with a huge smile. He pulled me in via handshake and slammed my back with his other hand in a man hug.

"Anteros," I said, the shock apparent in my voice.

"Look at his face," another laughing voice said.

"Himerus," I greeted. I got another man hug, this pat on the back more like a pummeling. "What are you guys doing here?"

"Pops invited us," Himerus said.

"Even you?" I directed at Anteros.

He was the god of slighted love, my opposite in powers but almost identical in looks, and Ma's child with her mortal lover Adonis. Zeus made him immortal pretty much to drive a wedge in between my parents. Himerus, god of lust, was the same; he was my dad's kid with some mortal woman, and he looked a bit like dad but much more like his mother—not that I'd met her.

"Even me," Anteros said, warily looking behind me as if worried my dad would be right around the corner, ready to pulverize him. Honestly, I wouldn't put it past my dad—my old dad, the warmonger, not this new somehow...normal man.

"Come in." I opened the door wider and got out of the way. "There's only one extra room."

"We can bunk together. Depending on how things are with your dad and me, we might try to get a place if needed, but we're scant on funds right now," Anteros explained.

"My dad is...different lately."

"I hope you mean in a good way, Archer," Dad said, entering the room.

"Of course," I floundered, but it was the truth.

Chase smiled and annoyingly gave me noogies until I dodged a further attack by weaving out of his reach.

"Himerus," Chase nodded awkwardly to the son he had ignored for most of his life. Then he looked at Ma's son and said so calmly that it was kind of eerie, "Anteros."

It was a perfect example of how different he had become. I remember screaming matches between my parents and my father wanting to tear Anteros to pieces. That was right before a massive fallout where the muses took my brothers in and raised them with Lucien's son Hymenaios.

Anteros's thoughts must've been akin to mine, because his face was stunned.

Himerus was pink-cheeked, either embarrassed or intimidated by our father. "You sent for us...sir?" He awkwardly shifted his weight and avoided Chase's gaze.

"Call me Chase, both of you."

Awkward silence.

"Archer, get us one of those nectar whiskey bottles that Heph bestowed upon us."

I went to the kitchen, which was eight feet away, wondering why he needed me to do it when he was right there. Not normally a lazy god—if anything he always had energy to burn—I found this weird.

"Boys, sit," my dad commanded.

They sat awkwardly on the edge of the sofa.

"Are you all in?"

"Yes," they said in unison.

"There's no turning back. You need to be sure." Chase was quite intimidating when he wanted to be, and right now, the bobbing Adam's apples of my siblings proved he was on point.

"What in Hades is going on?" I asked, almost dropping one of the glasses I was getting out of the cupboard.

"Try not to break the bottle, and get over here with those drinks," Chase ordered, making me feel as if I were a mere servant.

I didn't care much for his tone or how he was leaving me out of something that sounded serious. He had the audacity to speak over me. I threw a glass at him. He caught it, so I threw another, which he again caught. He smirked at me, so I threw the third and fourth glasses simultaneously. Chase had to scramble to place the others down as these flew at him. He was only able to snag one out of the air, and the other hit his hand awkwardly and shattered on the ground. He glared at me.

I took a fifth one—considering we only had six glasses in all before I had snapped—and walked over with the bottle in hand. "Stop hiding things from me, damn it!"

"Sit down, you little..." Chase took a deep breath and calmed down. For a moment, his anger was as it had been in the past.

Perhaps I shouldn't poke the bear while he had been hibernating, particularly around Anteros. I walked over and poured everyone a glass as my dad spoke.

"I called Himerus a week ago to see how the land lay in Olympus."

Fiji, but whatever; I didn't think I should correct him after my stunt.

"He said things weren't going well, for either of them in particular. I convinced them they were needed and gave them a choice. They chose us over Zeus, Archer."

I overpoured my father's drink in shock. He took the bottle from me and laughed before he drank some carefully from his glass. My brothers, unwanted and tread upon for three millennia, were here supporting me, without money or regard for the comfort and luxury my grandfather bestowed upon those he favored.

"We are needed, though, right?" It was clear from Himerus's firm grip on his glass he was terrified about giving up a place of security for the unknown.

"Himerus, ease up," I warned him.

He looked at his hand and lessened his grip on the glass that could shatter with his strength.

"In a sense, yes. But it was more of me being afraid Zeus will use you against me and Dite."

"We would never go against you!" Anteros said, full of emotion. "I don't care what you both think of me. I don't care how shitty either of you have been to me and how much you hate me. She's still my mom!"

"You misunderstand me," Chase said. "I don't think things will bode well in the future between my father and me."

I withheld my "duh" comment for Dad stating the obvious and just watched silently to see where he was headed.

He looked at Himerus. "I didn't want him to hold you over me. As much as you think I don't care, and I know I haven't shown it, you are my son. If Zeus..." Chase couldn't finish. He cleared his throat and took a swig, actually viewed Anteros objectively. "And I love your mother more than anyone in the world, Anteros. I would never want to see her hurt or be forced to choose protecting Eros over your wellbeing. Himerus said both of you were getting a lot of grief from Zeus about us. He would use both of you to get to us." Dad paused. "Anteros, I regret being so hateful toward you in the beginning. None of it was any of your fault."

This was too much for my brother, and he lost the courage to return my father's intense gaze. "Nice speech and everything, but my mother cares nothing for me. I came for Archer," Anteros replied. His jaw was stubbornly set, and he was staring at the floor. Able to read the emotions off the face that looked so much like my own, I knew he cared way more about being accepted by us, including Ma, than he would've liked to admit.

"Dite is the most complicated female in existence. She drives me crazy as much as I love her. She cares. She doesn't know how to show it and often shuts down and gives others a cold façade. Regardless, I know her better than anyone. She would not do well seeing you harmed."

I nodded. This was all true. Despite her flaws, my mother loved her children, bastards and all—even if she was terrible at showing it.

"So what do you mean the future not going so well with Gramps?" Himerus asked. It sliced through the seriousness and the awkwardness of my father's admission.

"It's just a precaution. I don't think Zeus will let this Callie issue lie." He had been hiding something from me. His apologetic expression confirmed it. "There's something about her, Archer. Zeus is hoping you fail to stay away. He wants her dead, and I have a bad feeling you staying away from her won't be enough. He'll find a reason to get rid of her."

I swallowed the lump growing in my throat. So staying away from her was pointless. Trying to protect her was pointless. My dad's info probably had the opposite effect he wished for. He'd expect me to fight for her, be with her, but I was tired. I felt done. What was the point of living if Callie would die? What was the point of any of this? Zeus always got what he wanted in the end. He was the god of gods.

My brothers' presence also had the opposite effect that my father most likely desired. He probably hoped they could distract me or lift my spirits, but nothing worked. They did help him watch me. When I went to be alone, one of the three of them tailed me, either trying to hang out or unsuccessfully hiding in the shadows. I doubt they knew what was on my mind; they probably thought I'd give them the slip to New York again.

I had a plan, though, and they couldn't stop me—a crafty plan that took a couple days in the market, chatting to some mortal teens and paying them and trusting them with my things. The morning of my plan, I convinced my brothers to take the trip to Caye Caulker for a day at the beach. I went down to the beach immediately, knowing they would be sucked in by the water sports. They lagged behind, talking to the proprietors about pricing, but I knew Anteros and Himerus were watching me. I sat down in the sand with my little notepad and pen, planning to hang out long enough for them to ease up in their surveillance.

I took pen to paper:

Dear Callie,

This is the last communication you'll get from me. I tried desperately to let you go, but neither my powers nor my heart will set you free. You must be the most stubborn mortal in existence, but that is one of the many things I love about you. That love has destroyed our lives, but I will never regret it. Meeting you was the best thing to happen in my 3,270 years. There is no company, never was any, that matched yours. You have become my life, my reason for existence, and without you, I'm miserably adrift.

Please, in receiving this letter, do not think ill of me. I must do what is necessary to free you from me and to stop feeling this way. I have run out of options and hope. Please, remember a promise you made me that last night we were together. I need to know you go on in the world.

*With all my heart
forever and always,
Your Eros, Archer Ambrose*

I knew what kind of note it was going to be the second I started writing it, but the weight of those words wore heavily on me. I wanted to tell her about Zeus and how he would destroy her anyway, but I could not frighten her or make promises about my family protecting her that I couldn't see through.

I turned my attention back to the notepad and tried to draft a letter to my mother, but no words came. How does one say goodbye to the woman who has borne and raised him, spent thousands of years by his side? Guilt festered inside of me. How would she react after she found out?

And my dad? No words came for him. Our reconciliation was short-lived, but we had grown close these past months. He'd blame himself, and Ma would too. I scribbled a note to both of them, apologizing, but it wasn't enough. No words would ever be.

I saw the speedboat, knowing it was waiting for me since it did not pull into a dock, the teenagers coming through for me in the end. I put the notepad in a Ziplock bag with my money and sealed it. I put it in my velcro pocket and stripped down to just my bathing suit. I ventured out into the sea and dove into the waves. The water was clear and warm, soothing over my anxiety, but nothing could assuage the guilt and desperation that overwhelmed me.

I swam parallel to the shoreline as if I were simply going for a swim, keeping an eye out for my brothers. The girls I had paid to talk to them at this very hour walked up the beach toward them. Once I could see them chatting up Himerus and Anteros in the distance, I dove under water and swam as fast and as long as I could while still passing as a mortal. I made it to the boat in minutes. They hoisted me into the speedboat and kicked the motor into full throttle. We shot up the coast for about twenty minutes. They had the backpack I had given them filled with my passport, a change of clothes, and other necessities for travel.

THE IMMORTAL TRANSCRIPTS: FEVER

They took me into a small marina area, and I thanked them. I climbed onto the dock, walking away mortally slow when all I wanted was to create more distance from my brothers. Once I was clear of people, I ran for the highway so fast that no mortal eye could see me, stopping when I was about a mile outside of Ladyville and walking the rest. I should've hurried, but I covered my trail carefully. By now, my brothers would've noticed my absence and called Chase. Likely, he'd summon the wind gods—the three who were against Zeus at least—to see if they had taken me anywhere. When he learned they hadn't, first, they'd check Caye Caulker Airport. With no leads, Belize City Municipal Airport and bus and taxi services would come next. By the time they discovered I went to Philip SW Goldson International instead, I'd be on a plane out of the country.

They wouldn't be able to stop me. Of that, I was sure.

CHAPTER 22

Callie

The night of graduation, there were parties. Lucien tried to get me to go to one, but I opted to hang out with my dad instead. I read his mind to find out he was worried about me. There probably was a reason to be. Aroha's vindictive but honest thoughts wounded me. As the night wore on, I tried to let it go, to let it heal, but it was like an itchy scab that I had to keep picking. It wasn't just a fleeting thought of hers either. She had wanted to do something to celebrate graduation, and yet she didn't call me. She was angry with me. What stayed with me was the accusation that I'd lied and how she wanted me to open Persephone's box.

After I'd found out Archer was Eros, I'd revisited all the mythology my father had taught me. Aroha (Aphrodite) had given Psyche false promises to get Eros back if she completed impossible tasks, merely to torture her. The final task was to retrieve Persephone's box, which Aroha said contained beauty; only, it really contained eternal sleep—whatever that was—and Psyche foolishly opened it. Archer was able to wake her, so Zeus made her immortal, and they lived happily ever after...for a while.

The fact Aroha wished this box onto me had severed the maternal-type friendship that had blossomed. I was devastated. I couldn't be close friends with Lucien either, because of his feelings for me. Dad was not long for this world. I had no one.

Restless, I got up off the sofa, hardly watching the action film my dad had on. I examined the artifacts in the glass cases: the tiny arrowheads Aroha said had been Archer's as a child, the figurine carved by Chase, the lyre that was Lucien's. We had found their things, thousands of years later, entombed in a mountain. Now, a decade later, we stumbled across the immortals who had lived there. How was this possible?

I continued to inventory all the items as I pondered on serendipity and chance...on fate. I'd ask Lucien about the Fates later. Pottery fragments, a broken necklace, spearheads, coins, and more. Then I saw it. I hadn't thought about it before. There was the box Dad had said was a jewelry box sealed shut by time and calcification.

I stared at it through the case. It looked bronze, turned black and tarnished with age. Carved into it were animals, ferns, and the gods in ornate detail. I sought out recognition of the faces, but they were too small and nondescript to discern. I noted one holding a lyre, Lucien; a woman holding a bow and, in her other arm, a baby holding an arrow, Aroha and Archer; Dionysus holding a goblet and vine; Athena with the wise owl perched on her shoulder; Zeus and his thunderbolt were at the top of the lid in a place of prominence. There were more figures wrapped around the sides and back and maybe even the bottom that I couldn't see. I didn't see a Persephone, though. One would think her image would be on her own box, so it probably wasn't hers. Dad would have a theory (as always).

I went back to the sofa to see my father was asleep. He slept a lot these days. I texted Raphael.

Raphael was there in minutes and lifted my father up and carried him to his room. Raphael was a large, strong man, but my father had lost so much weight, he didn't weigh much more than me. Once Dad was settled in bed and Raphael left, I turned in early for the night (some graduation day). Without school to distract me, tomorrow was going to be a long day.

Sleep would not come, so I tested out my powers as I often did during my sleepless nights. I closed my eyes and thought of Archer, begging whatever gift I had to let me see him.

I saw his face, full of determination, but his eyes were unfocused. He stood at what looked like the base of a mountain. He unslung a bookbag from his shoulder, fished inside, and took out a plastic Ziplock bag. Inside, there was a small notepad. He placed it under a rock. He left the bookbag by the rock as well and walked up an incline.

What was he doing? I tried to call out to him, but this was a dream or a fever or some kind of vision. I wasn't actually there.

The morbidly resolute expression on his face told me he wasn't mountain climbing for fun. I was scared. I wanted to stop him from walking, but I had no body to put between him and whatever doom he was attempting. I was only there in mind.

Then I saw it. I knew what he was up to, and my blood ran cold. *Black billowing smoke rose above the volcano that I had mistaken for a mountain. From the amount of smoke, it was clearly active . There would be magma, which, like fire, probably could kill an immortal. Archer was going to kill himself.*

I followed him helplessly as he trekked up the mountain. He neared the top and hesitated a moment, then continued climbing, disappearing into the smoke.

I woke up with a jolt. It was real (No, no no!). In my mind, I knew this was happening or would happen. I had to stop him. Only, I knew he wouldn't listen. I picked up my phone and texted two words to Lucien and Aroha: **Soufrière Hills**. Then I went into my bathroom and splashed my face with some cold water. How could I stop Archer? How could I make him come back to me, want to live?

Like a thunderbolt to my brain (poor analogy, Callie), it clicked.

I quietly snuck into my father's office and felt around his desk in the dark, only illuminated by city lights that were cast through the large windows. I found the key and hurried to the glass case. Time was of the essence, an immortal life on the line. I grabbed the box and hurried back into my room, slipping back under the covers. I examined the box under the lamplight and located more gods around the sides of the box.

On the bottom of the box, there was a girl; a man and a woman were pulling her in opposite directions by her forearms. The woman's other hand held a tuft of grain, the man's holding a scepter with a skull on the tip. It was Persephone being torn between her husband, Hades, and her mother, Demeter. Persephone clutched something round in her hand, and I realized it might be a pomegranate—if I remembered my mythology correctly. I ran my finger along the little pomegranate, because it looked strange, to find it was slightly raised.

I pressed the pomegranate and heard a click, as if the box had unlocked. I hesitated. What would happen if I opened it? And yet, what did I have to lose? Archer might be gone, and without him alive in the world...promises be damned. Maybe, just maybe, I could stop him. I did before. By repeating a myth (real history), I could do it again: get him to come back to me.

I was nervous. I took a deep breath, unsure of what to expect as I opened the lid of the box. It was empty. Inside was blackness, darker and thicker than any cloth, paint, or manmade material could be. It was an open void, dark space, nothingness, an absence of light. I held my hand on the lid in case I had to close it. I didn't know if whatever power this might have could spread to others. At first, nothing happened.

Quickly, though, my eyes grew heavy, like cement was weighing the lids shut into permanent submission. My breathing was forced into deeper slower breaths, and my head felt heavy. I imagined it felt like going under for surgery—not that I'd ever had to before. My eyes closed, and I was unable to open them. I didn't fight it. I would sleep and hope that when I woke, Archer would be there with me. My body went limp, and I felt myself slipping away from consciousness.

The last thing I heard was the lid of the box snap shut and click, locking itself again (good). Thoughts were too hard to formulate. I floated away, not afraid of this sleep, but relieved, at peace.

CHAPTER 23

Archer

Soufrière Hills—the place on Montserrat I should've gone to the first time I was there instead of thinking Heph would help me. When I arrived, I wanted to head southwest to Plymouth, the former capital that was buried under the massive eruption of 1995, but was informed when trying to buy tour guide tickets that no one could go there currently. Soufrière Hills was still an active volcano, erupting now and then over the years since that fateful day. They were on an alert, level 4 for possible eruption, so not even all my money could persuade some of the private guides to take me there with the rangers patrolling. Luck was against me. However, I was able to find a tour to Jack Boy Hill, the most popular tourist spot to see the volcano, which wasn't too much farther away since the volcano was pretty centrally located.

While the tour guide was talking about the history of the 1995 event, I gave him the slip and hurried away and out of sight. I had to go on foot. What was a few miles at immortal speed? I followed a road until it dead-ended and the greenery gave way to a river, its east side a barren wasteland and west side flourishing with forests. I eventually abandoned the river when it curved west into full greenery. At this point, it wasn't like I needed directions to the looming smoking mass ahead. I followed a trail of long-ago-dried lava toward the volcano, watching my feet on the rocky terrain, and slowed down to a mortal pace. No one would be here to stop me; not even rangers would get this close.

When I hit the volcano's sharpening incline, I looked up in awe at its smoking power. Ash fluttered down on me like snowflakes. I sighed. I placed my bookbag on the ground and took out the sealed notepad with the letters, anchoring it under a rock so Chase would find it. I was sure he'd figure out where I was a couple hours too late. I tried not to think about his reaction. I tried to swallow the guilt, but it stuck in my throat, choking me. Then I started walking.

It was a steep incline and absolutely stifling. Even the ichor in my blood protested, unable to regulate my temperature anymore. I now understood the mortal saying "sweating buckets." What an odd sensation. I wiped the sweat from my brow; it stung as it went into my eyes and tasted of salt as it dripped onto my lips. I felt so human, so frail, able to die. As I climbed, I felt as if Callie were by my side. She was with me in spirit, and perhaps—if possible—we would see each other in Elysium one day.

I wondered if the ichor was hot enough to combust in my veins; it felt as if it were on fire, boiling from the inside. I paused, standing there. I knew I needed to climb farther, to perhaps throw myself into the magma if needed. I had known it would be a physical and mental climb to figure out the breaking point. Fire and accelerant were all that had worked in the past, but surely, the high temperatures would eventually make me combust, and the healing abilities would cease when the ichor no longer could sustain me.

I arrived at the smoking level and stepped into its thick coating. It was like barbecue smoke, full of tiny particles of ash and rock, but smelling of sulfur. It stung. My eyes and lungs both burned. I had expected a giant pool of magma I could just leap into, but no. Smoke choked me, and ash clogged my eyes. I stopped breathing—because I didn't need to—and closed my eyes. It was a bit better, but how would I find the hottest point? I had read once volcanoes went up to four thousand degrees. Surely, that would kill me. But what could I do? Stumble around until I fell into some lava? Stand here until eventually something happened?

A loud whooshing noise made me jump. My foot slammed into the ground, actually into it, and I sank into deep ash up to my ankle. It instantly ate away my clothing and started to burn my skin.

Then something pulled me back. Two arms, I registered, were wound around me in a full nelson, making my arms useless and immobile. "Eros," a labored voice said in my ear, drowned out by the air roaring around us and steam hissing somewhere nearby. I recognized the voice at once, though: *Bampás*.

Dad dragged me back down the incline. I didn't fight him; there was no point because he'd win, being the strongest Olympian out there. Once we were clear of the ash and I could see again, he loosened his grip, thinking me compliant and safe. I tried to pull away from him. He tightened his grip, and we fell onto the rocks, tumbling and sliding down about fifty feet or so. Someone clambered down after us—Zephyrus. That was the windy noise and how my dad got here so fast. One of my oldest friends and my father had ganged up on me. My mission was officially botched, but I hardly cared. Nothing mattered anymore.

"Calm down, you little fool, and listen," another voice barked. Proteus stood over us, looking uncomfortable and drenched in sweat. "You almost ruined everything."

"What?" I managed to get out. My voice was rough and throat sore, coated in the ash I'd inhaled. If I had been mortal, I'd be long dead already.

"Eros, please," Dad breathed in my ear, his grip on me vice-like. His voice was a desperate plea, and my throat plugged up with guilt for the pain I was causing him. "Come down to level ground."

"Why should I?" I mumbled. But I was defeated. I couldn't do this to him. I'd let him drag me down, tell me what to do, run my life, whatever. I was done fighting and done hurting him.

"I've got news. It's Callie." My father loosened his grip, letting me sit up. He sat up too, but his muscles were still flexed, ready to subdue me again if needed.

"You're lying." I couldn't believe him; he might just say anything so I would find the will to live again.

"He's not," Zephyrus joined in. He'd never lie to me.

"Kid, if you die, you ruin many more lives," Proteus said, crossing his arms. "Can we get out of here, now? I feel like every drop of me is evaporating. Um...water god, here."

"Look at me, Archer," Chase said.

I did. I was staggered by his expression. He was no longer Chase, though, as my mind had already shifted into calling him Dad, *Bampás*; for the first time, we were truly father and son. He was distraught, exhausted, tortured. He had thought I might die; that much was clear. And it affected him more than I had ever anticipated.

"I'm not lying. You die today, so does Callie in a sense." And his devastated face told me there was a silent addition of himself. My numb mind could hardly grapple the amount of feeling he now had for me.

Callie. She could die? In what sense? He was being purposely vague. But when I pressed, he refused to answer me. Even when we reached the bottom, he refused to tell me anything.

Proteus shook hands with my father, who thanked him. Then the dehydrated water god sprinted toward the coast. Zephyrus teleported my father and I to a hotel room, then wished us luck and vanished.

I had so many questions but no energy to ask them. I looked out the window and saw airplanes. We were in Belize again, at the Phillip S.W. Goldstein International Airport, which meant we were flying somewhere far. "Where are we going?" I managed to get out.

"Get a shower. We're going to New York."

"But—"

"You've both proven you won't live without each other quite effectively, so there's no other option at this point," Dad said quite bitterly. Now that he had me safe, his anxiety had rightfully shifted to resentment. I'd put him through Hades and back.

Then his words clicked. "Callie?"

"She's okay. Look, your brothers should be here soon with our tickets. Go get a shower."

If I looked half as bad as my father, I was black with soot from head to toe.

"Your brothers will hold the fort here. I'm not sure how long we can stay in New York, but we'll rendezvous here before we move on."

"To where?"

"I hardly know yet, Archer. You and Callie have forced my hand. I'm planning as I go. Go get washed up." He plopped onto the sofa, a cloud of ash swirling around him. He was exhausted but holding back the anger that had to be churning inside of him. No one had a temper like my father when he lost it. He was carefully planning something out that probably would take years, and I was forcing him to do it all now.

I went in the bathroom and looked in the mirror. Every inch of me was gray from my hair and beard—which I had let grow out, abnormal for me—to my skin and clothes. It finally hit me while I was in the shower. I had been depressed, then for a moment, running on shock and guilt, but the water helped me think clearly for the first time in months. I would see Callie, and I couldn't be sad about it nor think about what repercussions there might be. I would see her again, hold her, kiss her. I wouldn't let her go. I didn't care she was only eighteen or that we had only been together a few months. When you cannot live without each other, you know that person is the one for you. I would marry her as soon as she would have me.

As the inky gray water ran off me, it took the horrid cloud of depression that had smothered me these past months with it. I stayed in the shower for at least a half hour, until the water ran clean, the smell of sulfuric ash was gone, and my mood had lifted.

I would be with Callie. I was myself again, filled with excitement and clinging tightly to hope, which had eluded me since I had left her.

CHAPTER 24

CHASE

"Are you going to tell me?" Archer asked for the umpteenth time.

I had ignored his questions, deflecting the entire way through the airport. I kept telling him Callie was fine, circumstances had changed, and we were heading to New York. I knew I had to tell him everything and not let him be shocked when he arrived there, but I just wanted him safely contained on a plane with a lot of mortals around so he couldn't overreact. His mind needed to process what he had almost done, come to terms with and regret it, before he could grasp moving forward into an unknown I might not be able to protect him from. My son wasn't yet stable. Emotions about him as a sickly baby came back to me; that was how I felt about him: would he make it till morning?

Instead of indicating anything going on in my head, I told him, "Get on the plane, Archer. I'll tell you then." He could not handle knowing how much he had hurt me with this attempt.

"You're freaking me out, Chase. What is it, damn it?"

I motioned for him to walk down the jet bridge, and he did as he was told, although his iridescent eyes glared at me, his jaw set. I gave him a smug look, as I always had when he was younger and had been reprimanded by me. He was always the defiant sort—well, only when it came to listening to me—but knew he'd never win a fight with fists or weapons against me; with words, we sparred equally. It burned him up inside for me to wield my paternal power over him.

Once we were seated with our carry-ons stowed, he pestered me again.

I took a deep breath. "Now, stay calm."

"Obviously, or you wouldn't wait for a safe place. Lay it on me." Archer laid his head back against the headrest and closed his eyes. A small smile played on his lips.

"How are you...happy?" I asked, not trying to stall, but I was utterly confused by his mood shift.

"I won't be if you don't tell me soon." He opened his eyes a fraction to glower at me.

"But—"

"You assured me Callie's alive, and we're going back to New York. I don't care what is coming or what is in store anymore. I need to be with her, and my damn grandfather can kiss my ass."

I couldn't help but smile at his attitude. Aroha was right; there was more of me in him than I had previously seen. I would do whatever it would take to protect Callie, for she was his life now, and over these past months, he had become mine. I was free to be the father I had always wanted to be, and I was not going to let that feeling go. I would never let myself be bound by war again. I would choose to dabble—because I was good at it and old habits die hard—but at least now I could choose. To wake up and realize I had my own autonomy—there was no going back.

The future felt less daunting than this moment, when I had to tell my son what Callie had done. "Like I said, she's alive, but she needs you in order to be well."

His eyes fully opened, and his smile faded. "Are you going to leave me in suspense, or should I just go check on her myself?"

In front of mortals, we had to choose our words carefully, so explaining exactly what Callie had done was tricky. "She uh...opened a box...and..." Hang it! I couldn't reword this, so I leaned in and spoke at immortal speed and quietly enough to not be heard by mortal ears. "She opened Persephone's Box, and she's in a coma." I sat back, trying not to cringe, awaiting an outburst.

Archer's face went blank. He stared down at his hands. I gave him a moment to digest the information. It was a sore spot. My lovely wife had tortured the abandoned Psyche some three thousand years ago and made her do tedious things. We'd all had a laugh at Dite by helping Psyche along, but we didn't bank on the girl being vain enough to open a box she thought was full of beauty. Dite had lied, of course, and it had been full of eternal sleep. In modern times, that was called a coma.

"Why?" Archer asked me.

Not much to go on, kid. I had no clue what he was asking me.

I took a stab at explaining. "She didn't leave a note, so I don't think she was..." I couldn't say any more. A lump formed in my throat as I thought about what I had barely stopped my son from doing.

I hadn't given myself any time to even grasp what Archer had almost done. I could've lost him. It was a helpless and horrific feeling, a war I couldn't win unless I got him Callie. Mental wars were the hardest to overcome.

"I mean, why is it happening again?"

My spear, I wanted to tell him the truth, that Psyche was Callie's ancestor, but I couldn't. He was happy for the first time in months. But there was more to my hesitancy; there was no causality. Cause and effect. Every maneuver of every battle has actions and reactions. This was not a clear-cut cause-and-effect situation.

I spoke low and quickly. "Psyche was duped by your mother's twisted, overprotective mind. Callie—my guess, and we'll find out when she wakes—might have purposely repeated history to force your return."

Archer let out a breath. His mood seemed to improve. "I knew this would happen."

I was worried he had cracked. "How?"

"I saw it."

This was definitely worrisome. My son was no oracle. "Again, how?"

"Well, I didn't see her do it, but I saw something that made me know I'd wake her."

"You mean she told you?"

"No. Months ago, she saw us...getting married. I can somehow enter her dreams if I go in her mind while she sleeps. I had thought it was wishful thinking, a fantasy of hers." Archer depicted the scene he saw in enough detail for me to take him on his word. I listened intently as Archer boasted of Callie's abilities with admiration and pride.

I couldn't share the excitement. She was definitely useful—I'd give her that, since she'd saved my son's life twice now through premonition—but Callie shouldn't have been able to predict events with such clarity. The mind reading was weird enough, especially how she got into Archer's mind when her father couldn't; no demigod ever had before. Heck, most of us immortals couldn't read each others' minds. And the premonitions on top of it were downright unheard of.

I just listened instead of pointing anything out to Archer that might alter his positive mood. I didn't want to tell him I knew they would marry, that Lucien had told me the truth, the prophecy he saw, and that devastation and death could be the result for some. I had so many questions, but Archer's chatter blotted them out. He was full of questions I couldn't answer, concerns I could hardly ease, until he settled on the topic of future plans, most of them unlikely to nearly impossible. I listened, nonetheless, for the two flights and three-hour layover. It was a pleasant change to see him happy. I tried to ease his worries and offered my support. As strange as this was, I meant it. After decades, almost a century, where he was only a blip in my thoughts, my son was becoming the center of my world. It had been the same long ago when he was born and no one but Dite and I knew he was mine. This was how a parent should love his child, yet that warmongering part of me rarely had allowed it.

A couple times before, I'd had this paternal, this familial pang, and I couldn't figure out why. I'm not a terrible god, but war would distract me from what was more important. The longest period of time was the few decades around Archer's birth up until he went off on his own with Psyche. I had been a family man—mostly. Aroha and I always had fidelity problems, but I had a feeling this time we might stick. I wondered if our odd freedom meant Dite and I could still have a baby. My father controlled everything, even policing Olympian fertility. I had always wondered if he'd allowed Archer to be born to give me Dite. He hated Heph, the reminder of my mother's only indiscretion. Or had he lost control, and Archer was the fruit of freedom and love?

"Chase." Archer looked at me oddly.

"Reliving the past, sorry."

"No wonder you were gone so long," he joked. To see that smile on his face was priceless, although his joke was lame. "We're here."

Sure enough, we were on the tarmac, pulling up to the gate, and I hadn't even noticed the plane landing. I had always been called the brooding type, but I preferred the term "thoughtful" with an intimidating face. People see a temper, and they assume someone is shallow and impulsive, when really they are deep thinkers with aggression issues that have built up so long they boil over. That was me.

We met Aroha in the airport lobby, after clearing customs. She was exquisite, as always. She ran to me as I hurried to her, and I wrapped my arms around her. She clung hard, and I realized, underneath her false bravado, she was cracking, exhausted, and in need of my support. I pulled away and held her face in my hands, examining that breathtaking beauty that wowed me every time I beheld her. Every single time was like the first.

Words stuck in my throat. "You look...amazing."

Aroha blinked back tears and laughed. "Of course I do."

I kissed her.

"Gross," Archer moaned, shuffling beside us awkwardly.

I let go of her, reluctantly. Aroha didn't pull Archer in for a hug or dote on him in her usually overbearing nature, treating him like her eternal child. She even avoided his gaze. Something was up with her.

Archer tried to pry her now-crossed arms apart so he could hug her. "No need to get offended. I was joking. I missed you."

She finally met his gaze, biting her lip nervously—a tell-tale sign she'd majorly messed up.

He let go of her. "What did you do, Aroha?" So adept to his mother's moods, Archer beat me to it.

"Maybe not here," I suggested, nodding toward all the mortals milling around us.

Archer looked like he was about to explode from being denied the info, so I pushed him toward the exit and then reached my other hand back for my wife. She intertwined her fingers in mine. We hurried outside as slowly as mortals would. Once we were out of the building and in the shadows, Archer pulled up, starting to defy gravity. I yanked him back down.

"What are you doing?" he demanded.

"You're not dangling us up in the air at an airport, Turtle." I used the nickname I'd had for him as a kid.

The Greeks had been very meaningful and creative in their worship and ascribed us many symbols, one being a dove to my son, which at the time did not float well with me. Back then, I wanted my first born to be symbolized as something powerful, manly, so I altered it to turtle dove, then turtle for short. I mean, when your symbols are strong animals that attack or defend themselves well—boars, vultures, and dogs—or weapons, you don't want your first-born son to be likened to a pretty little weak bird.

"And your old pet names for me won't spare Ma." Archer yanked her from my grasp. "What did you do?" he shouted.

Mortals were looking.

I snaked my arm around his neck and yanked him back into the parking garage area. I let him go once I noted the security cameras and pushed him against the wall. His eyes were aglow, as were mine. "Don't lay a hand on your mother. Use whatever words you wish, I'll grant you that, but do not harm her."

Archer swallowed hard, and his eyes dimmed down slightly. "There's the war *hero* I'm used to, the tyrant who commanded me, walked out on me time and time again." His words stung. They were honest and true, which was why they wounded my pride.

This wasn't good, though. We couldn't afford to fight amongst ourselves.

"We need to stick together, Archer. Let her talk. Then you can say what you will."

He took a deep breath and seemed to relax. Aroha looked terrified. I had never seen her cower at Archer before, always being a complete matriarch of the house, which made us butt heads often. Still, I wouldn't have it any other way. I love a strong woman.

"Oh Archer." Her voice wavered. "I didn't mean to..."

Seeing Archer was ready to scream, and I was impatient myself, I urged her on. "Dite, get it out."

"Callie was talking about being able to read our minds, and I didn't believe her. Us! You know? She caught me at a bad moment. I was deeply disturbed by you going to Heph to try to die, Archer. I blamed her. I shouldn't have, I know. I challenged her to read my mind, and bad thoughts just popped out. I thought of the impossible tasks and Persephone's box—I'm sorry."

"Dite," I chided before Archer could speak. "What were you thinking? You knew the box was sitting there in the glass case in her living room! Do you ever think before you speak?"

"I wasn't speaking, was I? I was thinking. I can't stop thinking before I think!"

True, but she still didn't need to have such cruel thoughts. I loved the woman, but time and time again, she disappointed me with her lack of empathy and her self-centeredness.

"Stop," Archer finally said. He was oddly calm. "Everything is happening for a reason."

"What?" Aroha looked more upset at his response than she had been at mine. She wanted his wrath. The only reason I could imagine was to feel better about what she'd done.

"If Callie couldn't read minds and you didn't think of the box, then I'd be..." He didn't need to finish. In a twisted way, he was right. Aroha's catty thoughts had inadvertently saved his life.

"Archer," Aroha sobbed, holding her arms out for a hug.

"It doesn't mean I forgive you. Lucky for you, Callie foresaw what will happen. I'll wake her. Let's get to the hospital."

"Visiting hours, Archer," she said quietly, avoiding looking at either of us in her shame.

"They can't stop me."

"Discretion, Archer. You can't wake her and stay by her side unless it's visiting hours," I pointed out.

"It's midnight. Hours start at nine," Aroha said. "I've been there every day, feeding her fluids and their protein shakes, drops at a time. Her dad refused the IV because he said she was terrified of needles after her last hospital stint."

Archer looked as if nine hours would kill him.

I was suspicious but couldn't voice it, because Archer was about to throw a fit. I grabbed his shoulder. "Nine hours for a lifetime."

"Mine or hers?"

"I will do my best to protect her for the rest of her life. If I can work a miracle, forever. I promise the first and hope for the latter," I told him.

He growled but motioned for me to lead the way to show he was giving in to the wait.

On the way to their apartment, I pondered over our predicament. But what my wife had said niggled my mind more than what the future could hold. Why no IV? Dr. Syches suspected or knew something we didn't. Perhaps my thoughts were simply wishful thinking, because there was no logic behind my suspicions.

Back at Aroha's apartment, Archer secluded himself in his room to sort through the rest of his things. Without discussing it, he knew we'd have to flee, to hide, to start afresh. Things would need to be sold or disposed of, some put in storage, and we'd have to discreetly send some to Belize via Iris. He'd packed light. Long ago, we'd all agreed to limit our necessities—meaning things we cannot live without—to one box. Mine was in Belize at the moment, consisting of portraits of all my children, one of Dite, and tiny keepsakes from every major war I'd won: arrow- or spearheads, bullets, bomb fragments, and the like. I was suddenly curious what was in Archer's.

"Ares." Aroha gave me her best attempt of pouty remorse.

I was beginning to hate that name. It didn't feel like me anymore, but there were bigger fish to fry, like chiding my wife for her behavior. "Really foolish, darling. Callie is not the type to have airs, to lie for no reason. She's a wholesome, sweet girl."

"Are we really going to let him wake her?"

"Do we even have a choice?" I realized too late she was deflecting away from her mistake. Dite was never wrong...in her world.

"I meant more of what will happen? What will Zeus do?"

I shrugged. "We almost lost our last child, Dite. He will do it again unless we can keep Callie alive. The only war I'm prepping for is one of self-defense. No more seeking war. You and Archer are my life now." I felt as if I were reaffirming ancient vows. "And can you call me Chase? I don't feel like Ares anymore."

Realizing I had lost my resolve to chastise her, she draped her arms over my shoulders, facing me so I was forced to see her beautiful face. With my lips only a mere six inches from hers, I was distracted by her charm.

"How will you keep them safe?" Her words yanked me back out of my smitten stupor.

"The less you know, the better."

"You don't trust me." There was that pout of hers again that killed me. I kissed it away.

"Chase, seriously."

I sighed. "You will need to stay here with Lucien, watch over the father."

She was crushed at the news.

"Zeus will expect you, me, and Archer together, but she'll be hidden before he realizes we are apart. I will be off in another direction, a distraction, and I hope to gain a powerful ally." I was vague, not affirming where any of us were headed so Zeus couldn't torture it out of her. I wouldn't put it past him to hurt any of us at this point.

"So, Archer will be left on his own?"

I shook my head. "I've gotten some help. Don't you worry about it, and it's only temporary. If I can lock in the ally I need, we'll have a place to be for a long time. I'll come for you then. Zeus won't be able to get to any of us, but—"

"There it is," she muttered, "the infamous 'but.'"

I ignored her quip and continued, "But we will all be at great risk for a few days."

"I'd feel better if one of us were with him," Dite protested, pulling me closer by my jacket.

"We'll discuss it later."

"We'll discuss it now in my room." She knew I was now deferring.

How and why were relationships like treaty agreements? The way her hands smoothed across the planes of my chest, I knew exactly what she was up to. I'd let her amend my plans because I wanted to be convinced. I had missed her to distraction. When her lips came into contact with mine, I scooped her up in my arms—tried not to come undone by her squeal of delight—and was in her room at immortal speed.

The next morning, Archer was banging on Aroha's door at 6:30 AM. His hair was cropped very short—thankfully, because I didn't think the frizzy puffball hair he'd been sporting since Monteserrat had pleased my stylish wife. The beard was gone too, making him look more like my boy again rather than the unhinged man I'd been dealing with. There was no point in protesting his insistence that he must go to the hospital earlier than visiting hours, so we waited in the lobby for an hour before we were allowed to see Callie. Archer went off for a few minutes to talk to Dr. Syches, and when they came back, they both seemed happy. I wasn't sure what that was about, but Archer's furtive look told me I'd have to wait until later.

Finally, we headed upstairs to the waiting room in the ICU wing, since only two at a time were allowed in to see her. It didn't matter as Callie was stationed in the nearest room. The nurse came knowingly toward us, batting her eyes and smiling at my son as if he were the most adorable creature on the face of the earth. At that moment, Love exuding love and hope, he probably was irresistible to all mortals.

When she turned around to usher Archer and Dr. Syches in, someone was suddenly there in her way: Lucien. The poor nurse's mortal eyes betrayed her, but we had seen him zip up the hallway from the other direction at immortal speed.

The woman flustered as Lucien gave her a smile and said some flirty quip, and she went on her way, giggling and flapping the file in her hand as a makeshift fan. Lucien stood between Archer and the door to Callie's room, clearly blocking Archer from the only thing he lived for in this world. This would not go well. Part of me wanted to pummel Lucien into the ground, but the rational part of me knew people were watching.

"Archer, you can't. She'll die. Be rational," Lucien said, but there was nothing logical to what he was saying. When had the god of truth argued with emotion? Lucien's arms were crossed, and he backed into the door so there was no way around him.

"Move," Archer said. His calm unnerved me, like a wild animal that appears tame, only to launch itself at its prey seconds later.

"You can't let him do this," Lucien pleaded, looking at each of us in turn.

No one spoke, not even Callie's father.

Archer stared Lucien down, and Lucien began to falter. I knew firsthand the power of my son's gaze to move, dissuade, cajole, upset, or intimidate those who have beheld that luminous gaze. I often used the power myself.

The glow, whatever innate gift I had been given that I passed down to him—our eyes held a power not even we could understand. It was a gift of the Fates, my mother would boast, and my father had always been unnerved by it. He hated me. Many times, I think my father worried I would overthrow him, because if anyone could, it would be me. My mother wasn't very fond of me either, but she liked to brag a good deal, so I was that token-child since Hebe was a bit chill and boring, truth be told. Heph was her favorite, of course. Anyone could have foreseen that the resentment and cold attitude of my parents would've set me up to be consumed by the love Dite could offer me. I never had a love like that until her, and now, I would finally be able to reciprocate that sentiment to others. If anything was worth warring with Olympus over, it was love.

Archer walked up to Lucien, right into him, their shoulders bumping hard, and he shoved Lucien out of the way, discreetly making it appear as a simple bump. Instead of protesting, Lucien gave way and let Archer by. There were too many mortal nurses eyeing us up like candy to start a fight. I ignored the ones eyeballing my wife.

And so we waited.

"I can't believe you all." Lucien sulked.

"She'd never wake up if he hadn't come back, Lucien." Aroha soothingly rubbed his shoulder.

"She could have," he shot back, defensively shrugging her hand off his shoulder.

Aroha withdrew her hand quickly. "This isn't even about Callie. Your attitude is because you couldn't wake her, and you wished you could. Only true love can wake her, Lucien."

He said nothing in response but stared at the floor, his silence a full admission.

My wife continued, "Don't be such a selfish little snob. You know this is the only way for her to have a life from here on out."

"Takes a snob to know one. We wouldn't be in this predicament if it weren't for you. I know she read your thoughts, and they most likely were as selfish and cruel as you always are, Aroha. You drove her to this." Lucien spoke truths as expected.

"Hey, enough, you two," I interjected. I would not pick sides, for they were both right. "Fighting about it won't help. We need to stick together to protect her."

"Ha!" Lucien shook his head, laughing. "The god of war creating peace. Laughable."

"Shhh!" Dr. Syches said. "I heard something."

I strained my immortal ears, trying to hear what was going on in the hospital room. Was that two voices?

CHAPTER 25

Archer

When I walked in the hospital room, I hadn't thought about what I might see. Sure, Callie in a hospital bed was a given. I had expected her to be frail, almost lifeless, pale, and emaciated. It's the kind of thing television puts into our heads. It had only been around the latest century of my life, but these visual inventions really left an impression. Instead, she was breathtakingly beautiful. Callie looked as if she'd decided to take a nap; her natural beauty had never needed the assistance of makeup. There were wires hooked up for her heart rate and oxygen levels, but no tubes. There was no cannula, so she didn't need oxygen. She simply was asleep. Persephone's sleep, only breakable through love—the one loophole the goddess had never foreseen when crafting her box to punish the person who attempted to steal her valuables back during the Hellenistic era.

I couldn't stop staring at Callie, drinking up the sight of her. She was my life force. The rhythm of her heart on the vital signs monitor was in tandem with my own, or perhaps mine shifted to match hers. I felt myself pulled in toward her. I was by her bedside with one fleeting adrenaline rush of worry: what if it didn't work?

There was only one way to find out. I stood over her and took her hand in mine. "Callie," I breathed out. To say her name in her presence, to be here right now, touching her, when only hours ago, I had been prepared to die—I had no idea how to deal with the emotions inside me. I felt as if I'd burst.

I leaned down and kissed each of her eyelids, trying to ignore the déjà vu feeling that crept up my spine. Over three thousand years ago, I'd done this very act to save a very different woman I had loved then. The parallels echoed in time, unnerving me.

I drew back, hovering over her slightly, awaiting some kind of reaction; her eyes fluttered and snapped open. When I touched her cheek, my happiness overflowed, rendering me speechless. Her eyes danced about until they locked on mine.

We were frozen for a moment, both of us unable to speak, to unload the plethora of feelings that had built up inside us, to get over the time that was missed, to think coherent thoughts. Thousands of years of life, and I never could be prepared for a moment such as this.

Callie's other hand shakily reached up to touch me, and I met her halfway, pressing my cheek into her palm. It was not an endearing gesture but inquisitive; she was double-checking I was real.

"Am I dead?" she asked, her voice raspy. She smiled wide. I couldn't help but smile back. Seeing her happy made me lightheaded. Then the smile faded. She thought she was dead.

I grabbed up the Styrofoam cup, which rested by her bedside, poured some water in it from the plastic ice water pitcher, and stuck a straw in it. I placed the straw between her lips. "No, Callie, you're alive and well now."

Callie drank a couple sips, and then she pushed it away. Then her hand slid up my shoulder to my face. I had to restrain the urge to devour Callie's mouth and lie in the bed with her. I wanted to begin where we had left off, coma be damned.

And so did she, it seemed. She pulled me down to her, and our lips met. I tried to kiss her gently, but the way she kissed me broke me into a fervor of passion. It was as if we were compensating for every lost moment, every missed kiss.

I tore myself away first. "Callie, you were in a coma. Take it easy."

She finally took in her surroundings as if she hadn't realized she was in the hospital until then. "You kept your promise," she referred to my promise to see her one more time before she died.

The first tendril of regret wrapped around me. My presence, my coming to wake her might start some immortal clock that would count down her life—one year or less—since I breached my punishment terms. "You broke yours," I tried to scold her, but it came out weak.

She gripped my hand tightly. How could she fathom I would leave her side? "I'm sorry." She looked away in shame. "I thought it would make you come back to me. I didn't care if I died either; I won't lie. I had to stop you from climbing. Why would you, Archer?"

"I couldn't continue..." My breaths were rapid and shallow, full of emotion. "Not without you."

Her eyes welled up.

"Please. Don't cry." I couldn't handle much more emotion at the moment. "Callie, I've broken the rules, the verdict, I mean. My grandfather might hunt us down. He most likely will try to kill us, but I couldn't live without you. I'd rather cease to exist than to be apart from you one more day. And from the state of things, you seem to feel the same." My feelings came out of me without a filter.

I awaited a thunder peal for Zeus to indicate he was starting the doomsday clock on Callie's life or, worse, a flash of lightning announcing his presence. Nothing came.

"I don't know how much time we have together, but I want every second to count. I want to marry you, Callie, and spend whatever time we have left, together, with you as my wife."

Callie took in a sharp breath. The monitor showed a rapidly accelerating heart rate. Her mouth dropped. I had gone too far. I'd already gained her father's permission—after a short debate over how young she was—reasoning she would be safest with me, and he would be more comfortable knowing we were married if we were to flee New York without his supervision. I thought my proposal was secure, but this long pause Callie was giving me made me wonder if she wasn't ready.

"Say something," I pleaded.

"Oh, yes. Sorry. I was stunned. I want to marry you, a million times over." Then she sat up with energy I didn't know she had and hugged me to her tightly.

I held her to me, breathing in her scent—devoid of laundry detergent, perfumes, or body spray, just Callie. She smelled glorious, and I noted scents of flowers, honey, and sunshine. I pulled away to be showered by her kisses. I returned them and made sure to end on her lips again. Oh, how I had longed for and missed them.

When I finally drew away, she said, "I knew you'd come back if I opened the box."

I didn't want to point out how her stunt and my father's rescue mission had cut it much too close. "Callie, you should be mad at me. I'm putting your life on the line out of pure selfishness." We gods always act out of pure self-interest, part of the power trip we got being deities, I suppose.

"I could never be mad at you. And you're wrong. We had no life apart. Maybe we're sad and pathetic that way, but it's true."

"I know you are right, but it doesn't assuage my guilt." Although the guilt should've been unfathomable, I couldn't quite feel it yet. Seeing Callie, holding her, being back with her, made me much too happy to see the negatives of the situation.

A knock on the door told us someone else was eager to see her. Her father poked his head in. I tried to slip away. I was serious about marrying her instantly and needed to get things settled.

Callie's hand clamped on mine. "Don't."

"I won't leave. Just let me pop outside to tell them you are awake."

She looked like she didn't want to give in, but once her frail father hobbled into the room and took her up in his arms, she let go of my hand, and I slipped out.

My parents took in my face, and what they saw made my father beam and my mother start bawling—tears of relief most likely—and she threw herself into my father's arms. Lucien's look was indiscernible, a mixture of resentment, anger, relief, happiness, and who-knew-what-else.

The doctors ushered her father out, and there was a battery of tests. After my parents popped in to see her briefly, they left, and Lucien went with them. Callie's father and I remained with her until the afternoon, when they had no choice but to release her from the hospital because she was completely healthy.

As soon as we got her settled at home, Ma and Dad came over with a grumpy Lucien. I don't know why he bothered coming if he was so resentful of my return. I wanted to call him out, but I was still giddy with all the pleasant feelings one experiences when seeing the love of his life after such a long parting.

Aroha discreetly slipped me the tiny box, and I put it in my pocket before Callie could see. Lucien saw, of course, and his eyes narrowed. He said nothing. I found myself wishing he would leave so I could properly propose to Callie without him ruining the moment with his brooding negativity. I had only told her my feelings, and she said she wanted to marry me, but then the subject dropped. There would be lots of quick planning needed.

I wanted to be alone with her, but no one would let us. They were worried about Zeus coming for us, and frankly, I was on edge, awaiting Hermes or thunder warnings. My parents were so worried; Ma mortifyingly stationed herself outside of Callie's bathroom while she showered and stayed with her while she dressed. This did nothing to relax her father, who hounded my father about what could be done to protect her. He already knew I wanted to marry her and had given me his blessing, but I hadn't told him we were leaving New York almost immediately.

Callie came out, her hair wet and smelling of flowers. I pulled her onto my lap and leaned toward her, just smelling her. Under all the flowery soaps and body spray, I could smell her scent, something I had longed for and missed.

"We're in danger now?" she asked.

I nodded. "But we couldn't make it apart. From here on out, we stay together."

"Will we be on the run?"

"Chase promises to find a safehouse we can settle into. We could be fine for years."

"She won't be fine, Archer. She needs medical attention all the time, and hospitals register their patients. How long do you think it will take Hermes to hack and find her?" Lucien said. Gods, I wanted to punch him for raining on my parade.

"What, I don't have practice with making fake identities?" I shot back.

Lucien crossed his arms. "I'm not going with you, so you'll need to *use* someone else to keep her fevers at bay."

I frowned and looked to my parents. They hadn't known he was parting ways either.

"No one was using you, Lucien, but maybe it's for the best," I told him.

He looked at me guiltily.

"You can't be happy for us, and we'll be sickeningly happy. It would be torture." For him.

He looked to the floor, blushing. I embarrassed him, but I needed him to know I understood and didn't undervalue his heartache.

"We'll figure the fevers out," Aroha said.

A knock at the door made us all jump. Callie went rigid, most likely remembering what happened the last time we were in this situation and Hermes came for me. It was exactly what was going through my mind at that moment. We all peered around at each other, but no one said a thing or made a move.

Lucien's eyes were closed, the only one cool-headed enough to check. "Mortal." He opened his eyes and looked at Callie. "Dan."

Callie growled and stood up. I got up and followed her.

She turned to me, bemused. "You can't come to the door. He thinks you're dead."

"Well, maybe it's time for him to know I'm not dead. Give him some real closure."

"Or a heart attack," she muttered, making me laugh.

"I'll stay out of view. I just want to make sure you're safe."

"Dan won't hurt me," she scoffed. "Plus, Raphael won't leave my side." She pointed to the servant, who was opening the door.

I darted behind it as he opened it. I was afraid of gods being right outside the door with Eagen.

She turned her attention to Eagen, who stood in the doorway. "Dan," she greeted. Did she sound a little too sweet and receptive?

I frowned. That was how Callie was—all kindness—but Eagen would get the wrong idea.

Eagen stepped forward, and Raphael pressed the door closed a bit, giving me the perfect view through the crack between the door and wall. Eagen gawked at him.

Callie laughed awkwardly. "Umm, he's a bit overprotective, but who can blame him after my coma? I can't talk long."

"How are you feeling? We were all so scared you would never wake up. Linda and I visited you twice. I brought you flowers, the wildflower bouquet. They seemed...you." Eagen was turning red and floundering.

"Thank you. That was kind of you. I'm feeling good, great actually. Sorry I worried everyone with all my health drama."

"Don't apologize. I should apologize." He hesitated, all too well aware of Raphael's presence.

Raphael was looking around, trying to make it seem as if he weren't listening, making the moment even more awkward for the kid—not that I minded.

"The other day..." Eagen sighed. "I was unreasonably jealous, especially of your dad. You should be spending the summer with him."

Guilt crept over me. There was no way Callie's father could leave New York with his treatment and feeble state, and there was no way to protect Callie from Zeus here. I was tearing her away from her last days with her father, something this guy was apologizing for not understanding.

"It's fine." Callie's voice was hollow and weak. Her thoughts must've been aligned with mine.

"If I didn't say those things about your dad and Archer, you and I might be—"

"No, Dan. Please stop. You know I'm not over Archer—"

"I'll wait for you. However long it takes," Eagen said, desperation seeping into his voice.

"You can't."

"You can't tell me that. I know you think you'll never get over him, but—"

"I won't. Dan he's—"

I couldn't miss the perfect opportunity, so I stepped out of my hiding spot and said, "Alive."

Eagen went white as a sheet, his mouth agog, as he scanned me to make sure I was real. "How? What? You died in a fire."

I was glad he let that slip out, because I'd never thought to ask how I had "died" to the mortals here. I invented a story on the spot. "There was a fire, but I made it out. I hit my head hard while escaping and had temporary amnesia. I still don't remember everything, but I was able to recall my family and find my way home."

"That kind of thing only happens in movies." Eagen glared.

He was right. I should've gone for third degree burns that needed grafting and a long hospital stay, but I didn't have the scars to corroborate that story either. "It happens. It's called retrograde amnesia."

Callie gave me a stern look of warning. She was not happy with my antics. The sooner we got rid of Eagen, the sooner we could get things moving and leave New York. I needed her safe.

In hindsight, the dramatic reveal had been too much. I just couldn't quell the jealous beast in me and wanted to see him forget about her. He had spent time with Callie. He had loved her and tried to take her away from me. I'd even tried to let him. He had treated her badly due to his jealousy. Gods' resentment ran deep. I mean, look what Athena had done to Medusa.

"So, you're just back together, like that?" He snapped his fingers. "After all that he put you through?" He shifted his attention to Callie.

"He didn't do it on purpose!" Callie snapped. She'd had enough too.

I tried to rub the tension out of her shoulders.

"So, what happens when you decide to ditch her again?" he asked me, then directed his attention to Callie. "I might not be around as a shoulder for you to cry on when he comes back with another bullshit story while he probably was chatting up chicks wherever the hell he went."

"I never asked you to be that shoulder. I kept telling you I only wanted to be friends." Callie crossed her arms defiantly.

"I won't be leaving her, for your information. We will be going abroad for a while, an extended honeymoon of sorts," I said to wound him.

It was cruel, but he was delusional. I believed Callie, that she would never purposely give him false hope or lead him on. The relationship he'd had with Callie was all in his head.

"Honeymoon?" he choked out.

Callie's eyes were wide as saucers and boring into me.

"Well, she said she'd marry me, and I was going to properly propose, but you kind of interrupted."

Callie's mouth dropped, and she kept staring at me, trying to see if I was joking or if I was for real. Then she suppressed a smile as Eagen awkwardly shuffled to leave.

"Well. Uh...I'll just go. Glad to see you finally happy again, Callie. I hope you stay that way." Eagen's tone chided me as if I would make her miserable. He had sort of been a friend, but that was clearly over now.

Raphael closed the door and locked it. She smacked me in the stomach with the back of her hand and gave me a glare, but then she was grinning.

"What?" I feigned confusion.

"Bit overdramatic, no?"

We were alone in the foyer. The others would hear us, but at least I didn't have to see their faces while I officially popped the question. I pulled her into my arms to stop her from walking into the room.

"Telling him we're getting married," she scoffed.

"Well, we are since, you know, you said you'd be my wife."

Her smile dropped to a quizzical expression. "I thought you meant down the line, not now."

"I was thinking more like tomorrow if that's good for you?" I really shouldn't tease her so when really this was to be a serious moment, but I couldn't help myself. I was bubbling with mischievous bliss.

I went down on my knee, took out the little box, and opened it, revealing the ancient ring. It was gold with our Greek meander around the bezel, which held a warm red stone—carnelian—that had an engraving of a winged me on it. Heph had forged this long ago.

Callie's hands shot to cover her mouth, and her eyes danced from the ring to my eyes and back several times.

"We already know we cannot live without each other, that we would rather die than part again. It makes sense that we ensure we are together forever. Callista Syches, will you marry me?"

She still didn't speak, and I grew nervous. She was young, and it was sudden. Would she want a longer engagement? My heart started beating rapidly in suspense. Then she nodded, blinking back tears.

I was up and pulling her into my arms, kissing her. "Tomorrow?"

She nodded, then grinned as I slid the ring on her finger. It fit perfectly, showing me that this was meant to be. "Can we even get a wedding put together by tomorrow?"

"Oh, I can," Aroha pulled Callie into the living room, hugging her. "You should never underestimate the gods."

There were congratulations all around; Raphael hunted around for champagne, and we all settled down because Aroha wanted to lose no time in making wedding plans.

Lucien remained standing, pensively staring at the ring until he glared at me with pure hatred. Although the rage burning in his eyes was misplaced, he recognized the ring. "Unbelievable!"

The entire room went quiet. Smiles dropped from faces.

"That was *her* ring, Callie. Psyche's!" With those words, Lucien ruined my proposal.

Did he live to spoil everything? I no longer felt bad for his grieving heart, but fury at his petty jealousy and desperate attempts to break us up. It was clear this friendship of thousands of years had come to a close.

CHAPTER 26

This was self-inflicted torture. Part of me wanted to watch Archer and Callie together, probably hoping to find flaws in their seemingly perfect love. Another part of me was trying to accept that I had no chance with Callie. Somehow, my stubborn brain wouldn't let go of the idea of a chance, no matter how slim.

What bothered me most about seeing the two of them cuddling, Callie on the couch, lying back on Archer with his arms wrapped around her as if holding her together, were the lies—hidden truths—between them. What was eight months of a relationship when only two months of it were spent together?

Two months, and he had proposed. She'd said yes. They were getting married. Archer was making the same mistakes he had before, and no one was pointing it out to him. How would he react if he knew he was marrying his dead ex-wife's descendant? Would he go through with it? And had he even told Callie the real dangers of their marriage? That Archer was being selfish, and Zeus would kill her? All it would take was one bolt of lightning.

No, they did know these things, and they didn't care. They were in *love*. They were beyond rationalizing in their fantasy land. They would both agree to marry, even if they would die tomorrow. Hearts and hormones. Ridiculous.

Then I saw that all-too-familiar ring. It was ancient, the type of ring we had given to our beloveds when we exchanged vows, a wedding ring. It was the emblem of Eros—sometimes just Eros, him with Psyche as a butterfly, or a couple little winged cupids. We gods gave out many, but this one I distinctly remembered as Psyche's ring. It was preposterous and disgusting. Archer had no clue he was marrying the echo of his former wife and yet wanted to put the same ring on her finger.

I lost it. I burst out in front of everyone, shouting it was Psyche's ring. Callie was horror-struck and gazed at the ring; Archer looked confused, feigning it most likely; Aroha and Chase were furious, and Callie's father looked disappointed in me.

No one spoke.

Dr. Syches cleared his throat. "Correct me if I'm wrong—as I was not alive like you—but I believe I've never heard of rings given in marriage until Roman times. Before that, it was just a token of love or promise, or signets."

He was right, but still the ring was familiar.

"You really are a clever man," Aroha marveled. "And completely right. This wasn't a wedding ring—"

"Engagement, a token of love, whatever. I remember that ring. I had Heph make it for you. It's Psyche's!" I pressed.

"It was one of the most common ring patterns in all of Greece for hundreds of years, Lucien." Chase talked down to me as if I were a child. I wanted to tackle him for his condescension.

"Everyone, stop!" Callie shouted. "Whose ring was this? I know it wasn't made for me on this short of notice, and it does look ancient."

"Call it a family heirloom," Archer said quietly.

"Archer, you can't give that to her. You can't recycle a marriage and pretend she's Psyche."

"I'm not!" Archer was up so fast, Callie was shocked as she was unceremoniously dumped on the sofa. He grabbed me up by my shirt and pinned me to the wall.

I shoved him, knocking him off-balance into one of the display cases, glass splintering everywhere.

"Stop it!" Callie rushed to Archer's side as I was yanked back by immortal hands—Chase's—and my arms restrained behind my body.

I gave up. Been there. Done that. He was the strongest god, so what was the point in fighting?

"Calm down, everyone." Aroha had her hands out as if we were rabid animals she was trying to tame.

"I'm calm," I ground out.

Chase let me go but shoved me down into the loveseat.

Archer was cradling Callie's arm. She had a small shard of glass in it. He tried to pull her closer, but she pushed him away.

"Archer, you're bleeding everywhere." She backed away from him, Raphael gently cradling and examining her arm, then helping her to the bathroom.

Archer inventoried the damage to himself. His arms were embedded with glass. From wrists to elbow, ichor leached out, burning holes into parts of his shirt.

Aroha shot me a nasty look. "Shooting false accusations, ruining Dr. Syche's artifacts, and now look at him." She gingerly led Archer to the sofa and began helping him pull out the shards as fast as their immortal hands could.

Dr. Syches was blinking, his mortal eyes too slow to keep up.

"Chase, help me before they heal and we have to dig them out," Aroha said.

Chase was over at lightning speed, and Archer's parents helped him remove the shards, placing them on the table. They finished in about the same time it took for Raphael and Callie to remove the glass from her arm, bandage her, and return from the other room.

Callie stood watching, fascinated as Archer's wounds healed instantly. She was pale. Dr. Syches and Raphael exchanged a coded look I couldn't comprehend. The servant nodded.

"What in Hades was that all about?" Chase asked all of us, exasperated.

"Is this Psyche's ring?" Callie demanded, staring Archer down.

He swallowed hard and shook his head. *Liar.* He stood and took up her hands. "No. As your father pointed out, we didn't often exchange rings back when I married Psyche, nor did I gift it later. But Lucien is freaking out because he did go to Heph for me to have it made. He's just senile in his old age. He forgets he was not my best friend when I was with Psyche." The joke was told in a scathing tone, so no one laughed. "Callie, it was a gift I had made for my daughter, but she didn't live to receive it. It's a long story, but she would never marry, so I thought to gift her with a token of my love. She was lonely."

"Why couldn't she marry?" Callie asked him.

"She preferred the fairer sex, and it was illegal among the mortals then," Archer told her.

Like my sister Artemis, Hedone had preferred the company of women, but had it been made for her? So many memories jumbled together. Too many trips made by me for rings for mortals I'd later desert.

"Oh," Callie said quietly. "That's sad for her."

"I'll get you another ring if it bothers you. I just thought since it was for my daughter, I'd give it to my wife in trust for my next daughter. Hedone was my everything, literally joy embodied, and you are my everything now. I wasn't thinking reuse, but a rebirth of my love."

So nauseating, and yet from her teary eyes, Callie was lapping up his "romantic" nonsense. She pulled him in for a kiss that didn't seem to end. I couldn't stomach it, this much cheese-grating lovey-dovey symbolic crap. They'd forgive each other of anything in their state.

I looked away to see four other pairs of mortal and immortal eyes judging me. Then it hit me. I was an ass. It really was Hedone's ring, forged by Heph in the 1500s, which took quite some convincing since he hated Eros. The ring mimicked our ancient rings to remind Hedone her father was the male who would always love her and be there for her. Unlike my sister, who surrounded herself with a lot of adoring females, Hedone had felt ashamed, rejecting her nature for a long time. Archer had planned to give it to her for her birthday, a big one—maybe her two thousand and five hundredth had been coming up? It was hard to remember time, but she had died before she ever received it.

Even Archer's cheesy line about not finding love or joy after his daughter's death until Callie was true. It made perfect sense. I had been clouded by my own feelings. The desire to tell him who Callie's ancestor was faded with the self-discovery that I was too biased to proceed with anything.

"I'm sorry." It rose out of my mouth like bile. "Yeah, I'll go." I hurried to the door.

Callie rushed after me, grasping my hand. I looked down at it, wanting to kiss it, wanting to kiss her, and hating myself for it. She bewitched me. What was she?

"Please, no matter what you're thinking right now, be there tomorrow for the wedding. You are his best friend, and these past few months, you've been mine."

Tell him, I mouthed so immortal ears couldn't overhear.

She shook her head. "Please," she begged.

The others would think she was referring to the wedding, but really she was begging me to withhold the truth, and it burned inside me to ignore it. I couldn't handle the power of her probing gaze and muttered something that sounded like a noncommittal agreement before I raced out of that apartment and away from my broken heart.

CHAPTER 27

CHASE

We left the Sycheses' apartment not long after Lucien. It was tradition to allow the bride to have a goodbye party with her family the day before the wedding. Callie didn't seem to have any family but her ill father, although Archer said something about an elusive aunt and uncle, whom I'd come across in my research when I was trying to figure out Callie's ancestry. I felt a tad wary we didn't tell Archer that Callie was Psyche's descendant, but I knew he was in so deep, it wouldn't change a thing. He'd love Callie no matter whom her ancestor was.

But these fevers and visions were starting to make me wonder about who else I might find hidden in Callie's family tree. Athena either knew something or was hiding it for someone, but I would find out soon, even if I had to intimidate her. Thena was a powerful woman, and she was a great war strategist who was wise beyond belief, but she broke easily under pressure and was extremely antisocial. I could get what info I needed simply by cornering her in person, but I was also the master of intimidation, so who could blame her?

At home, Aroha went into her frenzied wedding-planning mode, freaking out when Archer tried to help and scolding me for not being at her beck and call to do as she needed. It was Archer's wedding, yet he hardly had a say. I tried to hear what he was saying over her screeches, to attempt to persuade her toward what Archer truly wanted. With her and a wedding, that was pretty much impossible.

I understood her stress once I was sucked into helping. Pulling off a ceremony in less than twenty-four hours, even small, was harder than planning a siege. Archer and I scaled her plans back, reminding her it had to be private, no reception, nothing outdoors. The less exposure to others, the better. I tasked Archer with arranging storage for their things and getting out of the lease. Most likely, he would not be back in New York for years—not to stay, anyway. This kept the two busy and not hounding each other, and things ran more smoothly.

The next morning, Aroha dosed Archer's morning tea with nectar. He needed it. He hadn't slept at all from the looks of it. If he tasted the extra sweetness or felt the positive effects, he didn't comment. He got ready, and we waited ages for Aroha to get ready, but it was worth it. She took my breath and words away with her beauty.

"I look that good, huh?" she commented as I pulled her into my arms, kissing her temple so as to not mess with her makeup.

"Always," I whispered.

"Can we go now?" Archer fidgeted, staring at the clock.

"The ceremony starts at one, Archer." She rolled her eyes at him but smiled.

"And we were only able to get ahold of one limo, so it needs to take us, then come back for Callie," Archer pointed out.

"And we have two hours, Archer."

"No harm done, and the time it took to get ready was well-spent, but why don't we just get going to be on the safe side." I tried to placate and please them both.

They looked at me oddly and then gathered up their things to leave. They still weren't used to the war god making peace. And neither was I. The old me would've said some snarky comment to Archer for freaking out needlessly and chide Aroha for taking forever. These remarks would just come out—like an uncontrollable impulse—and I'd instantly regretted them. Now I was in control. Oh, the beast within was still there. I could feel him, but he was subdued, only ready to come out when I needed him.

At one of those almost-insta marriage chapels, called Love Chapel, Aroha ran around, making sure flowers were correct, that the officiant had the documents she had helped ready yesterday via *Project Cupid*, and that everything was ready. Then she planned on joining Callie to vamp up the girl's makeup and hair, knowing the girl had too simplistic a style to please the goddess of beauty.

She also insisted on giving the girl a vial of nectar, despite Archer's romantic comment that she didn't need nectar and was naturally beautiful. Aroha went off, freaking out about a bride wearing a bandage since nectar can heal demigods, so Archer let it go. It was best to let Aroha make things perfect by enhancing beauty and removing blemishes like wounds. It was true that my wife was an artist; Archer would later be appreciative.

I waited with the anxious Archer. "If you keep pacing, you'll wear a hole in that carpet. Slow down too, in case a mortal walks in. You're somewhere in between mortal and immortal speed," I said quietly as I tinkered on my phones. I had bought a new almost untraceable stealth phone with top-notch encryption abilities and was transferring numbers into it from my old one. Aroha had one already that I'd set up the night before. I'd get Callie and Archer ones as soon as we settled them. Zeus would no longer be able to track us via phone.

"Sorry," he said. Then he slumped into a chair.

"And sit up straight. Your mother will kill us if your suit is creased. What's wrong? Cold feet?"

"No." He looked at me, aghast. Then he sat up straighter and unbuttoned his jacket to prevent creasing. "I want to marry her, need to. I love her and can't live without her. I'm just worried about everything. The fevers, whether she's too young, where we'll go, how we'll be safe. I just don't want anything to happen to her because of me."

That was a lot to think about. I had to take a systematic approach. "She is young, but this is best. It'll make her father feel secure that she is settled and cared for. Treat it like an engagement in your head if you think it's too soon. It's only a mortal marriage. Once we get her immortal—and I will find a way—you can immortally marry her when this nonsense with Zeus is over. As for her age, you don't have to, you know, do *it* until she's ready. Unless you already..." This was awkward.

"No, I haven't." He gave me a look for even suggesting it. "She's pretty inexperienced."

"Then, take your time. As for the fevers, we will figure it out. We won't let anything happen to Callie, and Zeus would have gotten her one way or another, even if you'd stayed away from her forever. He wanted you to fail and come back, but he's underestimating me. He always has, because he hates me and fears me deep down. He is powerful, but I was the first Olympian born, not made. I am stronger than him, and ironically, I have pissed off fewer gods than he has. I told you the plan, but I cannot reveal much. I don't trust Lucien, and I think it's time to break away from him for a while."

Talk of the devil, as they say, and he shows his horns. Lucien walked in not thirty seconds later. He was hesitant, avoiding our gazes.

"You came," Archer said quietly. I couldn't read him or how he felt about Lucien's presence.

"I promised Callie. Well, she forced me into promising, but nevertheless."

Archer smiled at the idea.

"And I have something to say. It needs to be said before you get married, and I won't see you for some time," Lucien began. Good, he was finally apologizing. His face screwed up in frustration as if an apology were beyond him. "I'm sorry, Archer, for my jealousy and lack of support, but there's something I have to say that might make you resent me even more. There's something about Callie that they aren't telling you, and it's not right. Everyone—"

"Stop, Phoebus," I hissed, the warrior coming to the surface. I used his first name, which he hated.

"He needs to know. Everyone else does, even Callie."

"What?" Archer demanded, standing, his shoulders tense, directing that luminescent glare at me, then Apollo intermittently.

"Don't," I ordered, but he was not much younger than me, and who knew if the blood-age obedience worked anymore since we could defy Zeus now.

I tackled him, trying to cover his mouth. It was childish and ridiculous, because Archer knew there was a secret now and wouldn't rest until he heard it. And it was cowardly, as Dionysus had falsely imparted to the poets about me. But here I was being a coward. I had won my son back, and instead of facing the fact I had hidden things from him, afraid to lose him again, I was ready to attack someone for telling the truth.

Lucien fought me, getting out words in between me pummeling him and trying to cover his mouth, "Callie...is...Psyche's."

"Dad, let him up," Archer said quietly.

I let go, panting. Lucien scooted away from me, blotting the blood off his healing lip. I took a good look at his black eye before it faded, wanting to mentally memorize it. I wanted to rip his head off for not only ruining my son's proposal with false accusations, but trying to ruin his wedding day too. I was seeing red, and I wanted that red to be Apollo's blood splattered upon the walls.

"He's doing this to try to break you up, Archer," I explained. "He's absolutely acting with selfish intent."

"I can't stand lies!" Lucien barked at me.

I growled and got up. I squeezed my hands into fists, trying futilely to suppress the warrior. I took deep soothing breaths. "I am barely holding Ares back right now, Lucien, so choose your words carefully. Don't provoke me. I know you can lie, just like I can suppress the warmonger in me. You're lying to yourself if you think you're doing this out of noble intent."

"So, you're trying to tell me Psyche is Callie's immortal ancestor?" Archer asked, looking between both of us. He was so calm. I had no clue what he was thinking.

Lucien scrambled up off the ground and away from me. "Yes."

Archer froze for a second. "Fuck off!" Archer laughed wholeheartedly.

"She's nothing like her, even the powers—"

"Reading minds," Lucien interrupted.

The smile on Archer's face died out.

"There's more unknown to it. Psyche never saw the future. We didn't want to tell you when we found out because you and Callie were forced apart. And you coming back was so sudden, and you were so happy..." I trailed off, knowing it was a lame excuse. Really, we were trying to protect him, but I should've told him on the plane to New York. "I didn't think it truly mattered if you loved her that much. You killed for her, were willing to die for her. Psyche was never that to you."

He ignored me. "How long have you known?" he directed to Lucien.

Good. I was in the clear for now, maybe forgiven.

"Since Nice," Lucien mumbled.

Archer shook his head.

"I should've told you. There is proof, just so you know. Callie's father has a letter of Psyche's preserved, written right before the end. You see, you can't marry her, Archer. You don't love her. You love that part of her that is Psyche."

Archer shook his head again. "I need to see her." Then he was out the door, us scrambling after, unsure of what he was about to do.

Would he be angry with her for hiding the truth? Break it off? I tried to talk sense into him, tell him to calm down and talk it out first before he spoke with her. But he had a one-track mind. He opened doors and slammed them, pushing me aside when I tried to stop him, his eyes alight with an emotion I couldn't read except for its intensity. When he opened the third door, finding what he sought, Archer froze on the threshold.

CHAPTER 28

Archer

Callie was Psyche's. The breath left my lungs. Shock rendered me speechless. I couldn't even think for a moment. The first thing that had come was laughter, stemming from denial that it was some kind of twisted joke. Deep down, I knew it wasn't. My father's expression told me all. I listened to them argue; they were both right. When could my father have told me and I would have accepted it? But Lucien should've as soon as he found out, before Zeus attacked. My father said it didn't matter, that I loved Callie more than I ever had Psyche, and he was right, but I had to see her. I couldn't walk down that aisle without sorting this out first. She'd lied to me or hidden the truth, and it burned inside me. One quick look at her would determine our fate.

I stormed out and tried the first doors I came across. Lucien and Dad followed me, the latter pleading with me to calm down. On the second try, I found her. I froze in the doorway of a tiny dressing room.

Callie stood facing me in a form-fitting white dress that had sparkling detail over every inch of it that dangled a little, making her look as if she were a beautiful water nymph shimmering in the sunlight. Her hair was tied up in some intricate updo that Ma was finishing. It reminded me of Greece, with laurel leaves woven in like a crown upon her head, and yet it reminded me of now and Callie's personality with the wild curls dangling out of the twists here and there. Her face had more makeup than I had ever seen on her, making her eyes vibrant and warm, her lips luscious and pouty.

I couldn't move. Want and need and love filled me, and my mind hardly fathomed anything until my mother stepped in front of Callie and broke my line of sight and the trance I had been in. Lucien and Chase pushed past me into the room, shooting worried glances all around, and shut the door, crowding us in.

"Archer!" Ma scolded. "It's bad luck to see the bride before the wedding. Get out."

"I don't believe in luck." It came out way harsher than I intended, and Ma's face fell.

"Archer?" Aroha was confused. "Don't anger Tyche." She referred to the goddess of luck.

"Get out," I ground out. "All three of you."

"What?" My mother was taken aback and probably mightily offended.

"I said get out!"

Aroha flinched, and Callie backed away into the wall, terrified. Gods, I needed to pull it together. I was scaring Callie to death.

I took a couple deep breaths as Chase urged Aroha from the room while giving me a look that said, *Don't do anything stupid.*

Lucien lingered for a moment. I gave him a look that could kill, resolving to never speak to him again—well, maybe for a century or so.

Once the door closed behind us, I crossed over to Callie and took up her hands. "I'm sorry I scared you."

"What's wrong?" Her eyes searched my face, and when they met mine, I was home.

There was no Psyche there, just Callie. Nothing familiar in her eyes, face, body—nothing. I wanted to kiss her but feared my mother might kill me if I added messing up lipstick to my outburst. I would need to apologize to her later. Instead, I pulled Callie into a tight embrace. "Why didn't you tell me?"

She said nothing for a moment and then went rigid in my arms, as if just realizing what I was talking about. "Psyche," she said in a breathy, trembling whisper.

All the anger had left me upon seeing her, and I didn't even care she'd lied. Callie had some bewitching power over me. I sank to my knees, my head resting on the stomach of her dress.

Her hands wound around my head, embracing me. "I was afraid."

I peered up at her solemn face, tears in her eyes, threatening to spill. "Of what?"

"I was afraid you'd realize you don't love me, that you love the only part of me that is her." She couldn't look at me when she said it, the poor thing.

I had forgotten how insecure mortals were when they were young. I would need to help her find confidence in herself. She was so much stronger and more wonderful than she would admit to herself.

"I can guess who put that idea in your head," I muttered. "You're wrong, and Lucien's wrong." I slid up her body, not daring to let go. "You can't cry, or Aroha will kill me for making your makeup run." I turned her ashamed face toward mine and prodded her chin upwards. "I love *you*, Callie." I rested my forehead down on hers. "Just please don't hide anything from me ever again."

"I'm sorry." She blinked back her tears, but at least she was meeting my gaze now. "But you need to tell me everything too."

"I've got a lot of time and things to cover. It'll take a while."

She seemed unnerved by my joking manner. "What now?"

"Well, now we walk down the aisle and promise our lives to each other."

"And just forget this? Can you?"

I shrugged. "Chase said he never told me the truth because he thought it wouldn't matter to me. And it only matters to me in one way: it means you can become immortal one day."

She was stunned.

"I'm sorry for the drama. Lucien got me angry, and then I just had to see you to know for sure, and Callie, I've never been more sure in my life about anything. You are the one I've been waiting thousands of years for."

She pressed up and kissed me, able to reach with whatever heels she was wearing. I kissed her back, making the most of it, until the door flew open and hit the wall. We yanked apart to see an amused Chase and a furious Aroha.

"Get your butt in there, young man, while I fix what damage you've done to my beautiful creation." She was fuming.

I gave Callie a sheepish look, despite the fact she looked exactly the same. Ma had the kind of makeup that didn't smudge even if you were in an immortal sparring match for hours. Callie looked fine, better than fine, but Ma just wanted to rib at me. Knowing better, I obeyed.

As I passed by her, I pulled my mother into a big hug. "I'm sorry," I whispered.

She squeezed me back, let go, and gave me a wink. Then she pushed into the room to "fix" Callie.

In the hallway, Lucien stood, hands in pockets.

"We're still getting married, so you ruined our friendship in vain," I told him so he would know I needed space and time to forgive him.

"He. Told. You?" Callie was in the hallway, her bouquet in one hand, the other curled into a fist. Her eyes fixated on Lucien in an icy glare.

Before he could respond, Callie was in attack mode. I thought she was about to punch him, but instead, she smacked him in the head with her bouquet. Repeatedly. Flower shrapnel was flying everywhere. Dr. Syches and Raphael arrived, staring in shock because they hadn't witnessed everything. They had been waiting in the chapel.

I turned to see Dad holding his phone up, recording the scene and smiling. "Please don't stop her."

Ma's face was full of horror. "Flowers," she gasped. "Stop ruining everything, Lucien!" Then she interceded and stopped Callie's attack and took the bouquet out of her hand.

Both Callie and Lucien were covered in bits of flowers.

"It's ruined," Ma lamented, holding up what remained of the bouquet: bent stems tied together.

"Don't worry. I'm on it," Raphael uncharacteristically spoke up. Then he hurried out the door.

Dad stopped filming, hugged Aroha, and took charge. "Darling, all will be well. It's not a Greek wedding until there's some kind of drama. Archer, help Dr. Psyches back to his seat, and get the officiant ready. I'll join you in a minute. Aroha, go get Callie de—er—I mean, unflowered and primped. When Raphael returns with another bouquet, we'll get started."

I nodded and did as I was told. I waited impatiently in the front of the chapel. My father, who was my best man, entered. Raphael showed up next, trying to catch his breath, and sat down next to Callie's father. Waiting for her to come down that aisle was excruciating. I worried there would be some kind of attack, that someone else would come and try to stop the wedding. It would be the last time she was away from my side. I would ensure that. I was again a bundle of nerves until some classical music came on, cuing the bride's entrance. The music faded away before I could tell what song it was. I could only hear my thumping pulse.

The nerves left the second I beheld Callie again, and I was full of bliss, pride, and excitement. Even though I had just seen her, Callie's beauty and my love for her were staggering and overwhelming. I took her in as she came up the aisle and saw how the dress poured over her curves as she moved, outlining her form, letting me see her body in ways normally obscured by clothes. The white contrasted with her bronze skin, making her glow with an ethereal radiance.

Her father was too frail to walk her down the short aisle, so Callie had decided she would boldly walk herself down it. Ma, as matron of honor, walked behind her since this wasn't your typical wedding party. When she reached the front, I took Callie's hands in mine, and they were warm. I hoped she wasn't feverish. We didn't need any more interruptions today. Ma fanned out Callie's train and took up her bouquet. Dad was on my other side, holding golden wedding bands that were simple but had the Greek meander pattern around them.

Callie's hands shook slightly in mine. She was nervous. I rubbed her fingers with my thumbs to soothe her. Neither of us dared to look away from each other. My parents sat down. The officiant began speaking, but I wasn't listening. I was absorbed by the beautiful being who was about to become my wife. I imagined an endless future for us: children, adventures, travel, aliases, many weddings and honeymoons just for fun. Tonight, tomorrow, fifty years from now—I needed her forever. I would do anything to make that happen.

Callie

The ceremony was almost over. It had felt seconds long, my excitement making things go by too fast. I couldn't remember the words or our vows. I was mentally recording Archer's face the entire time. I was lost in Archer's eyes, his happy smile—where just the corners of his lips tweak up in insuppressible joy—and his warm, strong hands holding mine. I was lost in him, just as I had been lost without him.

"You may kiss the bride" brought me back to reality, as did his lips when they softly pressed against mine. I pressed back gently, highly aware Dad and Archer's parents were watching. But Archer didn't notice (or care?) as he deepened the kiss and pulled me in against him. I was lost in his lips, in that honeysweet scent of him, and in his touch. One kiss led to another, and neither of us wanted to stop. How could I break free from him when we had no idea how long we had left, how many more kisses there would be? His arms tightened around me, his hands gently cradling my head—so tender, yet underneath, there was superhuman strength. He was heaven—or Elysium if I recalled my mythology correctly.

"I might live to see a grandchild after all." My father sniggered.

Mortified, I yanked away from my husband's lips. My face felt hot, flushing up more as I took in those vibrant azure eyes that so clearly wanted me. *Husband.* The wedding night came to mind, and my stomach churned with nerves (gulp).

I tried to back away, but Archer held me tight. He pressed his forehead against mine with a blush on his cheeks and a wide grin he couldn't subdue. Then he let me go, except my arm, as he guided me down the aisle. I saw my dad's watery eyes, his joking obviously just an emotional deflection. Chase wore a prideful smile, and Aroha was pure jubilation as she went crazy snapping pictures with her phone. They were my family now too. My dad was trusting them with my life, to protect me.

So weird to be married at eighteen...to a three-thousand-and-something-year-old god (wasn't going to ponder too long on that). It was hasty—at least I'm sure it would look that way to all the kids I'd just graduated with—but when I'd been forced to live without him, thinking he was dead, to know how it felt to live without him, I knew I had to spend the rest of my life with him. As long as I lived, starting as soon as possible.

As we made our way toward the exit, I espied Lucien in the back, leaning against the wall by the door. His face was a cross between bitterness and wounded pride. I'd never hated anyone before, but I did hate him at that moment. He'd tried to ruin everything, and I still couldn't understand why, except for utter selfishness and a deluded dream of us being together.

As we passed him, having to walk single file, Archer's hand involuntarily twitched in mine. I peered down at the floor as if I were afraid to step on my dress. After the stunts Lucien had pulled—trying to break Archer and me up (twice)—I didn't want to talk to him for a long time. He was no true friend of mine in the end, but a selfish god who looked only after himself. I was beginning to think the myths were true when it came to some gods suffering from conceit and hubris (ahem, Lucien).

I had believed that if Lucien told Archer I was a descendant of Psyche, the wedding wouldn't happen, but it backfired, proving to me how understanding and dedicated Archer was, a superior man to anyone I knew. He loved me, and nothing could threaten that adoration. I felt the same about him. Nothing would part us now.

Outside, a limo waited for us to head toward a mysterious destination. The chauffeur opened the door. Chase and Aroha were right on our heels. I thought they were riding with us until Aroha, happy tears in her eyes, pulled me into a way-too-tight hug.

"Crushing...me." I muttered.

She apologized, pulled away, and wiped her tears away. She made Chase take a photo of us together.

"C'mon, Ma." Archer rolled his eyes and huffed when she fussed over him and needed a photo with him.

She fanned her face to prevent tears from spilling. "It's not every day your son gets married." (Only a couple times within a few thousand years for him?)

As she and Archer spoke, Chase squared my shoulders. I could not see this kind, warm man as a god of war, but nevertheless, I felt comfort that he would make sure I was safe. "And it's not every day you gain a daughter." He pulled me to him and hugged me, his huge muscles squeezing me softly. He kissed my forehead sweetly and beamed at me with the same kind of pride I often saw in my own father's eyes.

My throat felt tight, and like Aroha, I had to blink back tears. I felt accepted, loved. I had been an outsider because they had to keep their identities a secret. Even after finding out, I had been prevented from being with Archer. Now I truly felt a part of their group, their family, and it made my heart swell. I would miss my father terribly. I would be uneasy and full of guilt not seeing him in his last months, but I would have Archer's family—a few of them at least—and I had promised Dad I'd return, no matter what, when a death god was made.

Dad waved to me, just having exited, leaning on Raphael for support. I hurried up the steps back to Dad and gave him a big squeeze.

When I pulled away, afraid I'd hurt him, he blinked back tears and took up my hands. "I am so proud of who you've become. You'll do great things, Callista. I know it."

"I'll miss you, Dad."

"I'll miss you too. Live many adventures for me, will you?"

I nodded. Unspoken between us, I realized I would only see him one more time. More tears threatened to ruin my day with these thoughts.

After Archer made Dad promises I missed hearing since Raphael was telling me all the things I wasn't allowed to do (like "piss any more gods off or die"), we climbed into the limo.

When the door closed, Archer sighed. "Sorry about them."

"They're great. They make me feel like family."

"You are, Mrs. Ambrose," he whispered and kissed my neck.

"Is that my real last name?" It hadn't dawned on me until that moment that his last name was an alias.

Archer pulled away to take me in. "Legally, right now, yes."

"What's your real last name?"

Archer shifted uncomfortably. "People didn't have last names back then," he said sheepishly.

"I don't care about your age."

"I'm technically a very old—"

"A god who looks my age. I'm okay with that. I mean, I probably will never stop hounding you about history since it's fascinating how much you've seen."

"I'll tell you everything you could ever desire." He probably would too, except what I truly wanted to know about: Psyche and Hedone.

He kissed me hard, and when he pulled away, eyes alight and focused on mine, he said, "We were called where we came from, so Olympus, or our family is referred to as Olympians, officially Eros of Olympus."

195

"Callista of Olympus," I tried out. "Badass."

And then his lips were upon mine, apparently extremely appreciative of the sound of my wedded name. I didn't pull away until the car stopped.

"Will you tell me now where we're going?" I asked.

"Sorry I was so secretive. I don't trust Lucien."

"I second that."

"We'll head to my place in Belize for a few days until my dad gives us the all-clear for the safehouse. I have no idea where it is, by the way. He's getting us secure phones, encrypted stealth ones, so you can call your dad and be untraceable as long as we stick to wifi. He's already told your dad we'll be off the grid for a few days, so no calls in Belize, I'm afraid."

I sighed, annoyed. I didn't want to acknowledge reality since I was still floating on cloud nine (which probably belonged to Zeus as well).

"Sorry." Archer squeezed my hand as the driver opened the door. "No more serious talks."

I nodded as the chauffeur helped me out. I looked over my shoulder to Archer. "Until tomorrow." I would be brave and face my tumultuous future, just not on my wedding day.

When I turned, I took in the building in front of me: The Plaza. Archer's hands were on my hips, his breath in my ear. "I wanted the best for tonight, but it was difficult on short notice. Ma pulled some strings to get us a room, but no suites or anything fancy."

I turned in his arms and wrapped my arms around his neck. "It's The Plaza, Archer. A closet is fancy here, at least from what I've heard. It wouldn't matter anyway. Being together is all that matters."

He kissed me and then pecked me away to usher us inside. I was so busy taking in one of the lobbies in, only having ever seen it in movies that didn't do the place justice. I was so engrossed checking out the tall ceilings, ornate molding, and the beautiful chandelier that I didn't hear a word the concierge said. Before I knew it, we were in front of the door to our room.

Archer had the keycard in hand but stopped and looked at me hesitantly. "Would it be too cliché to proclaim I'm a bit old fashioned?" He was smirking.

Before I could surmise what he was talking about, he scooped me up in his arms, swiped the door to let us in, and pushed it open with his foot. He slipped into the room, carrying me as if I weighed nothing. The door clicked shut behind us.

"Carrying me over the threshold?"

"So to speak, yes."

He let my legs slip gently to the floor and was over opening the curtains before I even saw him move. The superhuman speed. I still couldn't get used to that. Sunlight flooded the room. It was a small room but had a king-sized bed and was opulent. Our cases were already in the room, rose petals on the bed, and the small table had champagne on ice and a fruit-and-cheese board. It was a romantic gesture, but it made me nervous when I thought of what might ensue. A wedding night—or evening since it was only two o'clock. I was trying to stay cool, not freak out, but anxiety of the unknown was building.

"This," Archer moved his hands around but was lost for words.

"It's nice."

Archer laughed. I grew self-conscious.

He pulled me into his arms. "This reeks of Ma. She's cheesy and over-the-top. I'm more...genuine."

"It was kind of her."

"You're always eager to please." He sighed. "Fight for yourself, Callie, always. You mustn't let any of us push you around. You're among gods now."

I swallowed hard. To stick up for myself after months of illness and depression was hard enough. Add in marrying a god people had once worshipped, and it was even harder. I felt like nothing at times, or at least lesser. But then again—

"With that being said, I have a favor to ask of you, my darling wife. I feel it has to be done before you are truly mine."

(Right) I take that back about sticking up for myself, because if he was talking about sex in these terms, I'd smack him upside the head. A hesitant "What?" was all that came out.

There was a knock at the door, and Archer cursed under his breath in Greek I didn't recognize—ancient probably. "Hold on, sorry."

He opened the door, and in walked a young man holding a thick tattered book, an old knife, and a vial of something. I was getting freaked out (like eleven-out-of-ten freak-out level). What was even scarier was this guy looked a lot like Lucien.

"Uh, Callie, this is Hymenaios, god of the marriage ceremony, and yes, I can see by your face that you are perceptive as ever: he's Lucien's son."

"Hi." I pulled myself together to offer to shake his hand.

Encumbered, he awkwardly put his things down and shook my hand. "I'm sorry. I'm early. From my experience, it's never good to interrupt newlyweds who are alone. More than once, I've walked in on more than I

197

anticipated." He blushed. "And now I've embarrassed us all. I'll give you two a minute to talk things over then." Then Hymenaios went back out of the room.

Archer let out a breath. I hit his shoulder.

"What?" He held his arms up in mock surrender. "He is twenty minutes early."

"For what? I'm a little freaked out here. A vial, scissors? I feel like an exorcism is going to happen."

Archer laughed loudly. "By all the gods, I love you." He tried to kiss me, but I turned away. His hands touched my hair. "I'll explain as I get you ready."

"For?"

"Our immortal wedding."

I turned to look at him. He pulled a couple bobby pins from my hair. "As you pointed out with your last name inquiry, you married Archer, not Eros. It doesn't feel real enough. I want to marry you eternally, forever. I thought..." He stopped speaking and pulling the pins out.

"Yes," I said. "If I live forever with you somehow or only a year, yes, Eros."

Our lips mutually met.

He pulled away, reluctantly saying, "He's waiting, and I have to get you ready."

"Ready?"

"For an ancient wedding. They were very symbolic, three days long, four if a mortal becomes one of us." He took a deep breath. "Crash course: day one, to celebrate and say goodbye to your family; day two is the wedding ceremony and now your hair will be cut as a sacrifice and proof of...um...your virginity—only a little bit of hair, don't worry—followed by vows, and then um...bathe together with a dash of holy water...andconsummation." The last two words were said in such a rush, I almost missed them.

He blushed and then hurried nervously, "The third day is a gift-giving day by all the family, which will be postponed. In fact, all of this is a bit improvised and modernized. Sadly, day four, where you'd drink ambrosia and become immortal, won't happen for a while." (Or probably ever, really).

He looked at me warily as if expecting me to explode. "Callie." He pulled me to him.

I hadn't realized I had gone rigid from anxiety. I wasn't getting a wedding night but a freaking ancient sacrificial ceremony. I took a deep breath, trying to calm down.

"Anything can be postponed. This is all sudden. If you're not ready—"

"One thing at a time. Hymenaios will what?"

"He'll read ancient Greek, slice off a tad of your hair, and immortally marry us."

"How is immortal marriage different?"

Archer paused and then said, "Our souls join, but Callie, I feel like they already have."

I pulled him in and kissed him. His hands went crazy tugging my hair, and when I pulled away, I realized he had been pulling my hair loose from the rest of the pins. He tried to weave his fingers through it, getting them stuck on all the spray Aroha had coated me in to keep my hair perfectly placed. A bath to wash it off sounded good, until I remembered Archer was supposed to join me. We'd made out (a lot) before, but we'd never seen each other naked. A holy water bath was not the way I envisioned the first time someone would see me in the buff.

"Me too," I managed to get out.

"Shall we let him in?"

I nodded. I had forgotten Lucien's son was standing outside.

Archer let him in.

Hymenaios shuffled awkwardly. "Are you sure about this, Eros?" he asked quietly. I wanted to punch the guy (really?). "You've never done this before." (huh?)

"I've never been surer of anything ever in my life," Archer returned.

"You were married before, though," I cut in, unable to stay silent.

"Now is not a time for the past. I married her when she was mortal but never immortally. The myth has some truths in it. She was made immortal later. I want more with you, forever."

He wanted more, which lifted my heart, but his words did point out he had done all this before. A wedding, lifetimes with a wife, a child, whereas I'd had one sort-of long-term boyfriend before him. He'd experienced millennia and saw so much, and I, hardly anything.

And this experience also included sex. I hadn't been far with a guy at all, and there were expectations for a wedding night. I was worried I'd embarrass myself. Equally, I was concerned about how many partners he'd had over his three thousand years (if several a year, wow, his number would be staggering).

THE IMMORTAL TRANSCRIPTS: FEVER

These discussions should've happened before we married, but everything was done in such a rush. Now, with company, was not the time to ask questions. I took a deep breath. The answers or my insecurities could wait because they would never change my mind. We could not bear a life apart, and that was all that mattered. The rest could be sorted out as soon as Lucien's kid left.

Archer sighed and took my hands in his. His expression told me he could surmise my thoughts. "Callie," he breathed out. "I know how your mind works. Everything is new. Everything is different. I felt like I had been sleepwalking for more than five hundred years, and you have woken me. The past before, that was literal lifetimes ago and gone. I'm freaking out thinking about the future, as you might be too, but I'm focusing on here and now. This moment. Don't think about anything but right here, right now, in my arms."

His words were the balm needed to soothe my nerves. I had to take each moment as it came. Simple as that.

I took a deep breath and nodded, then looked at Hymenaios. "We're ready."

Hymenaios opened his thick book. He began the ceremony by reading in ancient Greek. It was too hard to figure out the words since I was still a novice at modern Greek. I had no hope of understanding, but Archer translated for me quickly and quietly. There were a few spots where a lot was said by Hymenaios and Archer repeated very few words, but I trusted him. The exact translation mattered less than the meaning.

Hymenaios gently took up a couple of my curls and sliced off about two inches of hair. It felt as if electricity filled the air, an energy, that spoke of real marriage. Something profound was happening. The feeling didn't leave after the hair sacrifice, nor after the vows. Before I knew it, Archer kissed me chastely, and Hymenaios said some concluding statement Archer didn't translate.

Archer gazed at me with an intense expression I couldn't read, but I knew what he was feeling, for I felt it too. More than ever before, I felt as if we were linked, closer than ever. The gods spoke of binds, immortal marriage, and the like, but none of it meant anything. Archer and I were soulmates.

Hymenaios shook Archer's hand and then pulled me into a quick hug. He whispered, "Welcome to the family." Then he gave me a small, timid smile before he walked out the door.

On being alone, I grew nervous and twisted my fingers. Archer moved away from me, but I didn't look at what he was doing. I was staring at the one massive bed we were to share. My face felt hot.

Pop!

I jumped, hand over heart.

"Sorry," Archer said as he made me jump again when he was right in front of me, moving too fast for me to keep up. A champagne glass with a ton of fizz was held up for me.

"Too much."

Archer's smile fell, and I instantly regretted saying it.

"No, the movement. Let my mind slowly get used to your superhuman speed." I took the champagne glass from him.

"Sorry, Callie. I just feel like I can be myself in front of you." (Great, I was a crap wife less than an hour into marriage). Aroha had said the same thing to me, so I should've known.

"I'm sorry."

"No, Callie. I need you to tell me when things are too much for you. And I'll tell you how I feel. I said no talk of the past tonight, but I've only had one real relationship and—"

"What?" I was flabbergasted. There was no way a god—as hot as Archer—had only been in one relationship in over three thousand years.

Archer laughed lightly. "And a lack of communication—among other things—ruined it. I learn from my mistakes. I will always communicate with you." He topped off the champagne after the bubbles fizzed down since he had poured it immortally fast the first time. "Too much? I will scale back what you need until you're comfortable."

I nodded. "Only one relationship?"

"No. I'm on my second and forever relationship now." He held up his glass in a toast. "To eternity together."

I didn't lift my glass. "But I might die one day."

He shook his head and looked at me with a wounded expression. "I killed Death so he wouldn't take you away from me. Obviously, I will do whatever it takes, Callie, to make you immortal."

I raised my glass, stunned by the conviction behind the words more than the meaning, which was huge to start with. Archer clinked his glass to mine, and we drank. It tasted of tart, dry, fruit juice that made the muscles in my jaw twitch like they did when I ate sour candy. I tried to hide my expression, but Archer noticed and took the glass from me and placed both of ours on the table. He picked up a strawberry and held it up to my lips. I bit into it.

"The sweetness will help."

Instantly, the bitter dry flavor left my mouth.

He held up my glass again. "Taste."

I gave him a look but drank because he was making a point. It didn't taste as bad this time. "Better, but I'm still not a fan."

"And if I said symbolically we had to finish a bottle tonight?"

I laughed and then tried to drink more but couldn't get more than a sip down. "Ugh. That's all you."

"Okay, my love." He took the glass off me with a smirk, downed it, and then his.

"Um."

"It doesn't affect us like you. That entire bottle will give me the same effect a glass would you. If this were nectar whiskey, however, we'd be in trouble."

"You have to finish it?"

"Gods are surprisingly superstitious." He sighed and poured another glass of champagne.

Then he removed his jacket and placed it on the back of a chair, slipped his shoes off and removed his socks. I simply watched my husband as he undid his tie, collar, and the shirt cuffs. He was beautiful. And mine.

Then his eyes locked on mine. Whatever he saw in my face dilated his eyes with need. My breath caught in my throat as he came over and pulled me in for a hug from behind. He moaned softly and kissed my neck where it met my jaw. It sent shivers down my spine.

He turned me around, scrutinizing my face and tipped my chin up so our gazes aligned. "Relax, Callie." He kissed me.

"It's our wedding night, and I haven't done much with a guy before, so—"

"You call the shots, whatever you're comfortable with."

"What of traditions and superstitions?"

"I don't think maritally-blessed holy water has an expiration date. The immortal marriage won't happen until it *all* does, but there isn't some innate law saying there's a timeframe. It's a process without a time limit."

An idea came to mind. "Did your mom pack our bathing suits?"

"I'm sure she did. Why?" His brow furrowed adorably.

"Does the bathroom have a jet tub? We could finish this bottle and fulfill weird rituals—most of them."

His eyes lit up at that. "My clever Callie. Whatever you want, you shall have."

"I could take that phrase and really run wild with it," I teased.

And his lips were upon mine again.

CHAPTER 30

Archer

Callie dug through her case and pulled out her bathing suit. It was a red two-piece from the looks of it. I closed the curtains and turned to her. There was no way she could get out of that dress without assistance, and she realized this when she tried to awkwardly bend her arms to get to the zipper. I stopped her hand and went to unzip it. Three buttons at the top had to be undone first, and I popped them slowly through the holes, trying to focus on the dress and not the idea that I was disrobing her.

When I unzipped it down to her waist, I swallowed hard and let go. She turned to me, clad in a see-through sleeveless slip. I could see her undergarments and every curve of her body. I was absolutely ready, but if she wasn't, what were a few more days after waiting for her thousands of years?

"You're beautiful," I said. There was so much more I should've said, but words weren't forming. Half my addled brain was fantasizing, and the other half was suppressing those fantasies so I would be a gentleman.

I couldn't help but kiss her with all my pent-up energy. Her rigor matched my own, each kiss seeming to ease away the anxiety that my strange traditions and our shaky future had built up in her. We were caught up in a fevered frenzy of kissing and touching between words of love. I wanted more, needed more of her. She was perfection. Her inexperience didn't matter; all that did was our love and our promises in both worlds to keep that love alive. Forever...

I awoke next to my gorgeous wife, who was fast asleep. I slipped out of bed, covering her up so she would stay warm, and slipped into my suit pants. I hung up her dress and the rest of my suit. I slipped out onto the terrace. The courtyard was a peaceful opposite of the bustling city. I had grown to love this city, mostly because of Callie, because of the things we had done together: our first movie, dinner, museum trip—our first everything. Every place we went together became ours. I vowed to myself once she was immortal and once we were safe, I would bring her back here. It was a more positive future to focus on than the immediate one. The sliding door opened, and Callie stood there in her skimpy, vibrant two-piece. I blew out a breath. She was gorgeous, and I wanted to get her back inside away from anyone lecherous ambling about in the courtyard.

"Bath?" she asked.

"In suits still?"

She put her hand on her hip, which accentuated her figure, and I would agree to anything in that moment. "I want to have a serious talk, and you'll get distracted if I'm naked."

"I'm distracted by that suit."

"See? So suits on."

"If I need one too, that means you're afraid to get distracted."

She gave me a side-eye and turned away. She totally was distracted by me too.

Callie went into the bathroom to draw the bath while I changed into my suit. I grabbed up the holy water and my champagne glass and joined her. I turned my attention to the running water and uncorked the vial of water Hymenaios had blessed to make our marriage lasting. I poured it in. There was no turning back—I didn't want to. Callie dumped a bunch of the hotel body wash in and instantly caused way too many bubbles, but I climbed in and offered my hands to help her in. The tub was small for two, so when she tried to sit across from me, she had to fold her legs over mine.

She was nervous about something again. I pulled her toward me—too quickly in hindsight—and kissed her hard. I pulled my mouth away, keeping her close.

"What is this serious talk about?" I asked, leaning back against the tub but keeping her legs on mine in that mutual comfort.

"I have a million questions."

"I'm sure you do."

"I don't even know where to start." She frowned. The myriad of questions about immortality must be plaguing her mind.

"Anywhere. Whatever comes to mind, ask."

"I want to know about Psyche."

It felt like a punch to my gut. "Of course you do." My tone was sardonic and cutting, which I instantly regretted when her face sank.

"If it's too hard..."

My ex was the last thing I wanted to talk about on my wedding night to another woman. But Callie looked so sad, and I was sure she thought my rebuff was from grief. Sure, it was sad to talk about, but my reaction was borne of regret and bitterness. I didn't want Callie to know how terribly wrong Psyche and my relationship had gotten, not today.

"It's not hard. It's just weird to talk about that on my wedding night with you."

"How about your daughter instead?"

If mentioning Psyche was a punch, mentioning my daughter was getting hit by an emotional tractor trailer. "I can't." It was all I could squeeze out.

Her gaze met mine, and she seemed surprised. "I'm sorry, you did say *anything*."

"I know, stupid of me. I'm not...I have never been able to talk about her death."

She was silent. I was shutting her out after promising communication. I was already messing this marriage up. The silence stretched for another moment, and I knew I had to open up to her and talk.

"Psyche was the prettiest girl I had ever seen back then: a red-haired, green-eyed, pale girl—unique looking for Greece at the time. Imagine you're eighteen and you meet someone you think is the most beautiful person alive."

She splashed me and gave me a look.

"What?"

"Imagine you're eighteen," she mocked me.

I was lost in my thoughts, not thinking about how I was saying them but what I needed to get across to her. Idiotically, I offended her. I went for a witty deflection. "Are you saying I'm the most beautiful person alive?" I teased her back, giving her a ridiculous model-squint that made most mortal girls' heart rates speed up.

"You know you are." She rolled her eyes.

I pulled her legs to bring her closer, making her squeal. "Well, the ladies do tend to treat me kindly."

"Callista of Olympus will murder said ladies," Callie said, giving me a glare.

"Eros of Olympus needs to assuage his wife's jealousy before she becomes an immortal, or she'll become the goddess of envy."

Her playful glare deepened. "Isn't there already a goddess of envy?"

"Nemesis, envy and revenge," I told her, dropping our game. "And best not bring her up in front of my parents."

"Why?"

Now this was a story I could tell without delving deep into my emotions. "Being Envy, I guess she must want what she can't have. She has a thing for my dad, like a forever crush, so she and Ma have had a few...catfights over the years. Dad can't quite steer clear of Nemesis because she's directly involved with most wars as well. But as far as I know, Dad's never been involved with her at all. She's pretty much the opposite of my mom."

"So anti-pretty?"

I laughed. "No, as you pointed out, most gods are attractive to mortals. But mortals and gods alike have varying tastes. Nemesis is kind of masculine in comparison to my mom—muscular, tall, slightly horsey-looking—"

"You're not describing her as attractive."

"I'm the god of love. Everyone is attractive to someone out there. I meant horsey in that dignified aristocratic way. Nemesis is...non-binary is your generation's term, I believe."

"Gotcha, Grandpa."

I looked at her oddly.

"Your generation," she mocked.

I yanked her even closer, and this time, she did not complain about me using superhuman speed to do so. "I think someone has had enough champagne." I knew she had hardly drunk any, but I was still in a teasing mood, and she was so close to me now that my thoughts were drifting off, replaying images from earlier that I wanted to repeat.

She kissed me, and I made the most of it, knowing she would pull away before things could get serious because she wanted answers. Indeed, she did. "You distracted me," she complained.

"You distracted me first. I was telling a story, and you cut in to mock me."

She gave me a look and backed up to lean against her side of the tub. I longed to have her closer again.

"Where was I?" I asked.

"She was the prettiest girl in the world." There was some underlying spite in her tone.

"To a naive eighteen-year-old—no offense—spoiled brat god, yes. I believe I was stressing my idiotic innocence more than her beauty."

"Go on," she urged. She took the champagne glass I thought I was consuming alone and took a swig. She grimaced.

I hopped out of the tub and raced into the other room, snatched up the champagne bottle, the extra glass, and the food plate, and raced back in as fast as I could without the fruit rolling off. I placed it down on the tub ledge and slipped back in to see her astonished face.

"I know, I know, mortal pace." I sighed. I poured a glass of champagne and held it up to her. "To Psyche, since this will hopefully be the only time we talk about her."

"May she rest in peace," Callie said, holding up her glass.

I froze. I tried not to react, but before I could plaster a fake expression on my face, Callie saw it.

"What? Does something different happen to gods when they die?"

This was so not where I wanted this conversation to go, today of all days. "Gods go to the Underworld and remain part of Hades entourage as spirits until they move on. If they have no unfinished business, they move on to Elysium. Psyche is apparently an attendant of Persephone."

"Well, what unfinished business does she have?"

I shrugged.

"You. You're the unfinished business, aren't you?"

"No. Not at all. Let me tell you the story, and you'll see the closure was complete centuries before her death. Hades must inform us if closure directly relates to us."

"And you know this because..."

"Because I know the rules," I said waspishly.

How could I admit to her that my daughter needed closure from me, and I could never bring myself to see her? I wanted to remember her alive, not some silver wispy cloud of whom she once was. I could not listen to her say goodbye, to most likely admit I was right for wanting her to stay with me and not go off with her carefree and wild mother, that she was sorry for breaking a father's heart. Five hundred years wasn't enough to get over a child's death; forever might not even be.

These words I could not share with anyone, not even Callie, so I went for another truth. "I saw my brothers and sister there. I never mentioned them and doubt Ma did to you—Deimos, Phobos, and Harmonia. Said goodbye to them after they died with the Spartans at Thermopylae. Xerxes knew about gods, so he burned all the wounded. It was the only time I stepped foot in the Underworld. I have no intention of going back."

Callie opened her mouth to speak, and I knew she was about to ask about Hedone, but her mouth closed. "To getting Psyche past us," she said instead, holding up her glass. "Past me, mostly. I'm sorry to ask this of you, but I have to know in order to stop feeling...second best."

I went to protest, but she put her hand up to stop me. "I know what you'll say, and it will be the truth of how you love me more, but I need to hear what happened, how things ended. I need to know. It's stupid, but as you said, innocent and naïve eighteen-year-olds..."

She was amazing. So much better than me at communicating and so understanding. I clinked my glass against hers, and we drank a sip. Callie grabbed up a strawberry and ate it. She put the glass down, the flavor not growing on her.

"I was too curious for my own good. On top of that, my younger brothers and I were always competing. Himerus—Russ that you met—is the god of lust, and he, well, being an ass, made me lust after Psyche when he saw I was interested. Despite the lust, I was a moral guy and would never think of pursuing her without marriage. Marriage wasn't a big deal to us, when it came to mortals. Gods were doing it all the time. I think Lucien had three wives at once back then, his sons being born back-to-back. Anyway, Psyche's father wouldn't let her marry me."

"Her dad said no to a god?"

"No, I posed as a lowly military bowman to test the family's worth. He was an arrogant king, wanting more lands through the marriages of his children."

"I remember the myth—uh, well I guess history, technically," Callie cut in. "Apollo made him believe she had to be sacrificed to some monster."

"A terrifying dragon," I amended. "And I took her away. Look, this next part is awful. I'm going to tell you the truth about it all, but save your judgment for the end, please. Some of it doesn't paint me in a good light."

She nodded. "If the myths are true, I know what you did, and your mother was even worse."

"I pretty much kept Psyche in a gilded cage and visited her every night. I see your eyes narrowing. You know me, Callie. I'm not pressuring you, am I? Even with my brother's arrow of lust in me, I refrained from indulging in those urges. We stayed up late talking, becoming friends, and then I knew she loved me. I cared for her a lot, but she deserved love, so I shot an arrow of love for her into myself and was head over heels.

"The marriage became real. I bound her to me with three words. Psyche was becoming a better person, not the silly spoiled princess her father raised her to be. But then she just had to see what I looked like. There was that blasted vanity that could not be stamped out. She knew her hair and skin were exotic, that men looked upon her favorably. She was afraid she had fallen in love with a hideous beast and let her sisters convince her that the lavish gifts I gave her and the large house were covering up for the fact I was revolting. Proving her sisters wrong and having it all in society outweighed her vow to me to stay in the dark.

"I'll never forget the way she looked at me: There was relief in her eyes, pride, and I realized in that split second what she truly valued. When I was good-looking enough for her taste, and she realized she was married to someone so much more profound and powerful than her sisters' husbands, she knew happiness. She failed. It was an unfair test, true. I was young, cruel. I left her wounded because I had made myself love someone for the first time, and she wasn't who I thought she was. I had been sucked in by her looks likewise, but it took me a long time to realize I was a hypocrite."

"While you sorted this out, your mother tortured her through the tasks, while the rest of your family helped her achieve them to thwart your mother?" Callie asked.

I nodded. "You know the myth, so after that, Zeus made her immortal since she had been through so much, and we had Hedone. I had loved Psyche then, even after my year-long arrow burned away. I realized I had acted just as she did. I had chosen her by looks alone, tested her, and found both of us wanting. I vowed to change my ways. I was a good husband after that. I loved her because she gave me Hedone, and Hedone stole my heart. She was my everything." I blinked back tears.

Callie scooted forward into my arms. She felt cold.

"Is the water cold?"

"It's getting there, but I think it might be one of my pesky fevers."

"Let's get you in bed, then."

"My hair," she said quietly. "I need to wash it." It was crispy due all the hair product my mother had put in, and a tangled mess as well.

"Allow me."

I wanted to do everything possible to make her feel comfortable. So much was changing for her. I was used to packing up every decade and starting afresh, but she was leaving her dying father just after starting over in New York. She would be completely dependent on me and would feel adrift.

I turned her around so her back was toward me and pressed her shoulders down. She slipped under the water enough to wet her hair and sat up. I took the hotel shampoo and began to lather her hair, which, due to her curls, was much longer when wet.

I wanted to finish the story before we crawled into bed. There, I wanted to talk about us, the future as if it were boundless, what we had done during our time apart, everything about *Callie*. I was done with the past.

"So, not long after Hedone was born, the fighting began. Psyche had been increasingly more demanding of attention and luxury. I preferred the quiet life. She wanted to party. She didn't like half my attention on Hedone. None of ours. Aroha, Chase, Zeus—everyone had to downplay their affection for Hedone."

"Her own daughter?"

"She didn't go as far as to resent Hedone, but she tried to compete with her. And when she failed with the gods—for she'd tried hard—she fell into a depression. Lucien, who you know by now has a weakness for all pretty girls, even turned down explicit advances from Psyche. I tried to rekindle our relationship, but she resented me."

I stopped lathering Callie's hair. She turned to me, her dark eyes feeling sorry for me, the last thing I wanted and completely unnecessary. Psyche had stopped hurting me two thousand or so years ago.

"Wash?"

She pecked my lips and then laid down her head almost in my lap. I ran my hands through her hair under the water to help the soap disperse. Callie watched me, and when our gazes aligned, she gave me a Cheshire grin, the little minx pleased with this simple affectionate exchange. Gods, I loved her.

I leaned back and closed my eyes for a moment, leaving myself and scanning the city. I sensed Aroha and Chase down the hall in a room, nearby in case Zeus sent someone. In The Champagne Bar, Dionysus, or Uncle D, was also on watch. I zoomed out to note two other immortals in Manhattan. Lucien was at his apartment, while Hymenaios was in my old place.

"Archer?" Callie's voice asked hesitantly.

"Sorry, love." I came back to myself and opened my eyes to see her hovering above me, hair wet, eyes sparkling, absolutely gorgeous. I kissed her, but she only kissed me back for a second before she asked where my mind had been.

"I'm not sure how much Ma or Lucien told you about our abilities, but we can 'scan' for lack of a better word and see souls, I guess—basically mortals and immortals show up on our 'radars.' I was simply checking on things."

"Is he coming for me already?"

"No. We're safe." I left off the "for now."

I was terrified Zeus would come for us. He could null-and-void my punishment since I had come back to her, despite promising a year in former negotiations. I couldn't live without her, and I could not feel guilty about jeopardizing our lives when they would've been gone had we not reunited.

Callie handed me the conditioner. "Be generous with the conditioner."

I followed her orders, knowing firsthand how much curly hair needed. "Let me finish this before we go to bed so we can talk about futures instead of pasts."

"I'm listening," she said as if I had been the major hold up.

I kissed her neck, making her shiver. I cleared my throat. "A few years after we married, Psyche proclaimed she wanted her normal life back, married to the man her father had originally chosen: a wealthy merchant with vast lands. He was now an old poor drunkard who abused his wife. I took her to see him to make a point. I had elevated her from mortal princess to goddess, given her a better life than being this lowly merchant's 'property,' so surely, she should've been thankful, even if she no longer loved me."

"I'm guessing she didn't like that very much?'

"Nope."

"Hang on." Callie dunked her head under and rubbed her hair.

I ran my hands through her mahogany locks.

She surfaced and wiped her eyes and then looked at her hands. She grabbed a washcloth off the rail above us and tried to wipe her makeup off. "Why won't this stuff come off?"

I shrugged. "Well, that is obviously a lip stain since it didn't come off throughout our activities today..."

She splashed me for the comment.

"And I'm guessing your eye makeup is clay-based or waterproof. I'm sure Aroha packed you makeup remover."

She was giving me a weird-out side-eye. "You know about makeup?"

Ah, that was why she was looking at me strangely. Modern mortal young men and their obsession with acting masculine and pushing down others who defy the status quo—so insecure.

"I am the son of the goddess of love and *beauty*. You pick these trends up after hearing about them all the time for a few thousand years, you know."

Callie went pensive for a moment. "The amount of information in your brain about everything throughout time must be..." Apparently, she lost her vocabulary.

"What do you want to know?"

"No, don't do that. You're distracting me. Back to your story."

I sighed, wishing I could spout out some interesting fact that would deflect my story completely, but it was best to get it over with. "Psyche became unbearable after that, neurotic, to be honest. She would destroy my things, make up lies about me, try to turn my own kid against me, and she would sneak out of Olympus to sleep with a different mortal every night. I refused to be with her intimately after she cheated the first time. She had the audacity to tell me right after to wound me. It was honestly one of the most hurtful things anyone has done to me; the things she said to me are etched into my mind forever."

"Stop, Archer. This is making you sad. I shouldn't have pressed. I was stupidly jealous, but I see now what you meant. I had this image in my head of you being brokenhearted by her death, and really—"

"She had broken my heart millenia earlier? Yes. I might as well finish now, and I want you to know everything."

I would even tell her about Hedone one day. I could imagine telling her while she was big with our child out of pure excitement of what could be. When another was on the way, I think I could face what had been. The image of a beautiful baby with my bright blue eyes, swaddled in my arms, came to mind as if someone had inserted it there. Unlike Hedone, this baby's locks were a warm light brown, not strawberry-blonde. I looked at Callie, who gazed at me fixedly. Her mouth didn't move, but I heard her voice whisper, *Philo*.

I jumped, literally half out of the tub and looked at her, astounded.

"Sorry." She had her hands up as if calming a wild animal. Her eyes were dilated and boring into mine. "I have a fever."

I stared at her, not making connections, a million things flying around in my brain.

"I see things when I do."

"Chase said," I commented stupidly. I shook my head. "You what? Put thoughts in my head just now?"

She shook her head and shivered. Damn her dislike of my immortal speed. I had her out of the tub, wrapped in a robe, and under the covers in seconds. I knelt beside her and felt her head. She was a bit warm but not alarmingly so.

She grasped my hand in hers. "I didn't put it in your mind. I recalled a dream. With me stopping the...volcano thing, I think my dreams are a bit prophetic."

I wouldn't argue with that. My sweet wife's visions had saved my life. And if this one would come to pass, my dreams of having a family with her would one day come true.

"Philo," I breathed out in a whisper. Another little boy god of love. She smiled.

"Show me again," I pleaded.

Her glazed eyes met mine, which shifted my attention to getting out of our wet suits first. I untied her robe. I pulled the three ties of her bikini and with all my willpower, turned away. She was sick and needed rest. At immortal pace, I rummaged through her bag, avoiding the lingerie, trying to not think about how my freaky mother had packed our cases. There were no pajamas in either of our luggage. It appeared Aroha was desperate for grandchildren.

I settled on the least risqué outfit for her and boxers for me. Then I fished out the fever-reducing medicine for her. I got her a glass of water and poured the last of the champagne in mine. She had just finished dressing and looked amazing. She climbed in under the covers and took the pill.

These fevers worried me. If Lucien—whom I refused to talk to at the moment—couldn't cure them, then that was troublesome—no, potentially dire.

"I'm fine." She assured me.

"Room service or go down to dinner later?"

"Dinner later."

She gave me the come-to-me beckon with her finger. I downed the champagne, instantly regretting how it rumbled in my stomach. Her gesture drew me in like a moth to a flame. I slipped into bed. She snuggled up to me, and I pulled her into the crook of my arm.

I felt tingly all over, a little light-headed, and giddy. *Love.* "I think we're now properly married."

"I feel it too." She smiled. Then her smile faded. "Oh, no. Finish your story."

"Only if you tell me about the Philo dream."

"After your story. Get done with the past before we talk about the future."

I was dying to know what she had seen, but she was right. I blew out a breath. "You play a hard bargain, wife." I adored calling her that.

"I left off with the crumbling relationship. I had told Psyche repeatedly if she wanted to leave, she could, but this time, I finally told her we were done. She tried to take Hedone, but Hedone wouldn't go. I was blamed for that, scorned by Psyche. She became by all definitions verbally, psychologically, and physically abusive toward me. I kicked her out of Olympus. After a hundred years or so, she came running back, begging to be remarried. I obviously didn't take her back, although Zeus let her stay. This was in Rome. She was more like an outsider who was tolerated. Soon as Rome fell and became a republic, all Olympians parted ways to different areas. We lost track of her for a long time, but she lived among mortals. In the 1500s, she demanded time with Hedone. I couldn't deny that, although I tried to convince Hedone not to go to Europe due to the Inquisition. You can surmise what happened. Psyche's flamboyance with her godly abilities, promiscuity, and big mouth most likely led to my daughter's death. When a mother does not put her child above herself, I cannot forgive."

"I can only imagine, but I would like to think I would give up my life and soul for my child," Callie said.

"Yes," was all I could say at first. "Yes, I would give it all if Hedone could live again."

Her arms tightened around me in comfort, her head on my shoulder. We were quiet for a moment. When she realized that was the end of my story, she pulled my face toward her so our gazes aligned. "Philo," she said and closed her eyes. I thought she was going to sleep until a montage of images assaulted my brain.

I was holding a swaddled little bundle, staring down at the adorable little face, a warm light brown curl resting on the baby's forehead. Bright glowing blue eyes, identical to mine, shone back at me with love. I closed my eyes to focus better. He cooed and flailed an escaped arm. I kissed his hand and tucked it back into the blanket. Callie placed her hand on my shoulders and peered down at the baby. He went wild on seeing his mother, wriggling and smiling. Her dark hair cascaded over my shoulder, and I pulled her into a long kiss.

It felt real, and yet when I opened my eyes, Callie was in front of me in New York in The Plaza. By the gods, I wanted this to be prophetic more than anything else.

"Beautiful." I pulled her closer, wanting to nap with Callie and dream of happy futures.

CHAPTER 31

I sat alone in my room, brooding. They were gone, the lovebirds, the newlyweds. Calling them that made the bile rise up from my stomach. The prophecy was coming true, but I had expected as much. Callie saved Archer, whom I had seen climbing toward a volcano, and the wedding I had seen happened anyway. I had to get the truth out, yes, but being the honesty god, I needed to be truthful with myself. I wanted the Psyche secret to stop the marriage because I was in love and drawn to Callie. I wanted her, and it burned me to even imagine what they had done after their wedding—something I fantasized myself doing with her.

There was one problem with the prophecy Themis had foretold: I hadn't changed sides. I was still on their side, no matter how broken my heart was, no matter how tattered our friendships were. Callie had to live, even if I could never have her. It would kill me if she or Archer died. I'd never choose a side against them. And yet...there were some dreadfully terrifying images that had not yet come to pass. Things were far from over.

My phone rang, breaking the silence of my apartment and making me jump. It was Aroha. I wanted to ignore it; in fact, I let it ring three times before it crossed my mind that something could be wrong. Archer and Callie were vulnerable to an attack from Zeus, even if Chase had an arsenal to protect them. They hadn't told me much ahead of time, and I hadn't heard from any of them since the wedding. They didn't trust me.

Even without hearing their plans, it was surmisable Chase would take the lovebirds to safety, most likely Belize, and either keep them moving or find somewhere off the grid Zeus would never suspect. The Anemoi—the four winds—would be used for transport since Callie could not risk flying in Zeus's skies. It would also be worrisome to travel by sea without ascertaining Poseidon's position, something likely on Aroha's to-do list.

The phone stopped ringing. I sighed and immediately called her back.

"Lucien?"

"Is something the matter?" I asked, sounding a bit more annoyed than I felt.

"I got a text message a minute ago, and I can't get ahold of Chase." Her voice was shaky.

I sat up, realizing she was scared.

"Are you okay, Lucien?" She said it with a loaded tone of voice, as if someone might be holding me hostage or something where I couldn't speak the truth.

"I'm fine. Dite, what is it?"

"The text was a threat. It said, 'Bring the mortal to the Brooklyn Bridge at midnight, or the Sun God dies.' It's from Zeus."

My head whirled in confusion. Threatening my life? It didn't make sense. "I'll be right over."

"No, let me come to you. Lock all your doors and windows, and arm yourself. We can't let them barter you."

I almost smiled, thinking of how Chase had worn off on her after all these years. Warmth spread through me that she cared so much for my well-being despite everything.

"Dite. He doesn't make empty threats."

Then it hit me hard, like a battering ram to my gut. I couldn't breathe. My heart squeezed in my chest. My hand involuntarily gripped the phone too hard, and it broke to pieces. I threw the shards to the ground as the realization—the threat, the prophecy, choosing sides—hit me. There were three Olympian "sun" gods aside from me: my sons. I was estranged from the other two, and they were rarely with Zeus, so he would go after Hymenaios, my firstborn, the one right here in New York, the one I was closest to. I looked at the clock, which read 11:45.

There was no time for doors. I launched myself out the window and slid down the fire escape to the ground. I fled at immortal speed to the street and kept going, not caring if any mortals caught a glimpse of the blur of my form. They wouldn't know what they were seeing anyhow.

I arrived at the Brooklyn Bridge in two minutes to see three forms standing on the bridge by the railing. Cars were whizzing by still, despite the hour. I had to walk slowly to not provoke them. As I drew closer, I could see the forms of Zeus, Hermes, and Hymenaios. I tried to read my son's body language. He was frightened, his arms awkwardly behind his back, most likely bound.

"Apollo," Hermes said with surprise, revealing to me they hadn't expected me to come. They had wanted Aroha on her own and perhaps thought I'd be with Archer.

I wished now I hadn't been so rash and broken my phone; I should've made a plan of attack with her.

"Expecting Aphrodite?" I feigned bravado. "Do you think she's stupid enough to steal the mortal from under her son's own nose and meet you without telling me you have my son?"

"Come. She's not labeled the wise one for a reason." Zeus laughed. "Her selfishness and vanity cloud that pretty little brain of hers. *You* figured it out after she called you as the damsel in distress." His last few words were mocking, and he placed his hands by his face, speaking in a creepy falsetto.

"Your son is a traitor!" Hermes spat.

Being accused of logic, I decided to exploit that trait of mine to buy time, to figure something out. "To be a traitor, lines must first be drawn. Tell me, *Zeus*, has the war begun, then?" I challenged, disrespecting him by refusing to call him Father. I hoped his ego would take the bait.

Surely, Aroha would be on her way here, but what could she do? She and I were no match in strength against a teleporting god and the almighty Zeus. Lightning rippled across the sky as a warning. Dad's temper for all of us to see, to intimidate and control us.

"Eros carved a line in the very fabric of our existence by marrying that abomination," Zeus growled. "Your son here officiated it." Zeus's pale face lit up with red-hot suppressed rage.

"It was just another mortal ceremony. He insisted he had to marry her as Eros too," my son said.

Officiated a second one? And Callie an abomination? This was news to me. Psyche's descendant was an abomination? I craved to know what he meant, but how could I trick the truth out of him in front of the god of trickery and thieves? Oh, how I loathed Hermes, my complete opposite.

"Abomination? Surely, the almighty Zeus isn't afraid of a measly little pest. And to start a war against the god of war, not a good move, *Pops*," I mocked him. I'd show Themis; I wouldn't turn on Archer, no matter what.

"Who said I'm starting a war?" Zeus's eyes narrowed at me.

I wanted to lash out to scare him. I wanted to shout at him that Themis had told me, but I didn't want the Fates to know. "Oh, an oracle or two," I said, gauging his reaction.

Zeus stepped closer to me quite aggressively, hands clutched at his side. Thunder boomed, despite the clear night sky, and lightning struck the bridge's suspension above us, the zing of electricity reverberating down.

Hymenaios's gaze met mine. His eyes bulged, and he shook his head slightly. I wasn't sure what his coded gestures meant except not to make any moves, not to provoke my father. Where in Mother Gaia was Aroha?

"Who would dare take on Olympus?" Zeus challenged.

"Who said anyone was taking anyone else on? To me, it seems like it'll be self-defense. You're the one threatening, *Pops*. Are you really threatening my son over a peon? A mortal girl who will age and die? She's a blip in our lives."

"No, you're right." Zeus smiled. It was an eerie smile that was feigned. His eyes were pale blue and cold. They did not crinkle as they should if he truly were happy or rethinking his rashness. "I'm going to kill your son if that mortal isn't brought to me by Aphrodite."

I faltered, the façade of my confidence crumbling. He was serious. He would kill my son, and I didn't know how to stop it. The prophecy had fire in it. Fire and water. I peered down at the road, trying to mask my expression. There was water below. This is where it would happen, and it was happening now. Archer was long gone with Callie in tow, so there was no possible trade-off. What was the use of this prophetic gift if I couldn't stop things? I'd never prevented one in thousands of years. No one was stronger than the Fates.

Then it hit me. Zeus didn't know, couldn't tell, Archer was gone. Rumors of him losing part of his sight, mind, or both were ringing true.

A blurred form stopped next to me. "And what if she cannot garner said peon? Archer and his wife are long gone. They didn't tell any of us where they went, save Ares, who is also gone." Aroha had arrived. She knew where they were or could make a good guess. And she would let my son die to protect her own.

"Took you long enough to get here if that were true," Hermes scoffed. "She hid her, Father, I know it."

"I was held up," she said, looking at her outfit, which was torn in places. "Had a lovely visit from your sister," she said pointedly to me.

So my sister Artemis was on Zeus's side. Not surprised that she was in his pocket, but floored that she would condemn her nephew to death.

"We're at an impasse." Zeus said. His quiet and calm voice was more threatening than when he shouted. "I think you know exactly where they are, and you will tell me." Zeus's eyes rested on me.

I shivered despite the ichor keeping me warm. Even if I had known where they were, how could I choose? My son or Callie and Archer? I would have to save my son, but telling Zeus where Callie was could result in more deaths and Ares storming Olympus.

"If I could tell you, you'd kill her, and a war as horrific as the one with the Titans would ensue." I knew who'd won that one, so we didn't stand a chance, even with Ares.

"Don't you dare, Lucien," Aphrodite pleaded, giving it away to me.

If she believed I knew, I must know, so it had to be Belize. I had no other idea where they could go on such short notice. The Great Blue Hole would mask their presence. They were off Zeus's shaky radar for him to come here too late.

"Dad, don't. He'll kill her!" Hymenaios finally spoke.

The desperation and horror in his voice pierced my soul. I couldn't choose. He was telling me to choose the others, planning to sacrifice himself to save them. He'd never forgive me if I chose him, and yet I couldn't let my son go. I was frozen, my heart breaking into a million pieces.

Hermes elbowed Hymenaios in the stomach to subdue him. When Hymenaios stood back up, his eyes were shining with tears. I couldn't look away. His gaze seemed to tell me he knew, he understood. Then Hermes proceeded to douse my son with gasoline. Despite my son's conviction to be a noble sacrifice, the fluid distressed him, and he started thrashing and screaming.

I snapped into action, racing to him. Something hit my chest hard, snapping my collar-bone and throwing me flat onto the pavement. Zeus's face glowered above me, his arm out; I had been clotheslined. Aroha launched herself at Hermes. They wrestled over the gasoline can for a moment, and then we heard a voice ring out.

"Stop!"

I heard the pull back of a bowstring, followed by a dozen more. I sat up to see we were surrounded by a bunch of beautiful young women armed with bows. In front of me stood my sister.

"Your own nephew!" I pointed, showing how cruel she was being to allow him to be put on the line.

"My allegiance is to Zeus and Zeus alone. Hymenaios is a traitor, as are you. Just tell them a simple location, Api, and save your son." I had no clue who this woman was in front of me. She was no sister of mine anymore.

"Don't, Dad," Hymenaios pleaded.

Hermes, holding a lighter, clicked a flame into being, one that would consume my child.

"I can't let you go, kid," I told him, my voice hardly above a whisper. I turned to Aroha, "The prophecy said I would betray you. I'm sorry."

Aroha shoved Zeus out of the way and tackled me flat to the ground, trying to cover my mouth. Then Aroha roared, rearing up, an arrow through her shoulder. She gasped in pain and pulled it out, screaming as she did so. She dropped it to the ground, staggering back and covering her wound.

"Belize City," I said simply, but the weight of those two words killed me. It was the ultimate betrayal. I would never be forgiven by them; if anything happened to Callie or Archer, I would never forgive myself. How could I let my child die, though?

Aroha fell to the ground with a defeated whimper.

"Now, was that so hard?" Hermes scoffed, letting the flame putter out. He untied my son's hands, and relief swept through me. It didn't matter that he had a look of contempt, that he was disappointed in me. My son would live. Alive and hating me was better than dead because of me.

Zeus grabbed Hymenaios before he could escape and held him in a chokehold. "I'm not sure I liked your hesitation, Apollo. You were almost able to withhold the truth from me. I don't like it. You're no longer a son of mine. All traitors must pay. I'm sending you all a message. Defy me again, and I will burn every single last one of you!" Zeus bellowed. Above us, lightning flashed, accompanied by thunder.

"I gave you what you wanted!" I shouted. "I didn't truly know! It was an educated guess, but Dite's reaction confirmed it. Please!"

I saw my son's eyes go wide. The hairs on my arm stood on end, and I heard the soft zing of lightning charging up—too quiet for mortal ears. Then there was a huge flash of blinding light, a cracking peel of thunder. My son had been struck with one of Zeus's bolts. He was engulfed in flames. His screams were drowned out by my own. Zeus and a shocked Hermes were gone, most likely teleporting to Belize to end Callie's life.

I stood, unmoving, unable to do anything but watch my son's agony. Aroha screamed, trying to crawl to him, but stopped, knowing it was a death wish. My sister ran past him, sneering, and gave me a cold look over her shoulder, her entourage following her.

Any moment, the ichor in Hymenaios's blood would ignite, and he'd be lost forever. His life flashed before my eyes—when I'd first held him, singing him to sleep, teaching him how to play the lyre, his constant and desperate need for my acknowledgment. I'd never been a good father to him, never told him enough that I loved him... All of these thoughts occurred to me in a second of time, as did the rest of the prophecy: water.

221

I ran at him at immortal speed, tackling him over the bridge, being sure to let go of him right away so I didn't ignite. As we plummeted to the water below, I wanted to pray he would survive, but there were no Olympian gods I'd trust to pray to. Instead, I cursed my father and closed my eyes as the water came up to meet me. I knew it would feel like a wall of concrete and break my bones. As long as I could heal in time to save Hymenaios, heal him with my power, that didn't matter. *Poseidon, Proteus, any water god. Help my son. Help Archer.*

Hitting the water hurt like Hades, and all went black.

When I came to, I was woozy, my vision blurry, and I felt drugged. I sat up and then fell over. I was apparently intoxicated, but how? My head ached from the sunlight streaming through the window. A hangover was starting to set in. Simultaneously drunk and hungover was not a good sign. I looked around to ascertain my surroundings and recall how I'd gotten here. It wasn't anywhere I had been before. Then it came back to me: Hymenaios!

I staggered out of bed, falling onto the floor. I quickly got up and walked crookedly to keep upright, the alcohol or drug keeping me from being steady. I had ingested something much stronger than human drugs. We can burn off that stuff much quicker than humans. I must have been given Nectar Whiskey.

The only place in New York I knew to get that was from Dionysus, my fellow outcast brother—different mothers, of course. He was a wayward party animal, and Zeus could never control him. I just hoped Dionysus was on our side. If he had nursed me back to life just to hand me over to Zeus, I'd kill him.

"Aios!" I called. My own voice felt like knives splitting open my head.

I heard some footsteps, and Dionysus appeared with a grim smile. "Humpty Dumpty's back together again!"

"My son?" I asked, my voice sounding slurred and gravelly.

"Alive, we've done the best we could, but he's got a long road of recovery."

"Let me heal him." I tried to push past him. I needed to see that Hymenaios was alive.

"Not yet, healer god. That would be a very bad idea in your state. His brother has been here and has done all he could. He refused to help you, though. I had to put two entire aged nectar whiskey bottles down your throat. All your bones were shattered, a few organs burst."

No, my other sons would not help me, and I deserved this pain for forsaking my friends. I closed my eyes, giving myself the equivalent to a CT scan. All seemed well, except my liver, which was working overtime on my inebriation.

"Well done, thank you. How did I get here?"

"Dite. She pulled you two out of the river, with the help of some naiads" he said quietly.

I could tell from his tone that I would never be forgiven by her. The water gods had come through to answer my prayers.

"Is she here?"

"No. She tended to Hymenaios through the night and left when your son arrived."

"And Asclepius? Is he still here?" I asked in reference to my other son, a talented healer who hadn't talked to me since he was a teen but far surpassed me in medicine and healing arts.

"No, gone too. What have you done to piss off so many people?"

"The worst. Dite didn't fill you in?"

"She didn't have time. She was on the phone all night between tending to your son. All I gleaned was that Archer's in it deep, which I already knew, but he was all she was talking about."

"Can I see my son?" I pressed, not wanting to talk about my betrayal or to think about what might be occurring in Belize.

He moved away from the doorway to let me pass, which I did quite awkwardly, my feet not listening to my brain. I used the walls for support as I staggered down the hall to an open doorway. In the bed lay my son, his skin bright red, hair gone, eyes bandaged. His chest did not rise and fall, nor was he wrapped in gauze like human burn victims. He could not get infected, and he had no need to breathe.

I scanned him quickly to see he was healing but still was a while from being back to his normal self. If he ever could be normal again. Ambrosia would do the trick, but there was no way I could get it. Only Zeus had access to it. My father had tried to kill his grandson. The thought of it was too much.

The important thing was that Hymenaios was alive, and I would ensure he would heal. None of us gods had been brought back from the verge of a death by fire, so I wasn't sure how he'd turn out. I had to give it my best. He looked so vulnerable and pink, like a baby.

I sat down next to him, trying to appear calm and collected when all I wanted to do was burst out crying about the state I'd put him in, the situation I'd allowed to escalate to this point. I should've sent him somewhere safe, away from all this. I had sent my current oracle somewhere Zeus wouldn't find her. I should've sent my son with her. Not that it mattered; Zeus would go after another one of my sons, then Euterpe, or my mother. I hated him.

"Aios, I'm here." I said, my voice cracking and still slurring.

His fingers moved slightly.

"Don't try to move. I'm here, Son. I'm so sorry." They were the only words I could say. I had so much more I needed to explain, but I never was good at putting my feelings into words. I needed him to survive, not to assuage my guilt, but because I loved him.

Then he spoke, a hushed whisper I hardly heard: "You're wasted."

I laughed out loud, taking his hand gently in my own. "You probably are too. We fell off the Brooklyn Bridge, kiddo. Well, I tackled you off it."

He winced at the thought. Then he sucked in air because the wince caused him pain. "Archer? Callie?" he asked a moment later.

I looked to Dionysus, who leaned on the doorframe. He shrugged. Aroha truly hadn't told him a thing.

"I dunno, Aios. I prayed to the water gods for them and for us as we fell. I had to see you first before I made inquiries. They may not even talk to me after what I have done." I awaited his remonstration as well.

"I'm mad, Dad." He paused to take a ragged inhalation of breath in order to talk more. "But then again, it proved how much I mean to you."

"It did. I'm not good with words, kiddo, you know that. Just because I don't say it, doesn't mean I'm heartless."

"I know," he said quietly.

"Now shut up before I give you something to knock you out. You've already expended too much energy."

He gave a throaty laugh, then lay still and silent. I got up to leave, but it didn't feel like enough. I leaned over and kissed the top of his bald head, hoping the thick black hair would grow back for him. Then I walked from the room, steadier on my feet than before.

Once we were out of the room, I closed the door and looked at Dionysus, reading him for truth. "You really haven't heard from them yet about Callie and Archer?"

"Nope. Would I lie to the god of truth?" He smirked at the thought.

I sighed, remembering I had crushed my phone and no one would be able to contact me, nor I them. "So what side are you on?" I eyed him, wondering whether they would even tell him any news.

"Haven't you heard? Hera has been summoning me for months to cure Zeus's madness, and I told her repeatedly to 'bite me.' After all he's done to me, she thought I'd help him? He didn't take too kindly to me saving Archer and the mortal from Zelus either. So, I'm on your side, I guess."

"I'm not sure what side I'm on anymore. I think I've been kicked out of the save-the-mortal group." The thought made me feel utterly alone.

"As long as she is moved before Zeus can kill her, no harm, no foul, right? I'm sure they'll need as many of us on their side as possible. Plus, if you're not on Zeus's side, you're on theirs. Whether they want your help or not, you can give it. We can do a lot away from them, you know." Dionysus certainly had a positive mindset.

I, however, had just watched Zeus try to kill my son for my insubordination. He'd kill Callie at the first opportunity possible.

"Can I borrow a phone?" I asked, determined to find out, to talk to one of my friends.

The prophecy was done. I would choose my side now and forever, no matter what. I was on their side, as Dionysus worded it, whether they wanted me to be or not.

"Sure, but by the way, you owe me $160 to replace my whiskey."

I gaped at him as he handed me his cell.

CHAPTER 32

Archer

My honeymoon wasn't going as I wanted. Sure, our first day and evening were spent in the privacy of our room, but things were awkward after Zeph took us to Belize. My brothers were with us for our protection and insisted we enjoy sightseeing activities and have fun. I wasn't sure what my father was thinking. I mean, with lighter cropped hair, some blue contacts, and boots with a heel, Anteros was my decoy, but how would they be able to protect us? It hardly seemed that they were paying attention to anything at all, and Callie was the one who needed a decoy more than me. I understood Chase's method—Zeus would be watching my parents and Lucien instead of my brothers.

Still, couldn't a god get more alone time with his bride?

I scanned the city relentlessly and saw two charities, Proteus, and a few of his many water-nymph daughters. I sensed both Naiades and Oceanids. Interesting that his daughters could give Zeus's barriers the slip too. I had never heard of many of Poseidon's kin surfacing, which was why mortals rarely saw them. But I didn't see anyone there who might alarm me.

I let my guard down a bit and took Callie to Caye Caulker for a day on the beach, then caught a boat to Ambergris Caye to go snorkeling, and my little daredevil of a wife insisted we go parasailing, much to my dismay. Humans are so fragile, and I didn't like her taking any risks, especially in the sky. Being on the touristy cayes was a reprieve from the city. I hated having her in Belize City.

When it had been just Chase and me, I wasn't worried about the violence or the gang activity, but Callie was human. My anxiety increased with Zeus's silence. Did he really not know what I had done? Had he simply started the timer on Callie's life without telling me? The unknown was more unnerving than an open threat.

On the second day, my brothers woke up hungry and moody, despite the fact we don't have to eat daily to survive. They had always been pampered; the muses had spoiled them rotten. We needed to go into town to go food shopping, but I wanted Callie to stay put and didn't want to leave her side either. As always, my wife was tenacious and didn't trust my brothers to shop. Neither did I. We decided all four of us would go together. Callie showered first, rejecting my invite for us to shower together after Himerus started on lewd jokes. I wanted to pummel him for that.

When I got out after my shower, I found Anteros alone in the living area. It was a small apartment, so I knew Callie was gone right away.

"Where are they?"

"Relax, we got a message. Iris sent some little errand boy. We're to meet her at the docks. She has a message only for your ears. You and I are to meet Callie and Himerus at the grocery store after."

"What were you thinking?" I shouted at him, yanking him up out of his chair.

His eyes went wide. "She is very stubborn. She said someone had to go with you in case it was a trap, and she was insistent that her hiding among the public was safer than staying here. She said 'sitting ducks,' to be exact. We figured they would be looking for you, and I'm your decoy, so Himerus was best to go with her. They blend in better. You know, the hair. She's very assertive and logically convincing. She just had a point, okay? And I'm worried. We gotta get out of here, so you need that message."

"Why wouldn't Iris come directly to us?" I reminded him.

"She'd give us away if she was being followed. Hermes—hacker extraordinaire—has been trying to find a way to track all the teleporters. Or your wife is right, and it is a trap. She's safer away from you."

I ignored his excuses. We should've all gone together. I closed my eyes, searching for Callie, and found her and Himerus in the market. I didn't note any sketchy immortals near her.

"She's okay," I took a breath, trying to calm myself. I was like a wound spring. "We're wasting time. C'mon. Let's find them."

I wouldn't feel at ease until Callie was by my side, in my arms. I knew my brothers and Proteus and his daughters would protect her to the best of their abilities, but I was the only one willing to die for her. Not to downplay their resolve to be heroic, but everyone has a breaking point. A foreboding feeling crept up my spine at the thought.

I ignored Anteros's insistent pleas to go meet Iris. I needed to see Callie safe.

We were out the door, running at immortal speed through the city until it became too congested with people walking out of the market. Then we walked—and got some stares, most likely because we seemed to appear from nowhere to their slow mortal eyes. It didn't help that we were identical blond twins in a city that was a mixing pot of Caribbean and

Central American culture and entering a local's area away from tourists. Callie and I had stuck to the touristy locations previously. They felt much safer. Prior to that, I had gained some looks when I entered this part of town, but now it would draw attention to her. There was nothing for it. I had to find her; we had promised never to part. I hurried my pace.

When we finally made it into the market, it was bustling with people. They had waited so they'd blend into the crowd, and it was working too well. I searched around, scanning everyone and everything in sight for Callie and Himerus. I double-checked everyone.

"The grocery store is up through here. Maybe they're there," Anteros said.

Living here longer than him, I wanted to smack him upside the head for talking down to me. I knew he was buying time. He was nervous as all Hades as well. His hands twitched, just like mine, feeling the same anxiety. Then I felt it, a strong immortal presence nearby, an Olympian.

"Do you feel—"

Anteros was cut off by a whistle to our left. In the alley, Iris was leaning strangely against the building and holding her arm, injured from the looks of it. She was not by the docks, so Callie had been right about a trap.

I raced over to Iris at immortal speed, my brother on my tail. I caught her as she slumped to the ground. "Iris?" What in the Underworld was happening?

She blew out a laugh. I knew something was utterly wrong. She wasn't incognito, but herself, the little sprite-looking teleporter. Her short black hair was up in the air like a troll toy.

"I'll live Archer, my gods." She coughed up blood.

Anteros looked at me with fright. He was so sheltered, a child raised by the muses, cozy and safe in Olympus under Zeus's ever-watchful eye.

I instantly reacted as my mind jumped to conclusions, so there wasn't a way to stop myself, like the dormant Ares in me woke up. I launched myself upon Anteros, screaming, "Traitor!" at him.

I had him pinned on the ground under me. He'd led me out on some mysterious note to separate Callie and me.

"No," he said, his eyes wide with innocence. "I swear it. Maybe I would've turned against you a year ago out of spite, but when I came to New York and you were nice to us...I was thrown off. I envied you but not in a bad way. Eros," he pleaded now. "I always wanted to *be* you. The fact you treated me as an equal, finally, it just...I dunno. I thought we were brothers."

Guilt flooded over me. I didn't have to be Apollo to see the truth etched in my brother's face, one almost identical to mine. He was just as lost and scared as I was, and my accusation hurt him.

I let him go, hopped up, and grasped his hand, yanking him up. "We are. We always will be. How my parents and I treated you was—"

"Neglectful."

"Yeah. I'm sorry I accused you, but I'm half-crazy about where Callie is."

"I shouldn't have let her go. I'm sorry."

Before I could assuage his guilt, a healed Iris stood up. "All right, you sentimental and idiotic love gods, you're wasting time. Zeus struck me with three freakin' bolts of lightning, and Hermes cut me up like five times, all to stop my message, so shut up!" She held her side, but her wounds looked healed.

Zeus had in fact fried her, obvious from the state of her hair. His bolts were deadly to mortals and pretty incapacitating to us.

"Chase said I had to whisper it in your ear and your ear alone. He made me vow on the Styx, so Zeus didn't get it out of me."

I leaned in as my brother huffed and walked to the alley entrance to stand watch and let her deliver it.

She leaned in and almost inaudibly whispered, "Thinking of your death will save your life. Go to that place."

I looked at her, lost, and she gave me a look that could kill. "Thank you, Iris. Did you send a messenger boy to my place?"

She shook her head, which made my blood run cold. This was definitely a trap.

"Callie?"

"They let me go so they could go after her. I'm sorry. I don't know anything else."

I let go of her, and she vanished, leaving a faint rainbow in her wake.

I knew my Dad was discreet for a reason. He had info, and he was telling me where to go next. Only, I had no clue what he meant and was completely absorbed by my missing wife.

"Archer!" Himerus's voice was sharp, and he was running down the street, frantic. Anteros intercepted him and yanked him into the alley.

"Where's Callie?" I demanded, also wary of trusting him.

"Hold on," Anteros chided. He felt over Himerus's body.

That's when I noted he was covered in blood and charred material, his hair on end. My stomach dropped. "What happened?"

"She's...I'm sorry." The big ape started crying.

I pressed him against the wall. "She's what?"

"It was an ambush! They knew we were here. Artemis and her gang were battling the nymphs, Proteus taken down by a bunch of muses—I think he's still alive—and Zeus got me. All it took was freakin' Hermes, Archer. He just appeared and took her. He and Zeus vanished with her."

I let him go. I closed my eyes, trying not to unleash my furious energy upon those who were trying to help me. I focused on scanning for Callie. Our souls were linked, so I found her immediately.

I took a deep breath. "I know where they are."

Both my brothers were looking at me with awe, and I realized I must be acting very much like my father—and so be it, damn it. I needed Dad's war mindset right now. "You should stay here."

"No way. Dad said we stick together no matter what," Himerus insisted.

"I don't have time to argue. It's suicide, taking on Zeus and Hermes. I'm getting my wife back, or I'll die trying. I'm not asking you to die too."

"Die by Zeus's lightning or be torn to pieces by the god of war for letting his son go at it alone? He already barely tolerates my existence," Anteros said with such nonchalance, you'd think we were talking about going on a stroll.

"And we're brothers. We have each other's backs from here on out. You can't do this without us," Himerus added.

"I can't let you—"

"Good thing you can't command us. Same generation. How do you think you're going to get her without us?" Himerus challenged.

The question left me dumbfounded. I needed them, damn it. And they were willing to risk it all for me and for Callie.

"Okay, here's the deal." I launched into hasty plans that would probably utterly fail.

There was no time for weapons or strategy. We'd have to rely on intellect and sheer random luck. I sent a prayer to Tyche, the goddess of luck, who was down in Atlantis. I hoped rather than expected her to hear my prayer.

CHAPTER 33

Callie

Himerus was nervous, making me feel even more anxious. We needed food. Sure, we could order to-go from a restaurant again, but I wanted the boys to have one nice home-cooked meal before we were on the run. I had no idea how many times we would relocate or where we would go. I had no clue if I'd live to see next week. I would cook a nice full breakfast because it would soothe me, and the boys would enjoy it. Everything was going to be unpredictable from here on out and unstable, most likely dangerous. Archer hoped we would hear today where we should go next.

In the Michael Finnegan Market, I hurried through the stalls, buying vegetables for the omelets and some fresh fruit. It had opened a couple hours ago, but we waited for it to become busy. I should've waited for Archer, and I knew he'd be mad, but the idea of a god sending a human messenger to where we were staying shook me up. Someone—friend or foe—knew my location. I needed to instantly get out of there. It took a bit of convincing, but the boys gave in. Archer and Anteros would be behind us in minutes.

I was okay with this plan until I felt eyes on me (just great). I turned to see a man with blond hair and pale skin in the shadows not far from us. My eyes went wide, and I tugged on Himerus's arm to get his attention. The man in the shadows put his finger to his lips to motion me to be quiet.

Himerus looked and simply whispered, "Proteus, our team."

I tried to roll the tension out of my neck, and I pulled Himerus's borrowed baseball cap farther down to hide my face. We left the market, but when we passed by a run-down jewelry store, I saw charms for sale in the window. I clasped the necklace my father had given me, the one that had belonged to my mother. It was a simple white gold chain with a tiny star pendant. I scanned the display, looking for the charm I wanted to add to it. I saw it, a little silver arrow. It would symbolize my past and my future. At some point, I would find a pendant to represent my father, a book maybe. Nothing there spoke Dad to me.

I stopped and headed inside, ignoring Himerus's snort of annoyance. He stood outside on watch as people milled to and fro, the crowd a bit thinner than in the bustling market. I made my purchase and joined him. His annoyed expression reminded me greatly of Chase. I removed my necklace to add the charm on.

Himerus shifted uncomfortably, wanting to move on to the grocery store to pick up more food, meet up with the others, and get back to the apartment. There was a shift in the air, the wind stopping, and the hair on my neck stood on end. A muggy pressure coated the air, like when a thunderstorm is coming. Himerus swore under his breath and pulled me as fast as he could into the shadows between buildings, going back in the direction of the flat rather than the grocery store. I fumbled with my necklace, trying to clasp it around my neck as I stumbled.

"No time."

"This was my mother's. She's dead."

Himerus yanked it out of my hand and shoved it in the pocket of his jeans. "C'mon. We have to get back. If I say hold onto me, you hold on for dear life, got it? I can outrun them."

"Who?"

"Don't panic." He took us down another alley. "I sense Zeus."

My breath hitched (crappity crap). Clouds obliterated the sun, moving in at an unnatural speed.

"Hold on!" He grabbed me.

A split second later, we were down the alleyway. More immortal curses flew out of Himerus's mouth, mentioning Hades, Poseidon's trident, and I'm not sure what else when we came to a halt. A stone wall blocked the way out. We turned around, but Himerus put an arm out to stop me. Lightning struck the ground not twenty feet in front of us—exactly where we had just been standing.

Where the lightning hit, two men appeared out of thin air. One was thin, lithe, with a mop of unruly light brown hair, dark eyes, and a smug demeanor. I recognized him immediately as the man who had come to New York a couple times, the messenger: Hermes. The other drew my attention at once. He was older than the other, in his thirties maybe, with pale blue eyes and long wavy platinum hair. He had a tidy short beard that matched in color. He looked like a movie star, perfectly formed, so I knew he was a god. I sensed I should fear him. Coupled with the lightning, I knew it was Zeus, the god of gods, the omniscient one who wanted me dead.

We were cornered.

"Himerus," the younger, plainer man said in a chiding manner.

"Sorry, Gramps." Himerus was tense, scared, but trying to hide it.

I was yanked into the air, and we were flying at such a speed, I had to close my eyes because they were tearing up from the wind. I was yanked this way, then that, like riding a roller coaster. And then it felt as if we slammed into a brick wall. I fell hard onto my butt. Himerus was being pinned to the wall by Zeus and Hermes. I saw a knife slice Himerus up as he fought them off, his strength and speed unbelievable, a blur of movement in front of my eyes like a crazy CGI action movie star.

I didn't want to leave him, wanted to help, but I ran. I was following his orders. If there was trouble, I was to run to the flat, and if I couldn't make it there, make it to the sea. There were nymphs protecting us, more in the water who couldn't come on land.

I saw flashes of lightning and saw Himerus smoking and falling to his knees.

"Zeus!" Proteus entered the alley.

I kept running, trying to follow the sound and the smell of the sea through the maze of buildings. The apartment was by the sea as well. I ran until I felt my lungs would burst, and then I tripped and fell when the solid ground gave way to sand.

I lay for a moment, my hands digging in the sand, before I came to my senses that I was so close to where I needed to be: the ocean. Belize City didn't really have beaches, just one manmade one, and this was not it. I looked up, squinting in the brilliant light. I was feet from the crashing waves. I jumped up and ran toward the mangroves that plagued the coastline. This meant no one was around—no tourists or locals, no witnesses. If I could reach the spindly water trees, I would be safe.

I was feet from the water and filled with hope. Some solid surface slammed into me. I was thrown back onto the ground, the wind knocked out of me completely. I struggled for breath and coughed, which allowed oxygen to flow back into my lungs. I looked up to see the smug man staring down at me with hatred. Cloud coverage obscured the brilliant sun. I knew the storm clouds meant lightning and that Zeus was coming, and perhaps my end. (The idea got me going.)

I tentatively stood, seeing if he'd attack. I tried to run, but Hermes was in front of me. I turned and tried to go for the ocean. Again, he reappeared in front of me. I tried two more times, and he simply laughed as if this unfair cat-and-mouse game was entertaining.

"Where do you think you're going?"

"Where's your buddy?" I mocked him.

He sneered. "He is Father, the god of gods, you disgusting peon." He spun me around so my back faced his front and wound his arms around me in a crushing grip.

The pressure became unbearable, the air left my lungs, and my ears popped. I saw darkness, and suddenly, we were back in the alleyway with Himerus, Proteus, and Zeus. It was a more painful process of teleporting than Zeph's soft and dizzying whirlwind.

Proteus looked dead—pale, unmoving, covered in blood, and his clothing smoldering. Himerus was holding his own against Zeus, punching him in the stomach, despite the bolts of lightning Zeus struck him with. Zeus shoved Himerus into the wall and turned toward us. My captor held his hand out, and Zeus grasped it. I was squeezed again, and it went dark, but the last thing I saw was Himerus shouting and trying to run fast enough to stop them.

I opened my eyes to see the ocean. I was let go. I tried to run, only to realize I was on a sailboat. I spun around and saw the ocean all around me and no glimpse of land, even on the horizon. Then my eyes rested on my kidnappers. I was in the middle of the ocean with the most powerful god, and he wanted me dead. (I was screwed.)

"There's nowhere to go, peon," Hermes said.

"*Tsk, tsk*," Zeus said, running his hands down his clothes, which were still smoking and blood stained. "Hermes, she has a name." (Right, good cop, bad cop routine.) "Callista Syches," Zeus said scathingly. (Never mind—bad cop, creepy cop, apparently.) He pronounced my last name as "*Psyche's*," as if he'd solved some huge riddle, not realizing we had all solved that one six months prior.

"What have I ever done to make you want me dead?" I demanded with fake bravado.

My mind reeled, trying to figure a way out of this. What if I dove into the water? Were there sea nymphs, Oceanids, there to save me? Was I too far from the coast to make it back if they weren't there? I had to find out, and the only way to know what would happen to me would entail breaking into the mind of the all-knowing god. Could it even be done? He might kill me at any moment. What was there to lose?

"Existed," Zeus said in such a simple manner, it was beyond insulting.

Then he sat down on the boat bench seat and crossed his legs as if he were completely at ease, trying to intimidate me (successfully). I focused in on him. I noticed his shoulders were stiff, his foot tapped, and he was discreetly biting his inner cheek. He did want me dead but was afraid of something—the repercussions?

"Where's Archer?" I had to buy time. For what, I didn't know. Any crazy idea. I was clutching madly at straws to survive, some crazy god to intervene like they did in myths, anything.

"Eros," he corrected me. "Don't worry about him. If I were you, I'd worry about myself."

I steadied my shaking knees, hiding my fear. The sky clouded over even more, casting a twilight feel, despite it being not quite noon yet. The wind whipped around us, and thunder roared. Zeus, god of the sky and chief of all gods, was summoning his powers to destroy me. All I could think about was what this would do to my husband, to Aroha, Chase, and even Lucien. They would retaliate. I destroyed Olympus through simply loving Archer. The worst part of it was, alive or dead, I couldn't stop it.

"So, no year as promised." I laughed bitterly.

My death was about to occur. I didn't fear it. Technically, I couldn't die yet until a Death was made. I dreaded being comatose, though. What if I could hear Archer begging me to wake up and knew I couldn't? What if this forced my dad into the same state as me? Out of all the possibilities, what bothered me most was the thought of not seeing my husband's face again, not living my life to the fullest.

"No," he said simply. "Well, it will depend on Eros. He has to choose a Death as part of his punishment."

It knocked the air out of my lungs. I closed my eyes. The tears betrayed me by leaking out. This psychotic god was going to make his grandson choose his own wife's executioner or keep her in an eternal coma. Archer didn't have the constitution to do either. He'd attempt to take his life again. That would never happen if I could help it.

My brain scrambled around for a way out. I decided I needed to get away, to trust in the water and just flee. I might've dreamed about drowning, which probably was prophetic, but at least it wouldn't let Zeus win. It would be on my terms.

I opened my eyes and glared at Zeus. Determination and a lot of raging defiance came over me. "My name is Callista of Olympus, not Syches anymore."

Zeus's jaw clenched. Hermes was the messenger and thief god (thanks, Dad, for all the mythology lessons) who was now hissing at me like a cat for my insubordination. It didn't intimidate me as he had hoped. I closed my eyes and took a step back. I wasn't religious, so I didn't know how to pray to gods, but I put a prayer up to Poseidon to help me, then one up to Eros to let love triumph.

"What are you doing?" Zeus asked, an edge in his voice.

I took a step up onto the opposite seat, ready to jump into the ocean if needed. The question was if I could do it before he could stop me.

Then a huge wave knocked the boat, and I almost lost my balance. I wasn't sure if I could do it under pressure, but I closed my eyes, thinking of Archer. In the past, I had been able to read his mind, find him.

He was thinking about me and was on the move, although his form and that of two others—his brothers—was blurry due to the speed. There was water. He was coming for me.

"Praying won't work, Miss Syches." Zeus disrupted my thoughts and insulted me by using my maiden name. He would not admit I was his family. "The gods are before you."

My eyes snapped open. Zeus stood there, arms spread, laughing.

"Not all of them," I muttered.

"If you think Eros will be of any help, you'll be sadly disappointed. Wings don't work well over water, which is precisely why I brought you here."

"Why bother? You're going to kill me anyway." I had to stall him, let Archer and his brothers get here.

The sun peeked through the clouds, reminding me of Lucien. What had he and Archer told me about Zeus? I should've asked Lucien more questions about him, not just about gods I knew. I thought back. He said Zeus used to be fair, rational, and he liked to bargain. Most importantly, he wasn't all-seeing as he professed, proven by his inability to see Archer coming for me now.

"Kill you? Not yet. That would set off my son and grandson. Unlike my son, I do not have a love for war. We're here to negotiate."

"I thought you negotiated in punishments, but I did nothing wrong."

"Eros broke my ruling. According to our deal, I could kill you right now."

I tried to read his mind, pushing into it, envisioning my thoughts stretching away from me like a rubber band. And then I was there. *I need to strike a deal, one she could never decide on, push her into choosing to die. Perhaps in exchange for Eros's life...hmm, her father's...or make her choose which one lives.*

His thoughts gave me chills, but I refused to flinch or react to give myself away. My stomach went queasy. How could I ever choose between

Archer and my father? I would die before picking one of them, but that was precisely what he wanted.

"As you said, you can't kill me now. So, what is your grand plan to get rid of me? Hmm..." I feigned thinking. "You'd have to get me to take my own life so that you'd be blameless. I wouldn't, so I imagine you would pit those I love against each other to make me choose. You'd expect me to beg and plead to take me instead of them. I'd hate to tell you, but it's not going to happen."

Zeus's face paled even more than its usual fair hue. His eyes went cold, almost lifeless looking. I felt static electricity building between us—the only sign of his rage. "They've told you a lot about me, I see."

"Only that you can't resist bargaining, are logical, and no longer omniscient."

"Zeus sees everything!" Hermes was suddenly inches from me, his face contorted in rage. (That was an obvious admittance through denial if I ever saw it.)

"Back down, Hermes," Zeus chided, his icy glare never leaving me.

I held his gaze, even though it unnerved me, to show him I was stronger than he thought.

"If that is all they told you, then you *see* too much, as I suspected."

He didn't deny my accusation, so I didn't deny his. Another wave rocked the boat. He leaned forward, cutting the distance between us in half, and there was no room to back up on this little boat. His irises moved, churning like a stormy sky. In fact, the sky was moving in circular clouds.

Where was Archer?

"What will you do for some precious time, Callista?"

I hated him calling me that. It ruined Dad's loving use of my formal name. Dad had been the only one to call me that, aside from teachers on first days.

"Not what you want me to."

"I find it highly unlikely you wouldn't nobly sacrifice yourself to save Eros or your father," Zeus sneered.

He thought he knew me, and in theory, I would give up my life in a heartbeat for either of them, but I'd be stupid if I believed either would live or that gods bargained fairly.

"Why would I? My father is so ill—thanks to you—that even if you stopped killing him, he could never heal. His heart is beyond repair. Apollo even said so. And you think Eros will live without me? He already tried to kill himself because of your stupid ruling. So no, Zeus, I say no to your bargain."

"Then you all die." He shrugged as if it were nothing.

"And you think Ares will just sit back and take that? You see, I don't think you're in a position to bargain."

Zeus laughed, but it was hollow (so I was right). "How about time? If Archer chooses a Death, I'll give you a year."

It was a simple request. He wanted Archer to fulfill his punishment and to replace the god he'd killed. And yet, the request was utterly complex. Death would kill my father and, in a year, me.

"You already promised him a year with me if he didn't stay away, so we gain nothing in this supposed bargain."

"Two years, then, but no more."

I swallowed hard. Two years. Would that give us enough time to figure out something else, a way around Zeus? I knew I could not make a deal with him, no matter what. Alarms were going off in my head.

There was a loud thump in the boat. Archer's water-drenched form landed right in front of me, making the boat rock. Relief flooded over me. Although I knew we were far from safe, I wasn't alone. Two more soaking wet boys climbed into the boat.

Zeus eyed them, a scowl on his face. "Found some help, I see."

"Blame yourself. You made them immortal." Archer's voice was tight. He was holding back his emotions.

"Made up with your little brothers, did you?" Hermes mocked.

Himerus and Anteros shifted closer to me, the boat rocking on a swirling sea. Waves lapped the boat, spraying us. The sky swirled with an upcoming storm.

"Enough formalities. I came for my wife." Archer turned to Hermes. "Don't even think about it." He knew whatever Hermes next move would be. Archer was so strong, unafraid.

"Hermes, don't," Zeus said.

Hermes gave his father an incredulous look.

Zeus looked down into the water. "Someone else is here. It would do you and me no good if this argument moved underwater."

So the storm was Zeus, but the waves weren't created by that alone. Poseidon was here, but on whose side?

"Didn't think you had it in you to keep disobeying me." Zeus glared at Archer. Something told me that when he was younger, Archer had been intimidated by that glower, but not anymore. "And you two."

I looked over to the brothers, and they looked down to avoid his remonstrative glower.

"Sorry, Gramps," Anteros said. "But don't see why he can't have her."

"At least we got rid of one of the trio," Hermes said.

Himerus gasped. "Aois."

The two brothers' postures slumped. We were losing them.

"I'll be happy to get rid of another one, Father," Hermes said.

"There was no Chaos." To keep his brothers steady, Archer affirmed that Lucien's son couldn't have died.

I didn't really get what or who Chaos was, but it appeared in their heads when an Olympian died. No Chaos, no dead gods.

Hermes and Zeus exchanged a coded look as if they had not even thought about the possibility of his survival (because all they had thought about was me dead, I bet).

Zeus's lips curled up in an irritated but smug expression. He had some trick up his sleeve. "You boys are interrupting. Callie and I were negotiating."

"She won't make any—" Archer began.

"I wasn't negotiating. I was wasting time," I said.

"I think you'll change your mind once this begins," Zeus said, lashing out. He was desperate and angry.

Before I could wonder what "this" was, lightning streaked out of the sky and struck Archer. He faltered onto one knee, his hands catching him on the deck, muscles twitching and steam rising off of him. He whirled around to look at me, eyes wide, expecting something horrific from the terrified expression on his face.

And then it hit me. My muscles went rigid, my bones ached, and I felt as if my blood was boiling, cooking me from within. My heart stopped, and I couldn't breathe. Then it started beating madly, thumping in my chest, its pulse unsteady, slowing and going too fast in turns. I couldn't hear or see for a second, but I felt someone catch me before I hit the deck. My ears rang, but through the ringing, I heard someone say, "What in Hades happened?"

I blinked and saw Zeus looming over us with a huge grin. "Oh, Eros, how stupidly romantic of you to immortally marry a mortal. Did you think it would stop me from killing her? I assure you, I will consider you necessary collateral damage, nothing more."

"I didn't do it for that." Archer hoisted me up, and I feebly stood on my legs.

My mind was processing their comments a tad slower than normal. It sounded as if Archer would die if I died, literally. Was that what immortal marriage was? If our souls were bound, would we always feel each other's pain?

"I did it because I will not live without her."

Zeus's anger abated, and his face fell. He looked sad. Maybe he was finally giving up? "You know, you used to be my favorite. It's such a shame."

I took it back. He was about to kill both of us.

He refused to look at Archer, the coward, as he sent another bolt of lightning through Archer. A large wave rocked the boat, splashing Zeus. Then the lightning passed onto me. Anteros caught me but placed me down quickly. I was momentarily blind and deaf again, but when it subsided, I saw all of them fighting.

"Love makes me stronger, remember?" Archer growled as he kicked Zeus into the side of the boat.

Hermes kept appearing and reappearing, but the brothers kept getting a punch or two in since the boat was limited in places he could reappear.

Hold your breath, child, a voice said.

But everyone around me was busy and not talking. It came from inside my head.

Hold your breath now!

I saw the tidal wave headed our way and took a huge gulp of air. I squeezed my eyes shut, praying to random gods, some not even Greek. I doubted it would work, but when you learned they were real, it was worth a try.

I felt upended, falling but then being cushioned. The ocean was cool. Something hit my leg. My stomach dropped, which meant one thing: I was being sucked down with a sinking boat. I kicked and flailed my arms, trying to get out of the boat's path, trying not to think about physics class when we talked about the inability to swim in aerated water. The fact I was falling through the boat's bubbles was no more comforting than the myth of being sucked down.

And then it stopped. I kicked as hard as I could toward the surface. I opened my eyes, and they stung terribly, but I had to find the way up. I saw light up above—the surface. It was so far away, and my lungs were beginning to burn. I kicked harder, but it made my urge to breathe stronger. I stopped, hoping buoyancy would pull me up.

Strong hands grabbed me, and I saw someone with white hair and beard in front of me: Zeus. I panicked, and a bubble of air popped out. I had no air left.

Stop, child, the voice said.

The face was up against mine, and I thought he was trying to kiss me for some weird reason until I felt him blowing into my mouth. My lungs expanded, and there was enough oxygen it seemed to prevent me from passing out. Then he yanked me, and we shot upwards. I had to close my eyes, the pain of the salt unbearable. I felt my face surface and took a huge gasping breath.

I treaded and wiped my eyes, gazing over to Zeus, completely confused. That's when I noticed it wasn't Zeus. The white-blond hair and beard were exceptionally long and tinged with green. His features weren't as sharp, and his eyes were a blue-green hue, like the ocean. And they were open wide, as well as his mouth, as he looked around at the sky and then me with fright and astonishment.

A swan honked, drawing our attention as it flew off frantically. Swans didn't belong in the open ocean (what the...?).

"Fly far, far away, Brother, like the coward you always were," the man murmured to himself, watching the swan disappear from sight. (Brother? Swan?)

Dad's mythology quizzes came back. Zeus could turn into a swan, a god in the water who was his brother...

"Poseidon?" I asked.

That snapped his gaze back to me, and he remembered I was there.

"Callie!" Archer was calling me.

I scanned the water and saw him when a wave dipped down. Then a large wave spiked up between us and was about to crest on top of me, but it stopped and sank back down.

"Archer!" I turned back around, and the Zeus-clone was gone. The sea was calm.

"Callie!" Archer's voice was full of relief as he closed the distance between us. "Himerus!"

He was in front of us in a flash. "Anteros!" Himerus called.

"Coming!" he said, swimming much slower than Himerus had.

Archer pulled me in and tried to kiss me, but treading made it awkward, so he went for my cheek. I looked around. We were in the middle of the ocean without a way to get back to land. Zeus and Hermes were gone.

"I have so many freakin' questions right now, but foremost, how do we get out of here?" I asked.

"We're ready, but *where to* is the question," Himerus asked Archer.

"Dad said, thinking of my death would save my life. Go to that place. Damn it!" Archer growled. "Why couldn't he just give it to me straight?"

"Archer, I can't tread water forever." I was exhausted. Being indirectly struck by lightning twice and almost drowning had taken everything out of me.

"Himerus, get started. We have to find land, regardless of where we're headed. Anteros, see if you can scan to see where we are."

While Himerus swam off at superspeed and Anteros closed his eyes, I asked Archer to repeat Chase's message.

"Soufrière Hills, Archer. Go where you wanted to die, and that will save our lives. Heph is there."

"You're brilliant, Callie." He smiled at me, despite the dire situation. In that moment, the way he looked at me made all the trauma we'd just experienced melt away.

"We're just south of Puerto Rico," Anteros said. "Montserrat is a few hundred miles, but possible."

"Um, not for me," I said. Did they seriously forget I was only a demigod?

"No time to explain. Hang on," Archer told me as he pulled me around to be on his back. "I mean it, Callie. Hold on for dear life, and don't let go."

I wrapped my arms around his neck. Surprisingly, he didn't go underwater from my weight but rose up. Archer gripped Anteros under the arms, and we literally rose out of the water, me on Archer's back, choking him from fright, and Anteros being picked up like a kid. I saw Himerus as a speck in the distance that disappeared on the horizon. We were fully out of the water, a hundred feet or so in the air (I was freakin' out), and then—*whoosh!* We crashed hard into the water.

I surfaced, sputtering out water. Anteros and Himerus were laughing about Himerus getting kicked in the head. He had been so far away, and now he was right in front of me.

"We call it island hopping," Archer explained.

Himerus sighed after Anteros told him the destination and took off again swimming.

"We discovered how to do it as kids. Himerus is exceptionally fast like our father. He swims so fast that he can get up and literally run on top of the water. Anteros, being the opposite of me in many ways, creates gravity, whereas I defy it. I pull us up out of the water because water would slow us down. Anteros pulls us to Himerus like a magnet. Only drawback is that he has to be able to see what he pulls himself to. The higher up I go, the farther he can see and control gravity's pull. So we're traveling roughly twenty miles at a time. It's going to take a while, love, but all you need to do is hold on."

I nodded, my mind not really understanding what he said. I grabbed on again, and they repeated the process. By the fifth go, I understood how it worked. Archer seemed to go higher each time so Anteros could see farther.

Also, he was beginning to shake slightly under our weight. The lightning had done him no favors either. When I could bear it no more, and my arms ached too much, Anteros shouted he saw land.

Sure enough, I saw some land on the horizon, a mountain—or volcano. It gave me a second wind, and soon we were crawling onto the beach by the volcano, all of us exhausted and spent. Himerus was winded and trying to catch his breath; Archer and I were immobile, heads turned looking at each other, and Anteros was counting his bruises before they vanished.

"We made it. We're safe here," Archer said quietly.

"Except the volcano," Himerus said.

"Are you referring to that one or Heph?" Anteros asked in a serious tone.

Archer laughed hard. Seeing the smile on his face brightened up my mood, and I started giggling. Heph wouldn't like any of these boys, and from what Lucien had told me, he'd hate Himerus the most of all.

"I'm serious," Anteros said, put out.

"I know." Archer laughed again.

The laughter died away, and we lay there, staring at the empty horizon, the warm sun drying us, while marveling over being alive, all silently wondering what the future held for us.

CHAPTER 34

CHASE

I knew I was being tailed. That was the whole point of me flying to California. I was leading away a couple spies—in the form of Alastor and Nemesis—quite fitting since the former was god of family feuds and the latter, goddess of revenge. Her, I could handle, but Alastor was freakishly sadistic. I was determined to lose him, or I might have to get as drastic as my son had and murder a god; that would make things even worse with Zeus. Part of me was longing for a good fight, but it would be best to wait for one I could easily win without effort.

After my layover at LAX, I flew eleven hours to Japan and landed at Narita International Airport. There, I jumped on the JR Narita express train to Tokyo station.

This was doing the unthinkable. A connecting plane was one thing other gods would turn a blind eye to, but to enter their territory without permission was seen as an affront. Being the god of war...I didn't want to think about how they would take it. The Japanese gods resided here, and they despised Zeus, and us by default. They kept to themselves mostly, rarely visiting other territories, so when you entered theirs, it could get messy. I didn't think Zeus's spies would dare to follow me there.

At Tokyo station, I hopped on the infamous bullet train, Shinkansen, to Osaka. Outside Shin-Osaka Station, I hailed a cab and directed the driver in my broken Japanese to get to the Kansai International Airport, extra money if he did it quickly. Traffic proved that impossible, and I saw another cab in my rearview trying to weave closer.

They did dare to follow me.

I told my driver to lose the cab. He seemed to understand, and without question, he started going down backroads and alleys that were almost too small for one car and weaved his way around the city. The normal forty-minute ride turned into an hour, but I was dropped off at the airport without the other cab tailing me.

Every moment I had led them on this goose chase was time I was leaving Archer and Callie vulnerable—a day so far, and adding in the connections still ahead of me, two days would pass. I was accustomed to long periods awake since sleeping amidst a war is not a great idea. In order to get to my destination, there would be a couple stops first, but after that, there would be even more travel. That last leg wouldn't be in my father's skies at least.

On the flight, I worried if my father might go as far as dropping my plane out of the sky, but Archer and Callie's safety overrode that concern. Even Aroha was left fairly vulnerable.

When I landed in London, I summoned Iris and imparted a coded message to Archer of where to rendezvous and made her swear on the Styx so Zeus couldn't pry it from her, even under threat of death. I then placed a call to make sure my children would be welcomed safely. It would be a pitstop for them until I lost this baggage following me and secured the real safehouse.

It had been too easy to lose Alastor and Nemesis, but outside Heathrow, while I headed to the bus station, to catch one to Gatwick for my next flight, I wasn't surprised I felt her presence—Nemesis, but she was alone. I had lost Alastor. Not wanting her to know where my next stop was, I veered away from the bus terminal. I nicked a man's cigarettes by swiftly picking his pocket and headed to the smoking area, pretending to need a smoke. I asked a smoking mortal for a light, got the cigarette going, and then wandered off, slipping into a dark area of the parking garage. I noted the security camera was busted, so I knew she was there, covering her tracks.

I turned to see her silhouette: strong, tall, broad shouldered, her hair in the same tight braid she'd worn for millennia. She put her hands on her hips to widen her stance, to try to appear more intimidating. "The wittle wabbit is finally cornered," she mocked me.

She was stupid to think she'd trapped me. Separating them, possibly losing them, had been the plan, but I'd be naive if I had thought I'd get out of it without a fight. Should I call her out now or bide my time?

I tossed the cigarette down to the ground and put it out with my shoe, letting the smoke out of my mouth like a formidable dragon. I tried not to think about Dite having a go at me for smoking again. It was a nasty habit I'd quit and picked up over a dozen times over the last couple centuries.

"Cornered?" I laughed. "Where's your friend?"

"The Japanese didn't take kindly to him."

No, they wouldn't. Family was everything to them, and Alastor has always disrupted peace within families.

"I figured as much. Ah, like old times, isn't it? You know, sometimes I love seeing you, Nemesis, and sometimes I *hate* it."

Stressing the word did its work. She flinched. I knew she had always had a thing for me. I never used it against her—well, to be honest, I may have slightly flirted to get her to switch sides a couple times.

"What are you up to, Ares?"

"You mean my father sent you without explaining why or what you were doing, and you jumped at the opportunity to see me? Aren't you cute?" I mocked her, knowing it would set her off—my intention—and braced myself for impact.

She collided into me, smashing bones in both our bodies. Foolish really, because I'd taught her how to roll with impact to minimize injury and to roll the opponent under to take advantage while said person was incapacitated. She forgot everything in her rage. I rolled her under me, pinning her down in a position that made her blush, and she could do nothing about it, her ribs most likely cracked. My collar bone and a rib or two were in bad shape, but from her shallow breathing, her lung had gotten punctured as well. I had the upper hand.

"No." She gasped for breath like a fish out of water, her dark eyes narrowing in anger. "I came because Hypnos evoked me."

By the beard of Zeus, I hadn't thought of that. Hypnos, the god of sleep, was Thanatos's twin brother. Since my son killed Thanatos, Nemesis had every right to be here if he asked her to retaliate as the god of vengeance. It was misplaced, though.

"Why would you be after me and not my son? Aww, Nem-Nem, I missed you too." I knew teasing her was the best way to set her off and end this in one way or another, so I kept at it.

She shoved me, healed now, but I pressed down into her. She blushed profusely. "Let me up."

"Not until you agree to walk over into a little restaurant and have a bite to eat, civilly. We can even call it a date if you insist, although sadly, it can't be."

It was cruel to torture her when I had no feelings for her, and I knew the woman had been mad for me ever since our Olympian days, but there are no rules in war or hearts. I was dealing with both, so I had to fight dirty.

"Date?" she choked.

I got up, pulling her with me in one fluid motion.

"Can't be?"

"Well, per my father's request, I was to shack up with Dite again and have a kid, but my son kind of interrupted that. I'm guessing his offer of a child—the first that would be born in thousands of years—is off the table. Why do you think he offered that?"

"Huh?" I had completely confounded her.

"Stop focusing on revenge for ten seconds. Zeus gave us the offer of a millennium if we kept our son away from a mortal. Think why."

"I dunno."

I had her grappling, not knowing her purpose and questioning everything. Either that, or she was still hung up on my date joke. Probably both with Nemesis. In fact, she might let me go. I could slip away while she questioned her alliances, so I went for it.

Nemesis was in front of me, slamming me down to the ground. "Don't distract me!" Then she started to pummel me.

I kept her at bay, but the gentleman in me never felt right about hurting women, even though she was a warrior who had proved her worth time and time again. I simply blocked her attacks, letting her tire and spend her rage. Then I faltered. I fell down when she wasn't even striking me. A horrific feeling of terror overcame me. I couldn't escape. Then pain radiated through me. Electricity. I knew the feeling all too well. I remembered my early days, as a boy at Olympus, my father instilling "strength" and "fortitude" in me via electrocution. And then the hypocrite had been a bit let down that I was a war god and lacked his lightning abilities.

The electricity reverberated through me while my mind deduced what was going on. "Archer," I gasped. The feeling vanished, and I was up, pulverizing the woman.

She was staggering away, confused by my weakness and then my strength. "Stop!"

I backed off, panting, and then fell to the ground in pain. Archer needed me, and here I was in England, five thousand miles across the world. Somehow, Zeus had found him. Callie would be dead, and Archer would want to be as well. He would blame me, and he had every right to. I had failed him. I was positive my father's weak sight would follow me, and by the time he'd realize I was alone, Archer and Callie would be off the grid. Something had gone wrong—a leak, or he'd stationed forces everywhere to find them.

"What's happening?" She was grasping my collar, holding me up off the ground.

"I have a profound connection to my son. I feel him dying."

"Dying?" Nemesis dropped me, and my head hit the pavement pretty hard. I saw stars for a second, and then she yanked me up. "Zeus wouldn't kill Eros."

"No?" I laughed.

My strength was returning. He might be okay—we hadn't seen Chaos, who would've been momentarily unleashed into our minds when an Olympian died—but Callie? I had started to equate her with Harmonia, and she was perfect for Archer.

"Ares?" Nemesis met my gaze, completely confused, but the fire was out of her eyes. "I'm supposed to want revenge—"

"But at times, you don't want to. Think what it might be like to live as you *want*, not how you have to. Things are changing, Nem. Start thinking for yourself and who you want on your team," I told her.

Then I planted a kiss on her lips, making the warrior turn to putty, and my hands that rested on those shoulders were completely holding her up for a moment. I pulled away, winking, before I ran off back toward the building.

She wouldn't follow me but sit in that parking garage, thinking about what I had said. The goddess loved and respected me. She would be angry when she realized the kiss was only an escape tactic, but she wouldn't blame me as it was for my son. She understood warfare of every kind, but she would hate herself for falling victim to my charm.

As soon as I created distance between Nemesis and myself, I scanned for my son. He was off the grid as he should be. I needed some info. I pulled my phone out of my back pocket to check in with how things were in Belize via Proteus. My cell was busted—not a cracked screen, but flat out in pieces that were held together by the case. I tried to turn it on, but it was pointless. *Thanks, Nemesis.* I chucked it into a trash can, then found my bus.

I hoped Proteus was protecting them; he was slippery as an eel at times and listened to no one but Poseidon. I hoped he didn't go back underwater. I was unsure of Poseidon's position on things. He could be laughing at us, hoping we'd go to war and destroy each other. Or he could want to stick it to Zeus and allow those who could break through the surface barrier to fight for us. I couldn't imagine how my suppressed uncles could survive mentally and physically down in their abodes. My father honestly was a dick for keeping them there. Yeah, Poseidon would definitely be on our side.

The hour-long bus ride and making my way through Gatwick to get on my plane was beyond frustrating. I got on my flight to Copenhagen. Nemesis didn't seem to be tailing me anymore, but for good measure, as planned, I exited the airport. It was my final destination, or I'd have my father think it was if he was somehow still following me or had Hermes trace my tickets. I was in Norse territory, but they weren't living in Denmark now, so they wouldn't be too bothered about any others coming and going.

I called out for Boreas, who showed up a minute later, giving me that bear hug he loved to bestow. Then I was sucked up into freezing wind and landed in a valley of lush green fields surrounded by mountains. I thanked him with words and coin, then set off alone on foot to the nearest town. I took a bus north to get to my destination, relaxing, knowing I was untraceable where I was, since the Norse were living where Boreas had brought me. The others would shadow my presence, but part of me was still in panic mode for Archer's and the others' welfare as well as the Norse being so close by. They didn't really like me all that much.

I arrived at a quaint little fishing seaside town with a couple ski slopes, not too popular during the summer months lacking snow. In the distance, I saw mountains on one side, sea on the other; in front of me was a lake and luxury cabins. I went up to one.

I took a deep breath. It was a nice cool temperature in northern Iceland. The last time I had been here was during the Age of Sturlungs. Warring chieftains and disputes with Norway had had me busy. Kind of hard to decide between the Aesir and Vanir sides to be honest. The Vanir lived in Iceland, last I heard, which would not bode well. I hadn't ended up on their side. They resented a foreign god meddling. This might go very badly. They might ask me to leave—or worse, make me—and I would if necessary, only after I got Callie and Archer here safely.

I was musing on the doorstep of the cabin, which overlooked Lake Ólafsfjörður. Taking a deep breath, I knocked. It took a few minutes for the door to open. She stood there. Her dark ebony hair was bound in a thick braid that was twisted up atop her head like a wreath of laurel, her regal demeanor in its habitual poker face. Nothing ever changed with her, a glutton for routine—no, obsessive with routine, facts, and puzzles; Athena should be named goddess of rigidity. And she was freakishly smart, which was why I was here.

"Athena."

"Ares," she breathed out in a whisper, which was the only moment of shock I saw upon the goddess of rational thought.

I should've expected more. She helped me with war, and often our paths crossed. We were siblings—half. Never knew her mother, but she didn't spring out of a head. It was a typical invented story of my father's, trying to explain away his infidelity to my mother. "I was a swan, so I had no idea what I was doing" was my favorite excuse that my mother bought. Ridiculous, the pair of them.

"What are you doing here?" Athena asked.

"Looking for refuge."

She bit her lip. "A few Norse are literally five minutes away."

"I'll take my chances. I need a place my son and his wife can stay for a while."

Her mouth rounded in surprise, but she closed it. "You better come in and catch me up. I..." she hesitated. "I saw the lay of the land, and I self-isolated. Zeus is..." she floundered for a word. The goddess of wisdom, smartest being on the planet, was lost for words.

"Crazy?"

"I was going to say having a psychotic break, but yes, Ares, in layman's terms, he does seem to be temporarily losing it." Then she pulled me into the cabin, looked around cautiously, and closed the door, locking it. She seemed a bit on edge.

"So, what is going on?" she demanded, not even offering refreshment or politely urging me to sit down.

These frivolous expectations of society had never taken for her. She was as antisocial as they came. I seated myself, which made her sit across from me.

"Obviously, Archer broke his punishment and married her, from your word choice of 'wife,' but what do you want from me? You wouldn't come all this way to simply ask me to hide them."

It was nice that I didn't have to tell the entire story since she was clever enough to deduce it. "In layman's terms?" I asked. "Two war gods looking for peace."

Her eyebrows shot up at my odd statement. "Peace?"

"It's time to break free from Zeus. He will kill this girl, no matter how much we try to prevent it. It will destroy Eros, and if I lose him, I lose everything. I'll storm Olympus."

"And what? You'll rule?" She eyed me suspiciously, rooting out my motivation.

"Am I the sort who could rule over immortal beings? No. Athena, I want a quiet life, an occasional war when I'm needed."

"But who would keep everyone in line, hold everyone accountable?"

"That's where you come in."

Her breath caught in her throat, and she stared at me, perplexed. I let it sink in for a moment as I watched her shock fade. Her grey eyes danced around, showing she was thinking a mile a minute, measuring probabilities, planning, strategizing, weighing outcomes. She pursed her lips and met my gaze, which had always been unnerving for her. She held out her hand and smiled at me. "Deal."

We shook on it. We were an unstoppable duo when it came to war. Reason and strategy, brawn and skill. For the first time since my son's sentence, hope sprang. We could do this, protect Callie and Eros. Even better, Athena and Ares combined could fell any foe. Without Zeus, I could be free, remain Chase rather than being enslaved to war as Ares. I would do anything for my child, but the dream of autonomy was just as enticing. It was time to dismantle the wrongs of millenia and break off all our shackles.

Never had I imagined I would say the words, but they slipped out, making Athena nod: "Olympus is going down."

CONTINURE THE SAGA!

THE IMMORTAL TRANSCRIPTS III

SHUDDER

BOOKS2READ.COM/SHUDDER

A MESSAGE FROM THE GODS

Anyone suffering from suicidal thoughts, such as ones portrayed in this novel, please seek help. Talk to someone.

If no one is available,
call the National Suicide Prevention Lifeline at

1-800-273 TALK (8255)

or

text the Crisis Text Line at

BRAVE (741741).

Never give up hope.

OLYMPIAN FAMILY TREE
(from the journal of Dr. David N. Syches)

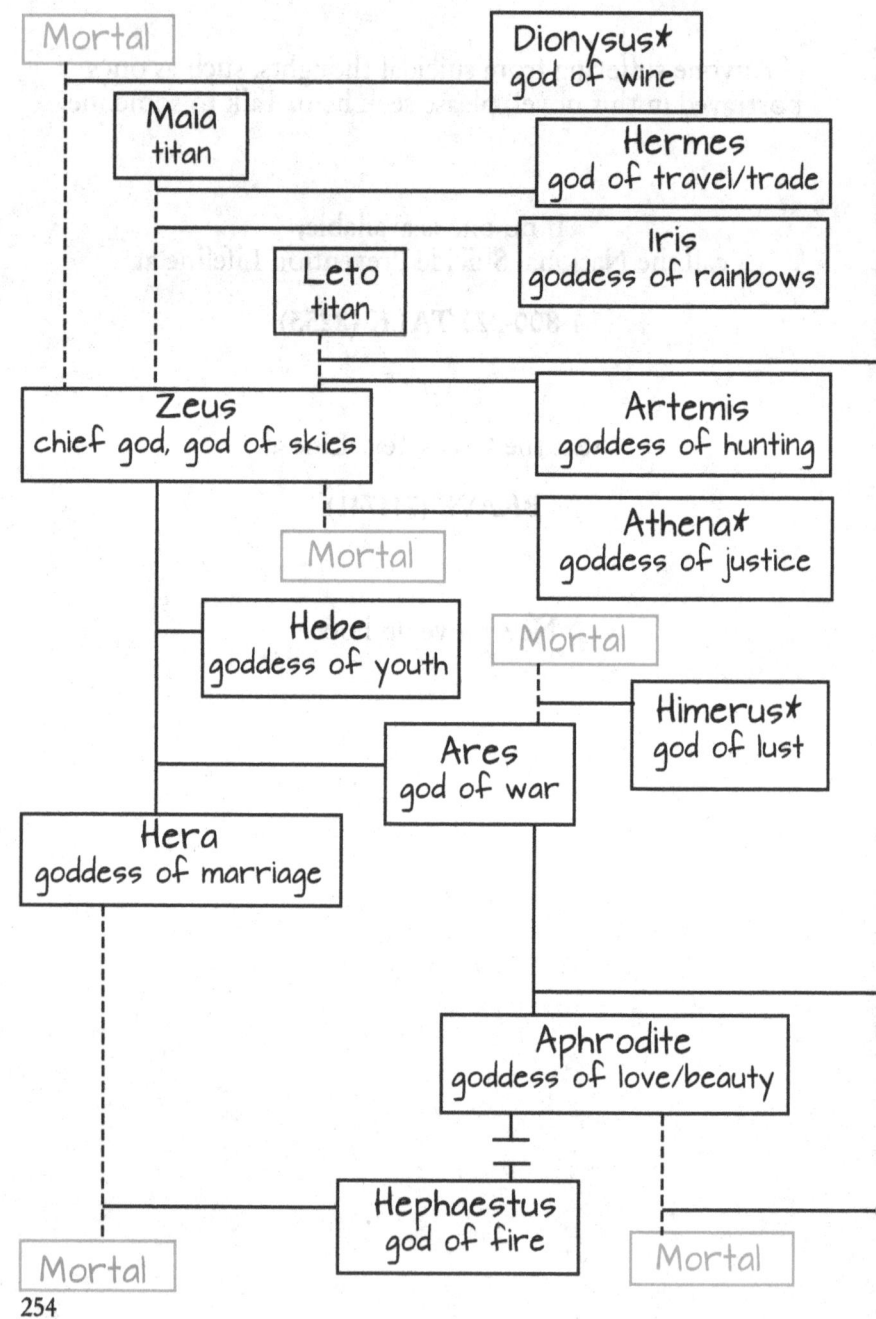

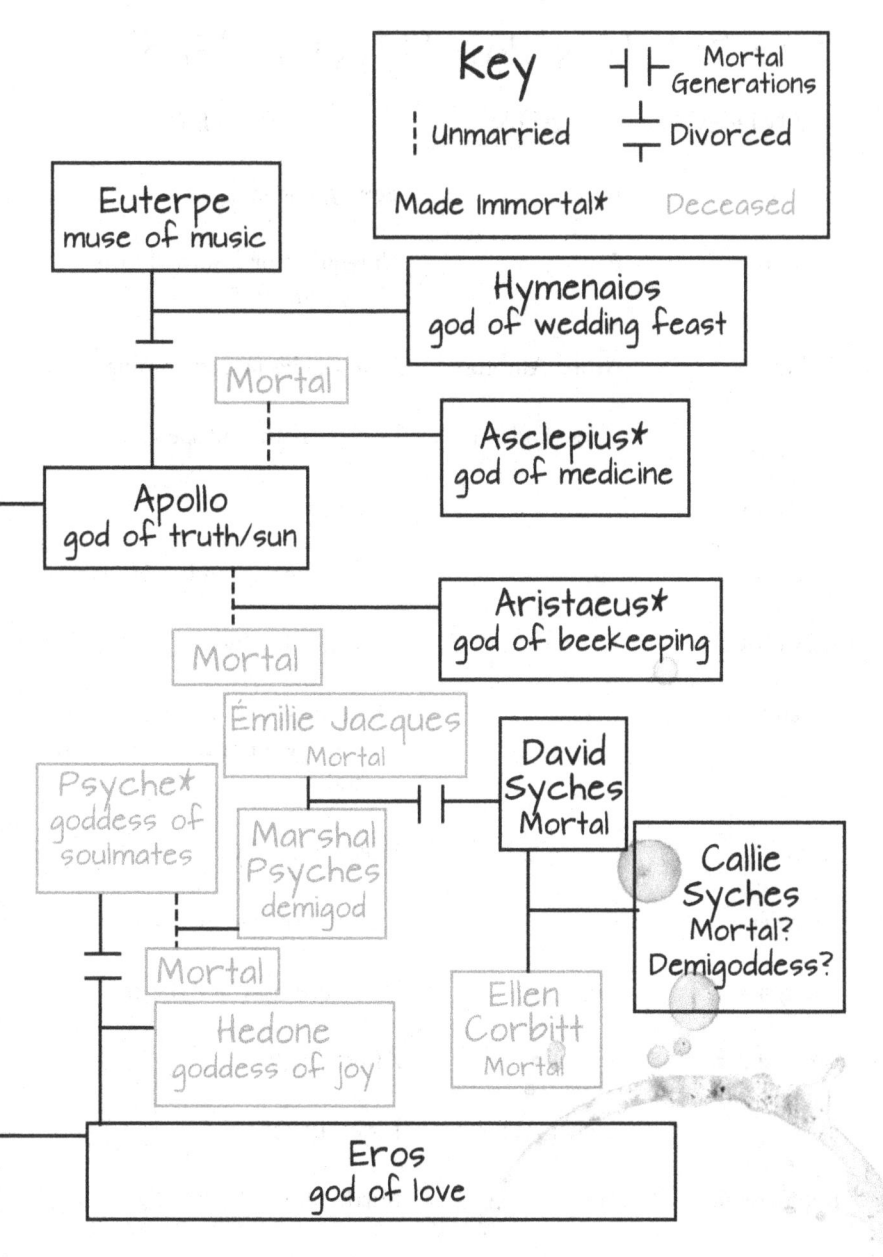

Key

Unmarried

Made Immortal*

Mortal Generations

Divorced

Deceased

Euterpe
muse of music

Hymenaios
god of wedding feast

Mortal

Asclepius*
god of medicine

Apollo
god of truth/sun

Aristaeus*
god of beekeeping

Mortal

Émilie Jacques
Mortal

David
Syches
Mortal

Psyche*
goddess of
soulmates

Marshal
Psyches
demigod

Callie
Syches
Mortal?
Demigoddess?

Mortal

Hedone
goddess of joy

Ellen
Corbitt
Mortal

Eros
god of love

Anteros*
god of counterlove

255

OLYMPIAN PANTHEON ALIASES

PANTHEON	ALIAS	POWERS
Aglaea	Belle	Beauty, splendor
Anteros	Antony	Unrequited or thwarted love, "magnetism"
Aphrodite	Aroha Ambrose	Love and beauty, swimming
Ares	Chase Gideon	War, strength, and speed
Aristaeus		Beekeeping
Artemis		Moon, hunting, and childbirth
Asclepius		Medicine, healing
Athena		Wisdom, justice, warfare, courage, inventions, arts, and crafts
Atlas		Holding the sky
Demeter		Agriculture, harvest
Dionysus	Uncle D	Wine, madness, and theater
Epimetheus		Afterthought
Eros	Archer Ambrose	Love, "flying"
Euphrosyne	Ada	Mirth, bliss
Euterpe		Music, lyric poetry
Hades		Underworld, scotopia, and invisibility

PANTHEON	ALIAS	POWERS
Hebe		Youth
Hedone		Joy, pleasure, and "flying"
Hephaestus	Heph(ie)	Fire, forging
Hera		Marriage, family, pregnancy
Hermes		Messenger, teleporting, theft
Himerus	Russ	Lust, strength, and speed
Hymenaios	Aios	Marriage ceremony, soul fusing
Hypnos		Sleep
Iris		Rainbow, teleporting
Janus		Duality, passages
Leto		Motherhood
Mnemosyne		Memory
Moirae	The Fates	Birth, destiny, and death
Muses		9 sisters of the arts
Persephone		Spring, plant life, and death
Phoebus Apollo	Lucien Veras	Sun, light, truth, prophecy, music, poetry, medicine, and healing
Poseidon		Sea, earthquakes

PANTHEON	ALIAS	POWERS
Prometheus		Foresight, prophecies
Proteus		Shapeshifting, foresight
Psyche		Soulmates, mindreading, and "flying"
Thalia	Thalia	Delight, charisma
Thanatos		Death, soul bearer
Themis		Justice, law, prophecy
Zelus		Zeal, ice, and "flying"
Zeus		God of gods, lightning, thunder, sky, and omniscience

ACKNOWLEDGMENTS

First, I'd like to acknowledge Cameron Scott Wright, who, as a grad student, was assigned to edit *Quiver*; Cameron didn't just do his assignment but went over the top by having great discussions with me about what he liked or would want to see. He was one of the few people I ever revealed the entire plot of the series to, and I'm glad for it. Cameron unfortunately passed away before the book was published, but in his final months, I was able to inform him that his hard work helped me get The Immortal Transcripts published.

The book is dedicated to my best friends. It may be pure happenstance that all of their names end in the *ee* sound, but they support my writing, accept me for who I am, and are always there, listening in the difficult times and celebrating the good. The honest vents about life makes writing so much easier; in fact, it would be impossible to focus on writing without our chats, ladies' nights, and support.

To my husband, who believes that I can do anything I set my mind to. I started believing and now accept that I can. With enough time, effort, and determination, I can fulfill all my dreams. He is my absolute support system.

My family has been instrumental in making this novel happen, with childcare, enthusiasm, and support. Also, they were the ones who fostered this intricate imagination of mine and helped it grow through encouragement and happenstance. I don't think I would've ended up an author if I hadn't been urged to read so much as a child and if my parents hadn't owned a video store—both inspired me to be a storyteller.

Thanks to Authors 4 Authors Publishing for such a collaborative process in polishing my novel to be its best. Without their assistance, it would still be resting on the shelf, collecting dust, to never be read. The story behind this series is a long one, but *Fever*'s first draft was written in 2008 while I was in grad school. Finally, it is out in the world for others.

I want to acknowledge everyone (and thing) who also made my story better. Thanks goes to the Carolina Forest Authors Club for the help and support, particularly those who critiqued it. Thank you, Kate, for being my dependable beta reader and first editor. Thanks, Google, for having street view maps and Google Earth satellite; it made my worldwide settings more realistic and allowed me to see places and describe them fully with more accuracy. Twelve years from first draft to publication tends to let some people slip through the cracks, so if I forgot anyone, know that your help was much appreciated.

Last, but certainly not the least, thank you, reader, for taking the time to read my novel. I hope you enjoyed it. Please leave a review through the venue where you purchased it or on Goodreads or other review sites. Much appreciated.

ABOUT THE AUTHOR

LISA BORNE GRAVES

Lisa Borne Graves is a YA author, English Lecturer, wife, and supermom of one wild child. Originally from the Philadelphia area, she relocated to the Deep South and found her true place of inspiration. Her love for all literature led her to branch out from the academic arena to spin her own tales. Lisa has a voracious appetite for books, British television, and pizza. Her inability to sit still makes her enjoy life to its fullest, and she can be found at the beach, pool, or on some crazy adventure.

Follow her online:

lisabornegraves.com
Twitter: @lisabornegraves
Facebook: @lisabornegravesauthor
Instagram: @lisabornegraves

Also by Lisa Borne Graves

CELESTIAL SPHERES
FYR

At seventeen, Toury arrives in Fyr, where magic is power, a prince's love is deadly, and female autonomy is a dream. Formerly a loner and burden to her adoptive parents, she ruins her chances of a fresh start by offending an ogler who just happens to be the prince.

Alex, the Prince of Fyr, is no novice when it comes to pressure. He has to face his father's ailing health, the expectation to marry soon, and the hidden necromancers trying to take over the realm by exploiting his dark curse. At least there's hope in a cheeky savior, but Earth girls aren't so easy.

Toury and Alex learn that the strongest magic cannot be conjured but must be earned. They must risk their lives, hearts, and futures to save the land from a darkness of apocalyptic proportions. But can they trust each other enough to save Fyr? Or will everything they hold dear turn to ash?

books2read.com/fyr

Authors 4 Authors
Publishing Cooperative

A publishing company for authors, run by authors, blending the best of traditional and independent publishing

We specialize in speculative fiction: science fiction, fantasy, paranormal, and romance. Get lost in another world!

Check out our collection at https://books2read.com/rl/a4a
or visit Authors4AuthorsPublishing.com/books

For updates, scan the QR code or visit our website to join our semi-monthly newsletter!

Want more romantic fantasy? We recommend:

KISS OF TREASON
by Brandi Spencer

Two forbidden lovers share the rare gift to heal others with a kiss—but at a cost. Odelia's life has been a lie. When the queen tries to remove her from the palace, Odelia uncovers the truth. Now she must decide whether to forsake her people or embrace a destiny that would pit her against the current heir to the throne...her best friend. Though her only hope of avoiding a civil war lies in winning his heart, revealing her secrets too soon could cost both their lives. And a kiss might not be strong enough to save them...

books2read.com/kisstreason